D0500284

# THE
# SIREN
# SONG

ALSO BY Anne Ursu

*The Shadow Thieves*

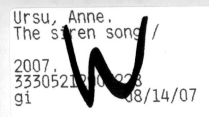

Ursu, Anne.
The siren song /

2007.
33305212        8
gi                08/14/07

# THE SIREN SONG

⇥ THE CRONUS CHRONICLES • BOOK TWO ⇤

## Anne Ursu

Atheneum Books for Young Readers
New York   London   Toronto   Sydney

Atheneum Books for Young Readers
An imprint of Simon & Schuster Children's Publishing Division
1230 Avenue of the Americas
New York, New York 10020

This book is a work of fiction. Any references to historical events, real people, or real locales are used fictitiously. Other names, characters, places, and incidents are products of the author's imagination, and any resemblance to actual events or locales or persons, living or dead, is entirely coincidental.

Text copyright © 2007 by Anne Ursu
Illustrations copyright © 2007 by Eric Fortune

All rights reserved, including the right of reproduction
in whole or in part in any form.

Book design by Ann Zeak
The text for this book is set in Hoefler Text.
The illustrations for this book were rendered in pencil.
Manufactured in the United States of America
First Edition
2 4 6 8 10 9 7 5 3 1
Library of Congress Cataloging-in-Publication Data
Ursu, Anne.
The siren song / Anne Ursu. — 1st ed.
p.    cm. — (The Cronus chronicles ; bk. two)
Summary: Thirteen-year-old Charlotte must rescue humankind
again when the evil Philonecron captures her cousin Zee, and
Poseidon himself sends a sea monster to eat the cruise ship on
which Charlotte's parents are trapped.
ISBN-13: 978-1-4169-0589-9 (hardcover)
ISBN-10: 1-4169-0589-8 (hardcover)
[1. Adventure and adventurers — Fiction. 2. Mythology, Greek —
Fiction. 3. Poseidon (Greek deity) — Fiction. 4. Animals,
Mythical — Fiction.] I. Title.
PZ7.U692Sir 2006
[Fic] — dc22    2006015841

For Gretchen Laskas and Laura Ruby
Proud Redheads

# Contents

# THE
# SIREN
# SONG

# PART ONE

---

## Fish

# No Way to Treat a Hero

ONCE, NOT SO LONG AGO, INSIDE AN ORDINARY MIDDLE
school in an ordinary city in an ordinary state in the
middle of an ordinary country, a small redheaded eighth
grader was doing something very ordinary indeed.
Charlotte Mielswetzski (Say it with me: Meals-wet-ski.
Got it? If not, say it again: Meals. Wet. Ski.) was in the
school office calling her mother. And lest you think she
was calling her mother for some interesting reason, let
me assure you she most certainly was not. For Charlotte
could be found in that same office calling her mother
every day after school. In fact, five months before, her

mother had contacted the Hartnett Middle School principal and asked him to make special arrangements to allow Charlotte to use the office phone, because Charlotte would be needing to call her mother every day and inform her when she was on her way home. You might think that after five months this would have become less embarrassing, but, as Charlotte would be happy to assure you, it had not.

You see, Charlotte Mielswetzski was grounded. *Very* grounded. She had to call her parents *right* after school every day and then walk *straight* home after she called. If her mother was at the office, Charlotte had to call when she got home as well. She was required to use the school and home phones, too, so Mrs. Mielswetzski would know she was calling from the place she was supposed to be. No cell phones.

And Charlotte actually had a cell phone now. For the last two years she had been begging her parents for one, but Mrs. Mielswetzski said it was ridiculous that kids needed cell phones and Mr. Mielswetzski said something about it just getting confiscated anyway (he was a history teacher at the high school and knew whereof he spoke). Charlotte suspected she was the only person in the entire world who didn't have a phone. But, as she soon learned, not having a cell phone is much better than being given a cell phone so your parents can keep track of you at all times. She needed permission to use it for any other reason, and they said they would know if she misused it because they would check the bills every month.

It was almost as if her parents didn't trust her.

The only things Charlotte was allowed to do were school-sanctioned activities, like gymnastics. She had been quite shocked that her mother had let her try out for the team, but, frankly, her mother had seemed even more shocked that Charlotte had wanted to try out at all and perhaps was not thinking clearly. Charlotte was fairly sure that if she'd been doing gymnastics all her life, her mother would have grounded her from that, too—but since Mrs. Mielswetzski had been trying to get her to do extracurricular activities for years and Charlotte had never had the slightest inclination to do so before, it suddenly must have seemed like a great idea. It's all in the timing.

"Hello, Charlotte," said Mrs. Mielswetzski when she picked up the phone. Her mother used to call her things like "honey," but not anymore. "How was practice?"

"Fine," Charlotte said. It had actually been more than fine. Charlotte had landed a cartwheel on the balance beam for the first time ever, after having tried for weeks. She was so excited she had almost fallen off, which would have made the whole thing a lot less cool-looking. But she didn't fall, and the whole team cheered.

And just then, Charlotte Mielswetzski felt like she could probably do a cartwheel anywhere—on a handrail, on a ribbon, on the whisker of her cat—and land it with grace and precision.

But she wasn't going to tell her mother any of that. The last thing she wanted to do was give her the satisfaction of thinking that Charlotte had had even a moment of happiness.

"It's a little late," said Mrs. Mielswetzski.

Charlotte winced. "Practice went long. You can call Coach Seltzer!" (If her tone wasn't that kind, you must forgive her; she had been a little irritable the last few months.)

With a sigh, her mother said, "Okay, Charlotte. Just come straight home. Do you want me to pick you up?"

"No!" said Charlotte quickly. The Mielswetzskis lived just six blocks from the campus of Hartnett Middle School, and when it was warm enough, Charlotte walked to and from school every day. But during the winter she'd had to get a ride from her mother, and it was often frostier inside the car than outside. So Charlotte was always quite eager to find other options. "Maddy stayed after to study. I can get a ride with Mrs. Ruby." Maddy, Charlotte's best friend, had already called her mother to come get them. Maddy had fallen prey to a lengthy and mysterious illness last October, and since then her mom had been all too happy to do just about anything for her. You have to work that sort of situation to your advantage.

Her mother paused. "All right, Charlotte," she said finally. "I'll be sure to call Mrs. Ruby and thank her later tonight."

Charlotte's cheeks flushed and she hung up without saying good-bye. Before she'd called her mother, she'd still felt a small glow from her accomplishment today— just a spark, really, but after the way the last few months had gone, a spark was good enough. But now that spark was gone. All gone.

Charlotte hadn't been lying. Mrs. Ruby was going to pick them up. Lately Maddy had been staying after school and working in the library while Charlotte was at gymnastics. Maddy was always happy to have an excuse to do homework (unlike Charlotte, who preferred excuses *not* to do homework), but really she did it just to get some time with Charlotte, since it was the only chance they had to see each other.

Maddy watched Charlotte as she glared at the office phone. "Everything okay?" she asked.

"No," replied Charlotte.

Maddy groaned sympathetically. "We should go watch for Mom."

Charlotte nodded, and Maddy led her out of the

office door. The school receptionist looked up and smiled at the girls. "Bye, Charlotte," she said. "See you tomorrow!"

Charlotte grunted.

"So," Maddy said when they reached the school vestibule, "your mom hasn't lightened up at all, I see."

"Nope," said Charlotte.

"It just seems kind of extreme," Maddy said for the hundredth time. "So you failed a math test. It happens."

Charlotte cast a look at her friend. Maddy didn't know the truth about why her parents were so mad at her; Charlotte would have loved to have told her the whole story, but then Maddy would think Charlotte was crazy and would lock her in a nuthouse, and that would put a serious damper on their friendship.

The only person who knew the truth was Charlotte's cousin Zee, but he didn't want to be locked up any more than she did. Oh, and her old English teacher Mr. Metos knew, of course. After everything had happened, Charlotte had hoped he would help her with her parents, but talking to people wasn't really Mr. Metos's strong suit.

The thing is, a few months before, in order to save all the sick kids, Charlotte and Zee had had to sneak down to the Underworld—the Underworld as in the-Greek-mythology Underworld, which is actually real. In fact, as Charlotte learned last fall, much to her surprise, all of Greek myths are real—Zeus, Poseidon, Hades, the whole bit. It's just that nobody knows it. Hades is the god of the Underworld, and a minor god named Philonecron tried to overthrow him, and to make an army he'd stolen and enchanted kids' shadows. That's why Maddy was sick—her shadow was taken, along with the shadows of pretty much every kid in the city, not to mention in London, where Zee had lived.

So, sometimes really bad things happen and, for reasons that are rather complicated, you're the only one who can stop them. And sometimes, in order to do so, you have to sneak out of the house late at night to get to the Underworld. And on those occasions, you, because you are a conscientious person, leave your parents a note explaining that you know what's making everyone sick and you have to go save the world. Helpfully, you also tell them you love them and not to worry.

The problem is, your parents don't really listen to this last part, and when you finally get back the next morning (extremely weird, because it felt like forever down there, but it turned out to be only one night in the Upperworld)—after Philonecron tried to throw you in the Styx, a few monsters tried to eat you, you met up with the Lord of the Underworld, and a whole shadow army tried to bring his palace down on your head—well, you find out that they have, in fact, worried. A lot.

After they call the police to tell them you have returned home safely, and then they hug you a lot and cry for a while, well—after that, they want to know where you've been. (And, for that matter, why you are covered in weird-looking slime, purple cobwebs, and Harpy poo, and why your cat's leg is broken.) And when you don't tell them, they tend to get pretty upset. And, after a few days, when you still haven't told them, they stick you in therapy. They're going to give you speeches about how *disappointed* they are in you and how family is all about *trust* and how you worried them to *death* and you don't have the decency to explain where you *were* and they have to assume the worst—which is that you can't be trusted. And then they ground you. A lot.

Charlotte Mielswetzski had once thought that she could talk her way out of any situation. This was before she came back from the Underworld. She would have liked to come up with something, something to make her parents feel better and to stop her from being grounded until she was thirty-five, but for once in her life, when she opened her mouth, nothing came out.

The thing that gets Charlotte is if she'd never left a note in the first place—which she did out of *concern* and basic human *decency*, mind you—and had just sneaked out of the house and come back in the morning, she could have told her parents that she'd gone to, like, a party or something (a very muddy, smelly, sooty, gross party), and then her parents would have freaked out and grounded her, but probably for only a month. Or maybe two. And she wouldn't have had to go to therapy.

As for Maddy, Charlotte had just flat-out lied. She was grounded, she told her friend, because she failed the math midterm and was in danger of failing the class. The problem was, Maddy was Charlotte's best friend, and Charlotte had to lie to her about the biggest thing that had ever happened to her. She had to lie to her about the whole world, basically, and what was the point of having a best friend if you couldn't tell her everything? And as they stood in the school lobby watching for Mrs. Ruby, Charlotte thought about what it might be like to tell Maddy the truth, once and for all. She could feel the words form in her mouth—"Maddy, I have to tell you something"—but she couldn't say them. There was no way she could say them. So Charlotte just sighed and shook her head. She'd been sighing a lot lately and was probably going to need oxygen at some point.

"How's Zee?" Maddy asked casually.

"Fine," Charlotte replied, just as casually.

Maddy, like every other girl in school, had a crush on Zee. Zee had come over from England last September to live with the Mielswetzskis; his parents sent him over when all the kids in London started getting sick. But a month ago Zee's parents had finally moved to the United States too, and Zee had gone to live with them in a house a mile away from Charlotte's. When Zee had first come over, with his perfect British manners and instant popularity and freakish girl-magnet-ness, Charlotte had wanted him far away. But they'd gone to hell and back together, or at least to Hades, and now he was the only one who knew the things about the world that she did, the only person Charlotte wasn't lying to on a daily basis.

But that didn't mean she wanted Maddy to date him.

"Was practice okay?" Maddy asked, in a come-back-to-the-light-Charlotte kind of voice. "Break anything?"

Charlotte thought again of her cartwheel, of the moment when she soared over the beam, when her legs began to come back to Earth on a perfect line, when she knew she was finally going to land it. Then she thought of her mom's voice saying, *I'll be sure to call Mrs. Ruby and thank her.*

"Okay," Charlotte shrugged. She felt sorry for Maddy. It must be hard to have a friend who spoke exclusively in one-word sentences.

"Oh!" Maddy exclaimed. "Listen! Are you guys doing anything for spring break this year?"

Charlotte grunted. "What do you think?" Spring

break was less than two weeks away, and it was going to be the same this year as it was every year. Everyone in Charlotte's school went off to some exotic locale every year and came back all happy and tan, while she stayed home and only got paler, which made her freckles even more pronounced.

"Because I was thinking, maybe I could ask Mom if you could come to Florida with us this year."

"What?" Charlotte turned. "Really?"

"Sure! We've got lots of room in the house, and Brian isn't coming. We have his plane ticket—maybe we could transfer it or something." Brian was Maddy's older brother. Much older. He was in his first year of college and apparently had better things to do than go to Fort Myers with his family. While Charlotte had nothing better at all to do. But . . .

"They'll *never* let me," Charlotte moaned. "Remember? I can't be trusted?"

Maddy rolled her eyes. "Maybe they will! I mean, hasn't this gone on long enough? You've been so good, too! Look, I'll have my mom call your mom. She can make it sound—I dunno, educational or something."

Charlotte closed her eyes and saw sandy beaches and sunshine and palm trees and . . .

Can redheads tan? Charlotte wanted very much to find out.

• • •

So it happened that Charlotte arrived at her house in a good mood, the first good mood she'd been in since she had returned from the world of the Dead and gotten Super-Mega-Grounded.

When she walked in the door, though, she found her parents sitting at the kitchen table waiting for her, and her good mood quickly dissipated. Charlotte had lived with her parents long enough to know that whatever this was, it could not be good.

With a loud squawk, her cat Mew came tearing toward her, and Charlotte quickly bent down to scratch her between the ears. Charlotte had a sort of joint custody of Mew with Zee, because when Zee moved in with his parents, Mew got upset and sulked around the house all the time. But now they switched off weeks and Mew was much happier. Charlotte's parents had suggested the arrangement; they were chock-full of good ideas about taking people's cats away from them.

"Welcome home, Charlotte," Mrs. Mielswetzski said.

"Hi, honey," Mr. Mielswetzski said. He, at least, still loved her.

Charlotte braced herself and looked up. "Hi," she said cautiously.

"How was practice?" Mr. Mielswetzski asked.

"Fine," said Charlotte, looking back and forth at their faces. They were inscrutable.

"Good, good." Her parents exchanged glances.

"Um," Charlotte said, tugging on her hair. "Well, I think I'm going to go upstairs. I've got a lot of homework." With a surreptitious bite of her lip, she moved quickly toward the door.

"Wait!" said Mr. Mielswetzski.

Not quickly enough.

Charlotte squeezed her eyes shut, then picked up Mew for defense. Mew would never let anything bad happen to her.

"Charlotte, we've got some news," said Mrs. Mielswetzski.

"Good news," said Mr. Mielswetzski.

"Really?" Charlotte couldn't help but feel a tinge of hope. Maybe she'd proven she could, in fact, be trusted. Maybe they were going to let her out of prison. . . .

"Well, your father has won an award," said Mrs. Mielswetzski.

Oh. Honestly, if people played with Charlotte's moods anymore today, she was going to actually *need* her therapy.

"Well, more like a prize," said Mr. Mielswetzski.

"Oh, Mike, it's an award!" said Mrs. Mielswetzski.

"Well, that's very sweet, honey," said Mr. Mielswetzski.

"You absolutely deserve it," said Mrs. Mielswetzski.

"Guys!" said Charlotte.

"Charlotte," said Mr. Mielswetzski, turning toward his daughter, "how would you like to go on a cruise for spring break?"

Charlotte almost dropped Mew. "What?" Mew scowled at her and jumped down onto the floor.

"Well," smiled Mr. Mielswetzski, "the Clio Foundation, a foundation supporting history teachers, has given me a prize—"

"An *award*," corrected Mrs. Mielswetzski.

"—a cruise for the whole family during spring break!"

Charlotte's eyes bugged out. A cruise! They would go to the Caribbean! Maybe the Bahamas! She would spend the whole time reading on the deck by the pool while cute waiters brought her smoothies! Sure, she'd be stuck with her parents the whole time, but they'd go off exploring, doing lame tourist stuff, and she would just sit in the sun and—

"It's an American History cruise!" said her father. "We'll go to see Mount Vernon and go to Colonial Williamsburg and we'll look at Civil War battlefields!"

"What?" said Charlotte. Clearly she hadn't heard right.

"An American History cruise!" said Mrs.

Mielswetzski. "Up the East Coast! Normally, a girl who is grounded doesn't get to go on cruises, but given the educational nature of this one, we thought we'd make an exception."

"Anyway," said Mr. Mielswetzski, "it will give us a lot of time together. As a family."

Her parents exchanged a happy look.

"Oh," Charlotte said. "Um, look, I've got to go to my room now. I'm not feeling very good."

"Oh!" said Mrs. Mielswetzski.

"Oh!" said Mr. Mielswetzski.

"You go rest!"

"By all means!"

"We can talk about the cruise later."

"Okay," said Charlotte weakly. And with that she walked slowly up to her room to call Maddy, to tell her of the latest cruel twist of fate.

Now, we know Charlotte Mielswetzski was not naive. She was by no means under the impression that she could just waltz down to the Underworld, thwart an evil demigod, chat up an Olympian, and waltz back up again without any repercussions. These things did tend to have repercussions. And since she'd gotten back from the Underworld there had been a part of her that was waiting for something to happen. Something like Philonecron—who had been banished to the

Upperworld—paying a call, or something like one of the gods—who really didn't seem that pleased with the idea of mortals traipsing through their realms—sucking her up to Mount Olympus and turning her into an aardvark. But as the months wore on and nothing happened, as she was confronted with the indignities of middle school and of having parents, Charlotte had begun to relax a little bit. Perhaps that's why she thought nothing of this strange gift falling into their laps so suddenly. Perhaps that's why the only thing that alarmed her about it was the close confinement with her parents and the forced march through Colonial Williamsburg. Perhaps she didn't even register that the organization that was sending them on this trip was called the Clio Foundation, because surely if she did she would have remembered that Clio was the name of the Greek muse of history. And that should have set off alarm bells, because Charlotte Mielswetzski, of all people, should know to beware of Greeks bearing gifts.

CHAPTER 2

# Something Wrong, Something Right

THAT NIGHT CHARLOTTE HAD THE CRAZIEST DREAM. Or at least, it would have been the craziest dream, had she not been having crazy dreams ever since her adventures last fall. In this particular crazy dream, Charlotte was one of the Dead, the vast numbers of nameless, faceless, aimless specters that inhabited the Underworld.

She was with a sea of Dead, all moving to a point up ahead that she couldn't see, but she was moving with them all the same. Her body felt weightless, strangely hollow, devoid of all the reassuring accoutrements of Life. It was not a pleasant feeling.

Together they all moved slowly along the red, rocky plain of the Underworld. Somewhere in the distance Charlotte could hear the screeching of Harpies. She knew she should be afraid, but she just felt so dull, as if she no longer had the power to feel anything. All she could do was move forward listlessly with her compatriots.

Then suddenly, up ahead, it seemed the ranks of Dead were starting to thin out. Charlotte sensed a change in the environment, something in the air. Steam, that was it—there was steam up ahead. Somewhere in the deep recesses of Charlotte's mind, an alarm went off, but she was too dazed to heed it.

And then the space in front of her cleared and Charlotte found herself face to face with the boiling, roiling River Styx. Across the banks were the Plains of the Dead. She had seen this view before, but last time she had stood here the Plains had been covered in a sort of glowing fog of Dead. Now they were completely empty. There had been so many Dead in front of her— where had they gone if not across the river?

Charlotte heard a strange hissing sound and turned her head—a group of Dead had walked right off the bank into the Styx. As they hit the river, their smoke-like bodies expanded, spreading apart until they lost their shape entirely, and then were gone.

Another hiss, another group went into the river.

Charlotte tried to shout but couldn't make a sound. Before her eyes the group of Dead melted into the air and became lost to oblivion.

Charlotte felt a shuffling around her, and before she could react she was being pushed toward the Styx. She wanted to fight back, to turn, to run, but she had no strength, no will. She could do nothing. She found herself on the banks, the heat from the river hitting her face.

She heard a voice somewhere over the crowd, and she turned to look. In the steam she could see a tall, dark form standing over the Dead's march, nodding, approving, egging them into the Styx. She stared, trying to make out who it was—she had been expecting it to be Philonecron, carrying out some terrible revenge, but it wasn't. It was Hades, the King of the Dead. Charlotte stared at him as she fell into the River Styx.

Charlotte awoke with a start, her heart pounding. She was in her room, in her bed, it was all right. She seemed to wake up like this every night these days; sometimes it was because she dreamed of Philonecron or one of his creepy Footmen, but often it was visions of dour, shadowy Hades that startled her awake at night.

Hades hadn't been *bad*, really. He just hadn't been *good*. In the Underworld, the Dead roamed in the Plains, aimless and lifeless, while all the endless series of Administrators (the gods and demons who made up the

Underworld's rather large bureaucracy) had everything they wanted. And Hades spent so much time in his palace he had no idea what was going on outside his walls. Nor did he care. Charlotte had wanted to do something, to help the Dead in some way, but there was nothing she could do—except, now, have nightmares all the time.

Mr. Metos, though, had gone off to try to help. Mr. Metos had been Charlotte's English teacher, and he was the one who told her and Zee all about the whole Greek-myths-being-real thing. He was also a Promethean—the Prometheans were descendants of the Titan Prometheus, who worked to protect people from the gods. After everything had happened last fall, Mr. Metos had left the school and gone off to the other Prometheans to discuss the issue of the Dead. He wasn't very optimistic, but he said he'd try. Charlotte had wanted to go with him—she thought maybe he could pretend it was a big field trip or something—but he wasn't nearly as excited about that prospect as she was. So he left her, full of all her terrible knowledge, while he went off to work and she went right back to middle school.

Mr. Metos had promised Charlotte and Zee that he would write, that he wouldn't keep them in the dark, but neither of them had heard anything yet. On top of being impatient, Charlotte was slightly offended; she thought he might be a little more interested in her well-being, given that Philonecron was now wandering around the Upperworld, but Mr. Metos didn't seem to be worried about Philonecron at all.

Which, Charlotte thought, must be very nice for him.

The next morning Charlotte woke up groggy. She'd had a very hard time getting back to sleep after her dream—every time she closed her eyes she felt herself being dragged off with the Dead again. Her morning wasn't improved when she got into the bathroom and found a gigantic pimple had appeared on her nose overnight. No need for Charlotte to go to Mount Olympus—Mount Olympus had come to her.

Charlotte tried to get out of the house as quickly as possible that morning. It was warm enough to walk, and, given her mood, it just seemed like a good idea to avoid her mother.

But Mrs. Mielswetzski came into the kitchen just as Charlotte was putting on her jacket. "What are you doing?" she said. "It's not time to go yet!"

"Oh," Charlotte said, "I'm going to walk today."

"Walk? Charlotte, it's winter!"

"It's really warm, Mom, look!" She pointed at the thermometer.

Mrs. Mielswetzski sighed. "All right. Just bundle up, okay? And be careful, it's slippery."

Charlotte rolled her eyes. "Mom, I *know*!"

Mrs. Mielswetzski's face darkened. "There's no need to get snippy, Charlotte."

Charlotte could feel anger swell up in her chest. "I'm not snippy. I just don't want to be treated like a baby. I can take care of myself."

"Really," Mrs. Mielswetzski replied flatly. "Then maybe you'd like to start acting like it." She let out a long exhale. "I don't know what's gotten into you these days. But I suggest that you can it. And, you know, this cruise is a privilege, not a right. Your father and I would be more than happy to leave you behind."

It was on the tip of Charlotte's tongue to say, "Promise?" but she thought better of it.

"I want to see you behaving yourself, all right?"

Charlotte glowered in response.

"And remember, therapy tonight!"

"Great," Charlotte muttered.

"What was that?" Mrs. Mielswetzski asked, in a way that implied she had heard just fine.

"Nothing."

"Charlotte . . . I want to see a better attitude from you. I mean it."

Charlotte opened her mouth to respond but then

realized she had no idea what might come out, so she quickly pursed her lips together and gave her mother a curt nod. And then got out of the house as quickly as humanly possible.

It wasn't even that cold outside. She was wearing her puffy lime green coat, with a purple hat, scarf, and mittens, and was just fine, thank you. Maybe winter was ending. Maybe it would only get warmer and she could walk to school every morning from now on and not sit in stony silence in the car while her mother explained to her how important it was to work hard in school.

The thing is, Charlotte just wasn't that interested in school. She never had been, really, but once you learn that humanity's troubles were created when Zeus sent Pandora to Earth with a sealed jar containing all the world's evils and an unhealthy sense of curiosity, it's hard to take history class too seriously.

But on the test, when they ask you to write an essay about the causes of World War II, you're not supposed to put down, "Because the gods don't give a monkey's butt about anyone but themselves." But Charlotte really didn't have anything else to say. So her teachers said she wasn't applying herself, and she couldn't exactly tell them she'd applied herself just fine in the Underworld.

This morning, as Charlotte approached the brick

facade of Hartnett, she found herself overcome with a great sense of dread. It hit her with a strange and sudden force, and she had an overwhelming urge to turn back, to get into her bed and not get out for about three weeks. She stopped in her tracks. The feeling itself was alarming to Charlotte—was she sensing something? Something dangerous? And was it something supernatural or just middle school? Sometimes it was hard to tell the difference.

Charlotte stood on the sidewalk across the street from the school, watching the stream of students head up the stairs and through the big, heavy front doors. School buses pulled away, cars unloaded their cargo and drove off, and the stream of students began to thin into a trickle while Charlotte looked carefully around for something unusual, something that could be causing her bad feeling. But there was nothing—just a few stragglers walking in the door, a lone car dropping a sixth grader off, someone's very strangely dressed grandfather coming out of the front door of the school.

Charlotte stared at the old man. He was in the oddest outfit she'd ever seen, and that included her father's disco costume last Halloween. He wore an old-fashioned three-piece suit and a bowler hat to match, which was strange enough, but even weirder was the ensemble's color—which was aqua. Charlotte was glad she didn't have a grandfather who dropped her off at school wearing aqua-colored suits.

When the old man reached the bottom of the steps in front of the school and turned toward the parking lot, he noticed Charlotte's gaze. Their eyes met, and as he looked at her, a slow smile spread across his face. Then the man nodded at her and walked away.

Suddenly Charlotte had a strong desire to be inside the confines of Hartnett Middle School. She didn't really want to add crazy people to her list of problems. So she slung her book bag over her shoulder and went across the street, up the steps, and through the heavy doors.

The halls were empty. Charlotte had missed the first bell and would be late, again. Her homeroom teacher would ask her for an excuse and she would say, "Overwhelming feeling of dread." That was going to go over nicely.

So preoccupied was Charlotte that she did not notice the person standing in the hallway studying a piece of paper—or at least she didn't notice him until she crashed right into him.

"Oh!" said the person.

"Oh!" said Charlotte, but not entirely for the same reasons. The person she had just crashed into was not a person at all, but rather a boy—a boy with dark rumpled hair, olive skin, and green eyes unlike any Charlotte had ever seen before. As she straightened, she couldn't help but notice they were very, very nice eyes.

"I'm so sorry," the boy said. "I wasn't looking."

"No, I'm sorry," Charlotte said. (Sorry you're so *cute*.)

"No, no," said the boy with a grin, "*I'm* sorry."

Charlotte had never really considered the advantages of having boys in the world. They always seemed like much more trouble than they were worth. But standing there looking at this boy, she wondered if she might have been wrong, if boys didn't have their place, because some of them had big green eyes and adorable grins, and isn't that really enough?

"I'm Jason, by the way," the boy said. "I'm new."

Charlotte gathered that. She was pretty sure she'd have noticed him if she'd seen him before.

"I'm Charlotte," said Charlotte.

The boy's eyes brightened. "Really?"

Charlotte blinked. "Um . . . yes."

"That's great!" he said enthusiastically. "It's so great to meet you!"

Charlotte didn't know what to say. No one that cute had been so excited to meet her before.

"Listen, do you know where the principal's office is? I'm supposed to go."

"Sure. Right behind you."

"Thanks," he said, grinning again. "Smash into you later!" With that, he turned and disappeared into the office.

It was at that point that Charlotte remembered the giant festering zit on her nose. She suppressed a blood-curdling scream. The cutest boy she had ever seen just magically appeared in front of her and she was hideously disfigured. No wonder she'd dreaded going into school so much today.

While Charlotte was standing in the hallway, the bell rang signifying the end of homeroom. Now she was going to have to go talk to the secretary before the attendance sheets got there and someone called her mom to ask why Charlotte wasn't in school. Because that would go well.

It took Charlotte some time to spin a convincing tale of woe to the school secretary, and as a result she was five minutes late for math, and when she walked in, Mr. Crapf eyed her fishily. Charlotte had a bad habit of being late to math, because the classroom was at the other end of the building from her homeroom and, well, it was hard for her to motivate herself to hurry to get to math class. It's just not something one does.

"Do you have a note, Charlotte?" Mr. Crapf asked imperiously.

She tossed her hair. "No, Mr. Crapf," she said, her

voice full of sweetness. "I'd be happy to get one from the doctor, though. I was in an accident this morning."

"I—I'm sorry!" he said, his stern expression falling. "Are you all right? Should you be here?"

Charlotte nodded primly. "I didn't want to miss math."

With that, she took her seat, the whole class watching her with the wide-eyed respect with which we regard those who have survived a brush with death.

After class Zee stood by the door and waited for her, an anxious expression on his face. Charlotte gathered her books and headed toward him.

"Hey, Miels-sweat-ski!" a voice called from behind her. Charlotte recognized the dulcet tones of Chris Shapiro, who was as short as he was obnoxious—and he was plenty short. Chris had been calling her Miels-*sweat*-ski since the fourth grade, which was apparently when he first learned how to rhyme. Charlotte rolled her eyes and ignored him. She used to be bothered by Chris, but once you've faced the King of the Dead, the school bully isn't quite so scary anymore.

"What happened?" Zee asked hurriedly when she reached him. "You had an accident? Are you all right? Is Aunt Tara all right?"

"Oh. No," Charlotte said, looking around surreptitiously. "I was just late."

Zee rolled his eyes. "You couldn't have thought of that one when we were gone all night?"

"Hey, Zee!" someone called from down the hall. Zee waved over Charlotte's head, and she turned to look. It was Jason! She turned back to her cousin.

"You know him?"

"Yeah. He's on my soccer team. Just moved here."

"Really?"

A sly smile crossed Zee's face. "Yeah. Why?" he asked, in a way that indicated he already knew the answer.

Charlotte narrowed her eyes. "No reason."

The cousins walked through the hallway together, moving resolutely against the endless tide of middle school students. Charlotte rarely got to see Zee these days. Even though he was *family*, she couldn't hang out with him any more than she could with Maddy—since her parents had decided she was clearly a bad influence on her cousin. (Which was absolutely ridiculous, by the way. Charlotte had never sneaked out of the house before Zee came along, so if you just looked at the facts objectively, exactly who was a bad influence on whom? Hmmm?) He had all the same classes as she did, but those weren't really a good time for meaningful communication, and Zee was too British to talk in class anyway. Charlotte could rarely catch Zee alone between classes because a pack of people always surrounded him, and seating was assigned at lunch. It was hard to do too much talking about the plight of the Dead when you were spending the whole hour passing Jim Foti the ketchup.

Still, whenever there was a chance, the cousins gravitated toward each other, huddling together instinctively, in the manner of two people who shared one awful secret. Maddy once asked Charlotte what she and Zee were always whispering about so portentously. Charlotte said Zee just took his science homework very seriously.

"How've you been?" Zee asked, lowering his voice conspiratorially.

"Same," Charlotte said with a shrug.

"Yeah. Have you heard anything from Mr. Metos?"

Zee and Charlotte asked each other this question every few days. It was silly, of course; if one of them had heard anything, they would have told the other right away. But still, they asked. And the answer was always the same.

"No." Charlotte shook her head.

There wasn't anything to say, really. They'd been over it a thousand times with each other; they were stuck. There were things to fix in the world, and no one was going to let them even try to fix them because they were kids. Except they were kids who had defeated a coup in the Underworld; none of the grown-ups had done that. As far as Charlotte was concerned, it was the Prometheans who should be forced to endure algebra, cruel and unusual groundings, and school bullies with major Napoleon complexes, while Charlotte and Zee worked to save the Dead.

Zee glanced at Charlotte furtively, as if he were trying to make a decision about something. "Look, Char," he said, his voice even more secretive. But then he stopped himself and, shaking his head dismissively, said, "Ah, nothing."

"Oh, come on, what?" Zee went all reticent at the weirdest times.

Zee opened his mouth, but before he could speak, a melodious, dual-toned "Hi, Zee!" came floating down the hallway. Approaching them were two of Charlotte's classmates, Ashley and Ashley, who did just about everything in unison. Charlotte didn't know why they bothered being interested in Zee; they'd either have to share him or he'd need a double.

As the girls passed, they flashed huge smiles at Zee, and he blushed. He did that all the time. When he first came to the school he had happily interacted with every member of the female contingent of the eighth grade—until Charlotte mentioned that half the girls had a crush on him. She was trying to be nice at the time; she had had no idea that he turned into Zachary-the-Stammering-Nincompoop around any girl he liked or who liked him. And, since Zee didn't know which girls belonged in that dread half, he had had no choice but to be embarrassed by all of them. As weird as it was, Charlotte found the whole thing rather reassuring, because it meant he would never, ever have a girlfriend.

They arrived in the hallway outside the gym, and Zee let out a small sigh and pulled Charlotte aside. "Look, Char," he whispered, "this is probably nothing, but . . . I saw something. . . ."

Charlotte's eyes widened. "What?"

"I mean, I didn't really see it, but—"

"Char! Zee!" The cousins moved apart as Maddy came hurrying toward them, wide-eyed. Zee gave Charlotte a dismissive wave of his hand, as if what he had to say really wasn't that important. "Char, are you okay? I heard you got hit by a bus!"

Maddy and Zee listened while Charlotte reassured them of her safety. She couldn't really explain why she'd been late that morning; what was she supposed to tell them, that she had a bad feeling and was distracted by an old guy in an aqua suit? Maddy would think she was nuts, and Zee might get a little too concerned.

At least Zee could be around Maddy. She was the exception to Zee's girl weirdness—maybe because she was Charlotte's best friend, Zee just had never thought of her romantically. Charlotte was glad, as it would be mighty uncomfortable if Zee went all social anxiety disorder every time Maddy was around. Plus he would probably freak out around Charlotte, too, and she didn't know what she'd do without Zee.

"Come on, we'll be late," Maddy said, motioning to the locker rooms.

"That's all right," Zee muttered.

"Oh, you'll be great," Charlotte said with a grin.

"Oh, yeah, brilliant."

On this day Zee was the one dreading gym, while Charlotte quite looked forward to it. For the last two weeks they'd been doing a gymnastics unit, and for once Charlotte was actually better at something athletic than Zee. Much better. (Gymnastics was one of the few units in eighth-grade PE that everyone had to do, boys and girls, and Charlotte thought that it was because Ms. Pimm enjoyed watching the boys try to do pirouettes as much as she did.) Her cousin, while he was able to manipulate a soccer ball like a virtuoso did a violin, performed a cartwheel with all the agility and grace of a morbidly obese grizzly bear.

After dressing, Charlotte strode out of the girls' locker room wearing her school-issue scratchy Hartnett T-shirt and polyester shorts with pride. Maddy, too, had a degree of saunter in her walk—she was no gymnast but had had some years of ballet and would acquit herself quite nicely. They settled themselves cross-legged on the mat.

The boys emerged from their locker room, not in the usual parade of small groupings arranged by social status, but rather in one large group—united, at last, in fear. Zee, who usually wore athletic gear like another skin, suddenly looked gangly and awkward. Charlotte grinned and motioned him over.

"Hey!" she called. "Sit with us!" She patted the empty space next to her.

Zee looked sideways at her. "I've never seen you so happy to be in gym."

"I'm just a naturally happy person," she said.

"Uh-huh," said Zee.

But in truth, his routine proved to be not half-bad, though he couldn't be said to be any good, either. He stumbled a bit on his split jump, and his cartwheel was really more of a three-hundred-and-sixty-degree spaz, but it could have been worse. In fact, for most of them it *was* worse. Lewis Larson got stuck trying to work his legs down into an attempt at a split. His twin brother, Larry, seized up during a back somersault and had to be helped out of position. Dov Stern leaned too far forward during a front fall and hit his face on the mat. Jack

Liao spent a good thirty seconds trying to kick himself up into a headstand before rotating all the way over and falling on his butt.

As for Charlotte, she sailed through her routine, landing her front handspring perfectly (which she didn't always do), and when she sat down, Maddy grinned at her.

When Maddy got up to do her routine, it was Charlotte's turn to grin. Maddy was awfully graceful for someone who studied so much, and suddenly it seemed they were in an auditorium somewhere with velvet-lined curtains instead of in the Hartnett gym with its pervading odor of feet. Charlotte looked casually over at the rest of the kids, making sure they were paying attention. Her eyes landed on her cousin, who was certainly watching Maddy. In fact, he seemed to be watching her rather intently. In fact, he had a very odd expression on his face. At first Charlotte thought maybe he noticed something wrong with Maddy, but he didn't have a there's-something-wrong look on his face. No, he had a there's-something-right look on his face, as if he had just seen Maddy for the first time.

Oh no.

## CHAPTER 3

### Charlotte Junior, Fish at Large

CHARLOTTE DECIDED SHE SHOULDN'T PANIC. MAYBE she hadn't seen what she thought she'd seen. Maybe Zee was just really appreciating the wonder of gymnastics. Maybe he wasn't going to turn into a complete freak around Maddy and make Charlotte's social life even more pathetic than it already was—which you wouldn't think would be possible, given she was grounded until she was thirty, but apparently it was.

She studied Zee carefully for some sign of change. She'd never seen him interested in a girl, so she didn't really know what sort of changes might manifest. Still, there should be symptoms. Was his face flushed? Were his eyes dim and unfocused? Were there little cartoon birdies flying in circles around his head?

But Charlotte couldn't get close enough to Zee find out. He bolted into the locker room after gym and always seemed to be with someone else between classes. Charlotte did notice that at lunch he very distinctly did not meet her eye, but she decided that that could be because of the pimple, which seemed to still be growing. She was surprised it didn't throw off her balance during her routine.

Charlotte decided not to think too hard about the fact that Zee was acting exactly how you might expect someone who'd just realized he had a crush on your best friend to act—at least, if that someone were Zee. In addition to the fact that he now had to be terrified of the last girl in school that he could talk to, Zee would be all neurotic about Charlotte and how she'd feel about the whole thing. Honestly. The girls were always complaining that guys weren't sensitive enough; Zee had enough sensitivity for the whole school, maybe the whole city.

And then, before English—which was the only class the three of them had together besides gym—Charlotte and Maddy were standing outside the classroom door talking (Charlotte may have waylaid Maddy there just to

see what would happen, but she'd never admit it) and
Zee came walking down the hallway. He was deep in
conversation with Charlie and didn't see them, so as he
got closer Charlotte whispered to Maddy, "Hey, call him
over." Maddy complied, and as her voice reached him,
Charlotte could see Zee's cheeks darken and his eyes
turn into small moons. He stood for a moment, frozen
in full fight-or-flight mode, and then called back, "Um,
I—I gotta go," and made a break for the classroom.

Maddy looked at Charlotte, eyebrows raised.
"What's with him?"

Charlotte shook her head. "Nothing." Maddy would
figure it out soon enough. She'd be all excited, too, and
Charlotte was going to have to break it to her that Zee
was never going to speak to her again.

To make the day even more annoying, Charlotte had
therapy after school. Every Thursday she had to miss
gymnastics, which was the only fun thing in her life, so
she could take a bus across town and have some woman
in a pantsuit ask her about her feelings for fifty minutes.
But since Charlotte had no intention of talking about
her feelings, they didn't have very much to do.

As Charlotte walked into Dr. Sorenson's office that
afternoon, she found herself in an even worse mood
than usual. Today was the last gymnastics meet of the
year and she'd be missing it. And the whole Zee/Maddy

thing was going to be a complete nightmare. Plus it bothered her a little that Zee was acting weird around her—they'd survived the Underworld together, they couldn't survive his crush on her best friend? He had to realize she couldn't do any of this by herself.

In other words, instead of being defensive and sullen the way she usually was when she walked into therapy, today Charlotte was defensive and *crabby*. She wondered if Dr. Sorenson, as a highly trained adolescent psychologist, would notice the difference.

Charlotte plopped down in the overstuffed blue chair and crossed her arms. Next to her was a small table on which always sat a box of Kleenex. After several weeks, Charlotte finally figured out that this box was there in case she needed to cry. Like that was going to happen. Charlotte Mielswetzski wept for no one.

Perched carefully on a high-backed armchair, Dr. Sorenson gave Charlotte a businesslike smile. "How are you this week, Charlotte?"

Every week, Dr. Sorenson started the session by asking her how she was, and every week Charlotte said the same thing, "Fine." Which wasn't a lie, really—she was totally fine, if "fine" meant she was grounded for eight million years, her parents treated her like a degenerate, and she was awash in her own helplessness in the face of evil. It all depends on your point of view.

The trouble is in normal conversation, when someone asks you how you are and you say "Fine," or some
such, the first person usually says "Good," or something
like that and moves on. But apparently no one had ever
told Dr. Sorenson the way normal conversations work,
because every week, after Charlotte said, "Fine," Dr.
Sorenson just looked at her as if Charlotte was supposed
to say more than that. Charlotte got pretty hip to that
game quickly—the doctor *knew* Charlotte didn't like
silence and would eventually start talking just so someone was saying something, and then Charlotte would let
something personal slip.

It was a devious plan, but Charlotte had outwitted
far greater foes than Dr. Melinda Sorenson this year. If
Dr. Sorenson wanted to play games, games Charlotte
could play. So the first few moments of her therapy
appointments were always spent in uncomfortable
silence while Charlotte proceeded to stare at the goldfish on the psychologist's desk and think of the many
places she would rather be.

In her first session, Dr. Sorenson went into a big
speech about how Charlotte should feel comfortable
talking to her. "This is a safe space for you, Charlotte,"
she had said. "You can say whatever you want. We can
talk about whatever you want. You should think of it as
blowing off steam, like writing in a diary or something,

except I'm even better because you can bounce things off me and ask me questions. I'm on your side here—I'll never tell your parents or anyone else what we talk about. I can assure you of that."

Uh-huh, Charlotte thought.

"And," she continued, "if you decide you want to tell me what happened to you last fall, I promise you that that, too, will remain between us."

Right. All her parents had wanted since Charlotte had come back was to find out where she'd been and what she'd been doing—because obviously it had been something deeply awful, possibly criminal—and they were clearly paying this woman to find out so they could learn precisely how much of a juvenile delinquent their daughter was.

"So," Dr. Sorenson asked after the requisite minute or so of silence, "how was your day? Did anything interesting happen?"

Yes. "No, not really." The goldfish did a lazy lap around the bowl. Charlotte sympathized greatly with the fish—swimming around and around and getting absolutely nowhere. In her head, she thought of Dr. Sorenson's fish as Charlotte Junior.

"Nothing at all?"

This was usually the time in the session where Charlotte thought of something completely random to talk about. Because, really, you had to fill the hour some-how.

"Have you ever seen anyone wear an aqua suit?" Charlotte asked.

Dr. Sorenson blinked. "A . . . what?"

"Aqua suit. Like aqua-colored?"

"No, I haven't. Why?"

"There was a really old man outside school today. He must have been someone's grandfather. He was wearing an aqua suit. An old-fashioned one with a vest and everything. And a bowler hat. An aqua bowler hat."

Dr. Sorenson raised her eyebrows skeptically. "Really," she said in an unconvinced voice.

Charlotte narrowed her eyes. "Yes, really!" She couldn't believe it. Her highly prized psychologist didn't believe her. What was that supposed to do for her self-esteem?

"Charlotte"—Dr. Sorenson sighed a long-suffering sigh—"I know you can be somewhat . . . colorful in the things you say. And I think sometimes you do that to mask what's really going on inside your head. It's a defense mechanism. But I think if you told me what you're really thinking about, you'd find it would feel really good. It can be a relief to tell the truth."

"Really," Charlotte said flatly.

"Really! I promise!"

Fine. Charlotte straightened in her chair. "Well, I think I'd like to tell you what I was doing when I was gone all night."

"Oh, Charlotte, that's great. I really think you'll be glad you did."

Charlotte folded her arms. "I was saving the world."

"You . . . what?"

Charlotte smiled and leaned forward, wide-eyed. "You see, Greek gods are actually real. Zeus and all that? Real. I know, I know, who knew, right? And there was this guy, Philonecron was his name. And he wanted to overthrow Hades, so he took kids' shadows to make his army."

Dr. Sorenson blinked at her.

"And Philonecron had these creepy clay guys that wore tuxedos. And they were following me and Zee, right? And stealing everyone's shadows. Because Philonecron took Zee's blood, you see, to lead the creepy clay guys to him. But Zee got back at him. He took charge of the whole shadow army and stopped Philonecron. It was amazing. So we were in the Underworld and trying to stop the whole thing. And we did! We stopped it! But Philonecron's walking around in the Upperworld now, and I'm not sure how the gods feel about me prancing through the Underworld, and plus it's really hard to know all this stuff about the world and not be able to tell anyone, so it can be hard to focus in school sometimes."

With a contented sigh, Charlotte leaned back in her chair. Wow, Dr. Sorenson was right. It did feel good to tell someone!

Dr. Sorenson eyed her coldly. "I see."

"You mean," Charlotte said in her best unsurprised voice, "you don't believe me?"

"Charlotte"—the doctor shook her head—"I think underneath your exterior lies a very mature girl with a lot to give the world, if you'd just give the world a chance. . . . I don't know what I have to do to get you to trust me. I'm on your side."

Right. The only person really, truly on her side was Zee. And he didn't wear pantsuits.

The rest of the session went like that, with Dr. Sorenson trying to convince Charlotte of her strength and maturity and Charlotte watching Charlotte Junior swim around fruitlessly. Time passed more slowly in therapy than it did in the Underworld.

On the way out of the building, Charlotte stopped into the bathroom to examine Mount Olympus. It was giant and red and seemed to be bigger than her nose itself. She was surprised Dr. Sorenson was able to focus on patronizing her. Grumbling, she walked out of the bathroom to find she was not alone in the lobby. There, standing and looking at the building directory, was green-eyed, rumple-haired Jason.

He grinned as soon as she came out. "Fancy meeting you here."

"Yeah!" Charlotte said, too surprised to worry about being hideously deformed. "What are you doing here?"

"Oh," he said vaguely, "I have an appointment."

"Right," Charlotte said. "Me too."

She wondered if Jason was seeing a therapist too. Except she couldn't imagine why someone that cute would be in therapy, for what troubles could he possibly have? Maybe he'd sneaked out to save the world and his parents were complete fascists and he was grounded for the rest of his life too. Then they'd have so much in common—though their relationship would be tragically doomed, since both of them were grounded. And it would be yet another way in which her parents had totally ruined her life.

"Hey," Jason said, "did you talk to Zee today?"

"What? Oh!" Right, Jason was on his soccer team. "Um, a little. . . ."

Jason leaned in, eyes sparkling. "I think he likes Maddy!"

Charlotte blinked. "How did you know that? Did he . . . tell you that?"

"Naw," said Jason. "I could just tell."

Charlotte didn't know how Jason could tell that, but she did know that somewhere, just because the words "Zee likes Maddy" had been spoken out loud, Zee was cringing and he didn't know why.

"Hey, look," Charlotte said reluctantly. "I gotta go. My dad's waiting."

He rolled his eyes. "Mine too."

Charlotte squinted at him. Didn't he have an appointment? She'd never known how confusing cute boys were.

"You were great, by the way," he said suddenly. "In gym."

Charlotte felt her cheeks flush. "Oh. Thank you!"

"Yeah, you must be really strong."

Charlotte felt her cheeks reddening.

"And," he added, looking around secretively, "brave."

She blinked. What?

"But of course"—he leaned toward her and whispered conspiratorially—"we knew that, didn't we?"

A chill passed through Charlotte. What did he mean? He couldn't possibly mean—

"Anyway," he said, grinning again, "I'll see you in school." And with that, he turned and walked away.

Charlotte's head was spinning when she crawled into the passenger seat of her father's sedan. She normally made an effort to sulk all the way home from therapy, so whichever parent was driving her understood the extent of her misery. And if they suffered as a result, so much the better. But tonight she was too preoccupied.

"Dad? Did you see a boy go inside? About my age? Dark hair?" (Impossibly cute?)

"Oh, you mean Jason Hart?"

"You know him?"

"Sure. I met him when I picked Zee up at soccer the other day. Nice kid. Likes your cousin a lot."

"Oh," Charlotte said. "Do you know anything about him?"

He shook his head. "He just moved here. Not sure from where. Lives with his grandfather, I think. Why?"

"Oh, no reason."

"Really?" Mr. Mielswetzski smiled slowly. "He's an awfully handsome young boy, isn't he?"

Charlotte gasped. "Dad!"

"Maybe I could introduce you? You could come to one of Zee's soccer games, and—"

"No!" Charlotte exclaimed. "No, it's okay."

"All right," he said. "Just let me know if you change your mind. . . . Oh! I have a surprise for you!"

"You do?"

"Yeah, look in the backseat."

Charlotte turned. She couldn't see anything but

stacks of library books. They were clearly from the high school library and had titles like *Revolution 1776* and *Thomas Jefferson Unplugged*. She turned to her dad and shook her head.

"The books, Lottie! I got you a bunch of colonial history books. I think it will really enhance your experience on the cruise. You'll have so much fun!" He was smiling so kindly at her that Charlotte didn't have the heart to tell him that it was the lamest surprise ever.

"The Jefferson one is particularly interesting," Mr. Mielswetzski continued. "Did you know he and Alexander Hamilton really hated each other? It's true! We think of our founding fathers as this big cohesive unit, but . . ."

And so he talked, all the way home.

# CHAPTER 4

## The Friendly Skies

Just a few days before, on a very normal transatlantic flight of a very normal commercial airliner, two very normal flight attendants huddled in the back room whispering about the somewhat abnormal passenger in seat 32E. Now, these flight attendants had seen it all over the years, and nothing and nobody fazed them anymore, including the guy in 32E. But that didn't mean they couldn't make fun of him.

"That's the oldest person I've ever seen in my life," whispered flight attendant A.

"I can't believe he can sit up straight," mumbled flight attendant B.

"I can't believe he's not drooling on himself," muttered flight attendant A.

"Did you see his suit? It looks like it's from a hundred years ago," murmured flight attendant B.

You cannot blame the flight attendants for whispering—you would have noticed him too. His suit was certainly nothing you'd ever seen before—an old-fashioned suit in the oddest shade of blue. Or was it blue-green? The color seemed to change slightly as you looked at it. He was thin and frail and, despite a lack of wrinkles, gave the impression of great age, and his skin seemed the texture and firmness of tissue paper. He was the sort of person you desperately hope does not sit next to you—and always does.

Indeed, the boy in the seat next to him looked none too happy. He was quite a handsome boy too, with dark rumpled hair and eyes that were a startling shade of green. The boy sat with his arms crossed and gaze lowered, headphones in his ears to discourage any attempt at communication. Every once in a while the extremely old man glanced at him and opened his mouth as if to speak, but the boy would not acknowledge him.

"He might *be* from a hundred years ago," whispered flight attendant A.

"I'm worried he's going to croak on the plane," agreed flight attendant B.

But the flight attendants were wrong. This man was not going to die on the plane, or anywhere else for that matter. For this man was not a man at all but a god.

Most gods, of course, do not avail themselves of mortal transportation—and when they do, they certainly do not fly coach. But this particular god loved mortals. He loved all their inventions and aspirations, their conventions and contraptions, their synthetic flavors and stain-resistant fabrics. They worked so hard at it too—like if they could just invent a way to keep white shirts white, they might keep from dying a little longer. But they couldn't, that was the thing—all the inventions and contraptions in the world wouldn't change the fact that they always smelled of death.

It was adorable.

No, this was not one of the gods who wished for the extinction of the species, for the world would be so sad without them, like a zoo entirely devoid of animals. And what kind of a zoo was that? A bad zoo.

There were those, of course, who didn't believe Immortals should travel in the human realm at all, literally or metaphorically. Because the whole point of this whole just-kidding-it's-only-a-myth thing is that you don't have to deal with mortals anymore. Because mortals are such lowly beings that even being around them gives you a rash. Because mortality as a notion makes you feel slightly oogy. And mostly because the next thing you know, your cover will be blown and you'll be at the mortals' beck and call once again, and no one wants that.

But this particular god thought they should all lighten up, for what was the point of having humans if you couldn't involve yourself with them? Oh, not *involve* involve—like, *I'm your god and if you sacrifice to me I'll really help you out when times are rough, you can count on me, I am your rock, a bridge over troubled water* involve. Don't be ridiculous. There are so many other ways for an Immortal to interfere. One might like to shoot a golden arrow at a woman's heart and make her love a man from a neighboring village, another might like to toss the Apple of Discord between the two lovers and break them up horribly, a third might like to start a war between their villages that resulted in the complete destruction of everything around them. Everyone needs a hobby. What's the point of having the ability to spread a horrid, pustule-induced pestilence across an entire famine-ravaged country if you're not allowed to do it, eh?

Officially, of course, the message from Up High these days was Do Not. Keep Away. Hands Off the Merchandise. Unofficially, the rule was simpler: Don't Get Caught.

In other words, one could not run willy-nilly through the mortal realm singing, "I am a god, bow before me, or else I'll turn you into a chicken." It just wasn't done. Subtlety was the key. If you really wanted to turn someone into a chicken, you had to do it *quietly*.

But even if this god wanted to, he couldn't turn someone into a chicken. He couldn't make people fall in love or make them hate each other, couldn't start a war or a plague. He had only one real ability, one wonderful ability—and he rarely got to use it anymore. For it was his job to serve Poseidon, the Lord of the Sea—which he was honored to do, really, truly, and he wasn't complaining by any means, and even if he was, you wouldn't tell Poseidon, would you?—not gallivant through the fields of mortality. And after one of his rare excursions some years ago resulted in a rather troubled mortal son who took his attention away from his duties, Poseidon had put the kibosh on any more adventures. And by "kibosh," he meant—well, you don't want to know.

But now Poseidon had forgiven him and given him a mission. A real mission. It was good for the ol' self-esteem, really. It was important in life to use your skills, to reach your full potential. He was all about reaching your full potential. As he kept trying to tell his son.

He had not been this excited in ages, really—he felt like a newborn child viewing the world for the first time. And he found himself whistling as he shuffled off with the mortals—talking to one another, reading their newspapers, plugged into their gadgets, entirely unaware of the Immortal in their midst. Sometimes he got the urge to reveal himself to them, to see their faces as they tried to comprehend his vast and terrible divinity, to—

"Sir?"

He looked toward the voice. A flight attendant was standing next to him, smiling a waxy smile. "Sir, do you need a wheelchair?"

He blinked. "A what?"

"*A wheelchair?*" she repeated loudly. "*It's a long way to baggage claim.*"

He eyed her coldly. "No," he said, "I'll be just fine."

Just outside of the gate, the green-eyed boy was leaning against a pillar, looking at the god suspiciously. The god walked over to him and whispered, "Wait here."

"What are you going to do?" the boy hissed.

"Reach my full potential."

A few minutes later he stood inside the men's bathroom staring into the mirror. If you looked at him, you might see a very old man with an aqua-colored bowler hat and a tuft of white hair sticking up from either side of his head, but he saw—well, he also saw an old man with an aqua-colored bowler hat and a tuft of white hair sticking up from either side of his head—but he also saw possibility. That is what it is to be a god—possibility.

There was shuffling in a stall behind him, then a tall, dark-haired man emerged, washed his hands, and exited while the god studied him. A few moments later, the god gave himself one last appreciative glance in the mirror and then strode out the door, heading back to the gate. He ignored the boy who shook his head disgustedly.

The flight attendant was still there, typing something into a computer. Straightening himself, the god approached her.

"Excuse me," he said, his eyes twinkling. "I couldn't help noticing you from across the room. Would you like to have a cup of coffee with me sometime?"

The woman looked up, and when she saw him a slow smile spread across her face. She raised her eyebrows flirtatiously.

"Well," she said, looking him up and down. "Hello, handsome!"

## CHAPTER 5

# The Perils of Being a Fish

When Charlotte came down to breakfast the next morning, her parents were still at the table, eating fiber-rich cereal and grapefruit. Every few months they went on a health kick, which meant that just about everything with any flavor at all disappeared from the house. Parents never considered how much their children suffered when they did things like that.

"Good morning, sweetie!" Mr. Mielswetzski said. "Would you like a grapefruit?"

Charlotte winced. "No, thanks, Dad. I'll just make myself a bagel."

"Your loss," he said congenially, plunging his spoon into the center of the fruit with such alacrity that a squirt of juice hit him in the eye.

Right. Charlotte fixed herself a bagel with strawberry cream cheese and settled herself at the counter, where she flipped through the newspaper and tried to ignore her parents. At least when they talked about their diet, they weren't yelling at her.

"We're going to have to be careful what we eat on the cruise," Mrs. Mielswetzski was saying.

"There's going to be so much food," agreed Mr. Mielswetzski.

"It's all about making healthy choices," said Mrs. Mielswetzski.

Charlotte rolled her eyes. If there was a lot of food on the cruise, she was going to make as many unhealthy choices as possible. She had to have *some* fun.

When she was done, she hopped out of her chair. "Um, I wanted to get to school early today, if that's okay?"

Both of her parents looked at her as if she'd said she thought she'd like to live out the rest of her days in a convent.

"Really?" said her father.

"Why?" said her mother.

"I'm supposed to meet Zee." This was technically

true, although Zee didn't know it yet. Zee usually took the early bus, and Charlotte wanted to ask him about Jason Hart. The night before, she'd decided he couldn't possibly have meant what it sounded like he meant by "but we knew that already"; she must have misheard him, or misunderstood him, or something. There was simply no way some random cute boy was going to appear in the halls of Hartnett Middle School knowing about everything. Or at least if he did, it would be to take her off to his evil lair and feed her to a Hydra, and Jason didn't seem to be about to do that. Plus—and this was hard for Charlotte to believe—he seemed to actually like her. Still, she wanted to talk about it with Zee.

"Oh," Mr. Mielswetzski exclaimed. "Your cousin called last night."

"He did?"

"Yes, when you were at therapy. I forgot."

She raised her eyebrows. "You forgot?"

"It happens," he said with a shrug. "Sorry, Lottie."

Charlotte grumbled inwardly. If she did that sort of thing, it was a sign of how irresponsible she was. If one of her parents does it, well, it happens.

"Did he say anything?"

"No, just to call him."

Charlotte frowned. Zee didn't call her much, nor did

anyone else; the terms of her grounding meant she could only talk on the phone for five minutes, total, which made it basically impossible to say anything at all. If he had anything to tell her, he usually waited until school.

But maybe something had happened, something that couldn't wait. Maybe Jason said something to him, or maybe he'd heard from Mr. Metos! With a quickening heart, Charlotte dashed upstairs to get ready for school.

But Zee was nowhere to be found in the morning. When it got to be time for homeroom, she waited outside the room for him, but when the bell rang there was still no Zee. Maybe he was gone. Maybe Mr. Metos had come back to get them, and it was a now-or-never thing, and since her father hadn't bothered to give her the message, Zee had left with him and now Charlotte was all alone. That would be typical of her life.

After homeroom was over, Charlotte headed toward math class by herself. As she was walking through the hallway, she heard someone loudly calling her name. Maddy was at the other end of the hall, waving frantically at her.

In moments she was at Charlotte's side, grabbing her arm and pulling her off into a corner.

"What? What is it?" Charlotte breathed, staring at her friend in wonder. Maddy's face was flushed and she was bouncing slightly on her feet, making her long, brown ponytail bob up and down.

A tremendous grin spread across Maddy's face. "It's Zee," she whispered, eyes like supernovas.

"Zee?" Charlotte repeated dumbly. She knew something about Zee? Had he said something about Mr. Metos to Maddy? But why would he—

"He asked me out!"

Charlotte blinked. "Out where?"

"Not out somewhere. *Out* out!" Charlotte looked at her, not comprehending. "We're going out! Me and Zee!"

Everything seemed to go strangely quiet in Charlotte's brain for a moment, as if someone had turned off the volume in the world and all that was left was some distant static, like a radio waiting to receive a signal. She felt her eyelids drop and open again—once, twice, three, four, five times—and each time they opened, Maddy was still in front of her, beaming at her.

"Can you believe it?" Maddy gasped. "He was waiting for me before school! We missed homeroom talking about it. I'm already becoming a delinquent!" She giggled wildly. "Char, he kissed me!"

Charlotte squinted at Maddy and slowly tilted her head to the side like a bemused cocker spaniel. "Are you sure?"

Maddy started. "What do you mean, am I sure?"

"I mean, are you sure? Did you misunderstand?" The fuzzy noise was back in her head, growing louder and louder, making it very hard to focus on the world around her.

"What," Maddy said, crossing her arms, "you don't think Zee could like me?"

Suddenly Charlotte could hear perfectly. "No! That's not it!"

"Really? Do you think I'm not good enough for your cousin?"

Charlotte shook her head frantically. "No!"

"Well, what? Are you jealous or something?" Maddy said, icicles hanging off her words. "Can't you just be happy for me?"

"No! I mean, yes! Wait . . ."

"Well, I don't know what your problem is," Maddy said with a sniff. "But whatever it is, I hope you get over it soon." And with that, she turned on her heel and stalked off.

It took Charlotte some time to remove herself from her position in the hallway. Students passed her by, talking and laughing, as if everything in the world was as it should be, as if they still existed in the same universe as this morning—then gradually, the stream of them slowed, and then stopped, and Charlotte was still in the hallway blinking toward the place where she had last seen Maddy.

Three full minutes later, Charlotte let out a long, strained exhale, shook her head, then headed toward math again. Maybe she would see Zee there and he would explain what was going on.

Of course she was late—there was that whole sojourn in the hallway, then as she'd tried to move again she'd discovered someone had replaced the air with some strange translucent goo, and that takes some time to walk through. Mr. Crapf glared at her when she walked in the door.

"Charlotte, do you have a note?"

"No," she said flatly.

"I'll have to mark you as tardy, then."

"Fine," she muttered.

As Charlotte sat down, she noticed that Zee's desk was empty—apparently he was still off reveling in his newfound love. Was that what he'd wanted to tell her when he called last night? *Charlotte, I've miraculously grown a backbone! Catch you on the flip side!*

Finally, a few minutes after Charlotte had sat down, Zee appeared in the doorway, gave the room a quick survey, and then strolled to his desk, a row behind Charlotte.

"Zachary?" Mr. Crapf turned around and eyed Zee. "Do you have a note?"

"No!" Zee replied cheerfully.

"I'll have to mark you as tardy."

"Brilliant!"

Huh? Charlotte spun around in her seat to stare at Zee, who grinned at her and said quite loudly, "Hi!"

"Charlotte!" snapped Mr. Crapf. "Turn around."

Oh, sure, *she* should get in trouble. Charlotte turned back around dutifully in her chair, but as soon as Mr. Crapf turned his attention back to the blackboard, she swiveled her head back toward Zee.

He didn't look like he'd suffered a massive blow to the head. In fact, he seemed quite cheerful as he took his notes. At least that hadn't changed—Zee was studiously copying down everything Mr. Crapf was writing on the board.

Except—Charlotte raised herself in her seat to peer at the notebook on his desk—those didn't look like notes. Was he . . . doodling?

Zee felt her gaze and looked up questioningly. "What?" he whispered.

Charlotte raised her eyebrows, shook her head at him slowly, and turned back around in her chair.

After class, Charlotte stood by the door, arms folded, waiting for her cousin. He bounced up to her and exclaimed, "Hey, Char! How are you?"

She stared at him. "I'm fine. How are *you?*"

"I'm great!"

"You are?"

"Yeah!" Zee turned his head and hollered down the hallway, "Oh, hey, Charlie! Be there in a sec!"

"I saw Maddy this morning," Charlotte said, her voice thin and high.

Zee's face lit up. "Yeah! We're going out! Isn't it brilliant? She's so pretty."

"Okay. Um, I'm just . . . surprised. I mean, usually you don't really talk to girls." There, there was that fuzzy noise in her head again. She really should have that looked at.

Zee blinked at her. "Sure I do!"

"No," Charlotte said. "No, you don't."

"Well, that's ridiculous! Why wouldn't I talk to girls?" He shook his head. "You know, Char, sometimes you just got to seize the day, you know? Go get 'em, tiger, and all that? You know?"

"Sure," she said, folding her arms more tightly.

"I just woke up this morning and felt so terrific," he continued, shaking his head in wonderment. "It's just so great to be alive!"

"Uh-huh," Charlotte said, eyeing him. "Okay. Hey, listen, what did you want to talk to me about?"

He blinked dumbly at her.

"You called last night? My dad didn't give me the message until this morning."

"Oh, yeah," he said, giving a dismissive wave. "It's nothing."

"Are you sure?"

"Yeah," he said, with a happy smile. "Positive."

All through the day, Charlotte studied her cousin, trying to figure out what in the world had gotten into him. He *looked* different. His shoulders had lost their slump, his face was bright and open. Gone was the heavy shroud of Zee-ness that he always seemed to wear, replaced by this aura of sunshine and daffodils and a whole lot of other things Charlotte couldn't parse.

Was it just love? Was that all it was going to take, this whole time, to fix whatever it was that ailed Zee? As he bounded through the hallways, enthusiastically greeting everyone in his path, as his voice boomed through halls and classrooms, Charlotte thought it seemed her cousin didn't have a care in the world, which was pretty impressive for someone who'd almost caused the eternal suffering of humankind.

As for Maddy, she was ignoring Charlotte. As soon as Charlotte walked into the locker room for gym, Maddy stalked off to change somewhere else. During gym, she kept a distance of at least ten feet between the two of them, as assiduously as if Charlotte had taken out a restraining order.

Meanwhile, the whole school was buzzing about Jason Hart. His presence had affected the school in much the same way Zee's had six months earlier. Wherever Charlotte went, pockets of girls were huddled together, whispering about the cute new boy. Charlotte kept her eyes open for him, thinking she would casually try to find out what he'd meant last night. If he was trying to tell her he knew, he'd certainly try again.

Plus, she really wouldn't mind seeing him again.

When Charlotte finally saw Jason at lunch, she was surprised to see he had changed too. When she'd seen him the day before, he'd been outgoing, cheerful—now he slumped in his chair with narrowed eyes and an aura akin to a black hole.

"Hi," Charlotte said warily.

"Oh!" Jason turned around. When he saw Charlotte, something passed through his green eyes—a flicker of something very like excitement, and suddenly he was the same old Jason again. Despite herself, Charlotte's heart leaped. "How are you?" he asked.

Fine now. "Okay, um . . . You okay?"

"Sure," Jason said, shrugging dismissively. He looked around and then leaned toward Charlotte and whispered, "So, have you seen Zee today?"

Unfortunately. "Yeah . . ."

He tilted his head questioningly. "Does he seem weird to you?"

A wave of relief passed over Charlotte. It felt good just to hear someone else say it. "You noticed it too? I don't understand it. He's just . . . changed."

Jason let out something between a laugh and a grunt. "He sure has. . . . Do you have any idea why?"

Charlotte threw up her hands. "No, but if you figure it out, please tell me." She shook her head. "You know he's going out with Maddy?"

"Yeah, I know. Gross, right?"

"Well—" That wasn't quite the word she would use. "It's just—"

Jason opened his mouth as if to say something, but just then Ms. Bristol-Lee came by and shooed Charlotte toward her seat.

When lunch was over, Charlotte walked out of the lunchroom talking with Julie and Kelly from the gymnastics team about the meet that Charlotte had missed the night before. Someone from the opposing team had face-planted on a handspring and split her lip open. Charlotte was always surprised when things like that happened to people besides her.

When they entered the hallway she saw Zee and Jason talking heatedly in a doorway. Zee had his arms folded and was shaking his head, while Jason was whispering something angrily, surrounded once again by the black hole aura. Charlotte stopped in her tracks. She couldn't believe her eyes; she'd never seen Zee fight with anyone before who didn't have demon blood. Jason's voice rose through the crowd. "I can't believe you would do that!" Then he stalked off, while Zee threw his hands up in the air.

The three girls exchanged a look.

"What's with them?" Julie asked, wide-eyed.

"No idea," Charlotte said, shaking her head slowly.

She couldn't figure it out. Did Jason like Maddy? Was that why he was being so nice to her? It would make sense. He noticed Maddy doing her routine and then he saw Zee watching her and got jealous. And he decided to be nice to Charlotte in hopes of winning Maddy—really, he was so cute there had to be an ulterior motive. But she sure couldn't ask Maddy, given Maddy wasn't speaking to her. Which Charlotte needed to do something about, and quickly.

She accosted her friend after English. "Look, Mad," she said, eyes wide with sincerity, "I was just surprised, okay? I'm sorry."

Maddy folded her arms. "Really?" she asked coldly. "Why did it surprise you so much?"

"It's just . . . Zee has always been really shy around girls."

"Well, he's never been shy with me," Maddy said flatly.

Except yesterday, Charlotte thought. "I just wasn't expecting it, that's all."

Maddy straightened. "Well, Zee doesn't tell you everything, you know."

Charlotte blinked. "He doesn't?"

"No. You think you know him so well, but you don't."

"Wha—"

"He said so."

"He . . . what?"

As Charlotte gaped, Zee appeared at Maddy's side. "Hi, Char!" he said brightly, then looked to her friend with moonstruck eyes and sighed, "Hi, Maddy."

Beaming, Maddy turned to him, and Zee took her hand and led her down the hallway, while Charlotte stood dumbly and watched them go.

When school was over, Charlotte walked to her mother's car lugubriously and flopped heavily into the passenger seat.

"Are you okay?" Mrs. Mielswetzski asked.

"Weird day," Charlotte muttered.

"Do you want to talk about it?"

"Not really."

She had never even considered what might happen

if Zee and Maddy went out. Maddy was her best friend, and Zee was—well, Zee was beyond that, he was her brother-in-arms, her confidant, swimming worthless laps with her in the great fishbowl of life, and he was the only thing that kept her from being smooshed by the terrible burden that had been placed on them both.

Charlotte exhaled loudly and sank deeper in her seat.

"You sure you don't want to talk about it?" Mrs. Mielswetzski asked.

Charlotte nodded.

"All right," her mother said softly. "Let's get you home."

Ten minutes later Charlotte was lying on her bed scratching Mew on the head. "Well," she murmured to the cat, "Zee has completely lost his mind."

"Meow," said Mew.

"What does he mean I think I know him so well but I don't?" said Charlotte.

"Meow," said Mew.

"I mean, after all we went through," said Charlotte. "Can you believe it?"

"Meow," said Mew.

"And I did technically save him from a lifetime of Philonecron mind control. That ought to be worth something."

"Meow," said Mew.

"Who's Philonecron?"

Charlotte started so violently she nearly fell out of bed. Her father had appeared in the doorway and was looking at her with an intrigued expression.

"Oh," said Charlotte tightly. "Nobody. Just something I read. . . ."

"That's an interesting name," he mused. "It's Greek. *Phil* is the Greek root for love and *necron* is the root for death. So this Philonecron chap's name means love or lover of death."

"Huh," said Charlotte.

"So I imagine he's not a very nice fellow!"

"No, I guess not," Charlotte said. "Um, did you want something?"

"Oh, yes! I was wondering if you have the Hartnett directory? I can't find mine."

"Oh, yeah, one sec." Charlotte pulled herself out of bed, careful not to meet her father's eye.

When he was gone, Charlotte plopped down in her desk chair and swiveled around to look at Mew.

"That was close," she whispered.

"Meow," said Mew.

A few minutes later Mr. Mielswetzski gave the school directory back to Charlotte. She had the desk drawer open and was about to put it away when she stopped short. She looked down at the directory in her hands and then quickly opened it and flipped to the faculty section.

Oh, she'd been so stupid! All she wanted was a way to contact Mr. Metos—well, she might not have his new address, but she certainly had his old one, right there in the school directory. Surely he'd be forwarding his mail, because that's just the sort of thing grown-ups did.

Charlotte sat down at her desk, got out a pen and paper, and began to write.

> Dear Mr. Metos,
>
> We haven't heard anything from you and we're worried.
>
> Is everything okay? Zee and I want to know what's going on. It isn't fair to leave us in the dark like this. We're scared. Please write.
> Charlotte

There. Short, sweet, to the point. The "scared" thing was maybe a little much, but adults ate that stuff up. Whatever it took to get him to write her. And then she'd have a letter from him and could tell Zee and everything could be back to normal.

CHAPTER 6

TotaLLy LuLu

THAT WEEKEND IT PROVED DIFFICULT FOR CHARLOTTE to focus on anything. She knew Mr. Metos wouldn't even get her letter until later in the week, and a reply would come, at the earliest, the following week while they were sailing the eastern seaboard exploring the wonderful world of American history. But she couldn't help but be impatient. As a result, she was on edge even more than usual and got in several fights with her mother and one with her father, who was disappointed that she hadn't read *Thomas Jefferson Unplugged* yet.

And then, of course, there was the matter of Zee

and Maddy. Maddy still hadn't forgiven her—and while Charlotte was pretty sure that she had, in fact, already apologized, and while the whole affair made her slightly annoyed with her friend, she was going to use her extensive anger management skills gleaned from five months of weekly therapy to bite her tongue and apologize again. Because Maddy was her best friend in all the world, for her—and only for her—Charlotte was willing to swallow a little pride. Any residual anger she felt she could just take out on her parents.

And she'd have to figure out what was going on with Zee. He was just not normal. Both of them had been walking around feeling as if they'd been bound up extremely tightly in very thick rope since they'd come back from the Underworld, and suddenly overnight he was skipping around like Lulu the Sunshine Girl. Didn't he care anymore? Had he forgotten about the Dead? How could he have? If she'd started going out with Jason Hart and been really happy and all the other girls got jealous because he was so cute and she was going out with him and they weren't, she wouldn't have forgotten. She would never forget.

So Charlotte was irritable all weekend, though for some reason her parents didn't notice anything was amiss. They themselves were quite busy making preparations for the cruise—or at least talking about making preparations for the cruise. Every dinner was filled with talk of the tasks ahead: They needed to stop the newspaper, find someone to pick up the mail and water the plants, her mother needed to reschedule all her patients, her father needed to put in for a substitute for the Monday after break, and everyone needed new raincoats. (Some people, Charlotte would like to point out, went on cruises where you didn't need raincoats.) It seemed to Charlotte that some wars had been launched with less planning than this. Sometimes while they talked, she liked to close her eyes and pretend they were actually taking her someplace fun.

"Oh, Char?"

"Huh?" Charlotte started. She looked up from her dinner—turkey burgers, no bun, and spinach, no salt. Her mother was peering at her curiously.

"Why were your eyes closed?" Mrs. Mielswetzski asked.

"Oh. No reason."

"All right. Well, listen, I spoke to Aunt Suzanne. We're going to have to get a catsitter for Mew while we're gone, because Zee's going to be staying at a friend's."

Zee's parents were going back to England during spring break, but he wanted to stay home for some soccer thing. Charlotte would never sacrifice a trip to

England in order to run around on plastic grass for an hour getting sweaty, but it's our differences that make the world go 'round.

"But—can't Charlie take Mew?"

"His mom's allergic."

"So?" That was a stupid reason. Didn't they have pills for that?

"Mew will be okay for a week. We'll take good care of her when we get back, don't worry."

Charlotte wanted to suggest she could just stay home with Mew instead, but she didn't think that would go over very well.

"Speaking of that," Mr. Mielswetzski said, "we'll have to drive her over tomorrow morning. It's Zee's week to have Mew."

Charlotte grumbled to herself. It hardly seemed fair that Zee got to go out with her best friend and steal her cat. If she'd known, she would have offered a trade— Mew for Maddy. It was only right.

"You know—I saw the funniest old man when I drove Zee home from his soccer game last week," Mr. Mielswetzski continued. "He was wearing an aqua suit!"

That got Charlotte's attention. "What?"

"A man in an aqua-colored suit!" he repeated. "And not just any old suit either, but a three-piece suit, you know, with a vest? And a pocket watch chain and a bowler hat! He looked like something out of an old movie—except aqua." He turned to Mrs. Mielswetzski and grinned. "I've got to get me one of those suits."

"Now, really," Mrs. Mielswetzski said.

"Wouldn't I look smashing, Charlotte? What would that boy you like think of me in that?"

"Dad!" said Charlotte.

"The what?" said Mrs. Mielswetzski.

"There's this handsome new boy on Zee's soccer team," Mr. Mielswetzski said, winking at his daughter. "I think Lottie fancies him."

"Dad!" said Charlotte.

"Mike!" said Mrs. Mielswetzski.

He looked at Charlotte, his face puzzled. "Don't you?" Turning to her mother, he stage-whispered, "I'm going to introduce them."

"No!" said Charlotte.

"Mike," said Mrs. Mielswetzski firmly, "I think you forget your daughter is grounded and not in any position to be set up with boys."

"Yeah!" Charlotte said.

"And she's too young to be dating, anyway."

"Mom!"

For the rest of the dinner, Charlotte sat there frozen in horror while her parents argued over whether or not her father should embarrass her to death, and when dinner was over she crept up to her room, closed the door firmly behind her, and crawled into the bed.

Charlotte passed another restless night, filled with her usual strange dreams of the Underworld. But this time, as the Harpies flew overhead, two of their faces morphed into those of Maddy and Zee. Maddy's narrowed its eyes haughtily and repeated, "You think you know him so well, but you don't," while Zee's said, over and over again, "Go get 'em, tiger!" while a man in an aqua suit laughed and clapped.

When she walked into school Monday morning, she didn't know quite what to expect. Part of her feared the whole place would have been hit with Zee's happy bomb, and everyone was going to be bouncing around like lunatics. But as she walked through the hallways, she found to her relief that everyone at Hartnett seemed to be quite normal, thank you; as she made her way to homeroom, she didn't see any unnatural exuberance in anyone, except Jasper Nix, who was always that way.

Right outside Mrs. Bryant's room, Charlotte's heart started to flutter. She so wanted to go in there and have Zee see her and smile slightly and nod in his British I'm-glad-to-see-you-but-I-don't-want-to-call-across-the-room way.

But when Charlotte walked into homeroom, Zee

wasn't at his desk at all. She scanned the room, only to find him crouching down in front of one of the book-shelves, looking deeply into Mrs. Bryant's fish tank.

At the beginning of the year, Mrs. Bryant had had ten fish. Then she brought in an angelfish, and every few days there was one less fish in the tank, until the angelfish was the only one left. Once Charlotte saw it had another fish's tail hanging out of its mouth.

As Charlotte carefully approached her cousin, she realized that he was not just examining the fish in the tank. He was talking to it.

She stared at him. "What are you doing?"

At the sound of her voice, Zee whirled around. "Oh, hey, Char!" he said brightly. "I'm talking to the fish!"

Charlotte looked into the tank and then back at Zee.

"His name's Tyrone," Zee added.

"What? . . . You named it?"

"Him. No, it's just his name."

"Okay." Charlotte looked around. There was no way to bring up her letter to Mr. Metos here. "So, um"—she shifted a little—"how was your weekend?"

"Oh, it was great!" he enthused, beaming up at her. "Maddy and I went to a movie!"

Something inside Charlotte deflated. "Really?"

"There were explosions!"

"Right," Charlotte said, eyeing him. "Zee, nothing fell on your head recently, did it?"

He scrunched up his face. "No, why?"

"No reason," she muttered. "Hey, listen. I have to talk to you." She motioned outside the door. "In private."

"Okay!" Zee exclaimed, so loudly that three people in the classroom turned to look.

The cousins went into the hall, where Charlotte pulled Zee into a doorway. "Listen," she said, leaning in, "I wrote Mr. Metos this weekend."

Zee blinked.

"I'm so stupid," she continued. "I should have thought of this earlier. I wrote him at his apartment here. They have to forward it, right?" The words came tumbling out of her mouth as if she had no control over them. Which perhaps she didn't.

"Right," Zee nodded.

"So I told him to write us. Maybe we'll hear from him now! Maybe he'll tell us what he's been doing." Charlotte looked at Zee, eyes wide with anticipation and hope.

But Zee looked as if she'd just told him she'd bought a new pair of socks. "Brilliant," he said.

Charlotte stared disbelievingly. "Brilliant?"

"Yeah, brilliant."

Charlotte stared at Zee, speechless, while he smiled happily back at her. Just as she was about to grab his shoulders and shake him, Mrs. Bryant walked by. "Bell's about to ring, guys. Come on in."

At lunch Charlotte looked for Jason Hart. She still hadn't been able to try to find out what he'd meant the other night. If he knew about the gods, about her, well, then his presence in the school was no accident. And if not, she needed to find out why he was there.

But Jason wasn't in his seat. Charlotte asked a few people if they'd seen him, and they all shrugged. Her heart sank. Perhaps she was slightly more disappointed at his absence than the situation warranted, but she did her best not to show it. Someone might tell her father.

When school was over, Charlotte once again found herself flouncing into the passenger seat of her mother's car. Mrs. Mielswetzski took one look at her and asked, "Are you sure you don't want to talk about it?"

Charlotte nodded and looked out the window.

They drove along in silence for a few moments while Charlotte watched the world go by. Then her mother glanced at her and said, oh-so-casually, "I talked to your Aunt Suzanne this afternoon. She says Zee has a girlfriend."

Zee told his parents?

Charlotte exhaled. There was no getting out of this. "Yup," she said, hitting the last *P* like a cymbal.

"She said her name was Maddy. Is this our Maddy?"

"Yup."

"Wow, that's really something."

"Yup."

"So, how do you feel about that?"

"It's a little weird," she said flatly, still gazing out the window.

"I bet. I mean, Zee and your best friend. That must be hard on you."

"It's not that, Mom," she muttered with a glance at her mother.

"Then what is it?"

"Zee's just . . . being really weird. It's like he's possessed or something."

"Oh, Char. Look, I know this sort of thing can be really difficult. People start dating someone and then it doesn't seem like they're the same person anymore. And it can be really lonely."

"All right, Mom," Charlotte muttered. There was no point in saying anything. She would never understand.

Charlotte stayed in her room most of that night, except for dinner, during which nobody mentioned a thing about handsome boys. Her father kept asking things like, "Why the long face?" but her mother always distracted him. Because it was the week before spring break, Charlotte had mountains of homework to keep her busy, including a paper due in English and tests coming up that week in science and math.

It was while she was practicing balancing chemical equations (as if she'd ever need to do that in her life) that she heard the scratching on her window.

Now, the last time there had been a noise on that particular window, it had been the tapping of the large black bird who lured them to the Underworld. But you could be sure Charlotte wasn't going to fall for that twice. Any bird scratching on her window was going to be sent straight back where he came from.

She slowly moved her head toward the window. The curtain was closed and she could see nothing. With a deep breath, she took a sharpened pencil from her desk (it was the best weapon she could think of) and crept slowly over to the window. The scratching grew louder and more frantic. Charlotte stopped right in front of the closed curtain, poised the pencil, and quickly pulled the curtain open—

—and promptly dropped the pencil in surprise. For it was not an evil bird scratching at her window, or even a not-evil bird. On the sill outside her bedroom window, scratching and meowing, was Mew.

Alarmed, Charlotte opened the window and lifted her cat in. "Baby," she whispered, "what is it?"

She examined Mew carefully. Her father had taken her over to Zee's in the morning before school. And it seemed like Mew had come right back. But the Millers' house was a couple of miles away—and that seemed like an awfully long way to go. Of course, Mew had also found her way to the Underworld, so really Charlotte shouldn't have been surprised.

"What are you doing here?" Charlotte whispered.

"Meow!" said Mew.

"Are you okay?"

"Meow!" said Mew.

Charlotte frowned. The cat seemed to be fine, but also extremely agitated.

"Did Zee do something weird?" she asked. "Is that why you're upset?"

"Meow!" said Mew.

"Poor baby. You can stay with me," Charlotte said, stroking her cat. She could think of no other explanation than that Lulu Zee had driven her out of the house. And frankly, she couldn't blame Mew one bit.

Eventually, Mr. Mielswetzski called over to the Millers to find out what had happened. Mew had gone missing right before dinner, it seemed. They offered to bring her back, much to Charlotte's dismay, but after conferring with Zee, Mrs. Miller said Charlotte could keep her, since she would be going away for so long. Charlotte went up to tell Mew the good news, only to find the cat had skulked under the bed to sulk.

Make room for me, Charlotte thought grimly.

The rest of the week, Charlotte did her best to stay out of Zee's way. He'd told her he didn't care about Mr. Metos anymore, so she really didn't have a thing to say to him. Anyway, even if she'd wanted to, he was pretty much always attached to Maddy. And when Maddy wasn't attached to him, she was always surrounded by the other girls in school, who now thought she was the coolest thing ever for going out with Zee.

Meanwhile, Tuesday passed, then Wednesday, then Thursday, with no sign of Jason Hart. Charlotte had no desire to ask Zee anything about Jason. Finally, at the end of the day on Thursday, Charlotte went into the school office and asked after him.

"We don't know, Charlotte. We haven't heard from him," Ms. Moran said.

"What?"

"Well . . ." The receptionist looked right and left to make sure no one was listening. Charlotte felt she was being let in on a secret, which made sense. She had, after all, developed a close relationship with Ms. Moran, since she was in the office every day after school calling her parents. That sort of thing really brings two people together. "Don't tell anyone, but he ran away. His grandfather called and told us."

Her heart pounding, Charlotte gasped, "Really?"

"But"—she leaned in closer—"the thing is, we can't reach the grandfather anymore either. The phone number they gave doesn't work, and there's no house at the address they gave."

Something on Charlotte's neck tingled. "Are you serious?"

"Weird, huh?"

"Yeah," said Charlotte.

Charlotte walked out the front door in a daze. Jason was gone. *Poof!* Disappeared. It was too weird. He did know about the gods, he must. Either he was working for them or they'd come after him. Either way, something had happened to him and his grandfather, too, and she wanted to know what.

Despite everything, Charlotte called Zee when she got home, but no one answered. She left a message and waited all evening for him to call back, but he never did. So on Friday morning Charlotte arrived at school early, determined to track down her cousin. Charlotte kept telling herself that Zee did still care, of course he did, how could he not? It was just that he was so happy to be with

Maddy that he couldn't really focus on anything else. Love does strange things to people. But once he heard about Jason, he would come out of whatever idiotic fog he was in and they could figure this out together.

But it wasn't Zee who Charlotte saw first that morning. When she got to school, she found Maddy waiting by her locker. Charlotte frowned; Maddy had barely said a word to her since Monday. She approached warily, then gasped as she saw that tears were streaming down Maddy's face.

"Maddy!" Charlotte exclaimed, hurrying over. "What? What is it? What's wrong?"

Maddy shook her head and began crying in earnest.

"Come on," Charlotte urged, putting her hand gently on her friend's arm, "tell me. What is it?"

"It's Zee," Maddy sobbed.

Charlotte gasped. "What's wrong with Zee?"

"He broke up with me!"

"He *what*?"

"For Ashley!"

"Ashley?" Charlotte blinked. "Which one?"

"It doesn't matter which one!" Maddy fell into Charlotte's arms. "Oh, Char," she whimpered, "I was so awful to you. I'm sorry. I just felt so weird that I was going out with your cousin, and I was afraid you'd be mad, and—"

"It's okay," Charlotte said soothingly. *Ashley?*

"I can't believe he did this to me," she bawled.

"Neither can I," Charlotte muttered.

After Charlotte had gotten Maddy together enough to get through the day, she tore off to homeroom to find Zee. It didn't take long. He was in the doorway of the janitor's closet with the blond Ashley, whispering in her ear, his hand resting on her arm.

Charlotte had no compunction about breaking that little scene up. "Excuse me," she said, tapping pointedly on Zee's shoulders. "Can I talk to you for a minute?"

Zee turned around as Ashley looked warily from Charlotte to her new boyfriend. "Uh, see you later, Zee!"

"You sure will, Ashley!" he called. "What's up?" he said, turning to Charlotte.

"What's up? What's *up*?" She shook her head. "What's going on with you?"

He blinked benignly at her. "What do you mean?"

"You broke up with Maddy!"

"Oh, right. I'm too young to be tied down, Char."

"You are?"

"Yes. Anyway, we wanted different things. But I'm hoping we can still be friends."

"But—" Charlotte stood there, her mouth hanging open, unable to even form words.

Just then Chris Shapiro strode by and called, "Hey,

Zee!" Then he added quickly, "Hey, Sweatski!" Charlotte shot Chris a haughty look.

"Ha!" Zee exclaimed. "Sweatski! Ha!"

Charlotte's head whipped back toward her cousin. *"What's gotten into you?"* she hissed, her eyes slits.

"What do you mean?" Zee asked, bewildered.

"What do I mean? You broke Maddy's heart. And there are things happening, Zee. Jason's missing!"

"Oh." Zee waved a hand dismissively. "He'll turn up."

"He'll turn up?" Charlotte repeated incredulously. "Zee, he's got something to do with our Greek friends, I know it! Either they took him or he's evil or—"

"Oh, Char," Zee said, shaking his head. "Can't you just get over that stuff?"

"What?"

"I mean, we're young. Who cares about all that stuff?"

"*You* do. Or at least you did."

"Well, I've changed." He shrugged.

She stiffened. "That's right, you have." She shook her head disgustedly. "Look, Zee, we're leaving for the cruise tomorrow, and—"

Something passed over Zee's face. "You are?"

"Yes."

"Wow," he said, eyeing her with great interest. "Are you sure you want to go?"

"What? Why?"

"Are you scared?"

"Am I *what*? Why would I be scared?!"

"Oh," he said, shaking his head. "No reason."

"Fine, Zee," Charlotte spat. "Fine. Just . . . whatever happened to you, can you get back to normal by the time I come back? Okay?" And then she gave him her most disgusted look, turned on her heel, and stalked off in all the fury she could muster.

That night, as Charlotte laid out her things for the cruise, she could not get her mind off her cousin. What had happened to him? If it wasn't a head injury, what else could it be? Do people really change overnight? Was it hormones? Did something happen at soccer to make him . . . weird? Or had he just decided to make a move with Maddy and then everything spun out of control after that? Was the nice Zee she knew just a product of everything he'd gone through in the summer and fall, and underneath it all was a jerk just waiting to come out?

Charlotte didn't believe it, not really. She didn't believe any of it. But, as she would eventually come very much to regret, she could think of no other explanation.

# PART TWO

——•◆•——

## Fishy

CHAPTER 7

## No Way to Treat a Hero II

IN THE IMMENSE SPRAWL OF SUBURBS SURROUNDING the town where Charlotte and Zee lived, there was an enormous mall. This mall—better known as the Mall—was the biggest mall in all of the United States. And if you were from London and were not used to malls at all, let alone malls the size of small towns, you would be properly horrified by the place. And if you had recently been led to the Underworld through a door in this particular mall, you would do everything in your power to avoid ever going there again as long as you lived.

Which is exactly what Zachary "Zee" Miller had

been doing for months. Every time his friends suggested they go, he came up with something else to do that day— soccer game, dinner with family, disfiguring rash.

But on this Saturday afternoon, exactly two weeks before the Mielswetzskis were scheduled to leave on their odyssey through America's past, Zee found himself walking through the doors of this very same Mall. It wasn't supposed to happen; Dov's mom was going to pick them up and he, Dov, and Sam were all going to see a movie at a nice normal-size suburban mall that had no doors to the Underworld at all (as far as Zee knew, anyway). But when he got into the car, Dov told him, "Change of plans. We're going to the Mall." And before Zee could open the car door and flee in the opposite direction, Dov's mom hit the gas and they were off.

It was silly, of course. Ridiculous. Normal boys aren't afraid of shopping malls. Normal boys go out with their friends and have fun and talk about sports and girls and music and video games and don't worry about whether a half-demon/half-god freak is stalking them. But normal boys just don't have Zee's fabulous luck.

As they parked in one of the mammoth parking structures that lined the Mall, Zee steeled himself to pretend it was an ordinary place and he was an ordinary boy and nothing at all extraordinary had ever happened to him there. He could do that. Zee had a lot of practice pretending his problems didn't exist—though, of course, his problems used to be a lot less weird. If he had only known what was to come when he was dwelling on his freakish inability to speak to some girl or another back in the good ol' days, he really would have taken time out to appreciate how lucky he was.

Sometimes he felt as if there were two Zees— Outside Zee, who was your typical teenage boy who hung out with his friends and played a lot of soccer and had a big music collection, and Real Zee, who missed his grandmother, who was harrowed by the Dead, who had almost caused the eternal suffering of the entire human race.

On this afternoon as they entered the Mall, while Real Zee's stomach was turning in a way it was not meant to turn, Outside Zee looked as if he was a normal boy out with his friends. If you looked at him, you would say, "There is a normal teenage boy out with his normal friends having an excellent time on a most excellent Saturday afternoon," not, "There is a teenage boy who needs immediate medical attention." Zee and his friends went to a movie (about some guy who hunts aliens even though he's *part alien himself*), ate some food court food (pizza), and then met up with Dov's mom outside one of the department stores to go home.

And Outside Zee patted Real Zee on the back—Way

to go, guy! You did it. You survived. No one suspected a thing. And Real Zee relaxed a little and thought only of the bright blue sky outside. And as they made their way through one of the Mall's long aisles toward the parking lot, for one moment Real Zee's heart was at ease.

Now, this was only the second time Zee had ever been to the Mall, and the first time he and Charlotte had come from the other direction, and he hadn't exactly been looking at the neighboring shops at the time, and besides the Mall is really quite enormous and people who've been going there for years don't know their way around, so there was no way for Zee to know that on the way out of the Mall they would pass the small non-descript hallway that led to the door that led to the interminable cold, dark passageway to the Underworld.

And then, there they were.

Zee could never forget it, never mistake it for some other dark corridor, some other door. He froze in his tracks and stared down the long dark nondescript hallway. In his mind, he was at the end of it—reaching for the handle, turning it slowly, feeling the cold rush of damp air as the door creaked open, plunging him into the absolute darkness.

Around him, shoppers strolled gaily by. No one else knew about this door, of course. None of the Mall employees had ever tried to open it; everyone assumed it was for someone else's department and left it alone. And the Mall customers never got close enough to it to look, for whenever they passed it they were always immediately possessed with a strange incuriousness and struck with a sudden urge to go somewhere else entirely.

But not Zee. For a moment he imagined running down the corridor, yanking the door open, and hurling himself down to the Underworld, back to the Dead, where he could free them all, where he could find his grandmother—who was the only person in the world who knew how to make the two Zees one again.

It was ridiculous, of course. There was no getting through the door this time. And even if he could, he was not exactly welcome in the Underworld. And even if he were, he would never find Grandmother Winter, who had died the previous summer. And even if he could, she couldn't help him now.

"What's wrong?" Dov asked.

"Nothing," Zee muttered. "I just . . . thought of something."

"I'm hungry," Dov's mom said suddenly.

"Yeah, me too," said Sam. "I really want a soft pretzel."

"That sounds perfect," said Dov's mom.

"Yeah," Zee said, casting a long look down the corridor. "Let's get out of here."

And then it happened. The voice. A breath, a puff of wind, a whisper. It echoed through his body, as if it were coursing through his veins. *"Ze-rooooo."*

Philonecron.

It had been happening almost every day for a month now. Zee knew the voice as well as he knew his own. Back in the Underworld, Philonecron had claimed he could control Zee because he'd spent so much time with his blood. And it was true. Philonecron could make Zee do whatever he wanted. He would speak, Zee's brain would soften, and Zee became entirely helpless in the god's hands—and if it hadn't been for Charlotte, Zee would still be down there doing Philonecron's bidding.

But they defeated Philonecron, got out alive, and Zee thought it was over, thought he'd never have that horrible voice inhabit his brain again, until one night, very late, he heard it echoing in his head.

*"Ze-roooo."*

That's what Philonecron had called him. Zero, as in Patient Zero, as in Your Blood Is the Key to My Evil Plan. And it was all the voice ever said. Just that name, over and over again. Was it just an echo? Some sort of trick of his mind? Or was Philonecron out there, some-where, calling to him? And why was it that still, upon hearing the voice, his brain would soften, his body would ready itself to do whatever his enemy asked?

He'd wanted to tell Charlotte—he just couldn't find the words. It felt wrong somehow. Like his own failure. Charlotte was ready to go off and free the Dead—but Zee still hadn't won the first battle. Philonecron had taken his blood, made his friends sick, used him to enchant the shadow army, controlled him. Philonecron had been defeated, yes, but not truly vanquished—and now he was wandering around the Upperworld, free, and his voice whispered inside Zee's head.

Like Charlotte, Zee wanted desperately to hear from Mr. Metos, but unlike Charlotte, it was because Mr. Metos was the only person who might know where Philonecron had gone. It wasn't that Zee didn't want what Charlotte did—he wanted to help the Dead, yes; he wanted to work with the Prometheans, yes. But first, before he did anything else, he wanted to find Philonecron and put an end to this once and for all.

Though he didn't exactly have a plan for that part.

When Dov's mom dropped him off at his house that evening, Zee opened the front door as quietly as he could and tried to sneak up to his room. He had in mind a night of lying on his bed with his headphones on, music turned up so high that if anyone were to be whispering inside his head, they'd have to be really loud about it if they wanted to be heard.

But as Zee crept up the stairs, he heard his father's voice call to him from the kitchen. With a sigh, he headed back down to answer his summons.

"You're being awfully quiet," Mr. Miller said from his post at the computer as Zee entered the kitchen.

"Didn't want to disturb you," Zee mumbled. "Where's Mum?"

"Having a soak in the tub. Did you have fun tonight?" Mr. Miller turned his chair around to study his son.

"Yeah," Zee said noncommittally.

"Dov and Sam, right?"

"Yeah."

"A movie and dinner?"

Zee shrugged in agreement. In England his parents had subscribed strictly to the hands-off style of parenting, but since they came to America they had clearly decided Zee needed them to be more involved in his life. Not that they'd asked him his opinion. Where the Mielswetzskis had responded to the whole gone-all-night incident by grounding Charlotte for the rest of her life, Zee's parents reacted by inserting him inside a giant fishbowl. They'd already worried about him, what with his grandmother's death and his strange fear that the mysterious illness sweeping over Britain had something to do with him (which, of course, it did, but Zee wasn't exactly going to explain that to them. See, Mum, I wasn't barmy, it was just weird clay Underworld men were following me!). So now, if his mother wasn't knocking on his bedroom door to find out how he was feeling at that particular moment, his father was grilling him to make sure his new friends weren't going to turn him into a delinquent. It was a little trying.

"Can I get you a snack or something?" Mr. Miller asked, standing up.

Plus they seemed to think he was five.

"No, Dad, thanks. Well"—he turned and started to head back out the door—"I'll see you later."

"Wait, Zee. I want to talk to you. Come here and have a seat," Mr. Miller said, pulling out a chair from the kitchen table.

Zee groaned inwardly, but there was no escape. With heavy steps, he shuffled over to the chair and sat down. His father sat down opposite him.

"Zachary," he said, folding his hands and placing them on the table, "your mother and I are concerned about you. We just wanted to make sure everything's all right."

"Yeah, Dad, everything's fine."

"Because you've just . . . seemed really preoccupied lately. You've been through a lot this year, so many really major things have happened to you, and it's perfectly understandable. It seems like there's a lot going on inside that head of yours."

If only he knew.

"It might really help to talk about it. If you can't talk to us, maybe we can get you a counselor? Charlotte's been seeing one and your aunt highly recommends her."

"Oh. Well, I don't really think I need that." Zee wondered what his aunt would think of the therapist if she knew that Charlotte made up most everything she said during the sessions.

"It can be very helpful," Mr. Miller added. "It's not just for people who hear voices, you know."

"Right," Zee said, his voice cracking. "Okay. Thanks, Dad. Well, I'd better go. Want to get a start on my homework!" And with that, he burst from his chair and fled the room.

Last October, after Zee and Charlotte had returned from their sojourn and all the kids had started getting better, his parents called and had a Talk with him. His father's transfer to the States was already planned for December, they'd said; he'd worked very hard to get it, and they'd found someone to fill his job in London. So it would be very difficult for them to cancel the move now, but if Zee wanted, if he really wanted to move back to London, they would see what they could do.

"No, that's all right," he'd said. "I don't mind."

The truth was, Zee didn't feel any more out of place at the very American Hartnett Middle School than he had at London's prestigious Feldwop and Egfred. Maybe less so. Charlotte thought the kids at Hartnett were snobbish, but she didn't know the half of it; Ashley O'Brien's parents might own a multinational corporation, but they hadn't ever lunched with the Queen. It made all the difference.

Not that he felt hugely *in* place either. There weren't many more black kids at Hartnett than there were at F&E (though when you're dealing with such small numbers, every little bit helps). He got a little tired of being asked if he was adopted when people found out he was Charlotte's cousin. He started keeping a picture of his black British mom and white American dad in his locker for a visual aid. And, of course, he talked funny and didn't have the right clothes and did everything wrong. He had finally stopped saying things like "knackered" and "bril" and had learned to say, "What's up?" instead of "All right?" and "soccer" instead of "football"—at least most of the time, though to tell the truth, he still felt funny about it.

But none of that mattered, because in America there

was Charlotte, and in England there was not. They were alone together. She had been through what he had, she knew what he did, and without her Real Zee would have lost his mind long ago.

The only other thing that kept him from going completely barmy was soccer. He'd been playing in a winter league at an indoor sports complex, and it was a great solace from the burdens he carried with him. Sometimes that made him feel guilty, too—the Dead were suffering and he got comfort by strapping on a pair of cleats and running back and forth on plastic grass?

But most of the time it didn't, because he was too busy strapping on cleats and running back and forth on plastic grass. Not that Philonecron was totally gone from him when he played; sometimes when Zee needed to land a particularly hard kick, he imagined the ball was his nemesis's head.

When he got to the sports complex after school on Wednesday, he went to his locker and got dressed quietly. The boys on the team were all right, but he didn't have a lot to say to them, really, and when they all went to the pizza place across the street after the games, Zee stayed pretty quiet. On the first day of practice, when he walked onto the field he was very conscious of being new, of being a head taller than anyone else, of being many shades darker than anyone else, of being from a different country, of talking funny. But by the end of the day, the whole team was acting like he was the coolest guy they'd ever seen, and Zee was under no illusion that it was because of his sparkling personality.

The new boy, though, Jason Hart, was a little different. He'd been nice to Zee from the moment he'd shown up at practice the previous Sunday—asking him tons of questions and just seeming really interested in him, well before he'd seen Zee play. The other boys took to Jason right away too—and since he was a terrible soccer player, Zee was sure that they did like him for his personality.

That night's game was against the Bears, the only team that had beaten them so far this year. (Zee's team, the Rockets, had been 8-12 the year before and were now, thanks to Zee, 13-1.) The Bears had won the league last year, and after playing against them, Zee determined their success was based on two players. The first was Mike Blum, a forward. In the last game, Blum had run circles around the Rockets' fullbacks and scored four times against their poor goalie Kyle, who seemed quite unable to speak after the game. The second was the Bears' goalie, John Sommers, who was over six feet tall, incredibly thin, and had arms that seemed to stretch out across the entire width of the goal. In the last game Zee had tried to score nine times, and Sommers blocked every single attempt. It was the only game that season Zee hadn't scored, and he had taken it very personally.

But this time, he had a plan.

When he was dressed, he ran into the stadium to find the coach. "Listen, um, I was wondering," Zee told him. "I'd really like to play defensive midfielder today. Do you think I might?"

Coach Johnson squinted at him. "What's this about, Zee?"

"Well," Zee said carefully, "I was thinking. That forward's pretty good, and—"

"And you thought you might be the only one who could stop him."

Zee winced slightly. That was exactly what he was thinking, but it sounded awfully arrogant. Yes, Zee knew he was the best in the league—but it was only because he actually was. He didn't take any pride in it, and he certainly didn't boast. It was just that Zee'd been playing all his life and working very hard in a country where the sport was much more important than it was here. Anyway, if you asked Zee, soccer was the only thing he was good at—and as it meant quite a bit less in his new home, it was hardly something to brag about.

"Well," the coach said, "you're right. Let's do it."

• • •

When Coach Johnson told the team of the change, the players seemed to think he was quite mad—no one saw the point of moving their best scorer to defense against such a good team, but people didn't always think these things through. Or, as the coach said, "This is the way it's going to be, so shut up and play!"

As the game went on, Zee felt the exhilarating quiet in his mind that happened every time he played. There was nothing else but this—him, the field, the opponents, the strategy, the ball. The harder he worked, the more he sweat, the better he felt. And his strategy was working; he kept Blum all tied up so he couldn't get in a good shot on Kyle. The Bears couldn't score.

Unfortunately, neither could the Rockets; no one on the team could do anything against their goalie. Zee felt his teammates looking at him, felt the weight of their expectations. With less than five minutes left to play, one of the Bears knocked the ball out of bounds at midfield, and as they were setting up for a throw-in, Ben sidled up to him. "Stewart's gonna get it to you," he whispered, nodding at the player behind the sidelines. "You've got to drive it. You've got to break away. You're the only one who can score."

"But—" Zee said.

"I'll get Blum," said Ben. "I'll cover him, it's okay."

Zee glanced around. His whole team was looking at

him. From midfield, Jason gave him a thumbs-up. Well, this is what Zee did. He may not have been much against Philonecron, but he could play soccer. With a quick nod, Zee shifted downfield, away from the Bears' forward.

From the sidelines, Coach Johnson started yelling, "Zee, you're out of position! If you want to play defense, play defense!"

As the coach's words rang across the field, Stewart kicked the ball right at Zee, and he leaped up over the defender, heading the ball toward his feet, then he attacked all the way downfield. Sommers was waiting for him, ranging around the goal, looking like an oversize monkey with a very high metabolism. His eyes flared, and Zee's flared right back, then he gave the ball a huge Philonecron-head kick. Sommers leaped up, stretched his arms out—and caught the ball.

An audible groan passed over the field; Zee didn't know if it came from him or the whole team. But there was no time to mourn the lost opportunity—Sommers had kicked the ball, and it sailed high and far over Zee's head down to midfield—right to Mike Blum. As Zee's heart sank, Blum began to drive down the field. Poor Ben tried to keep up, but within seconds the Bears' forward had broken away and was heading right toward Kyle.

Zee took off toward the Rocket end of the field as fast as he could, cursing himself out along the way. Blum was by the goal now, and Kyle sprang out in front of him, ready to block any strike. And when Blum kicked, Kyle was right there, his hands poised, and the ball shot right into his hands like a missile. Zee was about to let out a cheer when he realized that the ball hadn't stopped. It exploded right through Kyle's hands, struck his face, and ricocheted right off, dribbling right to Mike Blum. Kyle collapsed to the ground, and before Zee could react Mike shot the ball into the goal. As his team swarmed around him, the Rockets ran to their goalie, who was lying prone on the ground, coughing and splattering blood. The ref shooed them all back, then crouched next to Kyle while the team stood around helplessly. After a few long moments, he and Coach Johnson helped Kyle, who was spitting blood everywhere, up. As the two adults carried the fallen goalie off the field, Zee looked to the spot where he had fallen, and his eyes fixed on some small white things scattered on the ground. Zee had seen enough soccer injuries in his life to know that they were Kyle's teeth.

When Zee met his mother outside the stadium, he didn't feel much like talking. His mother, on the other hand, did. Her concern for Zee's emotional well-being stopped when it came to soccer. It was a difficult adjustment for her to watch games in the States, where the play tended to be less skilled, and after games Zee usually had to hurry her into the car so the other kids didn't hear his mum talking about how awful they were. It was always a relief for Zee on the days Mr. Mielswetzski picked him up—unfortunately, today was not one of those days.

"So," she said as he approached her, "you were out of position there."

"I know," Zee said.

"Hmmmph," Mrs. Miller said. "So, what happened to the keeper?"

"*Goalie*, Mum. His teeth got knocked out."

"Good!" she said. "Next time he won't have such soft hands!"

"Mum!" He looked around frantically to see if anyone had heard.

"Well, really, Zee, anyone could have caught that, couldn't they? Anyway, he'll be fine."

Zee just got into the car, glowering.

"You kept that skinny boy from scoring the whole game," Mrs. Miller continued, starting the car. "I watched you. What did he get on you last time, four goals? And this time he didn't score any, and you haven't played defense since you were eight? That's pretty good."

Zee shook his head. She would never understand. "I blew it, though. We lost. We should have at least tied."

"Yes, you botched it. You were out of position. Won't do that again, will you?"

"No," Zee muttered.

"You can't play every position, you know. You're not supposed to do everything by yourself. You have to be able to count on other people."

"All right, Mum," Zee muttered. This sounded dangerously close to a talk about his feelings.

They pulled out of their parking spot, with Zee staring out of the window, replaying his mistakes. The night was dark, and in the streetlights you could see a few snowflakes dancing around in the evening breeze. As they pulled out of the driveway onto the street, Zee noticed a man standing under a streetlamp. He looked like the oldest person Zee had ever seen. He didn't have a coat, either, and he looked like he'd walked out of Victorian London in his bowler hat and three-piece suit. The suit was in an odd color, too—like a swimming pool—but Zee knew his eyes must be playing tricks on him in the dark. Who wore an aqua-colored three-piece suit and bowler hat?

CHAPTER 8

## The Yacht

On any given day on the deep blue waters of the Mediterranean Sea, you can find boats of all kinds, from the smallest wooden fishing boat to the largest freighter headed for any of the seven corners of the world, from small pleasure crafts to mammoth cruise ships teeming with huddled masses yearning for the lunch buffet. You can also find many of the most majestic luxury yachts in the world, owned by movie stars, foreign princes, and congressional lobbyists. But there is one yacht on the Mediterranean that makes all the star/prince/lobbyist yachts look like small wooden fishing boats, and that yacht you will never find.

It's not that this yacht is lost, or sunken, or hidden somehow in a small cranny off the coast of Croatia—it sails right out in the open with all the fishing boats and pleasure crafts and freighters headed for those seven corners and mammoth cruise ships with their huddled masses. It's just that, unless you've been invited by someone from the yacht—and even if so, you might think very carefully about whether you'd really like to accept that invitation—your eyes would pass over the ship and your brain would think, *Look at that big puffy cloud,* or, *My goodness, the horizon's clear today,* or *Gosh, I'd like some couscous right now.*

And while right now you might be thinking, "Wow, I'd really like to see that yacht," let me assure you that— as remarkable as it is, as palatial and plush, glorious and grandiose as it is—this is not a yacht you particularly want to visit. For the people on this yacht—and I use "people" for lack of a better word—those who live on it and the vast numbers who drop in for a visit, do not like mortals very much. Except for the ones who do, and those are the ones you should avoid most of all.

One day, not so long ago, in a velvet-and-fur-lined bedroom on one of the many decks, there sat a man who had just arrived on this yacht. Or something very like a man. He was too tall to be a man, really, and too evil looking, with his impeccably tailored tuxedo and thin, cruel, gray face; with his black spiky hair and deep red lips that exactly matched the color of his eyes. In fact, even if you had never seen one before, you would swear that he was some kind of god. And not a particularly nice one, at that.

Of course, this man had one characteristic you don't normally expect of gods—he was in a wheelchair. In fact, if you studied the matter carefully, you would quickly realize that this man had no legs. You might also notice that he had a distinctly sour expression on his face—as you might if all your plans for world domination had been thwarted in a most embarrassing fashion, and your legs had gotten fried off in the process.

You see, once upon a time, this particular god-like man had had a dream. It was a simple dream, really, and a beautiful one—as dreams always are. All he wanted for his life was to overthrow Hades and rule the Underworld with a friend—a brave, strong, mortal boy—at his side. But the boy had been corrupted by his cousin, a nasty, horrible Gorgon of a girl with the most unpleasant complexion, and all this god-like man's plans—along with his legs—had been destroyed.

Ah, yes, you would think as you looked at his face, now I understand why he looks the way he does. But—

and here you might squint a little—what is that, lingering behind his eyes? That is not bitterness at all, but something else. Something quite the opposite. It couldn't be excitement. . . .

Could it? This man's Immortal life had been ruined, his whole Underworld lost to him forever, all his dreams had been cruelly destroyed—like a beautiful dove that has been shot through the heart with an arrow, the red blood marring its once pristine whiteness, letting out one final pathetic cry as it plummets to the ground and meets its doom. Like that. What could this man possibly have to look forward to?

And now, there, look—what is his mouth doing? That cruel, wide, red mouth spreading out upon his face. It looks like a grin, a horrible, evil grin—but it can't be. For what would this man possibly have to grin about?

Unless . . .

Unless that was anticipation in his eyes. Unless that man did now have something to live for. Unless that man had come to this very yacht in order to achieve one aim. . . .

Vengeance.

A few minutes later the man was rolling his way through a great doorway into a vast hall, and even if you had never seen one before you would know this hall was a throne room. The walls and ceiling of the room were covered in animate murals that all portrayed a blue-skinned man as he rode a golden chariot across the sea, or commanded a tidal wave as it threatened a small village, or sank an island to the bottom of the ocean. All around the room were solid gold statues of the same man—one of him wielding his trident angrily, one of him standing majestically, one seated with chin in hand as if deep in thought, one sprawled seductively on the ground like a supermodel selling blue jeans.

And there, in the middle of the room, seated on a massive golden throne, was the man himself. But he was nothing like a man—great and terrible, with deep blue skin and eyes like oceans. If you saw this man you would know, without a doubt, that this was a god. And an extremely powerful one, at that.

If you or I had seen this particular god, we would be quite scared indeed. But the man in the wheelchair was not scared, no, not at all—in fact, when he saw the god, another smile spread over his face. It was not a particularly nice smile, but since this god-like man was evil to his very core, we must assume it was the best he could do.

"Grandfather!" the god-like man exclaimed eagerly, as he rolled toward the throne. When he got close enough he held out his arms, as if to receive a hug.

The great and terrible god stood up imperiously, eyes flashing with rage. "Philonecron," he intoned, his voice rumbling like the ocean, "is it true? The stories I've heard? Did"—his nose wrinkled up as if someone in the room had not changed his socks in some time—"*mortals* do this to you?"

"Yes, yes!" Philonecron said, eyes wide with the horror of it all. "An impudent mortal! She destroyed everything!" He shook his head. "She's a sniveling little miniature Harpy! She has horrible manners. And," he added, eyeing his grandfather carefully, "she thinks she's the equal of gods!"

"I see," the god said, eyes narrowing. "Well. I will show her what happens when she interferes with my progeny."

Philonecron's eyes flickered. "That," he said, pleasure tingeing his voice, "is what I thought you'd say."

Now let's flash forward a few weeks—no, no, not quite that far, you don't want to see what happens before it's time, do you?—and look inside the same yacht to the same bedroom on the twenty-second deck, where the same god-like man (well, technically, half god, half demon) had made himself quite at home. The once fur-lined walls were now made of the smoothest ebony, the velvet-and-fur-trimmed bedding had been replaced with black silk sheets of impossibly high thread count and the otterskin rug with a Persian rug imported from the Underworld itself (just because Philonecron was banished from a realm did not mean he couldn't take advantage of its fine quality goods, after all), and a wall had been removed to add a whole wing for an evil laboratory—all at considerable expense, of course, but there were so many jewels just strewn around Poseidon's yacht that no one would miss four or five. Philonecron had changed too, since we saw him last. There were his legs, of course, which had grown two more inches since he arrived on the *Poseidon*. (If he were still in the Underworld, it would have only taken days, days! Here in the godsforsaken Upperworld, they grew more slowly than moss on Atlas's rear end.) But there was something more, something that couldn't be measured, something in his posture, in his face, in his blood red eyes. If you looked at him, you would not think, Ah, there is a man who had all his hopes for Underworld domination so cruelly thwarted by a sniveling freckle-faced miniature Harpy—no, no, you would think, Why, this Philonecron does not look so different from the Philonecron of old, from the Philonecron I saw in those halcyon days in the Underworld, when he collected human blood and gleefully plotted the eternal suffering of humankind.

He was not all the same, of course—there was the whole legs issue, and he didn't wear a cape anymore because it kept getting caught in his wheelchair—but the point is, if you looked at him closely, you would find the sour look of before completely gone, and you would never know that he had spent months wandering the Upperworld in despair and agony before coming onto the *Poseidon*. Could it be that his new evil plan had been set in motion? Could it be that he was moving closer to what his heart most desired?

Chimes sounded in the room—a few bars of Bach's Fugue in D Minor—and a grin spread across the god's face.

"Come in," Philonecron purred. The door swung open to reveal a man who looked as old as the sea itself. He was frail-looking and much smaller than most of the gods you would meet on the *Poseidon*, but you would not mistake him for a mortal. It was something about his skin, perhaps—pale and blue-tinged, with an almost translucent quality. Or his eyes—such a curious shade of blue-green, almost an aqua, really. That shade was perfectly matched in his suit, an ill-fitting three-piece suit with a pearl pocket watch chain attached to his waistcoat, and on either end of his small, shriveled head was a tuft of white hair, on top of which sat an aqua bowler hat. He looked like a hundred-and-twenty-year-old banker in his (oddly colored) Sunday best.

"Hello," Philonecron said, drawing out the word like a caress. "I am so glad you came. Please, make yourself at home." He smiled as magnanimously as he could, the effort straining his cheeks slightly.

The old man looked around the room suspiciously. "Looks different," he said, his voice crackling with age.

"Oh, yes," said Philonecron. "Well, I had to make some adjustments. It wasn't to my taste."

The old man eyed Philonecron warily. "He doesn't like it when people mess with the rooms."

"It's all right. You see, I am his grandson, and I can do whatever I want. Besides, I find tackiness so oppressive, don't you? Might as well be hanging out with . . . mortals." He shuddered. "Well, may I offer you anything? An ambrosiatini? Octopus paté? Mermaid caviar?"

"No, no," said the old man. "Let's—What are you looking at?"

"Oh!" said Philonecron, who had indeed been eyeing the old man with a trace of disgust on his face. "Excuse me, I'm so sorry, I don't mean to be rude. I"— he pursed his lips as if trying to suppress what lay just behind them—"I was wondering if perhaps you need the name of a good tailor?"

The old man blinked. "Why?"

Philonecron let his eyes roll over the baggy suit

again, opened his mouth, and quickly closed it again. "Oh, really," he oozed, waving his hand dismissively, "no reason at all. Well, let's get to business, shall we? I would like to thank you for entertaining my little proposition."

"Oh, it's my pleasure," the old man said, his eyes growing two shades lighter. "I always enjoy using my . . . talents. . . . Say, Poseidon's approved this, right?"

"Oh, yes," said Philonecron, eyes sparkling as they always did when he lied. "It was his idea."

"Good," said the old man. "Because I wouldn't want him to get angry."

"No, no," said Philonecron. "We certainly wouldn't want that."

"Well, then. The mortal boy. How much do you know about him?"

"Oh!" Philonecron exclaimed. "Everything."

"Everything?"

"Yes. We have a special bond, he and I." Philonecron reached into a drawer and pulled out a soft leather book. "Here's the dossier," he added, running his hand lovingly over the smooth cover. "I've been working on it for some time. It should have everything you need."

"Excellent," said the old man, grabbing the book and flipping through it. "This will do just fine." And with that, he opened his mouth, wide, wider, impossibly wide, so suddenly there was no face at all—just this massive gaping mouth, and before Philonecron could say, "Italian calfskin leather," he dropped the book into that mouth and swallowed it whole.

Philonecron let out a small, almost imperceptible whimper, then gathered himself and flashed the old man a tight smile. "Well," he exhaled. "I myself would have *read* the book, but to each his own. Now," he said, "is there anything else I can do for you?"

"No," said the old man. He let out a small belch and Philonecron winced. "I have associates who can take care of the other matter. You'll get your package soon after I arrive."

"Oh," breathed Philonecron, his voice betraying his excitement. "Yes, yes." He clasped his hands together, and as a smile crept across his face, he looked through his window out into the distant horizon, where dreams can be found.

"When do I begin?"

"Oh, right away," Philonecron said. "Right away."

## CHAPTER 9

# Hamsters "R" Us

Since they had gotten back from the Underworld, Zee had been having all kinds of nightmares. Every night his unconscious mind took the threads of the experience and weaved them in a new, more horrible way—and just when he thought there were no more possible awful stories his brain could tell, it found a new one to torment him with.

After a while, though, his mind seemed to get tired of all the relentless variety and instead took four or five of the most egregious dreams and played them in repertoire, a sort of greatest hits of post-traumatic REM sleep. You would think that after the tenth time you dreamed that Harpies were attacking your family while you were chained to a cliff and forced to watch, it would become less upsetting—but, Zee could tell you, it had not.

The night after the ill-fated soccer game, Zee was having one of these familiar dreams. This one began, as it always did, with him coming upon his grandmother in the Underworld. She looked like herself—not like the Dead at all, but as alive as she had ever been, beautiful, comforting, real. Just as he always was, Zee was overcome with happiness when he saw her—she was there, she was all right, it was all going to be all right now.

But just as she was about to enfold him in her arms, Philonecron appeared behind her, grinning his evil grin. He held up his hands menacingly, and Zee was about to yell, to warn her, when Philonecron put his finger to his lips and Zee was silenced, frozen.

In his dream-consciousness, Zee knew what came next. It happened the same way every time: Philonecron would wave his hands over Grandmother Winter and she would slowly fade into a hazy, dumb shadow while Zee watched helplessly. But on that night, after Philonecron put his finger to his wide, red mouth, just as Zee felt the terribly familiar softening of his mind that meant he was falling under the god's spell, something happened that had never happened before.

*Zachary, come over here!*

A young girl's voice, high-pitched and strong. His mind cleared, his head whipped toward the source, and just like that Philonecron was gone.

*Zachary! I have to show you something!*

Zee was standing at the entrance to a cave with a young girl whom he had certainly never seen before. She was five or six, with long, dark hair and bright green eyes, and she was entirely in control of the situation. As Zee stared at her, bewildered, she pointed into the cave.

*In there.*

Then Zee was inside the cave, walking through a long, black tunnel. He could see some sort of light source up ahead? No, no, a fire—there was a fire somewhere up ahead. As he moved along, he saw shapes begin to move on the cave walls—images. They seemed important, but something in his head said, *Later. You'll look at those later.*

And then the passageway opened up into a small room inside the cave, and right in the center of the room burned a small fire. The flames flickered and danced along the stony walls, and again Zee could see shapes moving behind them.

*I have to show you something else.*

The dream changed in a flash. The walls were gone, the cave was gone, Zee was gone. His mind filled with an image of a small boat fighting its way through the rough waters of a night-black sea. Inside the boat was a lone figure—a girl with red hair and freckles. Up ahead lurked some giant shadow ready to consume the boat, and Zee wanted to scream at the girl inside not to go any farther, to turn away—but he couldn't, he wasn't there, this was just a dream, and all he could do was watch as the girl sailed toward her doom.

Zee awoke covered in sweat, with that image still lingering behind his eyes. The girl was Charlotte—of course. Did it mean something? Was the boat some kind of symbol? Was it a warning? Or was it nothing? Just a dream. Just an ordinary dream.

Zee had been wary of his dreams ever since he'd learned that dreams came from a lake in the Underworld. Philonecron had used the lake to send him messages last year. Charlotte, too, had had strangely prophetic dreams last fall; she'd seen the Footmen well before they'd encountered them. But she and Zee were never able to figure out why—Philonecron must have had them sent, but it didn't really make any sense.

But of course, no one was sending him dreams now, for the Underworld was the one place in the whole universe Philonecron was not—and who else would possibly be sending him messages? Sometimes dreams were just dreams, and sometimes Zee just needed to go back to sleep and stop being such a ninny.

The next morning, as Zee was getting ready to leave for the bus, his mother stopped him. "Zee, we have to talk to you about our trip."

"All right." His parents were going back to London in two weeks to take care of some business. They'd invited Zee to come with them, but it was the league tournament and Zee didn't want to miss it. So he was going to stay with the Mielswetzskis.

"Your aunt and uncle are going on a holiday for spring break."

"Oh!" Or not.

"So we're going to have to get you a sitter."

"What?"

"I know a very nice woman who is going to stay with you. A Mrs. Pennywait."

"Mum, I can take care of myself."

"No, you can't. You're thirteen, Zee. I'm not going to leave you by yourself for a week. That's the end of the discussion."

"Can I stay with a friend? With Charlie Fornara? They're not going anywhere."

Mrs. Miller frowned. "Well . . . I could call and ask."

"Please, Mum." Zee didn't know why he was feeling

so desperate about this, but it just seemed that someone who'd been to the Underworld and back shouldn't have a babysitter.

When he got to homeroom, he was disappointed to find Charlotte wasn't there. He hadn't realized how much he relied on seeing her in the mornings; there was something that seemed to steady him about seeing her at the beginning of each school day. Every day when she walked through the classroom door she looked for him, and when their eyes met a message passed between them: *We have to live another day of this great big lie of a life, but at least we're not alone.*

Finally, a little bit into math class, Charlotte appeared in the doorway. As soon as Zee noticed her, his eyes went right to Mr. Crapf, who had been none too pleased with his cousin's time management skills lately. (Charlotte repeatedly said she had trouble getting to math on time because it was all the way at the other end of school from homeroom, but Zee noted that he hadn't been late once. She said it was because his legs were longer.)

Indeed, Mr. Crapf did not look happy. "Do you have a note, Charlotte?"

Charlotte drew herself up. "No, Mr. Crapf," she said, her voice full of sweetness. "I'd be happy to get one from the doctor, though. I was in an accident this morning."

Zee started. An accident? His dream flashed back to him again. As Charlotte walked to her desk, he tried to catch her eye, but she was too busy demonstrating her love of math. So after class, he waved on his friends and waited for his cousin.

"What happened?" Zee asked hurriedly when she reached him. "You had an accident? Are you all right? Is Aunt Tara all right?"

"Oh. No," Charlotte said, looking around surreptitiously, "I was just late."

Zee rolled his eyes. "You couldn't have thought of that one when we were gone all night?"

"Hey, Zee!" Jason Hart's voice carried down the hall, interrupting them. Zee sucked in his breath. He had completely forgotten that this was Jason's first day—Zee was supposed to show him around, but he'd been so distracted by the dream he forgot. Some friend he was.

"You know him?" Charlotte asked.

"Yeah. He's on my soccer team. Just moved here."

"Really?"

Zee couldn't help but notice that Charlotte seemed quite interested in Jason. He forgot his concern for a moment and let a deliberate grin spread across his face. "Yeah . . . why?"

Charlotte narrowed her eyes. "No reason."

"Uh-huh," Zee said knowingly.

They walked along through the hallways, talking of everything and nothing. Zee still felt the aftershocks of the vision in his dream. What if it was a vision? What if it was a prophecy? What if he was supposed to warn her? What if he was a complete paranoid prat?

Zee sighed, shook his head, and said, "Look, Char—"

But he couldn't do it. The words just wouldn't come. What was he supposed to say—I had a dream where you were in danger? Fat lot of good that would do. And Charlotte would say, "Zee, I had a dream you were a complete twit." And it came true!

Just then, Zee heard his name floating down the hallway in a decidedly feminine way. He stiffened. Ashleys! As they floated past him, the two girls waved and smiled at him flirtatiously, and Zee felt his face turn red.

What did they want from him, anyway? They didn't know him. They thought he was cool because he was new and an athlete and had a British accent, but they didn't have any idea what he was like. They barely even knew Outside Zee, let alone Real Zee.

And what was he supposed to do? Just walk up to them and say hi? He was never going to do that. He couldn't do that. Because then they would say hi back and expect him to say something else. And Zee had absolutely no idea what that would be. What in the world do you say after hi? And without some kind of plan, some kind of meticulously plotted, carefully researched, thoroughly considered plan, he would just stand there, frozen in time, while the girls slowly realized that he was not at all what they thought, that in fact he was clearly socially—and quite possibly mentally—disabled. Then they would shake their heads slowly, sigh with some combination of disappointment and pity, and walk off, while Zee stood there, still trying to come up with something to say, for a good two or three more weeks. Then he would have no choice but to move to a lonely mountaintop, where he would spend the rest of his days with no one to keep him company but an eagle and a cranky mountain goat named Mr. Thimbles.

When it was all over and the Ashleys had passed, Zee and Charlotte walked on, as if in silent agreement that they would pretend the whole thing had never happened.

"So, what was it you wanted to tell me?" Charlotte asked when they arrived in the hallway outside the locker rooms.

"Look, Char," he said, shrugging, "this is probably nothing, but . . . I saw something. . . ."

Charlotte leaned in. "What?"

"Well, I didn't really *see* it, but—"

"Char! Zee!" Zee and Charlotte both instinctively broke apart as Maddy came hurrying toward them, wide-eyed. Zee gave Charlotte a dismissive shrug.

Clearly the Fates were telling him he was off his head. "Char, are you okay?" Maddy breathed. "I heard you got hit by a bus!"

Maddy he could talk to. She was Charlotte's best friend, and of course she didn't think of him . . . in that way. They were just friends, plain and simple. He could talk to girls as friends all day long. He wasn't mental—it was just when there was a threat of something else that he was doomed to an eternity with Mr. Thimbles.

In England there had been a girl Zee had liked very much. Very, *very* much. Samantha Golton was a forward on the F&E girls' football team, and Zee would have liked very much to scrimmage with her. But, as you might expect, he had never spoken to Samantha Golton—at least not until she showed up in Exeter last summer, where he was staying with his grandmother and playing on a regional team. It was she who spoke to him; she came to one of his matches and invited him to a Grecians game, and then she fell ill and he never saw her again.

They'd taken her shadow, of course, and when Zee was down in the Underworld he found himself wondering which one was hers. He wanted to say something to it, something comforting, something protective, as if it would somehow carry the message back to her. She wouldn't hear it, of course—but it would get to her, and every time her shadow stretched out on the sidewalk in the afternoon sun, Zee would be with her. He had never been able to speak to Samantha, but he thought of all kinds of things he could tell her shadow.

Samantha was gone from his life forever, and there was no point in his old feelings anymore. But he still thought of her sometimes—she would linger behind a thought, flash by in a dream—Samantha Golton streaking down the soccer field, at once ferocious and graceful, her long ponytail streaking behind her.

Perhaps it was Maddy's ponytail that he noticed a half hour later while sitting cross-legged on the rubbery gym floor watching the gymnastics routines. As she was going into her cartwheel, she whipped her head around, and the flash of the hair flowing behind her head made Zee take notice. But it was not Samantha Golton he thought of, watching Maddy do her routine; for Maddy's grace was different from hers—controlled, elegant— and so was her strength—steady, quiet—but grace and strength nonetheless. Maddy was calm, confident, skilled, fluid, and . . . beautiful. Maddy was beautiful. And as Zee watched her, he felt a sense of contentment pass over him, a feeling that he could watch her all day, a feeling that he wouldn't mind if Maddy taught him how to cartwheel, and somersault, and even pirouette if she really wanted to.

And then Zee's heart dropped. His breath caught. His stomach flipped.

For the rest of the day Zee tried to avoid Charlotte. He couldn't face her. What was she going to think? How dare he develop feelings for her best friend? That's the exact sort of thing you're not supposed to do, because then Charlotte would feel excluded, and you can't exclude your cousin, because your cousin saved you from an eternity of Philonecron-induced mind control, and besides, it just isn't nice. And when, at the end of English, Maddy called out to him and he saw the two of them standing there, together, everything inside of him just froze up, like a hiker who encounters a bear in the forest—a very angry bear who had developed a taste for human flesh during a genetic engineering experiment that went horribly awry. Except there were two bears, and one of them was his cousin, and the other one was a *girl*, and he was going to open his mouth and something absolutely ridiculous would come out. Except he couldn't open his mouth—it had locked shut, and he was going to spend the rest of his life like that so he would have to be fed through a tube and instead of speaking would have to develop a highly involved grunting system— which would still be better than anything he could say to Maddy. So Zee mumbled something incoherent, and then turned and fled for the hills.

As he walked out of the front doors that afternoon, he decided he'd never been so happy to have the school day be over. He'd thought he had problems *before*, what with the whole obsessive evil demigod running loose in the Upperworld, but this—this he did not need. He was simply going to have to try to talk himself out of it, for what was the point, really—Maddy would never like someone like him. She was steady, together, the smartest girl in school. So smart, really—in science she always got things right away when everyone else was blinking dumbly at the teacher. Maybe she could come over in the afternoons and help him with covalent bonding—

No, Zee.

"Hey, Zee, wait up!"

Zee stopped just in front of the school bus. Jason Hart was running toward him. Again, he felt a pang of guilt. Tomorrow he'd make it up to Jason, tomorrow he'd show him around, tomorrow he'd introduce him to everyone. All the boys, anyway.

"Listen, mate," Zee said, "I'm sorry I forgot to show you around today."

"Oh, it's okay. It doesn't matter."

"But I should have introduced you around, and—"

"No, I met everyone. Charlie and Dov and Sam and Jack. They were all really nice."

"Oh!" Zee was impressed. Those were his best

friends at school, and Jason had managed to find all of them. "Well, I'll show you around tomorrow anyway."

Something passed over Jason's face, something Zee couldn't quite identify. "Sure," Jason said, looking at him oddly. "And, uh, you know. Good luck."

"What?" But Jason had already turned and left.

On the bus on the way home, Zee sat next to Jack Liao, who was gabbing on about a basketball game he'd gone to the night before (Zee did not understand basketball; you dribbled with your *hands*), and Zee tried his best to put ponytails and gymnastics out of his mind. Eventually Chris, who was sitting behind them, joined in, and Zee let his attention waver.

Suddenly, a burst of laughter interrupted Zee's reverie. He turned his head to look at his friend. "What?"

Jack blinked. "What?"

"What were you laughing at?"

"I wasn't laughing."

"Oh." Zee looked around at the kids sitting behind him, then shrugged. "All right."

Zee got off the bus slowly, thinking reluctantly about the long night ahead of him. He always felt so restless on the days he didn't have soccer, like a hamster without his exercise wheel. Today, especially, he needed to be running back and forth down a field kicking things—but instead he had a long night of homework and angst ahead of him. Maybe he needed to get a human-size wheel installed in his room. It would fit in perfectly with the rest of his life—run fast, look absurd, go absolutely nowhere.

Out of the corner of his eye, Zee saw a flash of movement across the street a few houses away from him. He wouldn't even have noticed it—for, after all, sidewalks do tend to have people on them—had not something in the back of his mind registered a familiar color. Zee glanced over and saw, standing next to a big oak tree, a very old man wearing an old-fashioned three-piece suit and bowler hat, all in the most striking shade of aqua. In the light of day, the color looked even stranger, no less so because it exactly matched the color of the man's eyes. His skin did not seem quite right to Zee. It was so pale and thin as to look translucent—indeed, there seemed to be shadows moving just underneath the surface. And while he gave off the impression of being terribly old, as thin and fragile as a glass skeleton, his face was as smooth as Zee's.

Then Zee heard the laughter again, the same laughter he'd heard on the school bus. But this time he knew it couldn't have come from Jack. Jack was long gone, sitting happily on the school bus, still waxing enthusiastically about three pointers and fast breaks. Anyway, the laughter wasn't coming from someone next to him, but rather from inside his head. And it was not laughter so much as a cackle—a very gleeful cackle.

Philonecron.

As Zee's stomach turned and his skin crawled, the old man disappeared behind the oak tree.

Eight months before, Zee had seen some extremely creepy and not very human-like creatures in tuxedos steal a boy's shadow, and he had done what anyone would have done in that situation—which was turn in the other direction and run as fast as he could. But now everything had changed, Philonecron was laughing, there was a not entirely human-like man lingering by his house, and so, finally, Zee jumped off his exercise wheel.

"Hey," he called. "HEY!" And then, without a thought, he took off across the street.

## CHAPTER 10

A Friendly Chat with Poseidon, the Second Most Powerful God in the Whole Universe

Once upon a time, it used to be that any sane person who ventured out on the seas would, before he embarked on his journey, make a sacrifice to Poseidon. It was only sensible. Since Poseidon is the second most powerful god in the whole Universe, you want to be as respectful to him as you possibly can be. Because you, after all, are a lowly mortal, no greater than sea scum on the tooth of a snaggle-toothed snake eel, of no more significance than a scale on the butt of a bottom-feeding dwarf suckermouth catfish—except the scum on the snake eel and the scale on the catfish butt both have the blessed privilege of being of the sea and therefore created by Poseidon himself, whereas you were made by Prometheus, a mortal-loving Titan freak, and nobody asked Poseidon whether we needed humans anyway, and you're lucky he doesn't drown you when you take a bath. Because he could, you know. And then you'd be sorry.

The point is, if you had lived once upon a time and if you weren't a moron with a major nautically related death wish, every time you even got near the sea—every time you even *thought* about the sea—you would drown your best horse or sacrifice your most prized bull in honor of Poseidon, in which case he might—just might—let you live.

Maybe.

One thing you could be sure of: If you chose to set out on the water making nary an offering to the great god of the realm, you could be pretty confident that that sea journey was going to be your last. For the seas are treacherous, and there are so many unfortunate things that can happen to a person on them—a sudden squall, an errant wave, a vicious attack by a flesh-eating giant squid. After all, there are so many humans out on the waters at any given time, and so very many dangers that they face, Poseidon can't possibly be expected to keep track of *all* of them.

All he wants is a little respect. You can't blame Poseidon; if you were the second most powerful god in the whole Universe (which you're not, obviously, because Poseidon is. And you're clearly not the first most, because then you'd be Zeus, and that guy has never read a book in his life) you'd want a little reverence and fear too.

And if you didn't get it, you'd be angry.

Really angry.

Take, say, Minos. He wanted to prove his right to rule Crete, so he asked Poseidon to send a bull out from the sea at his command, and all the townspeople would be like, "Ooh, bull!" and make him king. Minos promised Poseidon he'd then sacrifice the bull, so Poseidon did it, he made a bull come out of the sea, because that's just the kind of guy he is. Giving. But Minos liked the bull so much he decided to keep it, so Poseidon had Eros make Minos's wife fall in love with the bull. She had a hideous little half-bull baby and everything. It was pretty hilarious.

Or the king of Troy. Once, for kicks, Poseidon decided to disguise himself as a man and help build the walls of Troy. But when he was done, the king wouldn't pay him. So, he sent a Ketos to terrorize the town and eat all the inhabitants. That was pretty funny too.

There's a lot you can do when you're the God of the

Seas. Sea monsters are just the beginning. You can flood a town, like Poseidon did with Athens when they picked Athena to be their patron instead of him. (Why would anyone do that? Athena can't do anything cool, like flooding towns or sending sea monsters after people.) You can dry up all the springs in the area so everyone dies from thirst, which he did with Argos after they chose Hera to be their patron. You can make mountains grow around a seafaring town so they can't fish anymore and everyone starves to death horribly, which he wanted to do when the Phaeacians tried to help someone who had crossed him. But Zeus went on a big power trip and wouldn't let him. The big ninny.

It makes him so mad thinking about it, even now. Mortals just don't have any respect. They act like Poseidon's some minor god, some wimp, some puddle god or something. He's not. He's the second most powerful god in the whole Universe, and he is Not to Be Messed With.

And then, they don't just disrespect him, but they mess with his children, too! Disrespect him all you want, really—he'll only make your whole town die horribly— but what really ticks him off, what you really should never, ever, ever do, is disrespect his offspring. Because that's just like disrespecting him, and that's a good way to get yourself eaten by a sea monster.

Like that guy Odysseus. On the way home from the
Trojan War, he and his crew got trapped in a cave that
happened to be the lair of Poseidon's son, a Cyclops
named Polyphemos. Now, Polyphemos certainly had his
quirks, one of them being that he really really liked to
eat humans. Preferably raw.

And after the Cyclops swallowed a few crew members whole and washed them down with milk, Odysseus
stuck a hot poker in his eye and blinded him. Blinded
him! Poseidon's son!

Well, Poseidon was not going to stand for that, and
it took Odysseus a little longer to sail home than it
otherwise might have. Like, ten years longer. Take
that, Mr. Blindy Man.

The thing is, if one of Poseidon's sons wants to eat
you, you let him eat you. You're grateful. As you're
being slowly digested in his stomach, you look up to the
heavens—well, no, you can't really do that inside his
stomach, but you can look up *mentally*—and say, Thank
you, Poseidon, Great God of the Seas, for bestowing
upon me the honor of being eaten by one of your
descendants, and I can only hope that I am succulent
enough to please the sanctified taste buds of your offspring.

And if you do that, see, you're home free! Poseidon
will leave you alone, no problem. You're always welcome

on his seas then—or at least you would be if you hadn't been eaten.

Well, anyway, things are different now. The gods have gone Deep Undercover. Nothing to See Here, Folks. Move Along. Stay Behind the Yellow Line. You're Right, It's All Myth, Now Shut Up and Have a Cookie. So, if you've been to the sea, it's quite doubtful you made any sort of sacrifice to Poseidon. And you can't be blamed. You don't know any better. You can't be in abject terror of a god you don't know about. Poseidon understands, he does. He's not some kind of demon; he's a god—wise and beneficent. So he's not going to send a sea monster after you.

Probably.

Though a little more respect wouldn't hurt.

Like he said, no one asked him if he wanted there to be humans in the first place. Sure, when the Olympians took power after they defeated Cronus, everyone thought Earth should be repopulated; mortal creatures were amusing diversions, and one did want to be the god of *something*. Poseidon himself created all the creatures of the sea, which is why they're so great.

But the whole human thing was pretty much a big accident. Zeus gave the task of repopulating Earth to Prometheus and his brother, since they'd helped in the war—Zeus acted like it was this big honor, but really he was just farming out the labor. Zeus never does anything himself if he can help it. Not like Poseidon, who rules the seas single-handedly, and it's not an easy job, you know.

Anyway, Prometheus made his creatures—humans—in the shape of the gods, which was a nice idea, though kind of creepy. Looking down at Earth and seeing miniature versions of yourself walking around scratching themselves all the time is a little weird.

Well, the humans all started freezing and starving to death, and Prometheus felt sorry for them and stole fire from Olympus to keep them alive, like anyone cared about them. The fire caused humans to look up to the heavens and see the gods, and suddenly everyone whose fishing boat got stuck in a storm was like, "Oh, Poseidon, save me! Save me!"

It wasn't really the plan.

At the same time, it was nice to be worshipped. You know, you can get out of bed in the morning and have thousands of little beings praying for your mercy and extolling your supreme greatness, or you can not. It's not a tough choice.

All in all, though, it did get tiring—no, no, not the worship, but the other stuff. You're just minding your own business, trying to woo some beautiful sea goddess, and some mortal starts whining, *"Oh, Poseidon, my family's starving, please send me some fish! Oh, Poseidon, I'm drowning, help me!"* Come on, learn to swim. It all got so *old*. He wants to be worshipped, not *bothered*.

So the whole we're-all-just-a-bunch-of-myths-let's-forget-it-ever-happened thing wasn't his idea—like Zeus would ever adopt one of his ideas. But for a Zeus idea, it was a pretty good one. Without mortals nagging him all the time, it gave Poseidon a chance to focus on what's really important. Which is being a god. There's no reason to spend your time waiting on needy mortals hand and foot when you can be cruising the Mediterranean on the greatest luxury yacht the Universe has ever seen.

Zeus doesn't have a yacht.

Olympus is fine, really, if you like that kind of thing. But Poseidon is glad that when he, Zeus, and Hades drew lots for the Universe, he ended up with the sea. He wouldn't have wanted Olympus, anyway.

Really.

Well, anyway, the moral of this story is Poseidon and mortals have been staying out of each other's way for some time, and Poseidon is totally fine with that. He won't bother them as long as no one bothers him. As long as no puny, insignificant, worthless, sniveling, pathetic mortal does anything to disrespect him, everything's going to be just fine.

And for the longest time, no one did.

• • •

He'd heard about the events in the Underworld, of course. Everyone had. There was the attempted coup, the shadow army, the destruction of Hades's Palace— ha! That he would have liked to see! All of that was interesting, certainly, but nothing like the news that two mortal children had thwarted an Immortal. The incident sparked the whole Mortal Question debate all over the realms once again; gods were yammering about it all the time now, even at his parties, where they were supposed to be having a good time and basking in the glory of being so close to Poseidon, Lord of the Seas. Even Zeus had taken notice, and he wouldn't notice a Chimera if it belched fire right in his face. Poseidon doesn't care what happens to mortals—wipe 'em off the Earth or don't—as long as they stay the heck out of his way.

At first Poseidon had had no idea that Philonecron was his grandson. Such a handsome and powerful god as Poseidon will be very attractive to the ladies, and Poseidon had more children than he could count. And he can count pretty high. He's a god, you know.

So he was on the sundeck lifting weights one afternoon, as he is on so many afternoons. He has to cast a small spell on his skin to give himself a sheen of perspiration; gods, of course, do not perspire, but one's muscles do gleam so in the sunshine. As always, lots of Immortals of the fairer sex were sunbathing around him, but Poseidon knew it wasn't the sun's rays they were after. They might pretend to sleep or read or listen to music, but he knew they were there to watch him. Why else would they be there if not to check out the huge, rippling muscles of Poseidon, Lord of the Seas, eh?

So there he was, in the middle of doing some major reps on the bench press, with his personal assistant Delphin spotting him—not that he really needed spotting, but it looked cool—and he'd just caught the eye of a sweet young thing with big purple eyes, long black hair, and eight tentacles for arms, when Triton came prancing up to him, blowing on his conch shell as if Cronus himself had come to take his Universe back.

Triton was Poseidon's son, and if you wanted to do something to him, that would be okay with Poseidon. (Not really.) Because there's a pattern to life—you have kids, it's a beautiful thing, they grow up, they move out of the house and have kids of their own. Or not, but at least *they move out of the house.* Not Triton, though. No, he wanted to stay home with Mom and Dad and run around blowing on his stupid conch shell, which was cute when he was three, but not so cute at three millennia.

"Must you?" Poseidon said wearily, as Delphin added weights to his bar.

Triton put his hand to his chest and tried valiantly to catch his breath. His long fish tail flapped in his agita. "Dad," he breathed, "there's a letter for you." With a portentous look, he produced a rolled-up piece of parchment tied ceremoniously with a black silk ribbon.

Poseidon looked around. All the pretty young things on the sundeck were eyeing him with curiosity. "Can't you see I'm busy?" he said through clenched teeth.

"I think you should read it," said Triton in a grave whisper.

Well, he did, and he almost dropped the weights on Triton's hoof. The Immortal who had been humiliated and mutilated was the son of Cynara, who in turn was the daughter of the nymph Galatea (ah, what soft green skin she had!) and Poseidon, Lord of the Sea.

Quickly he summoned the dishonored pathetic wretch to his yacht, to his protective bosom, and the wretch told him everything that had happened. It was not two mortal children who had had the temerity to offend Poseidon, but just one. The girl! The girl had thwarted his plans, the girl had turned the boy against him, the girl caused Philonecron's disgrace, his banishment, his hideous dismemberment. And she had laughed in his face! She said the mortals would bring the gods down! She called Poseidon a pantywaist. Poseidon! The second most powerful god in the whole Universe!

This could not stand.

They were all laughing at him, he was sure. Zeus and everyone up on their precious Olympus were pointing and giggling at him. Well, not for long! Soon mortals would see what happens when you mess with Poseidon, the Earth Shaker!

It took him some time to come up with an appropriate retaliation. He couldn't send a Ketos to destroy her town; she lived in the middle of a continent, and sending a lake monster wouldn't really do the trick. He tried it once in Scotland, and the darn thing ended up settling down in the middle of the lake and raising a family.

But then the idea came to him. So beautiful, so simple. And full of entertainment value for his guests. Divine retribution and an excuse to throw a fabulous party. What could be better? Now, all he had to do was sit and wait. She would be there soon enough.

CHAPTER II

# Mirror, Mirror

Hey!" Zee shouted again as he tore across the street. He didn't have a plan, really—he was chasing down someone who might well be a henchman of Philonecron's and he didn't have a plan, which maybe wasn't the best idea. The old man could have any kind of powers—he could freeze Zee in place, blast him down the block, turn him into a tree, turn him into a common gray squirrel, and Zee would spend his days trying to convince people that he was not a squirrel but a boy, a real boy, and they would laugh and feed him bread crumbs and say, "Sometimes that squirrel seems almost to be trying to communicate with us," and then they would chuckle and shake their heads and fold up their picnic blankets and leave, and then a stray dog would come by and eat him.

But there was no time for a plan, no time to even think about trees or the life expectancy of a common gray squirrel, no time for anything but running toward the oak tree. Somewhere in Zee's mind a fantasy played out—he tackles the old man, pins him down, gets him to take him to Philonecron, and then Zee defeats Philonecron and traps him forever in a jar of very stinky olives.

But when Zee reached the oak tree, there was no sign of the man in the aqua-colored suit. Quickly he scanned the street. Nothing. He turned around slowly, trying to find some evidence of an escape route—but there was no way the man could have disappeared from sight in the time it took Zee to run down the street. Anyway, Zee had had his eyes fixed on the tree the whole time; he would have seen the man if he'd moved from behind it. Unless he'd stayed out of Zee's sight line and disappeared behind the nearest house—but no, there wasn't time.

Or, unless the man had simply disappeared. *Poof!*

Zee let out a gargled scream and kicked a large rock that lay under the big oak tree. He exhaled heavily, kicked the rock one more time for good measure, then, after scanning the horizon fruitlessly one more time, began to walk slowly home. Whoever the old man was, he would be back—Zee knew that for sure.

When Zee walked through the back door of his house, his mother was sitting at the kitchen computer. She had been a kindergarten teacher in London and had been working substitute jobs since they came over, so she was often home when Zee got home. Which would have been completely fine if his parents hadn't decided to go mental and treat him like he was made of glass.

"Zachary," she exclaimed as he walked in the door. "Are you all right?"

"Sure," Zee said.

"You look flushed. Zee, are you shaking? What happened?"

Zee stiffened. "Nothing, Mum."

The next thing Zee knew, his mother was at his side with her hand on his cheek.

"You're all clammy. Are you ill?"

"No, Mum," he said, pulling away. "Just hot. Jogged from the bus stop, you know. No soccer today and all."

She eyed him suspiciously. "Well, sit down. Let me get you some water."

"It's all right," Zee insisted. "Look, um"—he began

to edge toward the door—"I've got to call Charlotte. . . ."

"You can call her in a bit," Mrs. Miller said in a voice that would brook no opposition. "Sit down."

With a heavy sigh, Zee sat on the edge of one of the chairs at the small kitchen table, poised to spring at his first available opportunity.

"So," she said, handing him a glass of ice water. "Tell me how your day was."

"Um . . ." Zee said, wondering if he might actually burst open. "Fine, Mum." He began to gulp down the glass of water as quickly as he could.

"You still like it at Hartnett?"

"Yes," he replied tightly.

"It's a tough adjustment," she mused. "Everyone thinking you have an accent. Being new. Not a lot of black kids there." Her voice was casual, but Zee could feel her looking at him intently.

Zee almost rolled his eyes. One or the other of his parents said the same thing once every week now, always as if it was something that had just occurred to them that second. Except they hadn't cared about any of this at all when he was at F&E, where he actually *was* miserable. "Nope, I like it a lot. Good school." Zee finished his water, plunked the glass down on the table, and stood up, nearly knocking the chair over. "Anyway, I'm going to call Charlotte."

"Something important?" Mrs. Miller smiled benignly at him.

"Oh, uh . . . English project. See you later, Mum!" And with that, he made his escape.

After casting a glance back at the kitchen, Zee trotted up the stairs to his room, closed the door, and turned on his stereo just loud enough to mask the sound of his voice, but not so loud his parents would complain. Then he picked up the phone and dialed his cousin's number, uttering a silent prayer that she'd be the one to answer.

"Hello?"

No such luck.

"Oh, Uncle Mike. Hi . . ."

"Zachary!" Mr. Mielswetzski said, his voice full of cheer. "How are you?"

"Oh, I'm good," Zee said, squirming. "How are you?"

"Well, we're just fabulous over here."

"Great . . ."

"We sure miss you around here. How have you been? How's school treating you?"

"Good," breathed Zee. "All good. Hey, listen, Uncle Mike, is Charlotte around?"

"Oh, she's at therapy. I'm just going to pick her up now."

"Right," Zee said. "Can you have her call me? Tonight?"

"Sure thing! Oh, what?" Zee heard his aunt's voice in the background. "Hold on, your aunt wants to talk to you. She's going to pick up the other phone."

"Zachary!" exclaimed Mrs. Mielswetzski, her voice bursting through the receiver. "We sure miss having you around."

"That's what I said," said Mr. Mielswetzski.

"Well, it's true," said Mrs. Mielswetzski.

"That's why I said it," said Mr. Mielswetzski.

Zee bounced up and down on his heels. Shouldn't they be picking up Charlotte now?

"Oh, Zee," Mrs. Mielswetzski added, "did you hear? About the cruise?"

"Cruise?" Zee repeated. He glanced out of his window, looking for lurking shadows. But there were none—the street was clear.

"We're all going on a cruise! Uncle Mike won an award—"

"A prize!" Mr. Mielswetzski corrected.

"A teaching *award*. We're leaving a week from Saturday. Going up the eastern seaboard! All three of us!"

"Oh," Zee said weakly, "that sounds brilliant."

"It is brilliant," laughed Mr. Mielswetzski. "The Mielswetzskis, sailing the seven seas!"

"Well, really just one of them," said Mrs. Mielswetzski.

"It's a metaphor, dear," said Mr. Mielswetzski.

"I know, darling," said Mrs. Mielswetzski.

Zee kept bouncing while his aunt and uncle chattered on about their cruise—did they have any intention of picking up Charlotte at all? Were they going to abandon her in front of her psychologist's office? At least then she could have easy access to therapy to deal with her abandonment.

Zee finally extricated himself from the conversation and hung up the phone with a great exhale. He went right up to the window and peered out. The walls of the room seemed to be closing in on him.

"*Where are you?*" he whispered.

No answer. Still, the skin on the back of Zee's neck prickled. Hugging his arms to himself, he stared out of the window a few more minutes, then flopped down on his bed and tried to still his heart while the sun slowly set outside.

When darkness started to creep over the room, Zee sat up and went to look out the window again. Still nothing. Charlotte had to be home by now, he thought. Why wasn't she calling? Didn't they give her the message? What if Charlotte never called him back at all, didn't come to school, just went off on the cruise with her parents. . . . Mielswetzskis on the seven seas—

Zee gasped. The sea! The image from his dream appeared in his mind again, Charlotte on a small boat heading toward disaster. What if it wasn't a symbol at all? What if it was quite literal—Charlotte in danger on the sea? Why he was seeing it he couldn't imagine, but maybe someone was trying to give him a warning. (But who, who?) Or maybe it was a trap—they'd been lured to the Underworld by a message that Mr. Metos was in danger. Zee would do anything to keep Charlotte from danger.

But—he thought suddenly—would he really? He'd been hearing Philonecron's voice for months and he hadn't said anything. Just because he was embarrassed, just because he felt like he had failed. But he never thought about Charlotte at all. Philonecron had been weirdly obsessed with having Zee by his side, yes, but he hated Charlotte with a fury. And if Philonecron was nearby, was speaking to Zee, was sending more creepy men after them, well, Zee wasn't the only one who was in danger. He had to tell Charlotte.

In his head, he saw the old man in the aqua suit standing next to the big oak tree staring at him. The image sharpened, as if someone had changed the settings on the camera, and Zee saw quite clearly that the man was grinning.

His skin prickled again, as if someone were drawing his finger lightly across his neck. For some reason Zee froze, his whole body at attention—like a prey animal in the woods. The music from his stereo suddenly sounded dim and far away, as if it were coming from down the street. In fact, his whole room felt dim and far away, as if Zee had somehow been removed from that plane of existence and was now living somewhere just beyond it. His lungs felt stretched, his skin tight. Then the familiar sibilant voice:

*Soon*, it said. *Soon*.

Violently Zee snapped back to reality. He stood in his room, poised on the balls of his feet, looking all around him, as if the source of the voice might be there. But of course, it was not. Zee tore out of his room and ran down the stairs.

His mother's voice came floating toward him from the kitchen. "Zachary? Is that you?"

As he ran through the front hall toward the door, the lie rolled off his tongue like a song, like a Charlotte Mielswetzski classic, "Going for a run, Mum!"

"But dinner—"

Her words were interrupted by the sound of the door slamming shut. Zee was gone.

It was about two miles to the Mielswetzski house, and Zee could be there in fifteen minutes if he ran. Which he did—down the front steps, down the street, around the corner, down the block toward the busy street that they drove down to get to the Mielswetzskis'. Block after block Zee ran, barely stopping at street corners, dodging cars that got in his way as he crossed the streets. People honked, someone yelled at him out of a car window, but he just kept running. He was getting hot and clammy underneath his sweater and jeans, and the sweat on his face felt like it was going to freeze. Steam rose from his head. One mile down, another to go—his legs began to protest, his chest heaved, his side began to ache, his lungs felt battered and bruised by the dry night air, but still he ran on, turning up another street, now on the jogging path that ran along the lake near Charlotte's house. So focused was he on keeping his legs moving, on keeping his lungs working, on hurling himself toward his destination, that he did not notice the three human-like shapes—two large forms supporting one small and shriveled one—that moved along swiftly in the shadows just beyond the periphery of his vision. Nor did he see the small man break away as the two large ones set themselves up underneath a towering tree a few yards ahead of him. He noticed nothing until, two blocks away from Charlotte's house, the two large men moved themselves so they stood directly in his path.

Zee thought nothing of them at first—he would just move around them, go to the street—whatever those two big men were doing standing in the middle of the jogging path on a cold March evening, it would not slow him down. He was almost there, and even as the dull pain in his side grew sharp and his legs threatened to give out and his chest was ready to explode, he was going to get there and warn Charlotte—

And that's when he got close enough to get a good look at the men.

At first it looked like they had no heads. For before him Zee saw two forms, wearing black suits and broad-brimmed hats, but there didn't seem to be anything in between.

Then the men stepped toward him as one and Zee saw that they did, in fact, have heads—it was only that the heads were made up of a clear substance that looked a great deal like water.

Perhaps if Zee had continued to run he could have escaped—if he had turned away from the men and run full tilt toward the Mielswetzski house, gotten inside, and never left again, this story might be very different. But he did not, for the sight of the men with water for heads coming toward him stopped Zee in his tracks.

Then his body took its revenge for the abuse he had inflicted on it. His legs faltered, his side screamed, his chest began to suck in air desperately, and the two water-faced men were upon him, grabbing his arms with their gloved hands. With all the strength he did not have, Zee flailed and fought, but he could not shake himself from their grip.

"There is no point fighting, young man," a raspy voice said. Zee wrenched his head toward the sound and beheld the old man stepping toward him, rubbing his pale, bony hands together gleefully. "Hector Horatio and Otis are quite steadfast."

Zee stared at the old man, fear and hatred in his eyes.

"Ah, yes, you remember me," the old man said. "That was carelessness on my part. I should not have let you see me before I had my friends here to help me." He motioned generously to the water men.

"What do you want?" Zee hissed.

"I? I want nothing from you. I am merely doing a job. But don't be afraid; I'm sure Philonecron will take very good care of you."

As panic welled up inside him, Zee kicked his left foot back as hard as he could toward the knee of the man on his left. Instead of making hard contact, his foot kept going past the plane of the leg, plunging right into the watery body. He heard a rippling sound and felt a strange vibration on his arm and, for a moment, the man's grip loosened. Zee wrenched his body forward violently, bracing himself to kick the other man, when his eyes caught some sort of strange shifting in front of him. Suddenly the man in the aqua suit was gone, and Zee found himself face to face with—himself.

Zee's whole body went slack, his vision blurred, his stomach turned, his skin turned to ice. The Not-Zee in front of him grinned a very un-Zee-like grin and said in his raspy voice, "I know, I know, impressive, isn't it?" He twirled around, holding his arms out as if to model himself. "Sometimes I even amaze myself! Really, though," he added thoughtfully, "the point is not the ability, but the opportunity it presents. Remember that, Zachary— it's not your talents, but how you use them! It's what you do with your life that counts!" Not-Zee tapped Zee on the nose. "Don't worry, no one will even notice you're gone. At least . . . until your cousin leaves. Until then, we'll have loads of fun!" With twinkling eyes, Not-Zee leaned in, and suddenly his voice grew deep, young, and full. Zee's voice. "It will be *brilliant*."

CHAPTER 12

## Special Delivery

Once Proteus had left on his mission, Philonecron began to prepare himself for Zee's—or as he called him, Zero's—impending arrival. There was so much to do! He needed all new furniture—from a nice ebony dinner table for two, to an armoire for the boy's clothes, to another velvet-cushioned, high-backed chair in which the boy could sit while the two of them discussed the finer things: music, philosophy, art, and evil plans. And, of course, the six-foot-tall silk-trimmed glass case the boy would stand in when Philonecron did not require his company.

Then, of course, there was the issue of clothes. Philonecron did not understand how a boy with a soul so akin to his own (not that Philonecron had a soul, mind you) could dress like a blind Cyclops with a mental disorder, but that was easily solved. A quick visit to the ship's tailor and Philonecron had a proper wardrobe for him, from morning coats made out of the wool of golden-fleeced rams, to casual afternoon suits for deck parties and seahorse races, to carefully fitted tuxedos for evening wear—not to mention thirty handkerchiefs crafted from the silk of giant Indos worms, all carefully embroidered with a majestic Z. (Philonecron also had a new, short cape made for himself. It billowed behind his wheelchair as he rolled around.) The tailoring was not as it was in the Underworld, of course. Nothing was. There was nothing like the threat of eternal torment to really motivate a person to do his best work.

But there was nothing he could do about that, or any of it, really; not the tailoring or the crass ambrosia or the lounge singer's tendency to be one sixty-fourth of a note sharp on anything in her upper register or the fact that the ship had lounge singers at all—he had to play nice for the time being. It wouldn't do to be feeding Poseidon's favorite tailor to a tank of demonic piranhas, at least not yet. Not until he'd gotten what he wanted. He could only hope Zero would understand.

Then there was the matter of finding the boy a good valet—since, after all, he wouldn't be able to dress himself. It was not an easy task—most of the servants on board the *Poseidon* wouldn't know how to match a cravat to a handkerchief if their lives depended on it. Which, if he were running things, it would.

Greatness, you see, is not always a blessing. Oh, sure, if you are also blessed with, say, your own realm to rule, then greatness is certainly a boon. But if you are gifted with genius, vision, virtuosity, and, of course, exquisite taste, and you must toil in a world of others' making—and those others are so vastly inferior in every respect to yourself—then it will bring you nothing but torment.

Oh, how Philonecron wished he weren't so encumbered with brilliance! Then he might be perfectly happy in this world of puckered seams and inept regimes, lax standards and lounge music. He would not mind that Hades had let the Underworld sink in the bog of bureaucracy, that Poseidon was too busy glorifying himself to remember what glory really was. He would not mind that none of the Immortals—from the most minor puddle god to Zeus on high—had any real ambition, vision, had any sense at all of their power and potential, and were content to mire themselves in mediocrity. They were unworthy of being gods, they were pathetic, every last one of them—and do you know who suffered because of it? Philonecron, that's who. He's very sensitive, you know.

But, wish as he may, brilliant he was. It was his burden to carry, and he would carry it as best he could.

Of course, it was a lonely life. Perhaps that's why he noticed Zero in the first place. Philonecron never knew there was a hole inside his heart (again, if he had a heart) until he began to spend so much time with the boy's blood and realized what a wonderful specimen Zero was, how like Philonecron himself—an extraordinary creature in a disgustingly ordinary world.

He had never really thought about what it might be like to have a family. Plotting to overthrow the King of the Dead is very time-consuming and just doesn't leave much time for thoughts of settling down. But Zero made Philonecron realize that not only would he be a magnificent ruler of the Universe, but he might be a pretty darned good father as well.

Yes, Zero was someone who he could raise in his own image, who could share with him a passion for elegance, culture, and world domination, who could help him as he conceived of his next evil plan. Because Zero was clever, capable, strong. Because Zero was a hero—anyone could see that, and he could help Philonecron get what he wanted. It is, after all, a hero's destiny to do great things, and what could be greater than helping

Philonecron take over the Universe? And when Philonecron finally ruled, he would have a son by his side. And when he unleashed pain and torment on the Earth to show humanity what it really was to serve a god, when he threw the Olympians in the deepest, blackest pits and set loose upon them demonic rats who would feed on their entrails for all eternity, he would have someone with whom to share it.

For what is the point of ruling the Universe without love?

You may be surprised to find him so sanguine after all he had experienced, and indeed it had not always been thus for Philonecron. It had taken him some time to get to the point where he could dream of love and the eternal suffering of others again. When he first was exiled, when the horrible Griffins with their piercing claws and intolerable breath dropped him in a field in the ghastly brightness of the Upperworld, he found himself wishing that his life would end. Him. Philonecron! He did not say—Do not worry, Philonecron, for you are an evil genius and you have a destiny, and someday you will crush them all in your white-gloved hands. No. Philonecron despaired. And if you had come across him lying in the field on that bright afternoon (and I sincerely hope you did not) you might have noticed a single tear slide down his gaunt, gray cheek, past his wide red mouth, and fall to the ground—whereupon all the flowers within a one-foot radius quickly turned black and crumbled in a steaming pile of ash.

But Philonecron rallied. There was no point in despair. All would be well. For he was an evil genius and he had a destiny, that much was apparent. You could not be as brilliant and accomplished as he, with so many natural talents and virtues, without a destiny. And perhaps it was all for the best, really, for if he had ruled the Underworld, he might have been satisfied, he might never have spent enough time in the Upperworld to realize what despicable chaos it was in, that mortals ran around willy-nilly without even fearing the gods, that the gods had less interest in being gods than Hades had in ruling the Underworld. If that was possible. In other words, the Universe needed Philonecron.

But that was all in good time. For he could have no peace while that bad-complexioned little Empusa who had taken his Zero from him, who had turned the great golden castle of his dreams into a pile of rubble, who had caused his humiliation and mutilation, was still breathing. There was no point in coming up with a new evil plan with her on the Earth. Philonecron knew his history, his literature—the girl was his foil, his archenemy, his nemesis, destined to thwart all his plans and finally to destroy him—unless he destroyed her first.

Then he could get his Zero back on his side and the two of them could begin their path to conquest. As a family.

He had planned, originally, that the girl would be taken care of before he won back Zero. He would fill Poseidon's ears with talk of her shocking insolence toward the second most powerful god in the whole Universe, and the Lord of the Seas would take care of the rest—then whatever spell she had cast over Zero would be broken, and the boy would come willingly into his welcoming arms. But of course spells are not so easily lifted, and when Philonecron met Proteus on the yacht, he had an idea. (Typical of Poseidon not to make use of Proteus's talents. Philonecron was surprised Poseidon didn't make the old man take on his own form all the time, so he could look at himself all day.) If he could remove Zero without attracting the attention of the skinny-armed midget she-Dragon, then the boy would see her destruction for himself and have no choice but to turn to Philonecron. Or, as he liked to think of himself, Daddy.

And it was all working beautifully. Poseidon might be a vulgar self-obsessed half-wit with all the worth of a Gorgon's hairbrush, but he did know how to exact revenge. And even Philonecron had to admit that his plan was quite inspired—if not, of course, genius.

The day of Zee's planned arrival, Philonecron could not contain his excitement. He tried to pass the time in dignified contemplation, but mostly ended up pacing back and forth (well, rolling) in his room, thinking about all that was to come. And when Proteus's watery henchmen appeared in the room carrying their long, thin package wrapped in white cloth, Philonecron clapped his hands together and let out a sound that could only be described as a squeal.

"Where do you want it?" asked the men, speaking together. Their voices burbled like someone talking underwater.

"It?" gasped Philonecron. "*It?*"

"Yeah. Where do you want it?"

Philonecron sighed heavily. "Put him on the table, there." The men nodded curtly and began to drop their bundle on the long ebony dining room table. "Gently!" he warned, scooting quickly toward them. "Be careful!" He put his hands to his face as the men placed the package on the table. "He's not damaged, is he?"

The men shrugged. "Just as we found him."

Philonecron looked up at the men, his red eyes piercing. "Were you seen?"

"No," said the men together. "We were not seen."

"Excellent," said Philonecron, nodding. "Now for your reward. It's in that room over there." With a sweet smile, he pointed to a small door at the back of his stateroom. This was another addition he'd made recently, though it wasn't for Zero's benefit. Philonecron rolled over and opened the door for them. "You two go on in," he said. "I'll be there in a minute."

As the men headed into the small room, which was not really a room at all but more of a closet made entirely of cedar, with a small heating unit topped with steaming white rocks, Philonecron closed and barred the door behind them. Then he opened a small panel, turned the heat up as far as it would go, and closed the panel with a satisfied pat.

"Have a nice sauna, boys," he whispered. An unfortunate end for Proteus's servants, but, really, it was best not to leave any . . . loose ends. He'd have to open the door later to let the steam escape—for one couldn't have the dears condensing again, could one?

In a few moments Philonecron had his package unwrapped and was staring down at his prize. "There, there, my boy," he whispered, putting his hand paternally on Zee's forehead. "It's all right now. You're *home*. You have a place here, Zero. Finally, you *belong*."

Gently Philonecron leaned over him. "Now, don't mind me," he murmured. "It won't hurt a bit." Quickly, with a practiced hand, he extracted some blood from Zee's arm into a small vial, then tipped the vial into a small obsidian bowl. He added a small flaskful of silver fluid, whispered a quick spell over the now steaming liquid, then injected the entire concoction back into Zee's arm.

"We'll have to refresh that every day, of course," he murmured. "At least until your cousin's . . . untimely demise." He sighed. "I know, I know. I'm sorry you have to be like this, my dear boy. It's so unfortunate. I'd much rather have us speak of great things under the stars, but it is not to be right now. I know you, you see—you might run away, and then someone on board might eat you, and we couldn't have that, could we?"

On the table, Zee began to stir.

"Oh, Zero," Philonecron said, holding his arms out magnanimously. "Can you believe, after everything that's happened, that we're here together at last?" He shook his head wonderingly. "You know, I was angry at first. I'll admit that. I'd thought we'd had an understanding, you and I . . . I really thought we came to mean something to each other."

Zee's eyelids started fluttering.

"But"—Philonecron clasped his hands together earnestly—"it's not your fault. I know that now. You're under the spell of that horrible cousin of yours.

That's why you betrayed me in the Underworld. You never would have done it otherwise, after all we'd been through together. After all I'd done for you!"

He sighed the sigh of the greatly wronged as Zee's eyes slowly opened. "But it's all right. I've forgiven you. We're starting over, clean slate, a new beginning for the both of us. Finally, we're a family.

"What would you like to do first? Would you like to hear some music? Hmmm?" Philonecron wheeled himself over to the large ebony cabinet and got out his violin. "Yes, I think I'll play for you. Won't that be delightful?" He beamed at Zee. "Now, sit up!"

Slowly Zee lifted himself up and squared his body around so he sat upright on the smooth dining table.

"Oh, no, not there. Go to that chair." He pointed at the large black armchair resting against the wall. "I had it made especially for you!"

Zee pushed himself off the table and walked slowly, mechanically over to the chair. He sat down, his back perfectly straight, and stared at Philonecron, eyes dull.

"Oh!" Philonecron exclaimed, beaming at Zee. Zee looked dully back. "We're going to be so happy together!"

# PART THREE

―――――

## Fishier

CHAPTER 13

## Come Aboard

On Saturday afternoon, one week after Zee arrived on the *Poseidon*, the Mielswetzskis got into a cab for the airport. Mrs. Mielswetzski had used all of Friday to pack and Mr. Mielswetzski had left school after his last class, but when Charlotte suggested she might also leave school at noon in order to get ready, her idea was not received with much enthusiasm.

"You're already missing three days of school at the end of the cruise, young lady," said Mrs. Mielswetzski. "I think that's quite enough."

"Though it really is too bad we couldn't have left

earlier," said Mr. Mielswetzski. "There's so much history in Charleston to explore."

"Yes, but school comes first, Mike," said Mrs. Mielswetzski.

"I know, Tara, but given the educational opportunities . . ." said Mr. Mielswetzski.

"We've already discussed this, Mike," said Mrs. Mielswetzski.

"But I'm just saying," said Mr. Mielswetzski.

"Um, I think I better go pack," said Charlotte.

That was Thursday night. On Saturday morning she was all packed, while her parents were running around the house freaking out and calling to delay the taxi. Charlotte found it all pretty amusing.

While being trapped aboard a boat for ten days with her parents traveling through the wonderful world of American history was not Charlotte's first idea of a good way to spend her time, she was actually looking forward to a break from her current life—which shows you how well things were going for her. Zee's complete personality transplant was weighing on her heavily. Now that he'd taken a one-way trip to Lulu-town, she found herself feeling quite alone in the universe. She'd thought that what they'd experienced in the Underworld might stick with you for more than five months, but apparently once you discover girls, the eternal suffering of humanity just doesn't matter anymore. Meanwhile, Maddy was inconsolable, and Charlotte used up her five-minute phone allotment listening to her sob, which was a lot of fun. Maddy would say, "He's such a jerk!" and Charlotte could only say, "Yeah, he pretty much is." And then, of course, there was the whole mystery of the disappearance of Jason Hart and the unanswered question of what he knew about the gods. In other words, Charlotte was glad to be on vacation. Lame vacation, yes—but it was still vacation.

And Charlotte had prepared herself with adequate defenses against her parents. As soon as the Mielswetzskis sat down on the plane, she took out her headphones and a book for two hours of antisocial behavior. But Mr. Mielswetzski stopped her.

"Oh, Lottie, we need you present and accounted for. We have so much to talk about!"

Charlotte raised her eyebrows. "We do?"

"We have to pick cruise excursions!" Smiling, Charlotte's father took a brochure out from his bag. "There's so much to choose from!"

This was the first Charlotte had heard of excursions. She had assumed that when the ship docked, all the passengers would just get off and wander around—which seemed awfully humane, given that most of the on-ship activities consisted of historical lectures, bridge tournaments, and other stuff for old people. But apparently there were organized old-people activities at every stop too.

"See, this is the problem," Mr. Mielswetzski said. "We've got just one day in Yorktown, but that's not enough. You could spend a whole week! There's a tour of the Jamestown settlement, the Yorktown battlefield—that's where the British finally surrendered. The Yorktown Victory Center is supposed to have some really phenomenal exhibits. But then there's Colonial Williamsburg. Lottie, you'd just love it. It's a fully restored colonial town, complete with people in costume. It's just like going back in time!"

Charlotte could only stare at her father, bewildered. How he had gotten the impression that going to a town where everyone was in historical costume was something she'd just love, she couldn't imagine. Sometimes parents see what they want to see.

"Well, anyway"—her father handed her the brochure—"you should look through these and pick the ones you really want to do, okay? I'll let you be in charge!" He beamed at her. From the other seat, Charlotte heard her mother take in a quick breath, as if she was about to say something and then stopped herself.

With a groan, Charlotte started flipping through the brochure, looking at her options. Boring . . . boring . . . painful . . . boring . . . torturous . . . oh!

"Hey!" she gasped, pointing at the page. "Look, we can go to the beach!"

Her father started. "What?"

"The beach!" She pointed to the page. "At Yorktown! A bus picks you up from the ship and they'll take you to a beach! Right on the ocean!" Charlotte had never been to the ocean, but it seemed like it would be a very nice place to be.

Mr. Mielswetzski gave her a puzzled look. "I hardly think the Clio Foundation sent me on a history cruise so I could go to the beach, Lottie."

"Well, didn't they want you to have fun, too?" She gave him her most reasonable smile. "I mean, it's an award, Dad, not a punishment."

From her seat right next to Charlotte, Mrs. Mielswetzski coughed slightly.

"Charlotte," her father said, "we can go to the beach any time. How often do we get to *travel back in time*?"

"But"—she blinked—"I thought you said I was in charge."

Mrs. Mielswetzski leaned forward in her seat and looked at her husband. "Yes, you did say that, Mike," she said. "I heard you." Was it Charlotte's imagination, or did she look like she was enjoying herself?

"Well, yes, but I never imagined . . . You're in charge of picking whichever *historical experience* you think would be most fun, okay?"

Charlotte bit her lip. "Well, what if I went to the beach and you guys had a historical experience?"

The smile left Mrs. Mielswetzski's face. "Remember, Charlotte, you're still grounded. . . . We only let you come with us because of the educational nature of the trip, and also because we thought it would be good for us, as a family, to have some time together." She stared at Charlotte pointedly.

"Fine," said Charlotte, in a way that conveyed how incredibly not fine it was.

"Don't 'fine' me, young lady. You're lucky we let you come at all. Just because you're thirteen doesn't mean you have a license to be rude to your parents."

Charlotte slumped in her seat and glowered at the chair in front of her.

"Now," said her father. "About Jamestown. Do you know they have a recreated Powhatan village? The Powhatan were the tribe of Pocahontas, Charlotte, but of course the true story of Pocahontas has very little to do with the myth. See . . ."

It was going to be a long trip.

• • •

The Mielswetzskis spent the night at a hotel in Charleston. The next morning, they got up entirely too early and dragged Charlotte to some historical house where some guy had done something, then the Mielswetzskis had lunch and took a taxi down to the pier, and Charlotte had to admit that when she got out and beheld the cruise ship, she felt the tiniest pang of excitement. The *Isis Queen* seemed enormous to Charlotte ("Actually, it's a small-ship cruise, which means we can dock in many ports a larger ship can't!" her father explained cheerfully) and looked, well, not entirely lame. The ship was gleaming white, as long as a football field, and as tall as a three-story house. It seemed almost luxurious, almost—well—like something that could even be . . . *fun*.

They walked up a portable staircase and into the ship, where a bunch of crew members were lined up to greet them. A man in a tuxedo handed them each a glass of champagne, and as he saw Charlotte, he eyed the Mielswetzskis questioningly.

"Aw, give her one," said Mr. Mielswetzski.

"Mike!" said Mrs. Mielswetzski.

"Just a couple sips. For toasting!"

"She's thirteen! You want to start her drinking?"

"T, it's not going to kill her. Anyway, we don't want

to create some sort of mystique around alcohol, do we? We talked about this."

"Uh," said Charlotte, smiling up at the champagne man, "no thanks." Maddy's father had given her a sip of champagne once at New Year's and it made her feel like there were bubbles in her nose.

The crew directed them up another flight of stairs and to a lounge for check-in, and as they made their way, Charlotte scanned her fellow passengers for other kids whose parents had dragged them on this journey through the heart of lameness. Maybe there would be people worth hanging out with and they could stand at the back of the tours and make fun of everything. But as they waited in line at the check-in, she realized that the people closest to her age on board were her parents.

"Is this cruise all old people?" Charlotte not-really-whispered to her mother.

"Shhhh," Mrs. Mielswetzski hushed, then glanced surreptitiously around them. "Well, it looks like it, doesn't it? Frankly, I'm surprised. Given the educational mission, I would have expected more parents to jump at the opportunity."

"Right," said Charlotte.

"Well, it doesn't matter, because this is a family trip, right? Charlotte, think of this as an opportunity. Why don't you use this chance to show us how trustworthy you are!"

Charlotte was about to gag, when it occurred to her that perhaps she should play along. If her mother thought it was an opportunity, well, then, fine. Charlotte would be the model of good behavior, and then maybe when they got home she'd be able to leave the house without a police escort. Anything was worth that. Anything.

"You're right, Mom," she said with an innocent smile. "I will."

"Oh, Charlotte," said Mrs. Mielswetzski. "I'm proud of you. Now, let's get our rooms. . . . Where did your father get to?"

After reclaiming Mr. Mielswetzski, who had wandered off to chat up the people at the excursion office, they walked up one flight of stairs to Deck Five. Charlotte saw, to her immense relief, that she actually had her own room for the cruise. Her father explained that the rooms would be much too small to add a bed and the prize specifically allowed for an extra room for family members, which made Charlotte like the Historical Torture Association, or whatever it was called, a little better. The rooms were still right next to each other, and her parents would be able to knock at any moment, but at least she could shut her door and have some peace and pretend she was on a cruise to somewhere cool. Charlotte had a potent imagination and she was fully prepared to use it.

In the hallway, Mrs. Mielswetzski suggested they all adjourn to unpack, but Mr. Mielswetzski stared at her as if she'd suggested they all adjourn to cut out their own livers with nail scissors.

"Tara! We have to pick the excursions! They're first come, first served! The tour office told me the best ones fill up really quickly."

"Oh," said Mrs. Mielswetzski. "Well, look, honey, Charlotte and I really want what you want, okay? You're the expert here, so why don't you pick what you think will be the best and we'll go along?" She turned to her daughter. "Right, Char?"

Charlotte was about to sigh heavily, but she caught herself. It was her opportunity to prove she was trustworthy, which, translated from mom-speak, meant to be a total suck-up. She could do that.

"Right, Mom!" Charlotte grinned. "Whatever you think is best, Dad!"

"But it's so *hard*," said Mr. Mielswetzski. "I'd better check my guide books. . . ." He shook his head and disappeared into the bedroom.

Mrs. Mielswetzski smiled at Charlotte. "Well, that should keep him busy for quite some time. Why don't you unpack and then take a little tour around the ship, okay? I'm going to take a nap. The ship leaves in two hours, I think—we'll meet up then and watch it pull out, okay?"

"Okay, Mom." Charlotte couldn't believe her ears. Her mother was encouraging her to wander around by herself? No ankle bracelet or anything? This sucking-up initiative was fabulous.

Charlotte opened the door of her room and began to look around. It was kind of neat, actually—there was a nice double bed and a little sitting area with a stereo and a TV, and a huge window that looked out on the sea. Charlotte walked over to it and gazed out at the vista before her, watching a few seagulls as they flew by. After a few minutes a maid with some kind of European accent came by to give her some weird-smelling soap (okay) and a few chocolates (yum) and to tell her there would be a mandatory lifeboat drill in two hours (weird) and to bring her life jacket.

"My name is Bettina," she said, "and I'll be your stewardess. You call me if you need anything, okay?"

"Sure," said Charlotte, eating a chocolate. "Can I have another?"

Bettina smiled. "Of course."

Supplemental chocolate in hand, Charlotte flopped on the bed and began to read all the cruise literature that was in the room. She studied the map of the ship carefully and read through the room service menu (room service was free!) and looked at some of the spa offerings (not remotely free). There was a daily newsletter that had a schedule for the day, the dinner menu, another mention of the lifeboat drill, and some biographies of the crew. (The captain, Charlotte noted, looked like Santa Claus about a year after tummy stapling.) There wasn't a lot on the schedule; the ship was going to pull out at six o' clock, and dinner began at seven. That night there was a movie in one of the lounges and some singer performing in the Mariner Lounge on Deck Five. They would be at sea all through the next day and would arrive in Yorktown, Virginia, on Tuesday for all of your historical reenactment fun. The day at sea, the newsletter promised, would be filled with onboard activities to suit every taste.

Right, Charlotte thought.

There was a map of the cruise's route, and she ran her finger up along the path as it progressed up the eastern seaboard—after the day at sea on Monday they'd stop at Yorktown, Alexandria, Baltimore, Philadelphia, Newport, and end up in Boston. (Of *course* they skipped New York City. Why go to New York City? That would be *cool*.)

Charlotte fully intended to use her parent-free time

to explore the ship, but the whole flopping-down-on-the-bed thing felt really good, and she suddenly was overcome with a wave of exhaustion. That's what you get for hanging around old people.

Charlotte awoke to the sound of rapid whistle bursts and the voice of God instructing her from above. No, no, not God, but the cruise captain, telling her to get her life jacket and proceed to Deck Seven. Lifeboat drill. Right.

So she grabbed her jacket from the closet and went out of her room. The hallways were filled with old people already wearing their life jackets, which was so typical, and she followed them as they proceeded in a calm and orderly fashion up two flights of stairs to the main deck of the boat.

The drill wasn't much. Everyone was divided into groups based on the letter on their life jacket, and some crew member showed them how to put the jacket on, even though it was pretty obvious, and ran through the whole lifeboat procedure. While he talked, Charlotte looked at the lifeboats, which were suspended on the edge of the deck. There were big levers protruding from tall steel beams next to the boats, which Charlotte figured would lower them into the water. Good to know if this "proving she was trustworthy" thing got out of hand.

Her parents weren't in her group, and as the crew member talked, she scanned the crowd for them. It didn't take long; in the group kitty-corner from hers, she saw her mother's red head bobbing up and down, looking frantically for Charlotte. Charlotte waved. Her mother saw her and threw up her hands in a display of frustration.

Uh-oh, Charlotte thought. She didn't know what she possibly could have done in the past hour to infuriate her mother, especially since she'd been taking a nap. Apparently, Charlotte had now gained the ability to irritate her mother while sleeping. So much for her early parole.

When the drill was over, Charlotte stood by the rail and watched warily as her parents approached her, but she learned rather quickly that she wasn't the focus of her mother's annoyance. As soon as she got within earshot of Charlotte, Mrs. Mielswetzski threw up her hands again and exclaimed, "I can't believe we're not in the same lifeboat!" Three other passengers turned around to look.

"Oh," Charlotte said, "I guess not."

"Well," said Mr. Mielswetzski, reaching over and mussing Charlotte's hair, "I guess Lottie's going to have to survive on the deserted island without us!"

Mrs. Mielswetzski turned to him, eyes flaring. "This

isn't *funny*, Michael! We have to be in the same lifeboat. What if Charlotte got separated?"

"I can take care of myself, Mom," Charlotte grumbled.

"That's not the point," her mother snapped. "Charlotte, why don't you trade life preservers with someone in our group?"

"Mom!"

"I really don't think we're going to need the lifeboats, Tara," Mr. Mielswetzski said gently.

"That's what they said on the *Titanic*, Mike."

Just then a horn blew loudly, and the whole ship seemed to shudder awake.

"I think we're going," said Charlotte.

"Oh, let's go to the top deck and watch," said Mr. Mielswetzski.

"Fine," said Mrs. Mielswetzski, "but I want Charlotte to trade life jackets first."

"I can't, Mom," said Charlotte. "I mean," she added, thinking quickly, "no one else is by themselves, and no one's going to want to trade with me because then they'll be separated from whoever they came with!"

"Fine," said Mrs. Mielswetzski. "I'll go talk to the crew. I'll meet you upstairs."

As she and her father leaned against the rail, Charlotte had to admit that watching the *Isis Queen* pull out of the dock was pretty cool. She stood feeling the wind against her face as the ship slowly made its way away from the shore. Soon Mrs. Mielswetzski joined them, and they all looked on silently as they moved out to open sea. At least, Charlotte reflected, this was the one place where she wouldn't worry that Philonecron was trying to get her.

CHAPTER 14

# Stormy Weather

THE REST OF THE EVENING, CHARLOTTE WORKED hard on her total suck-up initiative. At dinner she was nothing but cheerful and compliant as her father waxed poetic about the wonders of Colonial Williamsburg (for after much deliberation he had decided that would be the destination for their first excursion). There was only so long she could keep that up, though, and when dinner was over she found herself quite tired of being so pleasant. It wears a girl out.

"Well, what now?" asked Mrs. Mielswetzski as they

got up from their table. "Should we go see the singer? She's in the Mariner Lounge."

"She's supposed to be *amazing*," said Mr. Mielswetzski. "The whole crew was talking about her."

Charlotte and her mother exchanged a glance. It never took Mr. Mielswetzski more than five minutes anywhere to befriend the people who worked there; he always seemed to prefer them to the people he was with. Every time they went to a restaurant, he was the waiter's best friend by the time they ordered. At a wedding last summer, he spent the whole time talking to the photographer.

"What about it, Charlotte? Do you want to come? I think it's fifties music tonight. That should be fun."

"Uh . . ." Charlotte said. This was difficult. She was doing her best, really, but there's only so much a girl can pretend to enjoy herself listening to old people's music. She might snap at any moment.

"Well, I'm kind of tired," she said. A flicker of disappointment crossed her parents' faces simultaneously. "Hey, I know!" she added quickly. "What if I use the time to read some of Dad's Williamsburg books? I could, you know, be the tour guide on Friday."

Her father broke out into a grin. "Oh, honey, that's great! I've got just the books for you. I completely understand, it's been a long day and sometimes it's really nice to just . . . hunker down in bed with some history."

"All right, sweetie," said Mrs. Mielswetzski, shooting Charlotte an I-don't-buy-it-for-a-second-but-you're-good-to-humor-your-father look, "you rest up. Your father and I will dance the night away!"

"It's fifties music, T," said Mr. Mielswetzski. "We're gonna *twist* the night away." He grinned and right there, in the middle of the dining room, started wrenching his body around as if he were having some kind of horrible attack. "It's not really my era, of course. Maybe they'll have disco night and I can really show them my moves!"

It took Charlotte some time to expunge the image of her father dancing from her mind that night, but once she did, she slept like she'd never slept before. The gentle rocking of the boat combined with the sound of the waves lulled her into a state of complete peace, without an Underworld nightmare in sight.

The next morning, after knocking on her parents' door and getting no response, Charlotte wandered up to eat breakfast on the terrace at the back of Deck Seven. She got a table right by the ocean, and as she sat and looked out at the waves while the sun warmed her shoulders and an extremely cute waiter brought her a stack of blueberry pancakes, Charlotte reflected that life, sometimes, wasn't a *total* loss.

Just as she was finishing her breakfast, her parents emerged onto the terrace looking sleepy and unwashed. Could they really not have eaten yet? Charlotte had assumed they'd already eaten and gone jogging and done Pilates or something, but apparently not. She'd never known them to sleep in so late before. She'd never known them to sleep in at all.

"Phew," said Mr. Mielswetzski, coming over to Charlotte's table. "I think we almost missed breakfast."

"Man," said Mrs. Mielswetzski, looking at her watch. "Just in time!"

"You guys are just up?"

"Yeah," said Mr. Mielswetzski. "We had a late night."

"Sure did," giggled Mrs. Mielswetzski.

"Oh," said Charlotte. "I knocked on your door. I thought you weren't there."

"We must have still been sleeping!" said Mrs. Mielswetzski.

"I wish you could have stayed up, Charlotte. Thalia was *amazing*," said Mr. Mielswetzski.

"She was!" said Mrs. Mielswetzski. "Captivating!"

"Who's Thalia?" Charlotte asked.

"Oh, the singer. She was incredible. Lottie, you have to come tonight."

"You do!" Mrs. Mielswetzski yawned, and then giggled again. "We were up so late!"

"Everyone was. Everyone stayed up until the end of the show. I think she sang until two a.m.!"

"It was like we were kids again!" said Mrs. Mielswetzski.

Charlotte didn't bother explaining to her mother that no kids would stay up until two a.m. listening to someone sing fifties tunes. Maybe it was the pancakes talking, but it seemed kind all of a sudden to let her parents have their little illusions.

"So, Char," Mrs. Mielswetzski said, sitting down, "it's a free day today! What do you want to do?"

"Um." Charlotte scanned her parents' faces quickly. She couldn't tell if that was a we-really-want-to-know-what-you-want question or a we-want-you-to-want-to-do-the-things-we-want-you-to-do question. "Well, I thought I might hang out by the pool? And read?" She eyed her parents hesitantly.

"That sounds nice," Mrs. Mielswetzski said vaguely.

"Mmmm," said Mr. Mielswetzski.

"Is it warm enough?" asked Mrs. Mielswetzski.

"Looks it to me," replied Mr. Mielswetzski.

Phew. "So, what about you guys?"

"I don't know," said Mr. Mielswetzski. "We might join you. Also, there's a lecture on Revolutionary Virginia that I want to go to, and we'll hit the fitness club. Mostly," he added, "I just want to see Thalia again."

"I know!" said Mrs. Mielswetzski. "I checked the newsletter. She's performing tonight after dinner. She's singing standards!"

"Oh, good," said Mr. Mielswetzski.

"I can't wait!" said Mrs. Mielswetzski.

"Oh, Charlotte, you have to come," said Mr. Mielswetzski.

"Really, she'll change your life!" said Mrs. Mielswetzski.

"Uh . . ." said Charlotte. "Maybe." She was a bit confused; she'd never seen her parents so excited about anything that wasn't educational before. "Well, um, do you mind if I go? I want to go get into my swimsuit."

"Sure, Char!"

"Have fun!"

"Don't forget to wear sunblock, Charlotte," her mother added. "And don't stay out too long!"

"Right, Mom."

They made arrangements to meet up for lunch, and then Charlotte got up from the table and left the terrace as soon as she could. Whatever had gotten into her parents, they were letting her do what she wanted, and Charlotte was not about to ask questions. The sea air, apparently, did wonders.

When Charlotte walked through the indoor restaurant that was behind the terrace and out onto the deck, the sun seemed to envelop her in its arms. She looked up into the sky, which was the brightest, purest blue she had ever seen. Next to her, the pool sparkled invitingly.

Charlotte walked along the deck, feeling the sun on her face. Already some passengers had staked out deck chairs, and a uniformed waiter was walking around giving everyone ice water. Even the waiter looked happy.

Wanting to explore a little more, Charlotte continued along the deck all the way around to the very front of the ship. The sea stretched out in front of her, and if she stretched her neck up so the railing fell out of her plane of vision it seemed like she was floating above it. She went up to the very peak of the bow and leaned slightly over the rail, feeling the wind push against her face as the ship pushed its way through the sea.

The bridge was right behind her, lofted above the deck, and as Charlotte turned to go back she looked up through the curved wall of windows at the captain and officers working within. There were eight of them lined up along the windows, dressed smartly in clean, white naval uniforms. They were all business, studying equipment, looking off into the horizon with binoculars, scrutinizing the waters ahead. Charlotte craned her neck up to try to see more, but she couldn't get a very good view. One of the crew members glanced down at her and gave her a discreet wave. Charlotte blushed and moved out of sight.

She made her way back around the bridge and went inside and back down to her room. It took her all of fifteen minutes to change into her swimsuit, shellac herself with sunblock, put on a T-shirt and jeans as a cover-up, and gather a book and her headphones to prepare for a day in the sun. Feeling generally positive about the world, she went back up to Deck Seven, not really noticing that the rocking of the ship had become decidedly less gentle, and pushed open the door that led to the outside, only to discover that her beautiful day had suddenly turned very ugly indeed.

Black clouds had rolled in and covered the sky, and the air was gray and thick with mist. As Charlotte stood there, rain began to pour down. There was a distant boom, and then lightning flashed overhead.

*"Great,"* Charlotte muttered. It *would* rain today. This was the only day her itinerary wasn't going to be filled with historical reenactments, museum trips, and freedom walks. Grumbling, she closed the door and, after considering a moment, headed up to the Observation Lounge to wait out the storm.

As Charlotte made her way up the stairs, a woman appeared at the top of the stairwell. Charlotte nearly stopped in her tracks — the woman was quite simply the most gorgeous person she had ever seen in her life. She appeared to know it too, dressed as she was in a sparkly green evening gown. Normally, Charlotte would have thought that was a little excessive for eleven a.m., but if Charlotte looked like that, she would have dressed up too. The woman was tall and statuesque, with long, shiny, raven-colored hair, creamy coffee-colored skin, and big cat-like emerald eyes. She looked like a movie star, like royalty, like both, and something about her made Charlotte feel at once attracted and repelled, like part of her wanted to go to her and learn all her secrets, and the other part wanted to turn and run.

As the woman approached, she caught Charlotte's gaze and raised one perfectly arched eyebrow. "I didn't know they allowed children on this cruise," she said, looking very much as if she smelled something bad.

Charlotte bristled and narrowed her eyes. She didn't know they allowed obnoxious people on the cruise. It was a surprising day for everyone.

The woman and Charlotte both straightened themselves, tossed their hair, and passed each other in haughty silence.

The Observation Lounge was filled with cozy-looking chairs and couches, and a few passengers were perched in various groupings, reading or playing cards or talking quietly. The whole room was surrounded by windows, giving a close-up view of the now full-on storm. As rain poured down, lightning cracked above, and the ship rocked in the high waves, Charlotte felt as if she and her fellow passengers had taken refuge inside a fragile glass bubble that floated inside the storm. A bubble with nice couches, of course, and all the soda you could drink.

There was a monitor in the middle of the lounge that had a tracking system to show where in the world the ship was. Charlotte looked at the screen carefully, studying the familiar coastline of the eastern seaboard. Off to the left was the coast of North Carolina, and as the ship blinked its way steadily on, Charlotte noted with some surprise that they were actually heading directly away from the shore.

Shrugging, she went over to the bar and ordered a ginger ale from the bartender (whose name was Ben, according to his name tag).

"Some storm, huh?" he said to her, raising his voice over the noise of rain beating down the windows.

"Yeah," Charlotte mumbled. "I was going to lie in the sun. . . ."

Ben smiled kindly. "I'm afraid you won't get much of that done today. But there are other things to do. Look in here." He motioned to a binder that contained the day's newsletter.

Without much enthusiasm, Charlotte skimmed through the events: trivia tournament, computer lounge orientation (Cute, she thought. Teaching old people to use e-mail!), bridge lessons, lectures, fitness classes. Nothing remotely interesting.

Just then the ship lurched to the right, and Charlotte's stool rocked to the side. Around her, passengers gasped and cups clinked and slid, while Charlotte grabbed for the side of the bar to steady herself.

"You all right?" Ben said.

"Yeah," she said. "But I'm afraid the floor isn't." She pointed. Her glass of ginger ale had slid off the bar and smashed on the ground.

"I'll get that," Ben said. "Don't move."

As the bartender grabbed a broom and emerged from behind the bar, Charlotte gazed around the room, watching people steady themselves. The ship took another lurch and Ben stumbled violently, while two teacups on a table behind Charlotte went sliding off the table and crashed to the floor. Just then her eye caught movement on the deck outside in the storm, where no one would want to be. She squinted. Someone who worked on the ship was standing there, someone dressed in the white coveralls of the crew. He was smaller than the other crew members and at first glance looked more like a kid, like someone Charlotte's age, than someone who would be part of the crew. Weren't there child labor laws at sea? She turned to look more carefully, but he was gone.

Another lurch, the stool bobbled, and the binder with the newsletters dropped to the floor. Charlotte thought this seemed like a pretty good time to get lower to the ground, and she hopped off the stool. The binder lay open and, as she picked it up, she noticed a familiar pair of cat-like eyes staring out at her. On the back of the newsletter was a picture of the woman she'd seen in the hallway—she was the singer her parents had been drooling over. Apparently they hadn't seen her manners.

"Beautiful, isn't she?" Ben asked. "Have you heard her?"

"No, no, I haven't." Charlotte looked up at him.

"She's supposed to be amazing. Our regular singer didn't show up, and somehow they got this woman. She's going to perform for the crew later."

Charlotte nodded noncommittally, then straightened herself and placed the binder back on the bar. The ship continued to rock back and forth emphatically, and she felt something inside her head lurch as if trying to catch up. The effect was making her rather queasy, so she decided she might go back to her room, and just as she moved toward the door she saw a flash of white outside on the deck again. Charlotte looked up to find the crew boy from before standing outside, peering at her. Then he was gone again in a flash, but not before she'd gotten a good look at him. She stood up and ran out of the lounge onto the stormy deck, but there was no sign of the boy. She stood, looking around wildly, as the wind whipped rain against her face. She needed to see him again; she needed to be sure. For the boy looked exactly like Jason Hart.

## CHAPTER 15

# Secret Agent Girl

CHARLOTTE STOOD ON THE DECK IN THE WIND AND rain looking around for the boy who might be Jason Hart. Who looked exactly like Jason Hart. In fact, if it weren't absolutely impossible that Jason Hart was there on the cruise, she would say that the boy she saw was, beyond a doubt, Jason Hart. But it was impossible. Wasn't it?

And if it was him—which would be absolutely, positively, one-hundred-percent impossible—what on Earth would he be doing there? Had he actually run away? If he had, running off to join a cruise ship made a certain amount of sense, like running off to join the circus or something. If you were going to run away, it would be a good way not to get caught.

But were cruise ships normally in the habit of employing eighth-grade boys? Charlotte doubted it. Maybe he lied about his age, maybe he had something forged, maybe he had connections. Maybe it was nothing.

But really. If it was him—if it really was him—was Charlotte supposed to believe that he had just *happened* to join the crew of the ship she was currently on? That it was all some sort of magical coincidence?

So if he was there, the question was why. Did he want something from Charlotte? Had someone sent him?

Jason Hart was on the ship. Yes, it was crazy. Yes, it was impossible. But so was, say, stealing children's shadows to make a giant army or taking a city bus to the Underworld to chat up Hades, so, really, as her gym teacher often said, nothing is impossible as long as you try hard enough.

Charlotte stood there in the storm, awash in befuddlement, as water poured down on top of her. The deck had become slick in the rain, and as the ship rocked to the right, she lost her footing and fell, hitting her head on the ship's railing as she went down. She yelped and sat on the soaking wet ground holding her head. Now she was befuddled and suffering from a major head injury. Charlotte grabbed onto the offending rail and started to pull herself up. What was she doing standing there? She had to find Jason. She wasn't going to be caught off guard again—whatever was in store for her, Charlotte was going to meet it head-on. How's that for taking responsibility?

Just then the door to the lounge opened, and Ben's head poked out. "What are you doing?" he yelled. "It's not safe out here. Get inside!"

"Right," said Charlotte, pulling herself up and ducking inside the lounge again. She was absolutely soaking, and the carpet underneath her grew wet in sympathy.

"What in the world were you doing?" asked Ben, not unkindly.

"I thought I saw someone I knew," Charlotte said. "I mean, a crew member."

"A crew member?" Ben shook his head. "We stay off the decks in weather like this. Sometimes people have to, but there's nothing out there"—he motioned to the bow of the ship—"for anyone to do. And even if there were, well, it's just not safe right now."

"Yeah," said Charlotte. "I mean, I was surprised. Do you have a new crew member, a guy in coveralls, about my age?"

"About your age? No, we wouldn't. The youngest crew member is eighteen."

"Well, maybe he lied. His name is Jason, and he's got dark hair and green eyes and . . ." Charlotte stopped herself. She was about to describe him as incredibly cute, but Ben might not see it that way.

"Not that I know of," he said. "Look, why don't you go dry off? You don't want to get sick for the rest of the cruise. Anyway," he added with a smile, "you're messing up my lounge."

"Right," Charlotte said, turning to go.

"And try to stay inside," he called after her.

She left the lounge, leaving a nice trail of water behind her like a wet dog. Whatever—she could shiver all day long; this was more important.

Charlotte stood in the hallway, studying the deck plan next to the elevator. On this level there were only three ways to access the strip of deck at the bow of the ship where Jason had been: the glass door in the lounge that Charlotte had gone through, and the doors on either side of the hallway. He didn't come into the lounge, obviously, and if he'd gone all the way around to the hallway door on the other side ("*Starboard*," her father would have said), Charlotte would have seen him. The Observation Lounge was all windows. (Unless, of course, he could transport himself, disapparate, or move faster than the eye could see. Charlotte wasn't ruling anything out.)

But if he didn't have magical speed-of-light/trans-porting/apparating abilities, and he didn't go through the lounge or the starboard hallway door, and there weren't any secret passageways Charlotte didn't know about, he must have gone through the door in front of which she was currently standing.

From there, there were a few places to go. You could walk about ten feet and be outside again. The deck was open from there all the way to the back, except for the engine room at the stern. Given what had happened to her, Charlotte thought that if anyone had tried to walk all that way outside, he'd be lying in the middle of the deck somewhere with bones sticking out.

Other than that door, there was the main stairway that Charlotte had come up earlier, an elevator, and a nondescript door marked CREW ONLY.

Well.

Charlotte studied the door, which was so plain and white it looked as if it were trying to hide its own presence, then looked to her right and her left and reached her hand out to the knob. It wouldn't turn. She started fumbling with it, carefully checking around her for any sign of company, when her eyes caught some drip marks on the carpet.

She was still leaving a trail wherever she went, she could tell that—there was a trail from the lounge entrance right up to the Sky Bar exit and back to the crew only door. But as she studied the carpet, she found there was another path, one that she had not made, leading toward the main staircase. Squaring her jaw, Charlotte followed it.

Down the stairs she went, past Deck Seven, Deck Six, Deck Five. The trail was growing fainter, but she could still see it, until about halfway down to Deck Three, and then it disappeared.

Charlotte climbed down the rest of the staircase to Deck Three. She'd stopped leaving a trail too by this point, but she still felt as if she'd been dipped in a vat of saltwater. She had passed a few passengers and some crew on her way down the stairs, and each one of them regarded her as if she were some kind of swamp thing. She found herself feeling grateful that the singer had not come by.

Charlotte looked around. She was standing in front of the main restaurant. They'd eaten there the night before, but they'd come down on the restaurant's other side. She'd never been down here before.

She stood in the middle of the hallway, chewing her lip. According to the deck plan, in front of her there was just the ship's doctor's office and then some officers' accommodations. On her other side was the restaurant, and behind that was the galley. Is that where he'd gone?

Was he a cook or a dishwasher or something? Charlotte took a step toward the restaurant, when someone brushed passed her. It was one of the waiters she'd seen at breakfast this morning, and he smiled at her in greeting as he headed toward the officers' quarters, then turned abruptly, got out a key card, and put it in a door that was so plain and white that Charlotte hadn't noticed it before. CREW ONLY, it read.

The door closed behind the waiter, and Charlotte hurried over to try the handle. No good. It was locked. But she was not going to be fazed; she got through the Underworld into Hades's Palace, she could get through a simple crew door. Charlotte tucked herself into a small passageway beside the door and waited for someone to come.

It didn't take long. Two stewardesses burst through the door chatting so intensely that they did not notice the redheaded girl who came around the corner and grabbed the door before it could swing closed, nor did they notice as she ducked behind it and disappeared from the hallway.

Charlotte was by a plain concrete stairwell. She could hear voices coming from the hall below. In front of her was another door that read SHIP'S OFFICERS ONLY. It had a space for a key card too, but Charlotte didn't need to go in there. She'd studied the ship's maps in all the cruise literature the night before, and what she needed was on Deck Two—the crew's quarters.

Slowly, carefully, she made her way down the stairs. She wasn't quite sure exactly how she was going to get away with sneaking around the crew's quarters. If Charlotte were a secret agent, she would find a nearby crew member of roughly her build, whack her on the head with something, and take her coveralls. But Charlotte, alas, was not a secret agent and didn't really want to go around whacking people on the head, anyway. It just didn't seem nice.

Or she could make her way over to the laundry and steal some coveralls or a stewardess outfit or something, and she wouldn't even have to hit anyone over the head. Of course, there might not exactly be outfits lying around, and even if there were, the people in the laundry might notice if some girl wandered over and took one.

Charlotte sighed. This would be so much easier if she were a secret agent. But there was nothing else to do but walk through the hallways and act like she belonged. Surely members of the crew had families. Surely the crew changed all the time, and no one could keep track of who was who. Surely there were different thirteen-year-old girls wandering through the crew's quarters every day.

Right?

With a shake of her wet, clumpy hair, Charlotte rounded the corner and descended the last few stairs. Before her was a tremendously long, wide, sterile-looking hallway, one that seemed to travel half the length of the ship. There was a door at the end, and she guessed that the crew's quarters lay ahead and the rooms here were dedicated to some of the ship's functions. Indeed, activity was everywhere; at Charlotte's end of the hallway, people were hurrying in and out of rooms looking busy. The first room was cavernous and filled with a cacophony of humming and banging noises. As she approached, the air thickened with steam. The laundry, she realized. There were no uniforms just waiting by the door for her to borrow, which seemed awfully inconsiderate. She pressed herself against the doorway and peeked in, trying to get a look at each person, but no one among the steamers, the pressers, the folders, the sorters, or the scrubbers seemed to be Jason.

On the other side of the hallway was a smaller room, from which the smell of baking bread oozed into the hallway. Inside, two people were kneading large lumps of dough while another was taking loaves of bread out of the oven. Charlotte was mesmerized—it hadn't occurred to her everything that must go into making dinner for the whole ship, and as she watched the man place the loaves of bread on the counter, he looked up, and his eyes seemed to meet hers. She gasped and quickly ducked away.

*Nice one, Mielswetzski,* she told herself.

She tried to look as nondescript as possible as she continued through the long hallway through the bowels of the ship, but as people kept passing her and no one stopped her, she became more confident. No one cared about a thirteen-year-old girl wandering the hallways; there was bread to be made and clothes to be washed and a ship to run! We're busy here, people! Let's move it along!

It was at that precise moment that a rough hand landed on her shoulder and a voice growled, "What are you doing here?"

Charlotte whirled around. In front of her was a mustached man in a white officer's uniform who looked very cross indeed. A badge pinned on his chest read, quite clearly, SECURITY.

"Oh, I'm sorry," Charlotte said, batting her eyes. "I got lost!"

"Lost, eh?"

"Oh, yes," said Charlotte. "I was supposed to meet my parents by the doctor's office—my mom's not feeling well, she says it's nothing serious, but I really can't help but worry, I mean, she's my *mom*. Since the operation, it's been hard. Well, anyway, if you could just point me in the right direction?"

As the security officer squinted down at her, Charlotte saw a flash of movement out of the corner of her eye. She turned her head and saw a small, dark-haired form move from a room at the end of the hallway through the door to the crew's quarters. Jason.

"Look!" Charlotte said. "That boy. Do you know him?"

The security man straightened. "Boy, huh? Did you come down here to see a boy? Aren't you a little young?"

"No!" Charlotte exclaimed, "it's not like that!"

"Come with me." With a curt nod, the man led her back through the hallway up the concrete stairwell, through the plain white door, and out into the carpeted hallway of Deck Three. "In there," he said, motioning to a small office marked SECURITY. "Sit. Let me see your room card." He swiped it into his computer, squinted at the screen, and muttered, "Meals-wet-ski, huh? Those are your parents you're with? Well, let's see what they have to say about this." He picked up the phone.

"Wait!" Charlotte said. "I'm sorry. I really am. I was looking for a boy, yes, but I thought he was someone I knew—"

But the man was not listening. "Yes, Mrs.

Mielswetzski? This is Lieutenant Rogers at the security desk on Deck Three. Could you come down here right now? Thank you." He hung up and shook his head at Charlotte. "Do you think you can just have the run of the place? There are rules, you know. There are procedures. I'm sure your parents let you do whatever you want at home, but out in the real world there are laws."

He continued his lecture while Charlotte slumped even farther down in her seat, waiting for the coming of her doom.

The doom arrived far too quickly for Charlotte's taste. She could never get them to, say, go out to eat on time, but there was nothing like a call from security to get her parents moving. They filed into the small office, and as soon as they saw their daughter, their faces grew dark. Of course, Charlotte thought, they automatically assume it's something bad. Maybe it was something good. Maybe Charlotte had just single-handedly thwarted a pirate attack and the security guy wanted to *commend* her.

"What in the world?" Mr. Mielswetzski said. "Charlotte? You were supposed to meet us for lunch. We were waiting!"

Charlotte felt Lieutenant Rogers's eyes rest on her. Lunch, doctor's office, same diff.

"I found her sneaking around the restricted deck,"

he said. "She seemed to be heading toward the crew's quarters."

"What?" Both her parents looked from the guard to her in perfect synchronicity.

"That deck is strictly off-limits to passengers," he continued. "I could have her thrown off the ship for this."

"Oh!" said Mr. Mielswetzski.

"Oh!" said Mrs. Mielswetzski.

"We have rules. There's a reason we have security precautions, you know. We can't have passengers running around everywhere."

"Of course," said Mr. Mielswetzski.

"Absolutely," said Mrs. Mielswetzski.

"We're so sorry," said Mr. Mielswetzski.

"We'll talk to her!" said Mrs. Mielswetzski.

"See that you do. One more incident, and I will have you all removed from the ship."

With that, he dismissed them. Charlotte got up and shuffled out into the hallway, while her parents followed grimly behind. At least, she thought, he hadn't mentioned *why* he thought Charlotte was down there. Because that would really—

"Oh, Mrs. Mielswetzski?" the lieutenant called. "A word, please. There's one more thing I think you should know."

*Great.*

• • •

Back up in Charlotte's cabin, she sat on her bed staring out of the window. It was still dark and stormy outside, and the boat seemed to be rocking more than ever. But Charlotte's vague feeling of nausea had nothing to do with seasickness. Mrs. Mielswetzski was pacing in front of the bed in full lecture mode, while Mr. Mielswetzski sat darkly in a corner, staring at the ground.

"We're on this cruise one day, Charlotte," said Mrs. Mielswetzski, "*one day*, and we're getting calls from security."

"I'm sorry," Charlotte said glumly.

"The lieutenant told me you were down there looking for a . . . boy."

"What?" said Mr. Mielswetzski, snapping to attention.

"It's true," said Mrs. Mielswetzski. "Charlotte snuck down to the crew level to meet a boy."

Mr. Mielswetzski groaned.

Charlotte straightened. "Look, you guys, it was important, okay? You don't understand."

"You're right we don't understand," Mrs. Mielswetzski snapped. "Would you like to enlighten us?"

"You're just going to have to trust me," Charlotte said quietly.

"Trust you?" said Mrs. Mielswetzski. "Trust you? You sneak off in the middle of the night and now this. You want us to trust you? We want nothing more than to trust you, but you need to begin *acting trustworthy*."

Charlotte couldn't help it; she was getting angry. Here she had risked her life a thousand times over *to save the world*, and if anything should earn a girl major trust points, it's that. "You guys don't know everything, you know," she snapped. "You don't know what things are like."

Mrs. Mielswetzski stopped pacing and sighed heavily. "Charlotte, I know there are a lot of pressures on a girl your age." From his corner, Mr. Mielswetzski groaned again.

"That's not it!" Charlotte was nearly yelling now. "I'm not some teenage girl you read about in your books. I'm *me*. You don't know what's really going on! You guys keep saying you want me to take responsibility, but when I do, you don't like it."

But she'd lost her mother again. "I don't see how sneaking into the crew's quarters to be with some boy is taking responsibility."

"He's not some boy!"

Silence then. Mrs. Mielswetzski stared at her, while Mr. Mielswetzski put his head in his hands. Charlotte cringed. Shaking her head very slowly, her mother said quietly, "Goodness, Charlotte, I thought you'd be a lot older before we'd be having this conversation."

"I'm a lot older than you think," Charlotte said through clenched teeth. She knew what it sounded like, and she didn't know why she was saying these things. Just last year, if this had happened—and of course it wouldn't have, but a lot can change in a year—Charlotte would have been able to make something up, anything, that could have convinced her parents that she wasn't having some kind of assignation and in fact her intentions were perfectly pure, as was only natural because she was a perfect angel. But there was something about learning the truth of the world that made lying to them just impossible. The truth was so much more absurd than any lie could be; everything else sounded weak in comparison.

But then Charlotte realized: Why not just tell them the truth? Not everything, obviously, but her dad had met Jason, and both her parents knew he had supposedly run away, and if they thought he was on this ship they would talk to someone important. Everyone wants to find a runaway boy, right?

"Look," said Charlotte, glancing from one parent to another to make sure she had their full attention. "I thought I saw Jason Hart."

Relief washed over her as she said the words; it felt good to tell the truth. Charlotte could just see it now— her parents would go right to the captain and they would find this runaway boy working in the laundry and they'd put him in a room somewhere and watch him very carefully so he couldn't *run away again* and Charlotte would be a hero and she'd ask to talk to Jason and of course they'd let her, because *she was a hero*, and she'd go all army interrogation on him and find out what was going on.

Her parents exchanged a glance. Mrs. Mielswetzski looked at Charlotte almost sadly. "Do you honestly expect us to believe that?"

Or not.

Charlotte's eyes widened. "Yes, I do. It's the truth!"

"Yes, and I believe you were also down on Deck Two looking for the doctor's office, right? Because I had had an *operation*? Oh, Charlotte, what are we going to do with you?"

"Come on, you guys. I'm telling the truth! You have to tell someone! Jason Hart is working on this boat. He must have run away and gotten a job on the cruise ship. You know, like people run away to join the circus?"

"Stop it." From his spot in the corner, Mr. Mielswetzski was staring at his daughter sadly. "Please. Don't use that, all right? Things are bad enough. . . ."

"But—"

"Charlotte," said Mrs. Mielswetzski, "I guess we're going to have to ground you on the cruise, too. I'd like you to stay in your room the rest of the day, all right? Your father and I will figure out what to do with you."

"But—"

"Don't argue, Charlotte. Really. Just stay in your room, okay?" Her parents exchanged another glance. "Your father and I will come get you for dinner."

And with that, they turned to go. Charlotte thought quickly. They were going to a lecture later, maybe she could sneak out, and—

"Oh, and Charlotte?" said Mrs. Mielswetzski, turning. "Your room key, please."

"What? Mom!"

"Your room key? You won't be needing it if you stay in your room, will you?"

Glowering, Charlotte reached into her pocket and handed her mother her key card, which she tucked ceremoniously inside her own pocket. Then her parents left, and as soon as the door closed behind them, Charlotte flopped down on the bed, buried her head in her pillow, and screamed.

## CHAPTER 16

# My Dinner with Philonecron

*Setting: an elegantly set ebony table in a vast stateroom. The room is tastefully decorated, if a little Gothic, and if you ignore the evil laboratory in the corner. Two people are seated at the table across from each other. They are **Philonecron** and **Zee**. Both are dressed impeccably.*

**Philonecron:** Oh, Zero, I'm so delighted you came to stay with me. It's been so trying here by myself with no one to talk to. They're all a bunch of Philistines and half-wits who wouldn't know sophistication if it crept up behind them, stuck its fangs in their neck, and sucked out all their blood.

**Zee:** . . . .

**Philonecron:** *(rolling eyes)* You don't have to tell me! Oh, here we go!

*A waiter comes in, carrying a tray on which sit two plates covered with large silver domes. He sets one in front of Philonecron and the other in front of Zee. Philonecron removes the covering on his and motions to Zee to do the same.*

**Philonecron:** Go ahead! Lift it up!

*Zee does.*

**Philonecron:** *(beaming)* Voilà! Doesn't that look marvelous? Would you believe you can't even get Hydra fillets up here? I had to have them ordered specially. But only the best for my boy. Eat, eat! You're a growing boy. You need your strength!

**Zee:** . . . .

**Philonecron:** I know, I know. It's not the same as it would be in the Underworld. It's overcooked, the sauce is much too rich—but what do you expect from these people? If only . . . *(sighs)* if only we could have made things work in the Underworld, Zero. We would have been so happy there. But . . . *(holding up hands)* I'm not holding a grudge. I think we've really been able to move past all of that. We have nothing but the future ahead of us. And what a beautiful future it will be!

**Zee:** . . . .

**Philonecron:** No, no, you're right. I know! If you hadn't foully betrayed me, we might have been content with just a nether realm, and our destiny is higher than that. *(Sighs happily.)* From the first time I smelled your blood I knew you were special, knew you were destined for great things. We'll rule the whole Universe together someday, father and son. I'll even get you a little throne.

**Zee:** . . . .

**Philonecron:** *(sighing dramatically)* I don't know how yet, my precious Zero. Overthrowing Zeus is not easy. That's why I need your help. You're a hero and I'm an evil genius, and together we will come up with the most wonderful plan the world has ever seen. Rest assured. *(He lowers his voice, like someone with a really good piece of* *gossip.)* Do you know my esteemed grandfather tried to overthrow Zeus once? It's true! He and the other Olympians trapped him and bound him up in a thousand knots. They hid his thunder bolt, too, so he couldn't fight back. I know! Naughty, naughty! Poseidon's a bad little boy!

**Zee:** . . . .

**Philonecron:** Oh, yes. *(Waves hand dismissively.)* Thetis got a giant to free Zeus, and everything was back to normal. In a way, it's for the best. Imagine if Poseidon ruled the Universe. We'd all be wearing leisure suits. *(He cocks his head.)* That's the rub, though, with Zeus. You need to separate him from his precious thunder bolt. *(Shakes his head.)* Or else confront him with an object of equal power. But of course, there are only two of those in the world. . . . *(Looks off thoughtfully into the distance.)*

**Zee:** . . . .

**Philonecron:** *(snapping back to attention)* I know! My glass has been empty for ten minutes! Where is that pathetic vermin of a waiter, eh? *Waiterrrrrr! (He stares at the door, which does not open, then sinks into his* *chair, defeated and disgusted.)* It's awful. Disgraceful! *(In a rage, he clenches his hand into a fist and starts banging it against the table.)* There. Are. No. *Standards!*

**Zee:** . . . .

**Philonecron:** Oh! Oh no, I'm so sorry. Don't be alarmed! I lost control, I admit it. I know how sensitive you are. Just like I am. That's why we make such a good team! *(Smiles.)* Now, tell me, what shall we do with humanity when we take over, eh? Enslave them? Destroy them? Enslave them, then destroy them?

**Zee:** . . . .

**Philonecron:** *(grinning)* Yes! Yes! Brilliant! We'll unleash the monsters and demons on them! *(He clasps his hands together, delighted.)* Oh, what fun that will be! Can you imagine the little dears running for their lives from Harpies and Gorgons and Minotaurs? Oh, my! Oh, what a show!

**Zee:** . . . .

**Philonecron:** Do not worry. We'll get there soon. As soon as you watch your cousin's untimely demise, we'll begin our work. Now. *(Clasps hands together.)* What would you like to do after dinner? Parcheesi?

**Zee:** . . . .

**Philonecron:** I couldn't have said it better myself.

## CHAPTER 17

# A Minor Course Correction

For the rest of the day, Charlotte paced around her room grumbling and pausing every once in a while to kick and/or punch something. She couldn't believe her mother had taken her key card. How was she supposed to get out and look for Jason if she couldn't get back into her room? Honestly. She thought briefly of propping the door with something so she could sneak out and get back in, but she didn't even want to think of the trouble she'd be in when her parents noticed that.

And she'd finally told them the truth—at least a part of the truth—and this is what she got? She couldn't imagine what would happen if she'd told them the whole thing. They'd lock her up in the attic until she was eighty.

Charlotte couldn't get over it. They were awful. They were impossible. They were always telling her they were there for her, and now when she truly needed them, they were treating her like a common criminal. Her mom was always so worried about her self-esteem, but she apparently didn't consider what it might do to Charlotte to have her own parents doubt her. Well, Charlotte thought, as long as she was willing to pony up for the therapy when Charlotte was thirty and suffered major trust issues.

Somewhere in the world there was a girl whose parents trusted her, who understood when she said she couldn't tell them everything, who believed her when she told them things that might seem unbelievable. Somewhere, that girl was very happy, and when she went out *to save the world*, she could do so happy in the knowledge that when she came back she wouldn't get in trouble for it.

Charlotte hoped that girl knew how lucky she was.

So what was she supposed to do now? Jason was on the ship, and he'd seen her, that much was certain. And now all she could do was pace around her room and wait for him to do whatever it was he was sent to do. When he came to kidnap her and feed her to his pet piranhas, then they'd be sorry. They would go around the country giving speeches and taping public service announcements: "Always believe your kids, no matter how crazy it sounds, because if you don't, they might get fed to piranhas."

Charlotte needed to find Jason, and she couldn't do that while she was confined to her room, that was clear—and she didn't want to wait for him to find her. She could call the security officer with an anonymous tip—but he wasn't going to believe her. They always knew what room you were calling from. Even if he didn't, she was just a kid, and adults don't believe kids, ever. It's like once you pass a certain age threshold some sort of brain chip kicks in and you suddenly start thinking that everyone under the age of seventeen is either a pathological liar or clinically insane. But, oh, once you reach adulthood, then you are magically gifted with sanity and become perfect in every way.

Charlotte paced. Well, maybe tomorrow when they went to the living hell known as Colonial Williamsburg—which was going to be a total blast, because the only thing worse than being dragged to Colonial Williamsburg was being dragged to Colonial Williamsburg by parents who thought you were a juvenile delinquent—she could find some nice-looking old person and tell her that there was a runaway boy on the ship, and she would of course tell security because, you know—runaway boy!—and they'd find him immediately and give *him* a lecture on rules, and then they'd tell Charlotte's parents, and then they would feel very, very bad for not believing their daughter. Not as bad as if Charlotte had been fed to piranhas, but she was willing to make some sacrifices.

It didn't take long for the universe to foil that plan too. Just as Charlotte had stopped pacing and gotten settled on her bed, slightly comforted in the knowledge that she had a plan of action, the overhead intercom system pinged three times signaling an all-ship announcement.

"Ladies and gentlemen," the voice said, "this is your captain speaking. You may have noticed we've landed in the middle of a storm. We're trying to navigate our way out of it, and I believe we should be clear of it soon. But unfortunately, we've had to make a course correction. Due to the storm, we're farther east than we should be, and unfortunately we won't be able to stop in Yorktown tomorrow. I hope to get us back on course soon so we can make our scheduled arrival at Mount Vernon on Saturday. I'm deeply sorry for any inconvenience. Our cruise director is working on an exciting roster of onboard activities for you. . . ."

*Wonderful.*

• • •

Charlotte's parents knocked on her door at six thirty. (Charlotte didn't know why they bothered to knock, since they *had her key*.) When Charlotte saw them, she felt her stomach twist up in rage again. For their part, her parents only looked solemn.

"Would you like to come eat with us?" Mrs. Mielswetzski said.

No. "Look, would it be okay if I got room service instead?" Charlotte asked icily. She was not going to sit there at dinner and pretend they weren't the worst parents in the history of the world

Her parents exchanged a look. "Sure, Char," Mrs. Mielswetzski said formally, "that would be fine. We'll come get you for breakfast tomorrow. Nine o' clock?"

Her parents stood awkwardly in the doorway, and Charlotte said, for no reason at all, "So, you guys must be pretty disappointed about the Williamsburg trip." As soon as the words were out of her mouth, Charlotte cringed. What was she doing? Why was she making conversation with these people? She was supposed to be slamming the door in their faces.

"Oh," said Mr. Mielswetzski. "Sure, it's too bad, but the cruise director says Thalia's going to sing during the day tomorrow. That's much better than Williamsburg."

Charlotte blinked. "It is?"

"Oh, sure," said Mrs. Mielswetzski. "We're going to go see her after dinner again."

"You guys aren't upset about missing Williamsburg?" Charlotte asked. She was so surprised she completely forgot she hated them.

"No," said Mr. Mielswetzski. "We can always go to Williamsburg. When do we get the chance to see a singer like Thalia?"

"Tonight!" said Mrs. Mielswetzski with a giggle.

"That's right!" exclaimed Mr. Mielswetzski. "Well, we better get to dinner, so we don't miss her!"

"We want to get a good seat! I think the whole ship's going tonight!"

"That's four hundred and fifty people. Three hundred passengers and a hundred and fifty crew. We better get our seat now!" Her father winked broadly.

"Well, I don't think *all* the crew is going. Someone has to pilot the ship!" her mother said with a giggle.

"Poor guy," said Mr. Mielswetzski.

Still talking, her parents turned to go, closing the door in Charlotte's face.

Charlotte passed a grim evening—as grim as an evening can be when your dinner is pizza, fries, and a chocolate sundae brought to your room. She halfheartedly flipped the channels on the television and tried to come up with a plan for the next day. Maybe at breakfast she would see an officer she could explain the situation to. Of course, she realized with a sinking heart, if she'd done that in the first place instead of running off half-cocked, she wouldn't be in this mess.

That night Charlotte was awoken a few times by some violent lurchings of the ship. Once she was almost thrown out of the bed, but after that things seemed to settle down again and, despite a few loud cracklings of the ship's intercom, which was right over her head, she was lulled quickly to sleep. When she was sleeping, she had a strange dream in which her house was picked up by a tornado and swirled inside the funnel cloud as it traveled across an open plain. Charlotte had had that dream a lot when she had seen *The Wizard of Oz* at an impressionable age, but this time there was a small difference. As the tornado blew the house around, Charlotte's dream-ears filled with the sound of wind, but there was something else, too. Underneath the wind, almost in harmony with it, was the soft sound of a woman singing.

When Charlotte woke up the next morning, she opened her curtains and found the storm had quieted. The sky still looked overcast and slightly menacing, but the rain had ended and the waves had calmed somewhat. The color of the water had changed, though, from the clear blue of the sea she'd seen yesterday morning to something richer and darker, almost the color of wine.

There was something else strange about the waves too, something about the appearance of the water, something Charlotte couldn't put her finger on, but she didn't really think about it too much. She was hungry.

It was fifteen minutes to nine—almost time to meet her parents. Charlotte was not going to let them yell at her for not being ready. So she quickly showered and dressed and waited for her parents to come fetch her for breakfast.

And waited. Nine fifteen, and then nine thirty, and her parents still weren't there. They'd had an appointment. For breakfast! Since Charlotte couldn't actually get back into her room without them, she was counting on them to come get her so she didn't *starve to death*. (Okay, room service was twenty-four hours, but that wasn't the point.) They'd had a *plan*.

Charlotte remembered yesterday's breakfast, when her parents had stumbled up to the café at nearly ten o'clock after being up late listening to their precious singer. Maybe it had happened again. Maybe they were sleeping happily after having fun all night, while their only daughter was stuck in the room next to them without her room key, starving to death.

Grumbling, Charlotte picked up the phone and called them, but there was no answer. Could they really be sleeping that hard?

Well, there was only one thing to do. She grabbed the cruise binder and opened the door to the room, and then carefully placed the binder in the doorway as a prop. Then she went into the hallway and knocked loudly on her parents' door. "Mom, Dad!" she called, knocking again. "Are you guys in there?"

Nothing.

They had forgotten her. They'd gone to breakfast without her. Charlotte couldn't believe it. Could. Not. Believe. It. First they treated her like a criminal, then they abandoned her. Completely abandoned. Was she such a disaster of a child that they no longer wanted anything to do with her?

Charlotte was in a fury now. She was going to go up to breakfast and yell at them. She was going to yell at them in front of the whole café, and everyone there would know what kind of people they were. The rest of the cruise, everywhere they went, people would point and whisper, *Those are the people who left their only daughter to starve.*

Charlotte barely noticed that the hallway was entirely empty—no one heading to breakfast or the deck, no stewardesses on their morning rounds, no crew members in the utility closets; nor did she notice how still the ship felt, almost as if it were just bobbing in those wine-dark waves. It wasn't until she got to Deck

Seven and entered the indoor part of the café that she realized something was wrong. For there was no one in the café at all, not even any waiters. The breakfast buffet was empty and the tables weren't even set. Charlotte ran onto the terrace, and it was empty too.

Well, she thought, maybe this café's closed today. It was a little weird that there wasn't a sign, but maybe she'd missed an announcement. Everyone was simply having breakfast in the main restaurant.

So Charlotte ran down there, becoming slowly aware of the extremely eerie feeling that she was the only person on the ship. She saw no one as she ran. There was obviously some great piece of entertainment or something, and a staff meeting. There was a reason no one was in the hallways or out on the deck or in the stairwell. There had to be.

It wasn't until she got to the restaurant and found it, too, entirely empty that Charlotte realized that something was very, very wrong. As she stood, looking over the empty room with its patiently waiting tables and chairs and its undisturbed place settings, looking so vacant as to seem haunted, a great shiver washed over her. Without a thought, she ran from the restaurant right into the galley—not caring who found her in a restricted area as long as someone found her—and it was completely deserted as well.

Charlotte would never be able to say what it was that led her back up the stairs to Deck Five and to the Mariner Lounge, but something did. In a fog, she ran right up to the closed double doors of the lounge and began to pull frantically on them. They were locked. But the doors had two windows like portholes in them, and as she pulled, Charlotte peered inside and saw what looked to be hundreds of people crammed into the lounge, all facing straight ahead. She yanked on the door again and then started pounding on it, but no one turned. No one even seemed to flinch. She pounded and she screamed, but to no avail.

Quickly Charlotte grabbed a chair from the library and placed it next to one of the doors, then climbed on it to get a better view through the porthole. She scanned the room carefully until her eyes landed on her parents' backs. Her heart leaped into her throat and tears sprang to her eyes. She pounded on the door again, calling their names, but they were completely still.

At the other end of the room, Charlotte saw movement. A head of raven-black hair swayed slowly back and forth among the heads of the crowd. The singer. Thalia. Charlotte stood on her tiptoes and peered at her, then pressed her ears against the door. Thalia was singing.

Right in front of Thalia, a row of white officers' caps peeked out above the crowd. That's when Charlotte realized that there was something wrong with the motion of the ship, that she couldn't feel the sense of movement she'd become accustomed to the day before. She remembered what it was she'd seen out of her window earlier and realized what it was that had bothered her: There was no wake. The ship wasn't moving.

After one last try of the door, Charlotte took off again, running this time toward the sliver of deck at the very bow of the ship. When she got there, she stared up into the bridge. She already knew what she'd see, of course, but it didn't feel any better to have it confirmed. The bridge was totally empty. She whirled around and looked at the waves below. The ship was just floating along in the current.

She grasped the rail in horror. She was stranded in the middle of the Atlantic Ocean on a cruise ship full of people in singer-induced comas. For the last month of her life, she had been feeling increasingly more alone in the world. Well, now she was truly all alone.

Charlotte sank to the floor of the deck, trying to get her breath again. There was no point in panicking, she told herself. If she was indeed all alone, it was her job to save everyone. Well, she could do that. She'd done it before. She was an old pro at saving humanity. Too bad there was no shadow army around, but you did what you could.

Closing her eyes, Charlotte calmed herself. The ship had to have a radio somewhere, right? She could find it and call someone. That wouldn't be hard. Someone would respond to the call of an abandoned cruise ship. Surely there was some kind of distress signal. And even if there wasn't, eventually someone would notice that the cruise ship wasn't where it was supposed to be and they'd look for it. An entire cruise ship with four hundred and fifty people can't just disappear. Someone would find them eventually.

With a beating heart and a burning stomach, Charlotte went back inside and tried every single restricted door there was. But nothing opened. She couldn't get in—there would be no radio, no distress signal. She'd just have to wait.

But she didn't want to wait. This had happened for a reason, and Charlotte really didn't want to find out why. She had to contact someone.

The Internet! The ship had a computer center, and Charlotte could go e-mail someone. But who? Who would believe her? Her cousin, Mr. Can't-We-Just-Get-Over-That himself? Well, she could e-mail the police or the coast guard or something. They'd be able to help. But first she needed to know roughly where they were.

That, she could find out. Quickly she dashed up the stairs to the Observation Lounge. She headed right to the monitor to look for the flashing white light of the ship next to the eastern seaboard. But when she looked at the monitor, she did not see the coastline of the United States at all. There was a coast, yes, but Charlotte couldn't place it.

Charlotte peered at the screen more closely. At the bottom were some latitude and longitude numbers that meant nothing to her, and then her eyes landed on some words right below those numbers. She took them in just as the map she was seeing registered in her mind, and she suddenly understood what she was looking at. It was entirely obvious, if you were expecting it, which Charlotte most certainly was not. The coastline she was looking at was the outline of Italy and Greece, and the words on the screen said, quite calmly:

LOCATION: MEDITERRANEAN SEA.

"Surprise!" said a voice behind her.

Charlotte whirled around to behold Jason Hart.

## CHAPTER 18

# Fish Boy Explains It All

As soon as she saw Jason standing there, smiling at her, Charlotte stumbled backward into the monitor, hitting her back on one of the corners—which, by the way, hurt. A lot.

"Get away from me," she said. The words came out in a rush and sounded something like "Geddoffamah!" She hoped the effect was clear enough.

Jason threw up his hands. "No, Charlotte, it's okay," he said, his green eyes wide like two verdant pools. "I'm on your side."

Right, Charlotte thought. "On my side? On my side?

How do you explain all this, then?" She motioned wildly at the monitor.

"I didn't do it!" Jason exclaimed. "I'm here to help."

"Who are you?" she hissed.

He blinked. "I'm Jason."

Charlotte rolled her eyes. "I know that," she said in her best *duh!* voice, "but"—she leaned forward—"*who are you?*"

"Oh," he said. "Well, I'm the son of a sea god."

"Right," said Charlotte, folding her arms around her chest. A sea god. What did that make Jason—Fish Boy?

"My mom's mortal, though, and I am too. I'm not a god or anything."

"I see," said Charlotte through clenched teeth.

"My dad's a big jerk," he said. "He abandoned my mother. He would have abandoned me if he hadn't decided I was useful. All he cares about is work."

"Work," Charlotte repeated flatly.

"Being a sea god."

"Right," said Charlotte.

"Anyway, he made me come with him. Said I couldn't be trusted on my own. I'm thirteen! And he made me spy on you. He wants me to be just like him. It's awful." He scowled. "I can't be my own person, you know?"

"This is all great, Jason," she said, spitting out the

words. "But if you're on my side, can you please *tell me what's going on?*"

"Oh," he said. "Right. You're in the Mediterranean."

"I gathered that," snapped Charlotte. "Why?"

"Poseidon," Jason said simply.

Charlotte straightened. *"What?"*

She listened, dumbfounded, as Jason explained that Philonecron had some powerful relatives indeed.

"But—but—" Charlotte sputtered. "But Philonecron was trying to overthrow Hades! Hades is Poseidon's brother!"

Jason shrugged. "That's different. Philonecron's a god. You're a mortal. The gods don't like it when mortals interfere with them. Especially Poseidon." He went behind the bar and started rummaging around.

"What is he going to do?" Charlotte whispered.

"Oh, you know," Jason shrugged, "strand you at sea, I imagine. It's his standard MO, really. Get someone blown off course and have them float around for a dozen years or so. . . . Unless some sea monster gets them first." He pulled out a soda from behind the counter. "Want one?"

"Sea monster," repeated Charlotte.

"Or whirlpool or storm. There's really a lot of ways the sea can kill you." He shrugged and took a gulp of soda.

"I see," said Charlotte, voice shaking. "Poseidon's mad at me, so he strands this whole boatload full of more than four hundred people, putting them all at risk for attack by a cruise-ship-eating sea monster, all so he can get revenge on me?"

"Yeah," Jason said. "He's a big jerk. They're all big jerks."

But Charlotte wasn't listening. The force of his words had hit her, and she half walked, half stumbled her way to one of the couches and promptly slumped into one, putting her head in her hands.

If Jason was telling the truth, which it seemed he was, she was adrift on the open sea in a large cruise ship with Poseidon, the Lord of the Seas, after her. The last Big Three god she met was scary enough, and he'd been on her side. She and Zee had escaped from Philonecron, thanks to a shadow army and a lot of luck, but Poseidon?

There was a plopping sound on the sofa, and Charlotte looked up to see that Jason had sat down next to her. He really did have very nice eyes, even if there was something fishy about him.

Charlotte tried to gather herself. She couldn't freak out, not yet. "Well, okay," she said slowly, "what about my parents? What about everyone on board? What's happening to them? They're all locked in the lounge with that singer."

"Oh, she's a Siren," Jason said offhandedly.

Oh. Charlotte put her head in her hands again. She should have known. Sirens mesmerized people with their singing; in the myths, their voices led sailors to their doom. And in real life, apparently, they could paralyze a whole cruise ship. Charlotte shook her head slowly, back and forth.

"She's been seducing everyone since she got onboard. She sang to the staff last night, then she went onto the bridge and got the captain and everyone, and then any holdouts she lured into the lounge by singing over the intercom while they were sleeping. Everyone was lured into the lounge, and they're all completely entranced."

"Oh." Charlotte remembered the voice in her dream. "But what about me?"

"It doesn't work on kids. Never has. I mean, you heard it over the intercom, right? It's like easy listening." He wrinkled up his nose.

"Okay," Charlotte said, exhaling. "So. Poseidon has it in for me, so he magically blows the whole ship into the Mediterranean, sends a Siren onboard to enchant everyone, and leaves me stranded and alone. That's the plan?"

"Yup," said Jason, taking another swig of his soda. "As far as I know. So I came to help you."

Charlotte stood up. She had heard enough. "Fine," she said. "Help me. We have to contact someone so we can get away from Poseidon, and then we can deal with Enchanto-Babe. I was going to go down to the computer center, but maybe we can break into the radio room—"

But Jason was shaking his head. "That won't work. There's no communication working on this ship, I can guarantee that. The Internet's not going to work, the transponder is off, the radar is off. The Siren would have seen to that. She can make people do what she wants."

"Fine," Charlotte said, "then you can help me break into the lounge. We have to get in there and wake everyone up somehow. Make Thalia stop singing!"

He shook his head. "That's not going to work. She's a three-millennia-old witch. There's only one thing that can stop her."

"Well?" Charlotte said. "What is that?"

"Poseidon's trident."

Charlotte gaped at Jason. Right. Poseidon's trident. When Zeus, Hades, and Poseidon tried to overthrow Cronus, the Cyclopses gave them each an incredibly powerful object: Zeus a thunder bolt, Hades an invisible helmet, and Poseidon a three-pronged spear. His trident was one of the three most powerful objects in the universe, and Charlotte seriously doubted he wanted to give it up.

"Oh, really?" she said. "Is that all? Well, you don't happen to have it on you, do you?"

"No," he said. "But I can take you to him. I know where he is, and it's not far. We'll steal the trident, come back here, and use it on the Siren."

Charlotte stared at him, openmouthed. "We're going to steal Poseidon's trident."

"Yeah," he said.

"And just how are we going to do that?"

"I don't know," Jason said. "I figured you'd have a plan. You defeated Philonecron and made your way through the Underworld! I mean"—he smiled softly—"that was pretty incredible."

Despite herself, Charlotte blushed. No one that cute had ever noticed anything she'd done before.

*Focus, Charlotte.*

What Jason was proposing was ridiculous. Absurd. Charlotte was not about to tussle with *Poseidon*. There had to be another way.

"Anyway," she said, "how do you expect me to get to Poseidon's palace? I don't scuba dive."

"He doesn't have a palace, or at least he never goes there. He's got a yacht. I can take you there."

"Look," she said, "you want to help me? You're

part sea god, right? You go back to Poseidon's . . . yacht and get me the trident and bring it back here, and then we can blast the song lady and get the heck out of here."

"Oh," Jason said, shifting in his seat. "Well, no, see . . . he's got an enchantment that will fry anyone with Immortal blood who touches it, and since my dad is an Immortal . . . He really doesn't like it when people touch his trident, you see. But," he added quickly, "he won't have protected it from mortals; it would never occur to him that mortals might even try something like that."

"Really," said Charlotte flatly.

"Yeah!" said Jason.

"Are you sure?" Charlotte was dubious.

He smiled brightly. "Positive."

"Right," said Charlotte. "Well, okay, I don't know about you, but I've met all the Greek gods I want to meet in my lifetime, so if you don't mind, I'm going to try to fix this myself. You can help or you can sit here"—*looking adorable*—"and twiddle your thumbs."

Jason shook his head. "It won't work."

Boys! "Well," Charlotte said, getting up firmly, "nothing ventured, nothing gained, right?" and with a toss of her hair, she strode out of the lounge, leaving Jason Hart, indeed, twiddling his thumbs.

• • •

The first thing Charlotte did was go near the bridge and try every single restricted door again, with as little success as she'd had before. The last door she kicked for good measure, ending up with nothing besides a sore toe underneath her sneakers.

Then she went back down to Deck Five, to the computer center. For she was not simply going to take Fish Boy at his word that the Internet didn't work. She didn't know exactly who she was going to e-mail now; the Greek coast guard? Her Greek was a little weak. But she'd figure something out.

She turned on the computer and waited impatiently for it to load up, while the ship drifted onward, and as soon as the desktop appeared she attacked the browser icon with the mouse. Her heart leaped as a blank page popped up on the screen. She closed her eyes and counted slowly to three, then opened them to see the words CONNECTION UNAVAILABLE.

With a gargled scream, Charlotte slammed her hands on the desk, then burst out of her chair and went back to the Mariner Lounge. She didn't have to stop the Siren, she didn't have to wake anyone up; if she could just get to one of the officers and get a key, she could get onto the bridge and turn on the distress signal. (Which, she hoped, was a large red button clearly marked DISTRESS SIGNAL, because otherwise there would be a problem.

Charlotte stood on the small wooden chair again and looked in. Nothing had changed—everyone was still completely motionless, riveted to the stage. As her eyes fell on her parents, her heart gave a little tug. It was horrible seeing them that way, completely in thrall to something beyond their control. She needed to get the ship moving again, she needed to get as far away from Poseidon as possible, she needed to free her parents. The lump began to rise in her throat again. They were so worried about what would happen if they let Charlotte out of their sight, but apparently they were the ones who needed worrying about. When they woke up, they were *so* grounded.

Thalia's dark head was still bobbing about on the stage. She'd been, Charlotte realized, singing all night and all morning. Didn't she get a sore throat? Eventually she was going to have to stop singing, right? And when she did, everyone would wake up and realize what had happened and they would revolt and then everything would be okay again, right?

Right?

Wrong. Who was Charlotte kidding? Thalia wasn't human. She was never going to stop singing, and unless Charlotte did something, everyone in there was going to be lost for eternity. How dare she? How dare she hurt all these people? How dare she hurt her parents? What kind of a monster was she?

"I see you, Siren!" Charlotte shouted, banging on the door. "I see you!" She scowled and added for good measure, "Your music's awful!"

And with that, the Siren's cat-like eyes glanced up toward Charlotte, and then she did the single most aggravating thing anyone had ever done to Charlotte, which is really saying a lot.

She winked.

She winked! The nerve! The gall! Red spots began to dance before Charlotte's eyes, and in one quick motion she hopped down, lifted the small chair up over her head, and bashed it against the door with all her might.

One of the chair legs splintered off with a loud pop. The door barely moved.

Charlotte let out a frustrated scream, then turned around and leaned against the double doors. There was nothing to be done. Nothing. Either she could trust Fish Boy and embark on his ridiculous, crazy, moronic, suicidal plan, or she could float out here in the Mediterranean until she was eighty.

Grimacing, Charlotte closed her eyes and buried her face in her fists, took a deep breath, then straightened and stalked off to her room.

As soon as she walked through the propped door, Charlotte grabbed her backpack and emptied it of all the things she had put in there for her ill-fated afternoon in the sun the day before, then reached into her closet and pulled out a rain jacket, a sweater, and her life preserver. (It seemed like a good idea.) Then she went over to the mini-bar. Her parents had once given her a lecture about taking things from the minibar in hotel rooms — everything was ridiculously overpriced, they said. One time she hadn't been able to resist and had eaten a bag of potato chips, and they made her pay for it with her own allowance — and they were right, the chips had been really, really expensive. But these were extenuating circumstances. Charlotte unlocked the minibar, quickly ate a granola bar and drank some juice, and then emptied everything else edible into her bag, along with a couple of bottles of water.

Charlotte had done this before, of course. She had packed extremely well to go down to the Underworld just five months before. All she ever did, it seemed, was load up her backpack for journeys to meet Greek gods. If you ever wanted to know what to pack for a quick jaunt to the realm of one of the Greek gods, just ask Charlotte Mielswetzski.

Then, with a pounding heart, she left her room and went back up to the Observation Lounge, where Jason Hart was waiting for her.

"Ready?" he asked.

Charlotte exhaled heavily, and though her heart was throbbing and her stomach churning, she drew herself upward and nodded at Jason. "Ready."

A few minutes later Charlotte and Jason were outside on Deck Seven, studying the lifeboats. The storm was gone, but it had left behind a thick mist that hung over the deck.

Each lifeboat was suspended by a complicated series of pulleys about three feet above the deck. Charlotte had absolutely no idea how it worked—they didn't exactly cover that in the drill. It's like no one on the ship considered what might happen if everyone onboard but the eighth grader had been mesmerized by a Siren.

"Well," Charlotte said, "let's get the tarp off first."

Together, they reached over and started snapping off the bright blue tarp. At the bow of the boat was a console with a steering wheel and some buttons. Charlotte used the small staircase next to the boat to climb in and examine the console, while Jason watched.

As soon as she got into the boat, she saw a steel plaque on which was written, quite clearly, LIFEBOAT INSTRUCTIONS. Her heart leaped slightly. It was nice to feel that someone was watching out for them, even if it was some guy in a lifeboat-making factory. Charlotte would take all the friends she could get.

"Okay," she said, scanning the instructions, "see that lever?" She pointed to the lever on the steel beam she'd noticed during the drill. "That's the safety. Pull it and climb in."

"Okay," said Jason, his voice full of determination. Charlotte cast a glance at him. She still didn't know what to think about Fish Boy, but there was a chance that he was on her side, and if he was, he was going to be an excellent companion for this journey. He knew things about the gods. He was part god himself. Last time she'd done this, with Zee, he'd been as lost and clueless as she. And Zee was her cousin and therefore not cute at all, unlike Jason. And unlike Zee, Jason did not think they should just get over the whole thing.

Jason pulled the lever and climbed on into the boat. "Okay," Charlotte said, "now I press this—," and as she did so she heard the sound of hissing air, then turning gears, and then the beams on which the boat was suspended began to move slowly, steadily outward. In a few moments Charlotte, Jason, and the lifeboat were suspended directly above the ocean, swaying slightly in the mist as the ship rocked back and forth.

"All right," Charlotte said, her voice catching a little. "Now this will lower us down." And she pressed another button, the cables began to move through the pulleys, and the little boat began its slow descent into the Mediterranean Sea.

# PART FOUR

## Fishiest

## CHAPTER 19

# Strait and Narrows

WHEN THE LIFEBOAT HIT THE WATER, JASON AND Charlotte began to slowly unhook it from the cables and from the ship. They were so small next to the cruise ship, like a mouse next to a hippopotamus. Charlotte couldn't believe something so vast had been rendered completely helpless. Poor hippopotamus.

The lifeboat was white on the bottom, which Charlotte hoped kept it from looking delicious to any passing shark, and the entire interior was bright red. There were containers of various sizes built into the boat, and Jason and Charlotte poked through them.

One was filled with life preservers, another with a thick rope, another with clear packets of water and bars of something that looked like it might approximate food. Possibly. Charlotte was glad she'd raided the minibar. In a smaller box in the back of the boat lay something that Charlotte first thought was a handgun, but proved to be a flare gun. Charlotte was relieved; it didn't seem like you should have handguns on lifeboats. People might start using them to eat one another.

On the bow of the boat was a big red button, marked, as all distress signals should be, with the word BEACON. Charlotte reached for it, but Jason suddenly exclaimed, "Wait!"

"What?" Charlotte said. "Someone could find us and then we wouldn't have to go!"

Jason shook his head. "The yacht has a radio too. We *really* don't want them to know we're coming. . . . Anyway, even if someone did come for us, the Siren would just get them, too."

"Right," Charlotte said, pulling her hand away. "Well, should we go?"

Jason promptly took the passenger seat next to the console, meaning, Charlotte assumed, that she was going to do the driving. When they had gone to the Underworld, Zee hadn't let her do anything. He was obsessed with being chivalrous and had always insisted on going first all the time, like she couldn't take care of herself. Well, she could. Zee went and got himself taken by Philonecron, and Charlotte had gotten by just fine.

(Mostly.)

Charlotte stepped over to the console, took a deep breath, and hit the big green button labeled PRESS TO START MOTOR. That seemed clear enough. And indeed, when she hit the button, the engine began to rumble. There was a lever near her elbow marked as the throttle, so she pushed it forward, and the boat burst forward into the mist.

"Okay!" shouted Charlotte. "Now what?"

"Just go northwest," Jason said, nodding at the compass on Charlotte's console.

"Right," said Charlotte, moving the steering wheel around.

She had driven her uncle's boat on Lake Sissabagama the previous summer. He'd said knowing how to drive a boat could come in handy—and Charlotte had to applaud his prescience.

The trick to going to see Greek gods, Charlotte had found, was not to think about it too much. Because if you focused on the fact that at the end of your journey would be, you know, Poseidon the Earth Shaker, it would be a little hard to get going. What you had to do was focus on the journey itself—one step in front of the other, as it were. Which was, really, exciting enough, given a sea monster could leap out at you at any moment.

*Calm, Charlotte. Breathe.*

Today Charlotte Mielswetzski was supposed to be enduring Colonial Williamsburg with her parents, learning about blacksmiths and bakers and one-room schoolhouses and all that stupid stuff. She was not supposed to be taking a lifeboat with the cute new boy to Poseidon's yacht. Next time, she was going to better appreciate the opportunity to see some historical reenactments.

"So, the trident," Charlotte said when they were on their way. "Poseidon doesn't, like, leave it somewhere when he sleeps, does he? Or take it out to have it cleaned?"

"Nope. His power is bound up in it, so he's not really going to let it out of his sight, you know?"

"I see," said Charlotte, sighing. For all his information, Jason didn't seem to have much of a plan here. They were just going to have to go and figure it out on the fly. On the fly was usually the way Charlotte did everything, but getting out of your math homework and getting Poseidon's trident weren't exactly analogous. "And am I actually going to be able to work the trident? I mean, I'm not exactly a god."

"For a while," Jason said. "Every time Poseidon uses

it, the trident is infused with his power—so it will work for a little while. And without it, he'll be at about half strength."

"You've thought a lot about this," Charlotte said, casting a glance at him.

"I keep my ears open."

Not open enough to figure out how to get the thing, though, Charlotte noted as she squinted through the mist. They could be right on top of the yacht, and she wouldn't have any idea. "So how far is it, anyway?"

"I dunno," said Jason. "About ten miles. That's where I left them."

"What?" Charlotte turned to look at him. "Left them?"

"Yeah. I lived on the ship. Dad took me there when I was young so I could learn to appreciate being part Immortal. . . . Learn to appreciate it? As if. All they do is go to parties and watch surfers get eaten by sharks and stuff."

"Wait . . . who's your grandfather, then?"

"Huh?"

"Your grandfather. I heard you lived with your grandfather."

"Oh," he said. "No, that's my dad. He just looks old. Well, he is old. But, you know, he's Immortal. Anyway, he told me I had to take some responsibility, so he made me come with him and get to know"—he stopped himself suddenly—"get to know you. But then I met you and, well, I couldn't do it. I ran away. But Dad sent his goons after me and made me go back on the ship."

As he spoke, Charlotte eyed Jason out of the corner of her eye. She was no fool, of course—she'd been through enough not to trust a random cute boy who was thrown at her feet with all the answers for saving the day. It was just as likely that he was trying to lure her to Poseidon's ship. Charlotte knew all about being lured. But the fact was, it seemed like she was going to have to get there anyway, so she might as well go with someone who knew the way.

Plus there was a chance he was telling her the truth. Charlotte did hope he was telling the truth.

"At first I thought they just wanted to spy on you," Jason continued. "I didn't realize what they were doing, but when I heard what they were planning on doing to you, well"—Jason's voice softened—"I had to come."

"Really?" Charlotte turned her head toward him. Jason was looking up at her, green eyes wide, and whatever she was about to ask him slipped out of her mind. It's hard to concentrate when your heart is making like a possessed bass drum.

"Of course!" He inched closer and put his hand on Charlotte's shoulder. "I felt a connection with you,

Charlotte, even when we first met. I couldn't stand the thought of them hurting you."

"Oh," Charlotte said, her knees growing slightly weak. Was it getting warm in the boat? She tried very hard to pay attention to her driving, but Jason Hart's hand seemed to be radiating electricity into her shoulder. It was probably because he was part Greek god, Charlotte thought; he had some magical electricity-radiating power. And maybe that's why she was suddenly feeling so lightheaded. . . .

"I never thought I'd meet anyone who could really understand, you know? Either I could lie about it like he did to my mom, or I could tell the truth, but who would believe me? I thought in addition to ruining my life he'd also made sure I'd never have a social life. But Charlotte"—he gazed into her eyes—"you *know*. You know *everything*. And you're so strong and brave. You're amazing."

She was? And then, before she knew what was happening, Jason Hart's gorgeous face was leaning into her slowly and his eyes were closing and his mouth was reaching for hers, almost as if he wanted to—

*Thump!*

As the boat hit something in the water, both Charlotte and Jason were thrown forward. The mist lifted slightly, as if it had been spooked by the collision, and as Charlotte straightened, she saw that they seemed to be in the middle of a rocky, narrow strait. The boat must have run over a rock, which seemed like something to avoid doing in the future.

The strait was framed by two large cliff walls, and in the middle of the strait was a row of three-story-high rocks. As Charlotte looked back and forth, she noticed that there were matching caves gaping like mouths in the walls on either side. The lifeboat was currently heading right for the rocks in the center—not really a good place for it to be going—so, uttering a small thank-you to the mist for its timely departure, she turned the steering wheel to the right.

Suddenly the air filled with the sound of a tremendous rushing of water, and Jason stiffened.

"Charlotte!" he screamed. "Turn left. Turn away!"

Ever responsive, Charlotte leaned the steering wheel all the way to the left as, in front of her, the sea began to change. The water was moving, at first slowly and then in a rush, into the cave on the right, and as Charlotte steered the boat away, she saw that there was a smaller cave inside the first. No, no, not a cave, but a mouth. A huge, gaping mouth, rimmed with pointy yellow teeth. There was a monster in the cave—green and round and the size of a house, with six pink eyes on six waving tentacles and an open mouth that seemed to take up its whole body. The current was rushing forcefully toward the mouth, and as Charlotte watched over her shoulder, she realized that the monster was sucking in the sea. Charlotte hit the throttle as hard as she could before the current could grab them and carry them helplessly into that awful maw.

With blood rushing in her ears, she steered the little boat toward the other side of the wall of rocks. It was hard to control the roaring boat in the midst of the churning, rushing water, and for a moment it seemed they'd smash into the rocks that bisected the canyon. But Charlotte leaned on the throttle and in a moment they had dodged them and reached calm waters.

Charlotte and Jason were both gasping as they stared at the water on the far side of the strait, rushing into the small cave as if it were being sucked in by a giant vacuum cleaner.

"What was that?" Charlotte yelled to Jason, slowing the motor.

"Charybdis! She used to be a nymph, but Zeus turned her into a monster. She sucks in the sea three times a day and everything in it. And if that's Charybdis, then"—he whirled around to stare at the cave they were currently passing—"Charlotte, duck!"

"What?"

"DUCK!"

No need to tell her three times. She ducked down as Jason did the same. From her crouch, Charlotte peered over the lip of the boat and saw a great figure rush from the cave—a giant woman with blue skin, snakes for hair, and a broad red mouth. She seemed to be floating on a pack of large dog-like beasts—no, the bottom half of her body *was* a pack of large dog-like beasts. There was growling and gnashing, and then one of the black dogs separated from the woman's body and bounded toward the boat as if it were on solid ground. "Get down!" Jason shouted again, and she felt his arm push her into the floor of the boat.

As Charlotte tried to shrink herself up into the smallest, most unnoticeable piece of girl the world had ever seen, she heard a loud thud and felt the boat shake. In terror, she scrambled backward and pressed herself against the side of the boat as the hideous dog-beast, with fire eyes and glistening teeth, prowled toward her. Charlotte was hit with a wave of rancid breath. She froze, and then—

Then a cracking noise, a whistling sound, a flash of light, an ear-bursting howl, and a smell of something singeing—and the dog-beast recoiled. Charlotte sprang up in time to see a large splash where the creature had plunged into the sea.

Charlotte whirled around. Jason was standing in the

back of the boat with the flare gun leveled at the spot where the dog used to be. Charlotte stood, open-mouthed, staring at him. As one, all the dog-beasts let out a tremendous howl, and the woman began to move toward the boat and the fallen beast.

"Can you drive?" Jason yelled. "Get us out of here!"

With the taste of fear in her mouth, Charlotte sprang back to the console, her back aching from her desperate scramble, and without a look back she jammed the throttle as hard as it would go. The boat seemed all too willing to comply and burst forth in the water so hard that both Charlotte and Jason stumbled backward.

Five minutes later the lifeboat was back on the open sea. The waters were calm, and there was not a cave in sight. Jason was driving now, muttering frantic apologies as he stared at the water ahead, while Charlotte huddled in a blanket in the passenger seat, trying to recover.

"I'm so sorry," he said, shaking his head. "I should have known. We could have gone around the strait. I didn't realize where we were. . . ."

Charlotte glanced up at him.

"That was Scylla," said Jason. "The witch Circe turned her into a monster. She and Charybdis attack everything that comes through. It's the Strait of Messina, and it's death for everyone."

"Tell me about it," muttered Charlotte, shivering into her blanket. She could still feel the dog's hot breath on her neck and sense his teeth coming closer.

"I'm so sorry," Jason repeated desperately, eyes fixed ahead of him.

"No," Charlotte said, looking at him. "No! You saved my life."

"I wouldn't have had to if I—"

"Never mind that! You saved my life!" And despite herself, despite the whole terrible morning, despite all her doubts and fears, and despite the fact that a rabid sea-dog had just tried to turn her into a snack, she found a small smile crossing her lips.

Jason wasn't evil. He couldn't be. If Poseidon had wanted him to bring her to his yacht so he could get rid of her, well, it seemed having her get eaten by a rabid sea-dog would have been a good enough Plan B. Or Jason could have navigated her there on purpose and arranged for the monsters to get her, which is what an evil person might do—but that's not what happened. He'd saved her life.

Charlotte straightened in her seat, letting the blanket drop from her shoulders, and stared out into the horizon. There were puffy clouds lingering just above the edge of the sea, and each of them seemed to form a shape against the pale sky. That one was a face. That one a horse. And that one, just above the water, almost on the water really, was—

—a yacht.

Oh, yes, it was a yacht. A gorgeous, gleaming yacht. Charlotte's eyes couldn't quite get a fix on it; every time she stared at it, it seemed to change shape. It was a cloud, a fishing boat, a cruise ship, a sailboat, a shadow, it was nothing at all. Charlotte had better luck when she looked away from it, keeping the image in the corner of her eye—then she beheld a sleek and stylish yacht sitting on the horizon. There was something about it that made you want to be wearing a diamond tiara and furs (fake fur, of course).

Charlotte was not in a tiara, nor in a fur. She was wearing sneakers and jeans and a sweater. And as they drew closer to the yacht, which was only half the size of their cruise ship but somehow seemed three times as big, she began to feel, not like a mouse next to a hippopotamus, but like a dirt-encrusted worm next to the sky's most beautiful dawn.

"Do you see it?" Jason whispered.

"Yes," said Charlotte. "Sort of."

"It's hard to look at, even for me. It's like staring at the sun."

"Yeah." She squinted at it. "Can anyone see it?"

"Immortals," Jason said. "And mortals, if they've been

invited. . . . I'm going to bring the boat around the back; there's a place to dock there, and it should be open."

Charlotte blinked at him. "Open?"

"They're not really that big on security, because no one ever bothers them, you know? No one's going to mess with Poseidon. Anyway, people are coming and going all the time."

"They are?"

"Yeah. Poseidon entertains a lot. He's having a huge party tonight. He's inviting all the big sea gods and other Immortals. As opposed to, you know, the huge party he had on, say, Saturday. Or the one on Sunday."

"Right." Charlotte was so glad Poseidon had time to have big parties in the middle of plotting to ruin her life. You don't want that kind of thing to keep you from what's really important.

As they approached the back of the yacht, Charlotte scanned the windows for any sign of anyone trying to kill or eat them, but she saw none. Actually, other than the fact that she had almost been sucked into a hideous monster's mouth and had been attacked by a sea-dog, the journey so far had gone about as smoothly as could be expected. Maybe they'd just be able to saunter onto the yacht, waltz over to Poseidon, ask him very nicely if they could borrow his trident for a bit, and hop back to the cruise ship.

Or maybe they'd walk onto the yacht and Poseidon would feed her to a giant squid. It was really hard to say.

Jason eased the lifeboat up right behind the yacht, where two speedboats and a Jet Ski were already lashed on. Four large houseboats and a big bullet boat were anchored off the other side of the yacht—belonging to people, it seemed, who had reached the yacht by going around Scylla and Charybdis. Charlotte reminded herself to go that way on the trip back.

If there was a trip back.

Charlotte shuddered. *One foot in front of the other*, she reminded herself.

"You want to lash on the boat?" Jason asked.

No, I want to go home. "Sure," Charlotte said grimly, grabbing a long coil of rope and climbing over the bow. The hull shone an intense bright white, and something about it seemed to shimmer. Charlotte had to keep looking away lest the brightness get too intense. There were a series of hooks on the hull, and she grabbed onto one of them. It was surprisingly warm to the touch, and as she held on, she got the distinct sensation of sentience. She shivered.

Charlotte tied the rope around the hook at the front of the lifeboat and then lashed them to the yacht. The summer before sixth grade, she'd gone to an overnight camp. There was one activity period where they offered classes in nautical knots, and all the sailing-type girls had eagerly signed up for it, but Charlotte, who did not care for those particular sailing-type girls, had gone swimming instead. It didn't seem, at the time, like one of those fateful decisions that you'd regret later, but that's summer camp for you.

Without proper training, Charlotte did the best she could in fastening the lifeboat to the yacht, and once it seemed relatively secure, she examined the hull, looking for a way to climb onto the boat.

There was none. Other than the hooks, the surface of the yacht was completely smooth. Charlotte frowned and put her hands on the hull, which was as warm as the hooks and seemed to hum slightly at her touch.

"I don't see how we're supposed to—oh!" The gleaming hull had begun to move, and Charlotte stumbled back in surprise, nearly tumbling off the lifeboat's bow. Before her eyes, the hull seemed to rearrange itself so that in one moment it was completely smooth, and in another it had a series of rungs leading all the way up to the top.

"Well, that answers that," she murmured. She glanced at Jason, who didn't look at all surprised, then turned back to the yacht and looked up the ladder to where it ended at the lip of the deck. "Hey, Jason," she asked, turning back toward him, "how am I going to get around? I mean, aren't people going to notice me?"

Jason shook his head. "Not really. Like I said, there are people coming and going all the time, and lots of the gods have mortal kids. Everyone will just think you have some Immortal blood. But"—he raised his eyebrows— "I wouldn't mention your name to anyone. You're famous."

"Check," muttered Charlotte.

"Well . . . shall we?" He gave Charlotte a smile that was at once nervous and excited, and if her heart flipped a bit, it wouldn't have only been out of anxiousness over the task ahead.

Charlotte began to climb up the ladder, feeling its rungs seem to reach out to her as she made her way up. Just as she was about to climb onto the deck, she saw Jason leaning off the ladder—the rung he was standing on had grown into a platform to accommodate him— and starting to untie the lifeboat from the yacht.

"What are you doing?" she hissed.

"Huh?" He looked up. "Oh! I didn't want anyone to see it. It's got stuff from the cruise ship on it!" He pointed at the name stenciled across the hull.

Charlotte couldn't believe her eyes. "Yeah . . . but we're going to need that to get back!"

"Oh." Jason blinked. "I hadn't thought of that." Jason, Charlotte had noticed, wasn't so good with the actual thinking. Which was okay, really; Charlotte could think just fine and Jason could sit there and be cute. That way, everyone had something to do.

As Jason retied the little lifeboat, Charlotte raised her head above the lip of the hull and slowly peeked through the rail at the edge of the deck. Whereupon she found herself looking at two glossy black ball-like eyes—eyes that were staring right back at her.

CHAPTER 20

# Lifestyles of the Rich and Infamous

GASPING, CHARLOTTE TRIED TO CLIMB BACK DOWN the ladder, but before she could move, something had grabbed her by the back of her sweater, and the next thing she knew she was being suspended in the air above the sea. She let out something between a scream and a squawk as she dangled two stories above the Mediterranean, then whatever had her began to move her back over the yacht, and suddenly she found herself staring at the face of a gigantic crab.

The crab seemed to have Charlotte in one of its legs . . . or arms, or whatever . . . and she was dangling from its front pincer. The crab was bright red and roughly the size of Charlotte's living room, with black eyes on what might be its face, if crabs have faces. At this particular moment, Charlotte was most concerned with whether or not crabs had mouths, because if they did, it seemed very likely that she was going to wind up inside it.

The crab's eyes fixed on her, and then he lowered his body in front of Charlotte in a strange motion that seemed to be almost a bow.

"*Geia sou, bonjour, konnichiwa,* greetings," the crab said, studying Charlotte. Yes, he did have a mouth, and out of that mouth words were emanating in a tight, dry voice that could really best be described—and Charlotte never thought she'd use these words in quite this way before—as crab-like. "Welcome to the *Poseidon.* Do you have an invitation?"

A what? A who? "I—"

"She's with me, Kark," said a voice to her left. Charlotte quickly turned her head. Jason was suspended by the crab's other pincer over the top of the deck.

"Ah, Master Hart." The crab bowed once more. "It's nice to see you again. You've been missed." This time when the crab lifted himself, Charlotte noted there was something black right below his head-like area that seemed, upon further inspection, to be a bow tie.

"Can you put us down?" Jason asked. Really, he sounded very polite, much more than Charlotte felt. But at least it seemed that she wasn't going to get eaten, which was a serious plus. At least . . . she wasn't going to get eaten *right now*.

"Certainly, Master Hart." And with that, the crab gently lowered Jason and Charlotte to the ground. Charlotte gasped as her feet hit the teak deck and she quickly grabbed onto the rail for support (physical and moral). "Master Hart," the crab continued, "will your friend be needing a chamber made up?" His eyes swiveled over to Charlotte.

"That would be great," said Jason. "Thank you, Kark."

The crab nodded—and nodding, for a crab, is not that different from bowing—and turned his eyes back to Charlotte. "Do you have any . . . special needs?" he asked.

"What? I—"

The crab gave her a look of barely restrained impatience. "Do you, say, grow six times your normal size at night or turn into a codfish after eating or have a lion head for a stomach that must devour everything in sight or . . ." He held up his front crab legs as if to indicate the wideness of the possibilities.

"Oh," said Charlotte. "No."

"Very good." The crab reached to the wall and a

phone appeared under his claw. He grabbed the receiver and, pulling it close to his face, said a few words in a language Charlotte didn't understand (Greek? Crab?), then bowed again. "The Shell Room on Deck Eighteen will be ready for her . . . momentarily." He blinked. "And . . . now. It's ready now. Does *mademoiselle* have any luggage?"

"Uh . . . no," Charlotte said.

Kark eyed her ensemble crabbily. "I see," he said. "We'll have a wardrobe provided for you." And with that, he turned away and began muttering into the phone again. They had clearly been dismissed.

Charlotte quickly moved toward Jason. "Deck Eighteen?" she whispered. "This doesn't look like it has eighteen decks." She motioned to the yacht around her. "It can't be more than three or four decks high."

Jason shrugged. "It has as many decks as it wants to have."

"Right," said Charlotte. Hades's Palace had seemed to be about six times as big on the inside as it was on the outside. She needn't have bothered to ask. "So, uh"—she nodded toward Kark—"he seemed nice."

"Aw, he was just showing off. I'm sorry about that. Are you all right?" he asked, putting his hand on her arm and gazing at her.

Something inside Charlotte's chest turned gooey. "Of course!" she said. "I've been thrown around by crabs twice his size."

Jason grinned. "I thought as much. Come on," he said, nodding toward the inside of the yacht, "let's go. . . ."

Other than the giant, talking, bow-tie-wearing crab, from this vantage point the yacht seemed like something any normal foreign prince or movie star might have. From the lifeboat, Charlotte had seen that the yacht had a tremendously large bow and three decks that rose above the ship's hull, with a three-level circular interior section covered in dark windows that looked like a weird wedding cake or a series of UFOs stacked one on top of the other. At the very top, behind the signal tower, was a round platform that Charlotte guessed was a sundeck. Each level had a big outdoor deck jutting out in the back, and it was on the bottom one that Charlotte currently stood. Besides the giant crab, the deck also had a big whirlpool, some lounge chairs of various sizes, and something in the back that Charlotte thought at first was a bar but proved, upon closer inspection, to be an extremely large aquarium filled with tropical fish.

"It's serve yourself," Jason explained, motioning to the aquarium.

"Oh," said Charlotte, looking toward the sky. There was a humming noise coming from somewhere; she couldn't quite place it, but it seemed to be heading toward the boat. It was growing louder and louder, and Charlotte finally realized what it was, but it seemed too weird, for what on Earth would a—

"Helicopter," Jason said as Charlotte stared upward into the sky.

"A helicopter! Here?" Charlotte's heart leaped. Maybe it would fly over the cruise ship, maybe they'd be saved, maybe Charlotte and Jason could get back on the lifeboat and go home, away from self-serve aquariums and snobby giant crabs and who knows what else that lay in wait for them, and maybe this time when Jason leaned his face into hers as they rode off into the sunset, they wouldn't be interrupted by a dog lady trying to eat her.

"Sure. Not everyone comes by boat." He squinted up at the helicopter, which was now heading directly for the boat. Charlotte couldn't be sure, but from where she was standing, it looked to be pink. "Probably a party guest."

"You mean"—Charlotte pointed upward—"that's someone coming to the yacht?"

"Sure. There's a landing pad up there, see?" He pointed up to the circular platform at the top of the boat that Charlotte had thought was a sundeck. Silly Charlotte.

She went over to the edge of the deck and leaned over the rail to look. The noise was almost overwhelming by that point, and the deck floor hummed as if in chorus. The helicopter hovered right above the small landing pad, then seemed almost to float down onto it. A man with dark hair and a dark suit got out of the copter and then reached up to help someone else out—a woman, tall and willowy with long, wavy blond hair, big sunglasses, and a long, silvery cape. Charlotte squinted up at her. She couldn't be sure, of course, but from this distance the woman looked a great deal like a certain movie star who had just won her second Academy Award for her performance as a deaf long distance runner who overcomes her handicap and her abusive father to find love and Olympic glory. Or something like that—Charlotte hadn't seen it, on account of how completely stupid it looked.

She stared up at the silver-cloaked woman some more. "Is that . . . ?"

"Yeah," said Jason.

"He invited movie stars to the party?" Charlotte whispered to Jason.

"Well, when the movie stars are Immortals. Her real name is Calypso."

Lacking anything real to say, Charlotte just nodded. She wondered how much the tabloids would give her for *that* story.

"Come on," said Jason, nodding at the doorway. "Let's go inside."

Charlotte did not know quite what she had been expecting Poseidon's yacht to look like; maybe some nautical version of Hades's palace, which looked on the inside like a (rather grim) Victorian manor. What she was not expecting was what she found when she walked through the door. While the outside had looked like any old billionaire's yacht, the inside, well, did not.

The hallway in front of her was all aqua, from the tall painted ceiling to the satin-covered walls to the thick shag carpeting on the floor. Suspended from the ceiling were large turquoise lights molded to look like the face of a man who stared down imperiously at the floor as he cast pools of blue light on it. Around each light were a dozen foot-long gold seahorses that dangled down from the ceiling. The satin walls were all covered in an appliqué to form giant glittering seascapes, with many different kinds of tropical fish in their multicolored glory, great gleaming dolphins and green sea turtles with luminous shells, a giant purple octopus and bright pink coral, and a great jungle of a sea floor made of sparkling plants of all different colors that seemed almost to sway in the nonexistent current.

As Charlotte examined the walls, she realized that every one of the flora and fauna before her was made up of countless small jewels. The red sea anemones were all tiny rubies put together with small diamonds interspersed for extra sparkle. The fish were made up of every color of jewel Charlotte had ever heard of, and some she had not. One of them, on a brooch maybe, a third of the size, might be beautiful, but all of them together, well—it looked like the student committee for the eighth-grade Under the Sea Dance had gone way over budget.

"Wow," said Charlotte.

"Yup," said Jason. "Kind of gross, isn't it."

"*Kind* of," said Charlotte. A booming noise rushed to her ears, and everything around her erupted in a tremendous shudder. Her body shook and her teeth rattled together harshly. Then, suddenly, everything was quiet again.

"What was that?" she asked, looking around. Charlotte had never been in an earthquake, but if she had, she thought that would surely be what it was like.

"Oh, nothing," Jason said, shrugging. "That's just Poseidon. He's got a bit of a temper."

"Oh, great!"

"Don't worry about it—shhh! Someone's coming!" A door a bit down the hallway opened—which was strange, since there weren't any doors in this particular hall that Charlotte could see—and an extremely large, lumbering figure made his way toward Charlotte and Jason. He was four times Charlotte's size, and as he entered the hallway, the ceiling seemed to grow to accommodate him. He looked, for all intents and purposes, exactly like the Cyclops Charlotte had seen in the Underworld, only the one in the Underworld hadn't had a patch over his one eye, nor was he being led by a Seeing Eye dog. As the blind Cyclops lumbered past, Charlotte and Jason pressed themselves against the bejeweled wall, though not far enough away to avoid the horrible smell of rancid meat that hung about him like a cloud. The Cyclops, not surprisingly, did not notice them.

"I'm just curious," said Charlotte, as they removed themselves from the wall after he had disappeared into another invisible door, "how many creatures are there on this yacht that might, at any time, eat me?"

"Well," Jason said, "not a lot." He paused a moment, considering. "There's one, two . . . maybe three. No," he corrected himself, "five."

"Five."

"Of the ones who wander loose, anyway."

"Right," said Charlotte.

"Jason! You're back!" said a voice. Charlotte whirled around to behold a tall woman with pale green skin, bright blue eyes, and a thick mane of long white hair smiling down at them. She was wearing a long, flowing, white dress with a shawl that looked like a fisherman's net made of gold, and small sea shells dangled down from her ears. Despite the green skin, the woman was beautiful, just as beautiful as the Siren, and Charlotte suddenly felt every one of her freckles burning like a pox on her face. She took a step backward into Jason's shadow.

Jason took a step forward. "Hi, Eunice. . . . I just went on a little trip. . . ."

"Well," the woman said, "you'd better go find your father!"

Jason blinked at her. "Is he back?"

"Just this morning. He's worried sick."

Jason scowled. "Aw, he doesn't care about me."

"Now, Jason," said Eunice, "your father loves you very much."

"Well, he has a funny way of showing it!"

"Didn't he take you on a mission?"

Jason rolled his eyes in response.

"Well . . ." the woman said, "he does the best he can for you." Her wide, deep, blue eyes glanced over at

Charlotte. "And"—she looked back at Jason pointedly—
"aren't you going to introduce me to your little friend?"

"Oh, I'm sorry!" He glanced back at Charlotte and
motioned her forward. Charlotte—very reluctantly—
complied. "This is Char—Charlene," he said. "She's my
date for the party."

His what? Despite herself, Charlotte felt her cheeks
reddening a bit. Well, what was he supposed to say—this
is my accomplice?

"Oooooooooh!" The woman beamed. "Pleased to
meet you, Charlene. I'm Eunice. I haven't seen you
around here before. Do you have"—her eyes looked
Charlotte up and down carefully—"Immortal blood?"

"Yeah," Jason said quickly. "Her dad's a river god."

"Oh!" said the nymph. "Oh! I see." She gave
Charlotte a sympathetic smile and lowered her voice.
"Well, that's all right, we don't have to tell anyone."

Charlotte opened her mouth as something flared up
inside of her. It was on the tip of her tongue to tell this
beautiful sea goddess (for that is what she looked like, and
in fact what she was. Eunice was a Nereid, if you want to
be precise) that she could tell whomever she wanted
that her father was a river god and she—Charlene—was
quite proud of it herself, and when you thought about it,
didn't freshwater gods have, well, a bit better *smell* to
them? But this seemed like an excellent occasion to heed

her mother's constant pleas to control her temper.

"Look, um, do me a favor?" Jason asked. "Don't tell my dad about Charlene? I want to surprise him at the party." Charlotte cast a glance at Jason. Sometimes, he thought ahead.

Eunice giggled. "I promise. It's going to be *some* party! Poseidon's going to be feeding a whole cruise ship to the Ketos."

Charlotte froze. "What?"

"Yeah, he's going to send in some helicopters and film it, and we'll watch the whole thing live! Isn't technology wonderful? We couldn't do that when it ate Troy, could we?" She let out a loud, gurgling laugh. "You're in for a real show, Charlene."

Charlotte stood frozen, her breath caught, as something in her stomach exploded in fear and horror. There was no doubt in her mind *which* cruise ship was going to be this monster's dinner.

"Wow, that's great, Eunice," Jason said quickly, grabbing Charlotte's arm. "Well, I better go show Charlene her room."

"Okay. Ta-ta!" And with that, the sea goddess gave a two-fingered wave and continued down the hallway. As soon as she was gone, Charlotte whirled around. "You said the ship was just going to float around for a dozen years or so!" she hissed.

Jason held up a hand. "I'm sorry, Charlotte, I didn't know!"

"What's he doing? What's the Ketos?" The words came tumbling out of Charlotte's mouth.

"It's a giant sea monster. And by giant, I mean several football-fields giant. Poseidon likes to sic it on people."

"He can't!" Charlotte exclaimed, as Jason held up his hand to hush her. She leaned in and whispered, "All those people! My p-parents!" As tears sprung to her eyes, she shook her head rapidly. No, Charlotte, there's no time. *"How do we stop it?"* she hissed.

"Same as the Siren," Jason whispered, looking around. "The trident. It's the only way."

"Okay!" said Charlotte. "What are we waiting for? We have to go." And she started to move down the hallway, as if she had any idea where she was going or what to do when she got there.

"Charlotte, wait," said Jason, scurrying up to her. A two-foot-high woman with bright white skin in a French maid's outfit walked past, and he lowered his voice. "I have to go find my dad before he hears I'm back."

"What?" Charlotte couldn't believe her ears.

"He's going to be so mad! Do you know what he'll do to me?"

"B-but"—Charlotte shook her head rapidly—*"sea monster!"*

Jason looked intently into her eyes. "Look," he said, "if my dad hears I'm back, he'll get really suspicious." His eyes widened in something very like fear. "He'll send everyone out looking for me, and then we'll be sunk. You should go to your room and rest, okay?"

*Rest?!* Charlotte thought. *"Rest?!"* she said.

"Just for a little while. We can't do anything now. Poseidon will be in his throne room later, and I know a place to spy on him there. Then we can figure out what to do. He'll be wandering around the ship now, greeting guests, and if he sees you now, Charlotte, it's all lost. The party's not till late. We have time."

"Time?" Charlotte felt her temper flare again, and she breathed it back. She couldn't yell at Jason; he was the only person on her side—plus he had saved her life, plus he had almost kissed her. He had gone to so much trouble to warn her and save the ship, he wouldn't lead her astray now, would he? Did she mention he had *saved her life*? If he said they had to wait, they had to wait. Charlotte might not like it, but it didn't sound like there was any choice.

"Okay," she said, breathing. "Okay."

"Come on," he said, "I'll take you to your room."

• • •

On Charlotte's cruise ship, there was a bank of elevators to take you from one deck to another. On the *Poseidon*, three floor-to-ceiling elevator-size glass tubes stood where the elevators were supposed to be. Two were empty, and one was filled with blue-green seawater. On the wall next to the tubes was a panel with two fish-shaped buttons cut out of sapphire, one with the fish pointing upward, another with it pointing down. Jason pressed the first button, which promptly lit up.

Out of the corner of her eye, Charlotte saw a figure move through the water-filled tube, and she turned and saw what was without a doubt a mermaid swimming inside of it. The mermaid had blue skin, bobbed black hair, and, of course, a long, scaly fish tail, and she moved quickly up through the shaft until she disappeared from view. Charlotte was in no mood to wonder at mermaids, but she still couldn't help but stare.

"There are whole floors on the ship that are all seawater," Jason whispered, "and that shaft connects them."

As he was talking, something began to rise up in the tube in front of Charlotte, something golden and lumpy and quite large. She watched as it rose slowly up into the ceiling, revealing itself to be a giant solid-gold head. It was the same face that had been immortalized in the hallway lights, with wide-set eyes, curly hair, and a wavy beard. The head stopped moving when it filled the length of the tube, and from somewhere above came a mechanical pinging noise. The glass tube parted in the middle, and as it did so, the great golden mouth began to open. The mouth methodically stretched all the way over the face, and when it stopped Jason nodded at Charlotte. "Well?" he said. "Get in."

As she stepped in, the mouth closed again. A low voice rumbled, "What floor, please?" and then they were off.

"This place is . . . something," Charlotte muttered, tapping her foot. Everything inside of her seemed to be moving very quickly—her heart, her blood, her breath, her thoughts, and as she stood in the elevator, she found she couldn't stop moving.

"Yeah," said Jason. "Everything is like this. And my dad wouldn't raise my allowance, can you believe it?"

Charlotte didn't say anything. She was sympathetic to Jason and his evil sea god father, and she knew he didn't mean anything by it, but it was difficult when her own parents were about to be fed to a giant sea monster. It just made all other parent troubles pale in comparison.

When the elevator let them off on Deck Eighteen, she found herself in a coral hallway—not coral colored, but rather with coral all over the walls and giant coral-shaped lamps casting a pink glow over everything. In the elevator landing stood a giant marble head about the size of Charlotte, with the same face as the gold elevator head they'd just ridden up in, and smaller versions of the same head sat decoratively on small tables throughout the hallway. Charlotte was beginning to get a good idea exactly whose visage that was.

This hallway had doorways set into the coral walls, and each door they passed had a different golden icon in it—there was a seahorse, a seal, a fish, an otter—and when they reached one marked with a seashell, Jason stopped. "The Shell Room," he said, motioning to the door. "I'll come get you soon. You rest up, okay?"

"Sure," Charlotte said, her heart speeding up again at the thought of a delay. She was conscious that her hands were trembling.

Jason reached out, picked up a strand of Charlotte's hair, and tucked it behind her ear. "You're the best," he said softly. "Don't worry. We'll go to work later this afternoon, okay? We'll have our chance then."

"Okay," mumbled Charlotte. Her brain was threatening to overload. Fear and anticipation and anger were making it difficult for her to breathe properly, her heart felt like it was trying to set some kind of speed record, and her stomach was churning harder than all the butter makers at Williamsburg. And meanwhile, despite everything, a small part of her heart still found the energy to leap at Jason's touch.

When Charlotte entered her room, she found that they called it the Shell Room for a reason. It was decorated with as much taste and subtlety as the rest of the yacht, which was to say, not much. The room itself was in the shape of a shell, and the walls and ceiling were covered in a light pink colored velvet. The floor was bumpy and strange, and when Charlotte looked down she found that it was made out of a giant fan shell sculpted in pearl. There was a large pink conch shell in the middle of the room that upon closer examination turned out to be a bed—once you climbed inside. A gold shell door led to what Charlotte assumed must be the bathroom (she didn't want to think what the toilet was like). The lamps, the light fixtures, and the doorknobs were shells, and shells made out of various jewels lined the tops of the walls. And on the far wall, opposite the bathroom, was a giant painting of a muscular blue-skinned man with a now very familiar face lying naked inside a big clamshell.

Charlotte was supposed to wait, and to rest, but there was no way she could do that, so she paced around the room and studied everything in it. On the shell desk, there was a binder much like the binder she had seen in her room on the *Isis* just a few days before, only this one was solid gold. Poseidon's head was engraved on the front, and inside was a single sheet of parchment with only the words THE POSEIDON written across the bottom. Charlotte was about to close the book when suddenly some words appeared on the page.

*Hello, and welcome to the Poseidon, the finest yacht in the Universe, designed by the Divine Lord of the Seas himself, Poseidon the Earth Shaker. How may I help you?*

"Uh," Charlotte said. She was already jittery enough; she didn't need inanimate objects talking to her.

*Would you like to see a room service menu? Would you like a schedule of tonight's entertainment? Would you like to see tonight's dinner menu?*

"Uh, no, thank you." And she quickly closed the book. She opened up the shell-door wardrobe, which was empty except for a life jacket and a full-length mirror, and just as she was about to shut it a face appeared in the mirror. Charlotte jumped.

"What may I get you?" it asked in a smoky and diffuse voice. This, for once, was not an image of Poseidon but a generic face that looked like a plain white mask.

"What?" Charlotte said, trying to regain her composure. She had an urge to slam the door, but it seemed like it would be rude. She didn't want to make the mirror face angry.

"Kark said you need a wardrobe. And"—he looked her up and down—"it seems that you might. What may I get you?"

"Uh, nothing now, thanks!" Charlotte squeaked, and closed the door as quickly as she could.

She leaned against the wall, panting. Her face was hot, and anger and fear stirred in her belly. It was no good. She couldn't wait. She had to stop Poseidon now. She wasn't just going to sit around and let him greet guests and scheme to feed her parents to a mutant sea monster. She had to do something.

With blood rushing in her ears, Charlotte dashed back over to the desk and picked up the binder again. The words appeared quickly on the parchment.

*Hello. How may I help you?*

She took a deep breath. "I need a map of the ship."

*Certainly. Would you like a map of the ship as it was yesterday, as it is today, or as it might be tomorrow?*

"Today," said Charlotte. "Right now."

*Thank you.*

Then, before her eyes, the words faded from the page and a profile of the yacht appeared, with the decks delineated. Without thinking, Charlotte placed her finger on the parchment to touch the ship, and as she did so, a plan of a deck appeared to her right. She moved her finger up one deck and the plan shifted.

Slowly, she traced her finger along the image of the yacht, watching the plans shift, until she found what seemed to be the main decks of the ship. She moved her finger over them, studying the rooms, and she saw quite a bit that looked like the deck plans of her cruise ship. There were several lounges, two restaurants, a laundry, a casino, a spa, a fitness center, but there was one room that was certainly not on the *Isis*—there, on Deck Six, the throne room.

Charlotte quickly put the binder down, opened the door to her room, and went off to find Poseidon.

CHAPTER 21

# The Earth Shaker

CHARLOTTE DIDN'T REALLY HAVE A PLAN PER SE;
Jason had said there was a place to spy in the throne
room, and she had simply decided to find it on her own.
She'd keep an eye on Poseidon and watch for when he
turned his back on the trident. Surely he didn't take it
into the bathroom with him, did he?

(Do gods go to the bathroom?)

And then what? Was Charlotte just going to grab the
thing and run? Wouldn't he try to stop her? Wouldn't
someone? Didn't he have, you know, goons? Sea goons?
What she needed was some kind of distraction, but she

didn't know what that could possibly be. Juggling probably wouldn't cut it. (And she couldn't juggle to save her life—and saving her life was, of course, the whole point.)

Deciding to take action hadn't exactly soothed Charlotte's agitation, and while she waited for the gold-head-a-vator, she found herself bouncing rapidly on the balls of her feet. She wasn't exactly calmed when the elevator opened and she discovered it wasn't empty; standing there, taking up almost the entire space, was a tremendous woman/eel creature with mud-like hair, gray skin covered in boils and what seemed to be leeches, and a long, thick, silver-gray eel tail that curled around the entire elevator floor.

"Uh," said Charlotte, "I think I'll take the next one."

The woman's swampy eyes narrowed. "Why?" she growled.

Charlotte blinked. "Um, no reason."

"Well, come on in, then."

"Right," said Charlotte, sidling into the elevator, desperately trying to avoid stepping on the tail.

Charlotte and the eel woman rode down two floors, with Charlotte trying to keep her eyes on the elevator panel as opposed to on the wiggling leeches on the woman's neck, when the elevator stopped again. The door opened to reveal a shark with man legs who grunted a greeting and strode into the elevator, standing to the other side of the eel woman. Four floors later a centaur with the tail of a fish trotted on, squeezing in between Charlotte and the eel woman. He was slightly less successful in the no-stepping-on-the-eel tail initiative, though he did excuse himself. The elevator only made it one floor before it stopped again, this time revealing three gray, shriveled hags who had no eyes in their faces or teeth in their mouths. One of them held up a glass eye and scanned the crowd in the elevator, and then all three waddled on, much to Charlotte's dismay. Everyone backed up to make room, and Charlotte ended up in a rather unfortunate position behind the centaur. Then the elevator started up again, and the whole crowd stood silently, facing front, watching the panel lights mark the elevator's descent—silently, that is, until the shark man started to whistle tunelessly.

When the doors opened on Deck Six, Charlotte found herself slightly relieved—at least until she stepped out of the elevator and remembered her mission. For suddenly she was in the foyer to Poseidon's throne room.

The foyer had a bit of a different feel than the rest of the yacht, in that it was not entirely covered in jewels. Compared to the yacht, it was almost tasteful; though it did have a vast blue rug on the floor with a forty-foot depiction of Poseidon's head. At one end of the foyer stood two imposing golden doors inlaid with pictures of dolphins.

Two huge marble statues framed the doorway, mirror images of each other, showing a well-muscled, imposing Poseidon with two dolphins at his feet and a trident in his hands. Charlotte wondered grimly if she could just take one of those. Though they did look rather heavy.

The only furniture in the room was a long bench that lined the walls. The benches had brass mermaids for legs, and the seats themselves were cushions made from a strange, shimmering leather (actually, it was the skin of the Ketos that Perseus had killed, which makes a rather durable upholstery, if you like that kind of thing).

The walls and ceiling were covered in murals—the ceiling was a skyscape with puffy clouds in a bright blue sky, and on the wall in front of Charlotte was painted a vast seascape, with an ancient town high up on a tall cliff face on one end, looking over the stirring sea. The sea itself was so vivid that it looked as if the waves were actually moving. No—they actually were moving. Before Charlotte's eyes, the waves rolled toward the cliff and crashed against its face.

Suddenly, at the other end of the mural, something began to rise up from the ocean and move steadily toward the town, something very large, something like a giant worm the size of several football fields, something with angry-looking eyes, a huge mouth, and tremendous sharp teeth. The Ketos.

Charlotte looked back toward the town and saw that something had appeared on the cliff face—a person. A woman. A woman was chained to the cliff, and the Ketos was moving toward her.

Charlotte knew this myth; this was the Andromeda story. Andromeda was a princess, the daughter of Queen Cassiopeia. Queen Cassiopeia was very beautiful but vain, and she proclaimed that she was more beautiful than all the sea goddesses, so Poseidon sent a sea monster—the Ketos—after the town. When the king and queen saw the monster coming, they decided to sacrifice Andromeda to the Ketos in the hopes of appeasing Poseidon, so they chained her to a cliff. But as the monster rose from the sea, the hero Perseus came by on his winged sandals and killed the Ketos, then freed Andromeda, and they lived happily ever after. Though Andromeda did have some issues with her parents.

And there he was on the mural, handsome Perseus, flying through the air on his winged sandals. He stopped when he saw Andromeda chained to the cliff and the monster coming out of the sea, then he swooped down toward the Ketos and—

—and the Ketos ate him.

Charlotte scowled. Talk about your revisionist history.

As the mural reset itself into the original seascape, Charlotte heard a loud creaking noise—the doorway to the throne room was opening. Quickly she ducked behind one of the statues. She was staring at its thighs, but if she looked up, she would be staring right at its statue butt. She chose not to look up.

A woman's tinkling laughter emerged into the hallway, followed by a booming male voice, and Charlotte carefully peeked out from between the legs of the statue. Right in front of her was a woman with wavy blond hair, a silver cloak, and big black sunglasses. The movie star—Calypso. And the man next to her, well, Charlotte had seen his face many times that day. This man was about ten feet tall, with light blue skin, dark blue curly hair, and a thick wavy beard with wide-set eyes, and he was the image of the statue Charlotte was hiding behind, only this man was—fortunately—clothed. Or, rather, unfortunately clothed; he wore white silk pants and a white silk suit coat and absolutely nothing else—except the three huge gold seahorse necklaces that hung down on his chest, dangling among a thick carpet of dark blue chest hair. On his head was a tremendous gold crown that had starfishes cut out of jewels all around the brim, and in his left hand he carried a solid gold trident.

Poseidon.

Charlotte's heart flipped as several emotions welled up inside her. There was fear, yes—one might even go as far as to say there was horror, for it is one thing to know intellectually that you have to take on the God of the Seas, another thing to see that god in the flesh, see how very god-like he looks, as if he could turn you into a water beetle at a glance, and, in fact, he probably would.

But along with the fear, there was also anger—one might even say rage—filling Charlotte's small frame, from her toes to the very tips of her ears. There was Poseidon, the man (okay, the god) who would so callously murder hundreds of people, who had put her own parents in mortal danger—just because he didn't like people messing with his descendants. Even if his descendants were *evil*. He was going to imperil people—her parents—for the sake of his own ego, and the thought made Charlotte's very eyes burn. She wanted to run out, to scream, to kick him and pound on him and tear him apart—but of course she could not. So she merely stood behind the statue and seethed, thinking of all the things she could do to Poseidon when she got the trident.

"I'm so glad you could make the party, Calypso,"

Poseidon was saying. "It's going to be huge! Everyone will be talking about it."

"I wouldn't miss it!" said Calypso brightly.

"Of course you wouldn't. Everyone's going to be there. Everyone who's *anyone*, anyway!" With a loud laugh, Poseidon casually placed his hand on the mural-covered wall, and before Charlotte's eyes the wall opened up to reveal a wide, gleaming staircase topped with a lush red carpet.

"My designer told me not to make the staircase of solid gold," Poseidon said as the pair mounted the stairs, "that it was impractical, but I said that nothing is impractical when you're the Lord of the Seas! Then I threw him in the ocean. The next designer didn't complain at all. HA!" As he laughed, he pounded his trident on the stair, shaking the whole floor. Even Charlotte's statue trembled.

"It certainly is beautiful!" Calypso enthused.

"Yes, yes, it is. It's magnificent! The *Poseidon* is the grandest, most beautiful yacht in all the Universe! Of course it is. It's named after me!"

Poseidon and Calypso were disappearing up the staircase, so, mustering all her secret agent skills garnered from years of television and movie watching, Charlotte took a deep breath and ducked out from behind the statue.

As she crept up the staircase, she was particularly glad she had worn sneakers—as opposed to, say, her clunky boots or slappy flip-flops. If you're going to prowl around a Greek god's yacht, sneakers really are the only choice.

Charlotte stayed a flight behind Poseidon and Calypso, peeking up at them through the railing as the staircase circled around, ever watchful for any stray centaurs or sea hags who might come up from behind her. But no one did—this staircase seemed to be For Poseidon Only.

"I'm thinking of getting into movies," Poseidon said, his voice floating down the staircase. "Strictly behind the scenes, of course, but everyone important will know who's responsible. You don't see Zeus making movies, do you?"

"I don't," said Calypso.

"Of course you don't! Zeus doesn't have the imagination. That's what you need to really make a name for yourself, you know. . . . I'll have to set up a front company, of course. Poseidon Productions! What do you think?"

"It's wonderful. I hope you'll let me be in your movies."

"The best actress in the world? Of course. Only the finest. We'll get you another Oscar. And one for me, too!"

"Just one?" Calypso asked flirtatiously.

The pair reached the landing two flights above the throne room deck, and as Charlotte watched, Poseidon motioned Calypso down the hallway. Deck Eight, Charlotte calculated, remembering her map—on which lay the casino, the fitness center, a souvenir shop, and the Constellation Lounge.

Charlotte darted up the stairs and into the hallway just as the wall was closing in around Poseidon's staircase. When she emerged, she found that this hallway was surrounded by a foot-deep tank that demarcated the walls, floor, and ceiling. The tank was filled with bright blue artificial-looking water and a bunch of mechanical sea life made out of jewels and precious metals. It would have been something to stop and consider (as in, consider *why*) but Charlotte didn't have time to look at the scenery.

As she moved down the hallway, she heard light footsteps coming up rapidly behind her, and then someone brushed quickly past her.

"*Signomi,*" said the offender in a high, musical voice. Charlotte had no idea what that meant, but she was too busy staring at the woman before her to really consider it. She was not that remarkable, really—she was a delicate-looking woman, only slightly taller than Charlotte, with a bone white face and elfin features.

She wore a white button-down shirt, black pants, and a bow tie, but what was so interesting to Charlotte was her hair—long, flowing, and a deep, rich shade of red.

The elflike woman scurried past and down the hallway, slipping into a side door, while Poseidon and Calypso went through two big glass doors at the end of the hall. With a passing glance toward the disappearing back of the redheaded creature, Charlotte dashed through the long faux-aquarium hallway and into the Constellation Lounge.

Poseidon and Calypso were standing right in the doorway, so Charlotte ducked behind the nearest potted plant to listen. Poseidon still had his trident firmly in his hand, which he waved around as he talked.

"As you see," he declaimed, "I've decorated the lounge with replicas of the constellations, but my constellations are made out of illuminated diamonds, and I think they're much more beautiful than the ones in the sky, don't you agree?"

"Oh, yes!" breathed Calypso. "Much!" Charlotte got the distinct impression that she really liked diamonds. "And . . ." Her eyes searched around the room. "Your waitstaff. Are they . . . mortal?"

"Goodness, no!" Poseidon said. "They were once. They're from an island whose king failed to make a sacrifice to me after an auspicious year, so I sank the island

and enslaved the females. HA! They were such good workers that I made them Immortal. It's so hard to find good help these days."

"You're telling me!" Calypso enthused.

Charlotte peeked through the leaves of the plant at the lounge and almost gasped at what she beheld. Milling around the lounge setting the tables were two dozen of the creatures she had seen in the hallway, all in the same black-and-white uniform, with the same dark red hair.

Now, Charlotte, as you may recall, had always enjoyed being a redhead; in fact, she found it truly preferable to any other hair color. It was a state of being one could really embrace. It had made her almost unique, or at least interesting. But these women were from an island where everyone was redheaded, and now Charlotte realized that the only thing better than one redhead was twenty redheads. The island these women had been from must have been a wonderful place. Before Poseidon sank it in an egomaniacal rage, that is.

"Well," Poseidon said, "I believe the entertainment should start soon. Would you like to sit here with me and have a drink before dinner?"

"I'd be honored, my Lord," gushed Calypso.

"Dinner's going to be something really special. I got a shipment of the finest caviar in the world. The whole dinner will be caviar tonight—caviar mousse for the first course, caviar soup, caviar salad, caviar with caviar sauce for the main course, and caviar ice cream for dessert. Only the best on the *Poseidon*!"

As Charlotte watched, the two gods began to move through the lounge to a group of plush seats on an elevated platform in the front corner. One of the waitresses immediately rushed toward the pair, and as Poseidon ordered, Charlotte saw him do something absolutely extraordinary: *He leaned his trident against the wall.*

Charlotte's heart skipped a beat, her breath caught, her every nerve stood at attention. The trident was right there, out of his hands, just leaning there minding its own business, completely unaware that it could be snatched.

Charlotte's hands clenched as if she were holding the trident already. She could taste her victory. She wanted so badly to get it, to thwart all his plans, to make him pay for what he had done. It was so close.

But how? She couldn't just run into the room, grab the thing, and dash out. Poseidon was right there, and he was certainly going to notice. There just wasn't any way for Charlotte to get close enough without causing suspicion, and she really didn't want to get zapped or fed to something icky.

But she had to get it now. Poseidon was going to be here until dinnertime with his trident out of his hands—and who knew when Charlotte was going to get another chance.

She bit her lip and studied Poseidon, studied the trident, studied the room. And then the idea came to her in a flash—Charlotte had a plan. And there was no time to think about whether or not it was a good one.

A few minutes later and Charlotte was back in her room. It was getting dark now—outside her shell-shaped window the moonlight danced over the blue-black sea. Night was falling on the *Poseidon*. Time was running out.

Charlotte went over to the wardrobe, opened the shell door, and stood in front of the full-length mirror.

"Hello?" she called.

A moment, then the familiar face materialized. "What may I get you?" it asked. "Perhaps a gown for dinner?" He eyed her up and down. "I think green satin might be just the thing. . . ."

"No," Charlotte said, "no. Can you get me one of the waitress outfits? That they wear in the Constellation Lounge?"

The face frowned. "Why would you want something like that? It's for the staff." His nose wrinkled up slightly, and Charlotte rolled her eyes. Wasn't he staff too? Charlotte didn't know where a magical mirror face wardrobe attendant fit in the whole hierarchy thing—but apparently *he* did.

"Can you get it or not?" Charlotte snapped.

"Of course I can get it," he said haughtily. "Will you be needing anything else?"

"No. No, thank you."

"My, so polite," he said drily. "Wait one moment." The face in the mirror disappeared for a second, then returned holding in its hand (and no, it had not had a hand a few seconds before) a suit bag. "Your outfit," he said, nodding slightly as if to bow. And then the white hand reached out through the mirror and handed the suit bag to Charlotte.

Well.

She quickly undressed, shutting the wardrobe door first for a little privacy, and put on the uniform—which fit perfectly. (Charlotte wasn't exactly surprised; it wasn't like she was expecting the magic mirror face to bring her an outfit from magic mirror land that was a bit snug around the waist.) Then she opened up the wardrobe again to study herself.

She looked like she was about to play at the eighth-grade band holiday concert.

It might work, Charlotte reflected. It would be dark in the room. But if she got too close, someone would notice it was all wrong; Charlotte's face was not exactly elfin, and she hadn't seen a lot of freckles on any of them.

"Um, sir? Mr. Mirror Man?" she asked, and the face appeared again. He eyed her outfit, and a white eyebrow went up. "Do you have any, um, makeup?"

The other eyebrow rose. "Ask the bureau," he said laconically.

So Charlotte closed the wardrobe door and went over to the bureau mirror, and in a few moments had secured herself some very pale foundation and some powder, which she applied quite liberally. Then she stepped back to admire her handiwork.

It was still more eighth-grade-band-concert than elf creature—or maybe now it was eighth-grade-band-at-vampire-school—but it was going to have to do.

Charlotte was about to let herself out of her room when she suddenly remembered—Jason!

She'd been so busy thinking about Poseidon she'd completely forgotten about him. Had he come by? Had he found her gone? Did he think she'd been eaten by a giant squid? Was he worried? He was probably very worried; Charlotte would certainly be worried in the same situation, and she was smarter than he was.

If she waited, just a little bit, maybe he'd come. He could help her; maybe distract Poseidon while she ran off with the trident. Even if not, well, it would be nice to have him along. Plus she was going to have to make a quick getaway, and she didn't intend on doing that without Jason.

In a fit of hope, Charlotte poked her head out and looked down the hallway, but there was no sign of him. She closed her eyes and sighed. She had to go; it was now or never. She had to get the trident, run to the lifeboat, hurry to the cruise ship, battle the Siren, wake everyone, and get the heck out of Dodge long before any Ketos tried to make lunch meat out of the *Isis Queen*.

Charlotte went over to the desk and pulled out a *Poseidon* notepad and a *Poseidon* ballpoint pen and, after making sure the paper wasn't sentient, scrawled:

> Jason—
>     Went to the Constellation Lounge to watch the show. Meet me there?
> —Charlene

Charlotte folded up the note, wrote Jason's name on the outside, attached it to the shell on her door, then headed back to the Constellation Lounge.

CHAPTER 22

Pucker Up

When Charlotte arrived, she found that in
the time she'd been gone it seemed every sea god and
creature on the yacht had come to the Constellation
Lounge for some before-dinner entertainment. A
quick scan of the room showed you could pretty much
put a fish tail on just about any animal if you tried hard
enough, from a lion to a wolf to a goat to a kind of
giant iguana-kitty thing. There were humanoid creatures in just about every shade of flesh (sometimes on
the same person) and various combinations of extrane-
ous appendages, from fins to horns to scaly body

armor to tails to extra heads. A giant tank came out of one wall, and inside it a whole group of mermaids and mermen sat in some lounge chairs of their own. It was a lot like the City of the Dead, except fishier.

Charlotte's eyes quickly went over to Poseidon, who was still in a corner with Calypso. Others had joined them—a tall goddess with a crown and what looked like lobster pincers coming out of her forehead (Poseidon's wife, Charlotte realized, Queen Amphitrite); a younger god with a horse bottom, a fish tail, and a giant conch shell around his neck; and what seemed to be a huge dolphin sitting in a chair, munching on some peanuts. All five were listening intently to the singer onstage. Meanwhile, the waitresses bustled around the room, bringing drinks back and forth from the bar to the tables.

It was nice and dark in the room, with the only illumination coming from the stage lights, the artificial stars, and some small table lights (actually, they were luminescent jellyfish swimming in little fish bowls, but Charlotte wasn't close enough to see that)—dark enough, perhaps, to mistake a thirteen-year-old vampire school band concert refugee for an Immortal sunken-island waitress elf.

Perhaps.

So, her heart in her throat, Charlotte plunged into the lounge and made her way toward the bar.

Her plan wasn't that complicated. In her outfit, she'd be able to move around the lounge unnoticed. She'd keep her eye on Poseidon, and when he seemed to be engrossed, she'd move over quickly and take the trident. No one was paying attention to anything but the singer and their food and drink, and with any luck, Charlotte could just sneak out and make her way to the lifeboat as quickly as she could. And Jason—well, Jason would come and find her.

Charlotte knew it wasn't the greatest plan ever hatched, but it was, at the very least, a plan—and it wasn't like anyone else was coming up with anything better. It was the best she could do under the circumstances, and as her gym teacher always said, all you can ever ask of someone is that they give their best.

Resolutely, Charlotte made her way through the seats toward Poseidon's box; she'd seen a nice corner behind the box where a girl could hang out relatively unnoticed, but as she passed by a table full of fish-tailed monkeys and other assorted simians, she was suddenly yanked back. Something had her by the shirt.

As she jerked violently, trying to right herself, she saw the creature that had her—it was a giant, grayish blob with what must have been a hundred hands, and its slug-like eyes stared at her dully.

"Touch-y," it drawled, releasing Charlotte. "I just wanted to know what someone has to do to get some ahi tartare around here."

"I'm sorry," said Charlotte. "I'll be right up with that." (Not.)

The slug's eyes narrowed. "You don't sound right," it said.

"Oh, I have a—a cold. Let me get you your food."

Charlotte started to step away, but a hand grabbed her again and she was thrust right up to the blob's face.

"You don't look right either."

Charlotte froze. Suddenly, from the corner of the room, there was a loud thumping sound, and the whole room trembled. Everyone and everything in the lounge went still, from the singer to the waitresses to the mermaids in the tank to the jellyfish candles.

"Uh-oh," the big slug muttered, dropping Charlotte and turning languidly over to Poseidon's box.

Poseidon was standing up, clutching his trident, and staring down at one of the waitresses while the other people at his table did their best to look away.

*"What is this,"* Poseidon growled, menacing the waitress with a small tumbler of a yellow, creamy liquid.

The waitress took a step back. "It—it's your ambrosia, my Lord."

He pounded his trident on the ground again, and

once more, everything shook. "I ordered it *on the rocks*," he spat.

"No, Sir, I'm sorry, but you ordered it straight."

At the sound of her words, everyone in the room gasped. Charlotte's every nerve was standing on end.

"*What?*" Poseidon yelled.

Realizing what she had done, the woman gasped and clasped her hands over her face, backing up two more steps. "My Lord, I'm so sorry," she breathed. "I was wrong. Let me get you your drink. I'm so sorry." She took another step back, as Poseidon seemed to grow before all of their eyes.

"You dare correct me? You dare? In front of all these people? On my yacht? You think I'm stupid or something? You think I'm crazy? You don't think I know what I ordered?"

"No, no, Sir, I—" The waitress had backed into a chair just two feet from Charlotte and was pressing against it.

"I'll show you," he boomed, lifting the trident up. The waitress screamed, and in one fluid motion, Poseidon pointed it directly at her. As Charlotte watched, frozen, a stream of green light came shooting from the trident and hit the woman. A burst of light surrounded her, and before Charlotte's eyes she began to shrink. She shrank to half her size, and then more.

Her body was changing too, her arms shrank into her torso, her legs fused together, her face narrowed, and her eyes began to bug out. As one, every single person in the room turned their eyes away as the waitress shriveled up and fell to the ground. Charlotte didn't turn away, though—she couldn't even if she'd wanted to. She was absolutely frozen. She watched as just feet in front of her, what was once a redheaded elf woman became a small goldfish, its eyes bugged out in horror, flopping around on the ground and desperately trying to breathe.

"HA!" exhaled Poseidon majestically. He gazed meaningfully around the room, then turned to his entourage. "Come on!" he proclaimed. "Let's go." And with that, Poseidon stalked out of the room, shouting the whole way.

Silence in the lounge. The goddesses left quietly, followed by the dolphin, who scooted out quickly on his fins. More silence, the only noise Poseidon's voice disappearing down the hallway. Or almost the only noise; Charlotte felt she could hear the goldfish gasping and its tail pounding against the ground desperately. Of course she couldn't hear, of course it was too small to make any real noise, but nonetheless the sounds seemed to pound in Charlotte's head, in her whole body.

And then the piano started playing again, and the singer started singing, and chatter filled the room. Charlotte heard someone say, "A goldfish again?"

She looked around. No one was going to do anything. Resolutely, she rushed over to the goldfish, whose tail was now beating softly against the ground and whose gills were open as if to the heavens, and picked her up by the tail. A yellow-skinned god with a rainbow-colored shirt saw her and gaped.

"What are you doing?" he hissed.

"Saving her!" Charlotte hissed back.

The god looked right and left, then back at her. *"He'll know!"*

Charlotte glared at him, her eyes flaring. *"I. Don't. Care!"* And she stood up, dangling the fish by her fingers, walked over to the nearest table, and gently plopped her into the small fishbowl lamp.

And then, from right next to Charlotte, came a silky voice. "Well, well," it said. "What have we here?"

The skin on Charlotte's neck prickled, and a great shudder passed through her body. She knew that voice.

Charlotte's head rose slowly, almost unwittingly, to find the source of the voice, and her eyes beheld what her heart already knew. She had come face-to-face with Philonecron.

It had never occurred to Charlotte that he might be

on the yacht; she'd been so occupied with her new enemy, she'd forgotten all about her old one.

She could not move—terror and shock had completely frozen her, and she simply stood there, staring in horror at the god-demon who had been haunting her nightmares for five months.

Philonecron was no happier to see her, and when her eyes met his, the sneer on his face was replaced by surprise, then pure rage.

"*You!*" he breathed.

Charlotte began to back slowly away, as if somehow that would help matters, as if she could turn time backward with each step, as if Philonecron would simply shrug and give up if she moved away from him.

But he did not give up. He straightened and narrowed his eyes and hissed, "You can't have him back. He's mine now."

"Wha—" said Charlotte, her terror replaced for a moment by bewilderment. For no reason that she could identify, a very ill feeling washed over her, as if somebody had run his fingernails down the great chalkboard of the universe. Suddenly Philonecron was next to her, grabbing her arm and wrenching her away. Something in Charlotte's brain registered that he was in a wheelchair and his legs hadn't quite grown back, but somehow that didn't make the situation any less terrifying.

"Aren't we brave," Philonecron whispered, pulling her over so her ear was right in front of his lips. Charlotte was aware of a great and terrible coldness surrounding him. "Coming all the way over here, playing the hero again. It's very touching, really. Inspiring, even!" He wrenched her arm up farther, and tears sprang to Charlotte's eyes. "But, alas, it is all for naught. You are going to die tonight, my plucky young friend." Philonecron ran a long, cold finger along her jaw. "You were going to die on your mortal ship, but here is just as good. Either way, my dear, you are going to die."

And with that, Philonecron threw her to the ground, tapped twice on the table, and called, "Security!"

Suddenly a hole in the ground opened up underneath Charlotte, and she plummeted into darkness. She was inside some kind of metal tube, half sliding, half tumbling downward in pitch blackness. Down she went, turning head over heels, slamming against the metal walls, flailing for something to grab onto. Her left hand hit one part of the smooth, cold wall just as her body bounced off the other, and her wrist twisted, sending pain shooting up her arm. Still she fell on.

It may have been only a few seconds, it may have been an eternity that Charlotte fell through the twisting, turning tube before she saw light again. It was streaming from somewhere below her, and she was falling into it—no, she was falling through it. And then, suddenly, the tube ended, and Charlotte tumbled out into a vast, bright room. She landed on the floor with a bang, her whole body crying out upon impact. Cradling her wrist, she looked upward and realized she was lying in a heap right at Poseidon's feet.

Charlotte was in the middle of the vast throne room, and it was impossible, really, that she could have landed so far in the middle of the room, it was impossible that she was here at all, for there was no evidence of any tube, any chute, any opening in a wall—there was just Charlotte, huddled and broken, and Poseidon, towering and terrible.

The throne room was like the rest of the boat, only more so. Images of Poseidon were everywhere, from the murals on the walls and ceiling to the carvings in the trim to the statues and busts, even the relief on his throne. At the end of the room, two great iron automatons with long spears blocked the big golden doorway. And in a nook in the back corner of the room, the giant dolphin sat at a desk flipping through Poseidon's correspondence.

Poseidon stared down at Charlotte, eyes flaring.

"Charlotte Mielswetzski," he intoned threateningly.

Charlotte huddled on the floor at his feet, shielding

her eyes from the strange glow his blue skin seemed to give off.

"Who do you think you are?" he spat. "How dare you? How dare you come on my yacht?"

Charlotte opened her mouth, but nothing came out. It didn't seem like he wanted an answer anyway.

"Did you want to humiliate me in front of my guests, is that it? Did you think that you would show me up?"

Poseidon's voice filled Charlotte's ears and reverberated through her head, then her whole body, so at every word she trembled.

"You want to take us all on? Is that it?" he sneered. "You thought that you could just waltz around my ship like you did the Underworld? You thought I might let you go like my pantywaist brother did? Hades is nothing. Nothing!"

He hit his trident against the ground, and the whole room shuddered so hard Charlotte's teeth knocked together.

"How did you get here? Who helped you? *Who?*" He banged the trident on the floor again.

"N—nobody," Charlotte stuttered.

"Nobody? Nobody? You're a mortal. You didn't get here by yourself."

"Why not?" Charlotte said, gasping slightly. "I got to the Underworld by myself."

Poseidon raised his eyebrows. It wasn't entirely true, of course. Philonecron had lured them into the Underworld. And she had had Zee.

"You have powers, then?" Poseidon asked, beginning to pace back and forth slightly. "Vision? Prophecy? Does that make you feel that you somehow have the right to challenge the gods? You?" He banged the trident on the ground again—*boom!* "A mortal?" *Boom!* "A child?" *Boom!*

Charlotte's whole body convulsed with the shaking of the floor, every muscle screaming from her fall down the chute. There was nothing she could say. There was nothing she could do. Poseidon had caught her, and she was going to die. She was going to die right here, and her parents were going to die too, and Ben the nice waiter, and Bettina the stewardess, and a whole cruise ship full of parents and children and husbands and wives and friends and cousins were all going to be swallowed up by a sea monster.

And it was her fault. All her fault. She'd acted too rashly. She never should have gone out on her own. She should have waited for Jason; he'd told her to wait. He knew the ship. He knew what he was doing. They could have worked together. But no, Charlotte had to go off on her own in a head of steam, and now hundreds of people were going to pay with their lives. Her mom and dad were going to pay with their lives.

Tears sprang to Charlotte's eyes, and she bit her lip and tried to blink them away. She was not going to give Poseidon the pleasure.

But he noticed, and his mouth spread in a hateful smirk. "Are you going to cry? Are you? Didn't take much, did it?" he cackled. "You think you're so strong, but you're weak. All mortals are weak. Go ahead, cry. Show me how brave you are, Charlotte Mielswetzski." And then he burst out in a deliberate, mocking laugh.

Well, that was too much. It was bad enough that he was going to kill her, he didn't need to make fun of her as well. It wasn't like she had anything to lose by talking back to him. He couldn't kill her any *harder*. (At least, it seemed better to believe that.) Drawing herself up slowly, she scoffed, "Yeah, I'm pretty weak. Just ask your legless grandson." Poseidon stiffened and slammed the trident on the floor again so hard that Charlotte bounced up in the air, then came down with a crash.

"How *dare* you? How *dare* you? You are nothing! You are vermin! You are scum! You are *mortal*!"

"If I'm nothing," Charlotte coughed, trying to ignore the screams of her bones, "why did you go through all of the trouble of punishing me?"

"Why? Why? Because you meddled with one of my descendants, mortal, and you must pay for it!"

"What was I supposed to do? He was trying to overthrow the Underworld! He was going to throw the Dead into Tartarus!"

"It was none of your affair."

"Of course it was. I'm human!"

*Boom!* (Bounce.) "That is why it was none of your affair. You cannot meddle in the doings of the great gods!"

Charlotte's head was a haze now, a muddle of pain and fear and anger and grief, her body was battered and bruised, and Poseidon still stood over her. He was horrible, he was worse than Philonecron, he was worse than Hades, he was petty and vindictive and hateful and he was a god and he had all the power and she had none. But she was not going to let him see her break. She was going to keep her strength until he killed her.

"Why shouldn't I meddle? Someone has to! You don't care about people at all!"

"Care about people? Why should I care? It's not enough for you to be able to worship us, you *want* things." He set his face in a sneer, and his voice grew high and mocking: *"Poseidon, protect my boat from the storm! Poseidon, save my village from the tidal wave! Poseidon, I'm drowning. Save us, Poseidon, save us!"* He scoffed. "Why should *I* help them?"

Charlotte couldn't take it anymore. As Poseidon ranted, she picked herself up off the ground. One foot on the floor, then the other, then she pushed herself up—oh! Not with that hand—so she was standing almost at her full height, despite the loud protests of her muscles and bones. It was nothing, she was barely above Poseidon's kneecaps, but at least she was up. She stared up at him, eyes full of fire, and hissed, *"Because you can."*

"You!"—his eyes narrowed into little slits—"You vermin. You dirt. You think you can tell me what to do? You think you can speak to the gods? Well"—he spread his hands out—"if you are so eager to be in my world, let us see how long you survive in it."

And with that, Poseidon lifted his arm toward Charlotte, and an invisible force pulled her up from the ground. Up, up, up she went, then hung in the air for a moment, and Poseidon, arm outstretched, leered up at her. The wall in front of her began to open up, and before Charlotte could see what lay behind it, she shot through the opening like a cannonball. Room after room whizzed by her, and then suddenly she was through the yacht's walls and into the dark of the evening. The next thing she knew she was hovering several yards away from the yacht, staring down at the open sea. The water roiled beneath her, and in the blackness, she saw a large shape move just underneath the water's surface. And then, whatever force that had her let her go, and Charlotte plunged toward the night-black sea.

CHAPTER 23

## Sir Laurence Gaumm

CHARLOTTE WAS PLUMMETING THROUGH DARKNESS, this time with no metal chute to guide her way. She tumbled through the night air, head over heels over head, toward the moon-capped waves. Time slowed to a crawl as her body rotated in uncontrolled freefall, she was utterly conscious of moving slowly toward her doom. The air was thick with the rushing and roiling of waves, and some other sound too, something high-pitched and loud, something that Charlotte eventually recognized as her own screams.

As the surface of the sea came toward her, there was

some displacement of the water and the air and everything below her seemed to grow only more black, as if
the moon itself had been blotted out. Frantically
Charlotte tried to take in as much breath as she could—
as if that would help, as if there were any way out of
this—and then she lost control of her senses entirely. It
was just black, all around, and she was falling, and there
was no direction anymore, no sense of up or down, of
body or time, and then—

*Thud!* Charlotte hit something. Not water, but
something else, something soft and sticky. Then it was
as if the world suddenly collapsed from under her, and
she tumbled downward along a strange, wet surface. She
slid and slipped and slurped and then—

And then everything was still. Well, not everything—
Charlotte had a distinct sense of motion, of some sort of
pressure change happening around her, as if she was in an
airplane coming in for a landing. But she was no longer
falling, and the aftershock of her experience hit her and
she began to gasp for air, to shudder and shake, as tears
poured down from her eyes. Her stomach roiled and she
vomited—once, twice, three times—and then she collapsed on the strange, gummy floor.

Charlotte was insensate with residual terror, and it
took her some time to gather herself enough so that
she could process her surroundings. But even once she

had finally gone from gasping and crying to trying to analyze her current predicament, she found herself with absolutely no conception of where she was. She was in total blackness, and her eyes would not adjust. As she lay in a heap on the soft surface, she could not even see the ground inches from her face. She had expected to be in water, she should be in water, she had been falling toward water; yet as she waved her hands around in the air, it was clear that it was just that—air. But there was no moon.

No, she was not outside anymore. She was inside something, very definitely, something without an opening or even a crack for light. It was as if she had been sealed inside—which perhaps she had been, perhaps Poseidon had chosen to prolong her death by sealing her in a trunk and sinking the whole package to the bottom of the sea. If given a choice, Charlotte would have preferred the quicker death, but no one had asked her.

Slowly she began to crawl around, feeling her way with her hands, at least to get an idea of how big her current prison was. If she was indeed in some kind of weird container at the bottom of the ocean floor, she was really most curious to find out how much air she had left. The very thought made her lungs constrict, and she automatically took in a deep breath as if to reassure herself that she still could. Her lungs filled with strange, sour air, and Charlotte retched.

"Gross," she muttered to herself.

Then, suddenly, the ground beneath her feet moved, and Charlotte was knocked off balance. She let out a yell of frustration, and then something very strange happened.

Something spoke.

"Pardon me?" The something said in a voice that echoed all around Charlotte.

Charlotte fell back, and something came out of her mouth, something that might have been a "Whaaa?" but was possibly just a yelp.

"Pardon me," it repeated, "is there someone there, please?"

The voice seemed to surround her. It was somehow omnipresent in Charlotte's strange chamber, as if the walls themselves were speaking.

Charlotte leaped to her feet and looked around frantically. "Hello?" she whispered into the darkness.

"Hullo, hullo! Are you in there?"

Charlotte looked around wildly. "In where?"

"Oh, dear, oh dear. Oh, bother!"

"What?" Charlotte exclaimed. "Who are you? Where are we?"

"Oh dear," said the voice, "this is dreadfully embarrassing, but . . . well, dash it all—there's no really good way to say this, I'm afraid, so I'll just out with it. I seem to have swallowed you."

"*What?*"

"Quite. It's ill-mannered of me, but I'm afraid it was an accident, miss. Couldn't be helped, really!"

Charlotte narrowed her eyes, trying to pierce through the darkness. Was this a joke? If so, it wasn't a very funny one. But whoever was talking was, she had to admit, not inside the room with her. And if she were really to consider the matter carefully, she would determine that it wasn't quite like the walls were talking, as she had previously thought, but rather as if Charlotte were inside the closet of her bedroom back home and the house suddenly started talking. Or, frankly, as if she were somewhere inside the stomach of a very large beast that was now having a conversation with her.

Charlotte stood poised in the darkness, every nerve on end. "Did Poseidon feed me to you?"

"Gosh! No! Upon my honor—"

"Then who are you? What are you?"

A coughing sound, and the floor underneath Charlotte's feet vibrated. "My name, miss, is Sir Laurence Gaumm, at your service. I was once an English gentleman, but now, well, now, the deuce of it is . . . I seem to be a giant squid."

"Uh-huh," said Charlotte dully. After all her worrying, she had, in fact, been eaten by a giant squid.

"Well," Sir Laurence continued, "perhaps the naturalists might have a more technical name for me. But I am a something very like a squid, certainly, and I am most decidedly giant. In fact, I am twice the size of the yacht you just descended from so surprisingly. But my manners are beastly! The Lady Gaumm—that is my sainted mother—would be most appalled. Please forgive me. Whom have I had the honor of swallowing?"

"Uh . . ." Charlotte said, "I—I'm Charlotte Mielswetzski." This was absolutely the weirdest conversation she had ever had in her life. She didn't know what to think. The squid—Sir Laurence—didn't seem like he was going to kill her any time soon; unless, that is, he liked to talk to his food before digesting it. Charlotte wasn't that familiar with the eating habits of giant squid.

"Mielswetzski? Gosh! And you're American? I do so like the Americans. So spirited, our brethren across the sea!"

"Yes! Yes, I'm American. But look . . ."

"Sir Laurence."

"Yes, Sir Laurence . . . are you planning on eating me?" It seemed like a good idea to get to the point.

"Gosh, I mean, gosh! No! I assure you, this is a most unfortunate accident. You see, I—Sir Laurence

Gaumm, giant squid—was swimming close to the surface and saw you being tossed off the side of the yacht and I thought—well, it's very embarrassing, really—that you were a bag of parsnips. I am excessively fond of parsnips. Especially steamed with a good lot of butter—but, you know, you can't have everything."

"Right," said Charlotte, growing slightly impatient. She had to find a way out of there and back onto the ship, though it seemed in her current situation, it was best to humor Sir Laurence. As he talked, she began to explore her environment, looking for an escape route. (Preferably through the mouth . . .)

"But I now realize you are not a bag of parsnips, or if you are, you are an excessively well-spoken one, and I most certainly do not want to eat you. Do you think that you might remove yourself from the upper chamber of my stomach? I would hate to have you fall through and begin to digest you. I am a vegetarian. I didn't used to be a vegetarian, you know. I liked a good suckling pig and venison sausage just like the next fellow. But it is different once you've been turned into a sea monster and you are asked to eat your aquatic compatriots, who are really stand-up fellows—"

Charlotte stopped. "A sea monster?" she interrupted. "Are you the Ketos?"

"Oh, my, no. I am an English gentleman. The Ketos is

no gentleman, I assure you. He's not even English. Dreadful chap. I'd stay as far away from him as possible."

"Okay," said Charlotte.

"Well, by the by, Miss Charlotte, it seems we are in accord. I have no wish to eat you, and you do not wish to be eaten. A happy coincidence, what! So, if I were to open my mouth quite wide, perhaps you could see your way clear to wandering up to my mouth and then you might, as it were, swim off? I'll count to ten, and, well, off you go, then!"

"No!" exclaimed Charlotte. "It's night! I'll die!"

"Die?!" Sir Laurence exclaimed. "Are you mortal?"

"Yes!"

"Oh, well, that's a different kettle of fish. Mortal! Good gracious! I don't mean to intrude, but, times being what they are, well, young lady, I would recommend most heartily that you stay as far away from Poseidon as possible. He's quite dangerous, you know."

"I gathered that," Charlotte muttered.

"Mortal! Just think of it. I was mortal once! At the time I thought it was an unfortunate condition; now I realize it's quite something to cherish! Well, Miss Charlotte, that's neither here nor there. It would be most ill-mannered of me to deposit you in the middle of the Mediterranean Sea at night. What would Lady Gaumm say? So how's this: I shall gallantly swim over as close to shore as I can get, and we shall wait until the sun is up to warm your passage, then you shall swim the rest of the way to safety, and we shall all go on with our lives, such as they are. A bracing morning swim off the beaches of Sicily. Capital!"

"No!" Charlotte exclaimed. "No! I have to get back on the yacht!"

Sir Laurence paused. "My dear Miss Charlotte, why would you want to go back *on* the yacht? It seems to me you were just tossed *off* it. And believe you me, you got off lucky. I'm not sure the Lord of the Seas would take kindly to your reappearance. He's not a very nice fellow."

"Tell me about it," muttered Charlotte.

"Ah, very well, I shall," said Sir Laurence, clearly unfamiliar with idiom. "Many years ago I was a happy fellow, a decent sort. Perhaps a little overfond of a game of cards here and there, but being a sporting gentleman at heart is hardly something to earn one reproach, is it? But that's neither here nor there. The year was 1912. I was in Venice with Lady Gaumm and my sisters, the Miss Gaumms, and I got caught up in a game with a fellow. Well, it came suddenly to be between him and me and I staked quite a sizable sum, and the gentleman—if I can call him that—when he put his hand down, well—not to put too fine a point on it—but I saw him draw an ace from his sleeve.

"So, a gentleman cannot let those things stand, you know, so I said, 'Sir, I say, sir!' and, well, called him out! And, well, next thing I knew I was a small, squirmy thing with tentacles. Really, they're most unwieldy— I've grown quite a bit, you see. I've been following him around ever since, trying to convince the old boy to let it go, but there's no reasoning with that chap."

"Yeah, I know," muttered Charlotte. She'd hit upon a strange part of the stomach wall, something thin and elastic. She poked it.

"Gosh!" exclaimed Sir Laurence. "What are you doing down there? I don't want to be rude, but that tickles! Gosh!"

"Sorry," Charlotte said, smoothing her hand over the thin area. It was no use. Even if it was the exit, there was no way to activate it that she could find.

Sir Laurence sighed. "There's just not much to do down here, and a giant squid can only eat so much plankton. So I follow the yacht along, and every once in a while Poseidon comes out on deck. At first I thought I might sort of, you know, present myself to him as per- haps someone with whom one does not want to trifle. I do not think he intended for me to get quite so large, you see.

"But it matters not. The rogue shot me with that

dreadful trident of his, and the fact of the matter is, it hurt like a bear. Then he informed me, waving the dread thing, that if I made one move toward him, he would turn me into chum. Chum! I, Sir Laurence Gaumm! Well, I must tell you, I would rather be a giant squid than chum, so recently I changed my tack and tried to appeal to the man's better nature. Unfortunately, I don't think he has one. Usually he just waves his trident at me and laughs. Really, it's not very sporting."

"Uh-huh," said Charlotte, leaning against the wall.

"Well, Miss Charlotte," Sir Laurence continued, "the point is, I should not advise going back on that yacht. Whatever you have done to merit the undignified treatment you received earlier, I do not imagine Poseidon wants to see you again. So, shall we make for the shore, you and I?"

"No!" Charlotte exclaimed. She needed Sir Laurence to let her out, and there didn't seem to be anything to do but tell him why. Time was running out. "Okay, Sir Laurence, look," she said. "Poseidon is having a party tonight, maybe even now, and at that party he's going to be showing everyone a cruise ship being eaten by the Ketos. And on the cruise ship are hundreds of people including"—tears suddenly welled up in her eyes—"my mom and dad."

"That cad!"

"They can't get away!" she exclaimed, voice trembling. "He sent a Siren to the ship and she hypnotized everyone and suddenly we were in the Mediterranean and the ship wasn't moving and Jason appeared and he told me about the Siren and that the only way to stop her was to get Poseidon's trident. . . ."

There was a moment's silence. "The trident?" Sir Laurence said slowly. "You're going to steal his trident?" He paused, thoughtfully. "And how, pray tell, are you going to do that?"

"I don't know," said Charlotte. "I mean, I think I can get it from him. Maybe. I have an idea." The words surprised her when they came out of her mouth, but she realized they were true. She had an idea. Or at least the germ of an idea. Poseidon was angry, impulsive, proud— and it had occurred to Charlotte when Sir Laurence was talking that those were character traits she understood very well.

"But," she continued, "I don't know if it will work. And even if it does, once I get the trident, I don't know what to do. I don't know how I'm going to get away. Poseidon can stop me with his bare hands, he proved that when he dumped me in here. But I have a friend on board, Jason, I thought he could keep Poseidon busy somehow, I don't know how. But I have to try. Please," she said, her voice cracking, "I have to get back."

Sir Laurence paused. "Well, Miss Charlotte," he said slowly, "I wonder if perhaps we might help each other?"

Charlotte and Sir Laurence talked for a long time, working out the details. Charlotte was not going to run off half-cocked this time. Her anger had gotten her absolutely nowhere—except in Sir Laurence's gullet. She was going to have a plan, a solid, definite plan, one much better than grabbing the thing and running. She was going to have a plan that had a chance—maybe not a big chance, but a chance, anyway, of working.

It took some doing for Charlotte to get out of the upper chamber of Sir Laurence's stomach. The thin part of the wall where she had been poking around earlier led, in fact, to the middle chamber of the stomach, where he assured her she very much did not want to be. Charlotte had to feel her way to the opposite end of the chamber and find the flap that separated the stomach from the esophagus. Sir Laurence was kind enough to surface for a moment and open his mouth so a touch of moon shone through the top wall of the chamber, and to Charlotte the light seemed like an embrace.

She spent some time trying to make the flap open, to no avail—it was designed to be opened from the other side, after all—with Sir Laurence dissolving into fits of giggles as she poked and prodded. Finally Sir

Laurence suggested he might lie on his belly and take in a bit of water, and she could grab the flap as it opened—being extremely careful not to get flooded and swept down to the lower stomach chambers, which he said would be a nasty business indeed, so Charlotte pressed herself against the curved stomach wall and waited while Sir Laurence took in a gulp of the sea. Water rushed its way down the long esophagus, then pushed the flap open and entered the chamber.

Charlotte hung back until the rush had stopped, climbing as far up the wall as she could to avoid getting wet, with only moderate success. Then the flap began to swing closed, and she sprang forward and grabbed it, using her best gymnast strength to propel her way to the other side.

Charlotte had had a number of unusual experiences over the last few months, from having her shadow nearly stolen to journeying down into the Underworld to riding across the river Styx with the Ferryman of the Dead to being set upon by a shadow army to absolutely everything that had happened today. But none of those unusual experiences were quite like crawling up Sir Laurence's esophagus. It was dark and sticky and smelly, and there was seawater up to her thighs, and something in the air made Charlotte's eyes feel that they were going to burn off. Charlotte had to use the wall to guide her. It was an icky sort of pliable wall, covered in a gooey substance she dearly hoped was plankton. Sir Laurence did his best to hold steady, but every once in a while he bobbled, and water splashed all over Charlotte, covering her in goo. It was sort of like going down the long passage to the Underworld, only a lot stickier.

Eventually she found herself in Sir Laurence's mouth, which had a distinct odor of rotted plant. She hung on to something (she didn't want to know what) while Sir Laurence swam carefully right up to the side of the yacht. Then he opened his mouth, and moonlight streamed in. Slowly, carefully, Charlotte squeezed herself between two large teeth, then reached for the boat, and as her hand touched the hull, the ladder appeared.

"Well," said Charlotte. "Here we go."

"Quite," mumbled Sir Laurence. He held his mouth open carefully as Charlotte climbed out and onto the ladder, her lungs expanding to drink in the sea air as Sir Laurence's head began to submerge itself into the sea.

Charlotte quickly turned her head toward him. Before her were the top halves of two great lantern-like yellow eyes, which gazed at her gently, surrounded by a vast darkness. For a moment the two stared at each other, the girl and the sea monster, while the waves danced around them in the moonlight. Sir Laurence's big eyes blinked twice, then he began to rise out of the water again to reveal a long, dark mouth.

"Good luck, old girl," he whispered. As Charlotte hung on to the side of the yacht, the tip of a massive tentacle wrapped itself around her shoulders and squeezed softly.

Tears popped into Charlotte's eyes. "Thank you, Sir Laurence."

And with that, he was gone, leaving barely a ripple on the surface of the water.

## CHAPTER 24

# Party at Poseidon's

THERE WAS AN ENTIRE MARINA'S WORTH OF BOATS anchored next to the yacht now, and as Charlotte climbed up the ladder, she heard voices chattering, chirping, squawking, and growling on the deck. She prepared herself to be grabbed by Kark, but as she peeked over the rail of the deck, she saw the crab was occupied with six tall, green-haired sea goddesses in glittering evening gowns. Quietly she slipped over the rail.

She didn't have any idea what time it was, but the moon was high in the night sky and the yacht was aglow with festivity. Lights festooned the ship, some in the shape of sea creatures, some replicas of Poseidon, and some, rather mockingly Charlotte thought, in the shape of tridents. Colored balls of flame hovered in the air, and up in the night sky the constellations seemed to dance. The yacht, in other words, was decked out for a party.

With a pounding heart, Charlotte straightened herself up and began to walk down the deck, feeling her black cocktail waitress shoes splurch with water with every step. As she passed, heads began to turn and watch her, and noses began to curl up, almost as if there was something about her that was quite distasteful.

Charlotte looked down. She was completely soaked and covered absolutely everywhere in splashes of green goo. Strands of seaweed were intermixed with her long hair, and judging by everyone's reaction to her, there seemed to be something very strange about her smell.

Her heart sank. It was no good. For her plan to succeed, she had to look completely unharmed, and not look (and smell) like she'd recently been dragged through sea manure. But was there time?

She looked around frantically, then, mustering as much dignity as was possible, approached a small bass-headed man in a tuxedo.

"Excuse me," she said. "Has the party started yet?"

"Not yet," said the fish in a nasal voice. "Soon. We're going to make our way up there in about half an hour."

He gazed at her seriously. "You know how Poseidon likes punctuality."

"Thank you," said Charlotte formally, moving quickly away.

Half of her still wanted to rush to find Poseidon, to try to get the trident now, but she needed to orchestrate everything carefully. She needed to clean herself up, to change clothes, and she needed as many people at the party as could possibly be there. For once in her life, Charlotte Mielswetzski had to be patient.

She took a deep breath. *There's time, Charlotte,* she told herself. *Do it right this time.* Then she tossed her seaweed-filled hair, stalked through the deck door, and headed for her room.

Twenty minutes later, Charlotte had eaten a package of trail mix from her backpack and was clean, dry, and dressed. It had taken her a few moments to pick her apparel—after all, she had a magic wardrobe at her disposal—but after some consideration, she had settled on a black leather jacket, a white shirt, and crisp blue jeans. Mr. Mirror Face was not particularly happy about her party attire, but she wasn't wearing it for him. Then she stood in front of the mirror and examined herself; before her eyes was a small, pale, freckled girl with long red hair held back in a ponytail, green eyes flashing above a stylish black leather jacket. She did not look like someone who was going to take on a god, but she did look like someone who had a good personal shopper. And maybe that was enough.

Charlotte exhaled. *Come on,* she told herself, *it's now or never.* Then, with a defiant flip of her ponytail, she left her room.

Charlotte had just assumed the party was going to be in the Constellation Lounge, but when she got there the lounge was empty save for two octopi in a hot tub in the corner snacking on some lobster rolls. Frowning, she left the lounge and headed back toward the main deck. As she went through the aquarium-lined hallways, she passed by the glass windows of the library, and her eyes fell on two tremendous creatures—one who seemed to be all mouth, and the other an unpleasant-looking blue-skinned woman. Strange shadows leaped on the wall around her, as if a fire danced beneath her legs. There was something familiar about the two monsters, something that filled Charlotte with unease, but as she came closer her eyes left them entirely. For sitting next to them in deep conversation was someone small and dark-haired and indubitably human, someone with large green eyes and scruffy hair, someone who made Charlotte's heart stop. Jason Hart looked up, saw her through the window, and burst through the door.

"Charlotte!" he exclaimed, coming toward her. "Where have you been? I've been looking everywhere for you. Are you all right?" Jason was dressed for the party, and it looked like he'd made some attempt to get his hair under control.

Relief washed over Charlotte, and something very like happiness, if you are allowed to feel happiness when you are about to take on Poseidon. "Jason," she exhaled, "you're here!"

Jason enveloped Charlotte in a hug. She was quite glad she'd bathed. "Oh, Charlotte, I'm so sorry," he breathed, beginning to lead her down the hallway, away from the library. "My dad—he was so mad, and he wouldn't let me out of his sight. I should have known! I never should have gone to him, I was just so scared he'd get suspicious! And then I got to your room and got your note, but you weren't in the lounge and everyone was eating dinner and—"

"Jason, it's okay. I'll explain it all later. We have to go now. The party's starting. Do you know where it is?" Charlotte had done an excellent job of being patient, she thought, but it was time to act.

"Yes, yes, it's on the top deck."

"Good. Can you take me there? Now?"

"Charlotte"—he looked at her, eyes wide—"you can't wear that. You have to be in formal wear. If

Poseidon sees you like that, he'll be furious! You don't know what he does!"

"I have some idea," she muttered. "It's okay. I promise. He's already going to be mad enough when he sees me." The thought gave Charlotte a small chill. "Anyway, a girl can't exactly run in formal wear. Now, we have to go!"

"Okay, okay," Jason said, moving down the hallway. He looked to see if anyone was in earshot, then whispered, "Are you getting the trident?"

Charlotte set her jaw. "Yes," she said firmly. "Yes, I am."

Jason sucked in some air. "How?" he asked, his voice full of danger and excitement.

But Charlotte just shook her head. "There's no time. You'll see. Just be ready to run to the lifeboat." She stopped. "You are . . . coming with me, right?"

"Charlotte!" He stared at her, letting his hand slowly graze her arm. "Of course!"

She smiled. "Okay. Let's go."

Jason and Charlotte took the elevator up to the top deck of the yacht along with several other party guests, all of whom were careful to look disdainfully at Charlotte's outfit.

"Who is she?" she heard someone whisper.

"I hear her father is a river god," came the reply.

"Well, no wonder!"

When the elevator opened, Jason and Charlotte

stepped into the hallway. In front of them two vast doors stood open, and guests flooded their way inside. Jason stopped, grabbing Charlotte's shoulder. "Emergency exit," he whispered, pointing to a barely visible door in the wall. "It's just five flights down to the main deck."

Charlotte nodded solemnly, then the two entered the ballroom.

The party had already begun. The deck was filled with a menagerie of gods and sea creatures in tuxedos and long dresses standing and talking—you wouldn't think that a Cyclops or a man with a lobster for a torso could pull off evening wear, but you'd be surprised—while the elfin waitresses circled with trays of crystal champagne glasses filled with ambrosia.

The ballroom was a giant, glass-walled square room, not entirely conforming with the dimensions of the ship. Large, brightly colored seahorse-shaped free-floating lanterns moved through the air as if they were swimming in it, and a great crystal chandelier hung in the center of the room, looking ready to squash anyone who claimed it wasn't the most gorgeous of its kind. The floor was made of small pieces of coral in a huge mosaic that showed Poseidon riding his chariot over a vast seascape, and it was covered in a layer of diamond dust that didn't look that different from the stuff that

Charlotte used to paint her toenails for her eleventh birthday party. Like the lounge, the back end of the room was filled with a giant tank, and Charlotte saw a few mermaids with tiaras floating near the top. Against one wall was an orchestra that consisted entirely of human-size starfish who played their instruments with any number of their five arms. The stage was framed with two giant marble statues of you-know-who holding tridents up over the proceedings, as if to bless them. Or, perhaps, as if to turn everyone into goldfish.

"Where's Poseidon?" Charlotte whispered to Jason as they stood near the doorway, surveying the room.

"He likes to make an entrance," Jason said.

"Typical," muttered Charlotte. She surveyed the room carefully. "Okay," she said to Jason, "I'm going to go hide by the stage, behind the statues. You should mingle. Act naturally. Is there someone you can talk to? Is your dad here?"

"No," said Jason, rolling his eyes. "He's working. He doesn't like parties. Poseidon lets him get away with it because he's usually doing his bidding." Jason scowled while Charlotte stared at him impatiently. "But," he said quickly, catching her look, "I'm sure I can find people, no problem."

"Good, good." She surveyed the room quickly. "Okay," she said. "I'm going to go hide behind that statue and wait. I just want you to be near the door, ready to run, okay?" Her chest tightened with worry. But what was she doing? Jason could take care of himself just fine. He'd gotten to the *Isis Queen* all by himself, he'd saved her in the Strait of Messina, he could handle himself. But that didn't mean Charlotte wanted him any nearer to danger than he had to be. She was growing soft.

"Be careful," whispered Jason.

"You too," said Charlotte. And then she slipped through the crowd, heading toward the orchestra.

Despite her inappropriate attire, no one paid much attention to her as she moved through the ballroom—maybe because they were all too occupied with their own conversations, or maybe because most everyone was three times her size and didn't spend a lot of time looking down. For whatever reason, Charlotte made it to the stage unscathed, and she quickly ducked behind one of the well-muscled statue legs and prepared to wait.

More people flooded the room, and still more, and Charlotte had never known how many Immortals there were in the world. Nor how many people who seemed to be mortals weren't—she saw another movie star, a newscaster, some foreign minister, and a pop singer she'd liked when she was younger but would never admit it if you asked her now. The vast ballroom was packed with monsters and creatures and gods—and one small mortal girl, hiding behind a statue five times her size, waiting for the god it portrayed.

And then the trumpets sounded, a great rumbling passed over the room, and the seahorse lanterns moved into a circle in the air, all looking toward the center of the room. The fish-tailed, horse-butted god that Charlotte had seen earlier blew dramatically on his conch shell. Everyone in the ballroom moved quickly toward the walls—a good thing, as the mosaic beneath them began to spread apart. The orchestra broke into a fanfare, and as the crowd watched, a great hole opened in the middle of the floor. The seahorse lanterns bowed, and slowly, majestically, Poseidon came rising up from the ground poised imperiously on a golden horse statue. He might have required his guests to dress in formal wear, but Poseidon himself was wearing only loose white silk pants and one giant gold necklace bearing a huge medallion of his own visage. The ground closed in around the horse statue while Poseidon held absolutely still, giving everyone in the room ample time to admire him. Finally, after a full minute of this, he moved his trident around in the air with a flourish, then dismounted. Another flourish and the golden horse came to life, rearing up with a loud *neigh*, making all the party guests move farther back. With another whinny and a shake of his impressive head, the horse took off in a gallop through the great hall and out into the lobby, leaving party guests scattering in his wake.

Everyone in the ballroom burst into applause. Poseidon nodded gracefully, then strode over to the orchestra and picked up a microphone. Charlotte, her breath catching in her throat, instinctively moved farther behind the statue leg.

"Hello," Poseidon told the crowd, his voice booming. "Thank you for coming to my party. It gives me great pleasure to see so many people enjoying the finest yacht in the Universe!"

Everyone applauded again.

"Eat, drink, and be merry, for we are Immortals, and it is our due. I hope you'll say by the end of the night that this was the greatest party in the history of the gods!"

More applause. Poseidon surveyed the crowd and added, "Even Zeus himself cannot throw a party like this!"

At this, the applause wavered slightly, and people began to look around nervously. Poseidon stiffened, and something dark crossed his face. The crowd quickly amplified their clapping and he relaxed.

"Now," he proclaimed, "please enjoy yourselves. And at midnight we will have a small demonstration of what

happens when you cross Poseidon the Earth Shaker!"
Poseidon waved his hand in the air, and two giant wall-
size movie screens unfurled on either side of the orchestra. Another wave of his hand and an image appeared on
them of a cruise ship bobbing listlessly in the night sea.

Charlotte had to suppress a gasp. Murmurs of appre-
ciation filled the room while she fixated on the screen.
Her ship looked so strange—lifeless, like a corpse of a
cruise ship floating along across the waters of eternity.
But it wasn't a corpse, it wasn't lifeless, there were hundreds of people in there, including the two people
whom—despite their prodigious flaws—she loved best
in all the world, and who loved her best in all the world.
And none of those hundreds of people knew it, but
underneath their thick Siren-induced haze, they were all
counting on Charlotte to save them.

Poseidon was still talking, something about the party,
but Charlotte couldn't hear—her ears were buzzing too
loudly with grief and anger and fear. Poseidon waved his
trident in the air and as a school of dolphins jumped over
the yacht in perfect synchronicity, the starfish orchestra
changed suddenly into a five-piece sea nymph band, with
the musicians themselves also not in formal attire, or
much of any attire at all. If Charlotte had not had other
problems, she would have commented quite loudly on the
disgusting display of sexism.

As the band started playing again, Poseidon strode off the stage and into the crowd, while followers milled around him sycophantically. Charlotte, meanwhile, could not take her eyes off the screens. Tears filled her eyes as in the back of her mind she saw the Siren's victims sitting helpless and oblivious to their fate. How could she save them? She was just a girl, one girl, just Charlotte Mielswetzski, redheaded eighth grader, gymnast and cat owner, daughter and cousin, student and friend and victim of the world's longest and most unjust grounding. What could she do against the whims of a god?

Well, it didn't matter what she could do, for that was not the point. The point was what she had to do, which was pull herself together and get to work. And while it felt like she was alone, she was not, for she had Sir Laurence and she had Jason Hart. And that wasn't all—she had her friends and her family. Okay, they weren't there with her; most of them had no idea where she was and some of them weren't even conscious. But she could use them. She needed them all, every single one of them. She needed her mother's careful rationality, her father's unalloyed optimism, Maddy's intelligence, and Zee's—yes, Zee, her Lulu cousin, whom she would happily forgive if she ever saw again—quiet strength. She needed them all—mixed with just a dash of Charlotte Mielswetzski impudence.

Tearing her eyes away from the cruise ship, Charlotte tried to pull herself together. It was hard; all her parts seemed to have their own agenda. Her stomach felt like someone had thrown it over an open flame, her throat was drier than any desert on Earth, her hands burned with cold, and her chest tugged as if she might vomit up her esophagus itself. Though her lungs were stiff and made of iron, Charlotte did the best she could to take a deep breath. Her eyes fell on a crowd of gods in front of the statue, laughing and drinking their ambrosia. One pointed to the stranded cruise ship and they all chuckled loudly, while Charlotte's eyes narrowed. Then she flipped her ponytail and climbed up onto the stage.

The band was in the middle of a song, and as Charlotte strode along the stage, full of bravado, the nymphs eyed her quizzically. Most of the people on the dance floor were consumed with flattering Poseidon, and the few who did notice her only glanced curiously at her. She skimmed the room for faces friendly (Jason) and not (Philonecron), but she saw no one she knew, besides Calypso, who was flirting with the foreign minister. Trying to ignore the thundering of her heart, Charlotte walked up to the front of the stage and, as the song ended, turned to the singer nymph and said, her voice cracking slightly, "I need your microphone."

The singer nymph looked at her skeptically. Charlotte straightened. "Poseidon wants me to have it," she added.

That was all it took. The nymph handed the microphone to her quickly, as a few more heads from the dance floor turned to investigate this strange interruption in their music. Charlotte stalked up to the very front of the stage, and two of the seahorse lanterns floated above her accommodatingly.

It's time, she told herself. You can do this, Charlotte. Of course you can. You have journeyed to the Underworld, defeated a Footman, confronted Hades, outwitted Philonecron, made a B+ in algebra. Charlotte Mielswetzski had saved humanity from an eternity of torment; she could certainly save a cruise ship full of history buffs. Adrenaline rushed through her, and suddenly everything in the room looked sharper, brighter. The roar of the crowd quieted, and she was distinctly aware of every detail of her own presence. She set her jaw and tapped the microphone.

"Hello," she said, voice calm and clear. "Could I have your attention, please."

Heads turned, first a few, then more, as the party guests took notice of this strange figure. Behind her the nymphs looked on curiously. In the back of the room, Poseidon, oblivious to the change in program, still held court, listening intently as a few Nereids admired his chest pendant.

"Good evening," Charlotte said, gazing steadily out into the room. "I'm Charlotte Mielswetzski."

Silence, then, for a moment, as her words spread around the room. Then a cascade of gasps, and Charlotte heard mutters of "That's the mortal," "Underworld," and "Philonecron."

A roar came from Poseidon then, and every single god, man, woman, beast, and all the combinations thereof ducked as one. He swung his trident in the air and yelled, *"How?!"*

Some of Charlotte's bravado faded, but she struggled to give no sign. "I guess I'm just tougher than you," she said, shrugging. "He tried to kill me," she told the audience matter-of-factly, "but it didn't work."

The crowd gasped as one, and Poseidon swung his trident around wildly. "Someone's helping you!" he roared. "Who is it? Who? Come forward and I'll be merciful."

Charlotte was pretty sure that was a lie. "No one's helping me. I told you before! I did it all by myself." Out of the corner of her eyes, she saw people surreptitiously scurrying out of the room. Over by the door, she saw a flash of scruffy dark hair, but then it was gone. "You tried to kill me, but I stopped you all by my mortal self."

"*Yearrrrgh!*" Poseidon gargled, pointing the trident at her. Charlotte blanched slightly as a murmur passed through the crowd. "Just tell me how you survived, you pathetic mortal," he spat. "Is Zeus helping you? Does he want to bring me down? Isn't he content with the skies and the Earth—now he wants the seas as well? I'll kill him. I'll flood Olympus. *Tell me!*" He shook his head and looked out at the crowd. "That's the only way she could live," he told the crowd. "Zeus must be helping her. I'm the second most powerful god in the whole Universe."

"Not true," Charlotte said. "I'm afraid you're just not that powerful, and now everyone here knows it." Now it was Charlotte's turn to address the crowd. "I mean, really, you're all scared of him, but I beat him and I'm only in the eighth grade. Besides," she added, looking back at Poseidon, "how much power can you really have if all you do is wave that trident around, huh? What kind of a god needs a magic wand?"

More murmurings through the crowd.

"I'll kill you with my bare hands," he growled, storming up to the stage, pushing people aside as he went.

Charlotte gasped, and for a moment the words she needed to say stuck in her throat. He was coming at her and he was going to kill her unless she could find the strength to say:

"I bet I could do anything with it you can."

The words tumbled out of her mouth in a rush, and Charlotte staggered as if to try to catch them. Stupefied by her gall, Poseidon stopped his rush toward Charlotte and stared at her, his eyes full of fury. She waited, heart in her throat as he contemplated her, his chest rising up and down rapidly with his fevered breaths. Meanwhile, the crowd around them looked from god to mortal, muttering darkly to themselves. What were they saying? Charlotte couldn't hear, but everything depended on it. Had she planted a seed of doubt in them, and if so, had Poseidon heard it? This was what she was counting on to save her, to save them all—his reckless vanity. Maybe, just maybe, if he felt his subjects had the tiniest bit of doubt, he would play Charlotte's game. It was the only way.

The murmuring spread through the room like ivy, and a tendril worked its way slowly up Poseidon's body until it reached his ear. Poseidon turned his head and began to look around the room, his eyes drinking in his guests' reactions, and something in him seemed to waver. Charlotte took in a quick gasp of air. She had him.

But just as quickly as the moment had come, it went, and Poseidon's head snapped back to Charlotte, his face hardening in a smirk.

"Oh," he growled. "You want my trident, do you? Is that what this is about?" He held his arms up and looked around, as if to let the whole room in on their conversation. "You think you can just use this and become like a god? You think you can defeat me with it?" He laughed cruelly. "Fine, then, mortal, take it."

And with that, Poseidon hurled the trident in the air, and it came spinning toward Charlotte. She reached for it, desperately, but, as if with a mind of its own, it moved out of her reach, then swung around in the air, and the handle hit her squarely on the back and knocked her down on the stage. A rumbling of laughter went through the crowd.

"Foolish mortal!" Poseidon proclaimed, cackling. "Did you think you would use my own trident to defeat me?"

Smarting, Charlotte picked herself up, but the trident dove at her again, sweeping under her legs and knocking her backward. She landed on her back with a thud.

"You wanted to play god, did you?" Poseidon thundered. "You humans are always overreaching yourselves. Can't you be content to be beasts?"

As Charlotte tried to stand, her every muscle screaming, the trident whirled around in the air so it was aimed spears first and sped toward her, then stopped, poked her tauntingly in the back, and spun around and banged into her stomach with great force.

All the air left Charlotte's body, and she crawled on the ground, trying desperately to put breath back into her lungs. Her chest felt as if it were made out of steel; it would not move. She gasped and gasped while the immense crowd looked on and the trident backed up, readying itself for another strike. Finally, her lungs filled again, and Charlotte slowly backed herself away, trying not to yelp as pain radiated through her back.

"That's all you are, you know. Beasts," Poseidon snarled. "It's not our fault someone chose to give you fire and make you aware of us. We allowed your creation, and how do you repay us? All you do is want. Want, want, want, want, want!" At his words, the trident moved back and forth in the air, as if to shake its finger at Charlotte. "Did you think you would take over my kingdom? You'll never understand. We're gods! There's nothing you can do to us!"

The trident dove in again, and Charlotte rolled out of the way. The thing zoomed past her and circled around again, hovering menacingly just out of her reach. Gathering every bit of strength she had, and quite a lot she didn't, Charlotte made a lunge for the trident.

"Oh, you still want it?" Poseidon said. "Well, take it! By all means!"

Suddenly the trident fell into Charlotte's outstretched hands, and as soon she touched it she screamed again. It was white-hot. Her hands recoiled, and the trident clattered against the ground.

"What?" he taunted. "What's wrong? Can't you handle it?"

Charlotte's hands were burning, her back was screaming in pain, her whole body felt broken. This was going to go on all night, he was going to attack her with the trident until she died. If she was lucky, she would die before the Ketos attacked the cruise ship and she would not have to watch, but Charlotte Mielswetzski was not feeling particularly lucky.

The trident sat on the floor a few feet away from her while Poseidon continued to berate her. She had one chance. Charlotte gritted her teeth, tucked her hands inside her stylish leather jacket, and, ignoring every pain in her body, lunged for the trident. Poseidon laughed again as Charlotte wrapped her jacket-covered hands around the handle. She picked it up—she expected to barely be able to lift it, but it was surprisingly light—and as the leather began to sizzle, she reeled backward and slammed the trident into the ground with all of her strength.

It was nothing like when Poseidon did it. The floor rattled, the walls rattled, but it wasn't like the whole ship was going to break apart. Still, it was something. She hoped it was enough. It had to be enough.

"Ha!" Poseidon proclaimed. "Good one, mortal! Now, why don't you bring that back to me. . . ." He held out his hand and suddenly a great gust of wind stirred behind Charlotte and before she could react, it began to push her toward the laughing god. "What shall I do with you this time, Mortal?" he said. "Clearly drowning was too good for you." Charlotte struggled to break free from the wind, but she was helpless as it pushed her toward Poseidon and her doom.

And then, *boom!* A green tentacle the size of a bus came crashing through the starboard wall. Glass shattered everywhere, and the tentacle swept through the room, knocking a group of gods off their feet. *Boom!* Another tentacle came through the port wall and landed with a huge crash on the stage, sending chunks of coral everywhere. *Boom!* A squid arm came crashing through the ceiling, sending the crystal chandelier smashing to the ground. Sir Laurence had gotten her signal.

"What the—" Poseidon said, whirling around. The wind stopped abruptly and Charlotte fell backward, tumbling to the ground. The trident dropped out of her hands on impact, and she scurried toward her prize, the pain in her body receding to the back of her mind. It didn't matter now. Nothing mattered but the trident. Charlotte grabbed it again, expecting her hands to burn, but Poseidon's spell had broken and now the gold handle was just warm to the touch, the temperature of life, and as her hands wrapped around it, it hummed eagerly. Charlotte held the trident close to her and tore off toward the door.

A loud yell came from Poseidon, and he turned to Charlotte, raising a hand to her, and then—*crash!*—one of the squid arms came flying out of the darkness of the night sky toward him, smashing him to the ground. People ran in every direction, as glass and coral and wood and crystal went flying everywhere. The sea-horse lanterns flooded toward the doorway. As Charlotte followed, a group of Immortals made as if to stop her, but she waved the trident around as if it were a torch protecting her from a roomful of snakes. And then a tentacle came bashing through the ceiling, and the gods around Charlotte scattered.

Poseidon was up off the floor now, screaming in rage, sending all the debris in the room sailing in a concentrated stream toward Sir Laurence's arms. But every time one got hit, another attacked the room again, knocking Immortals over like bowling pins. Again Poseidon went down on the floor and Charlotte sped toward the door. Later she would think of her injured back, her battered bones, her seared hands, her beat-up muscles. Later. It didn't matter now—all that mattered was getting through that door.

Around her, minor gods and sea creatures were scurrying everywhere, some trying to fight off Sir Laurence, others running for the doors. The air filled with shrieks, the sound of destruction, and the enraged yells of Poseidon.

Charlotte burst through the doorway into the hall, where, huddled in a corner, white and shaken, was Jason Hart. "Charlotte!" he exclaimed, relief washing over his face. "I—I thought he was killing you!" he stuttered. "I couldn't watch! And then people came running out and said there was a sea monster, and—"

"It doesn't matter!" She whirled back around and pointed the trident toward the two giant, heavy, wooden ballroom doors. She had absolutely no idea how to work the thing, but in her head she thought, *Shut*, and a burst of blue flame came out of the trident. And the doors swung closed. That was easy enough. *Seal*, she thought, then as more blue flame came out, she turned back to Jason and shouted, "Get me out of here!"

CHAPTER 25

## Surprises

Jason grabbed Charlotte's hand and led her through the emergency exit door and down the stairs. Every movement amplified the pain in Charlotte's body, but she had so much to worry about that the pain wasn't exactly at the forefront of her mind. There were five flights of stairs between them and the main deck, then once they got there, there was a long hallway and expanse of deck to get across and a ladder to climb down in order to get to the lifeboat. Nothing else mattered.

The walls shook, and crashing noises filled the air as they ran down the stairwell. Charlotte sent a mental message to Sir Laurence to keep the ship together long enough for her to get off it. Four flights of stairs left, then three, then two, then—

One flight above the main deck, Jason turned off and opened the stairwell door, motioning Charlotte through. "Come on," he shouted, "this way!"

"But the lifeboat's down here!"

"I know a shortcut! Come on!" A particularly loud crash reverberated through the walls, and the door Jason was holding open fell off one of its gold hinges. "Let's go!"

He started running down a long residential hallway, and Charlotte followed. Down the hallway they went, ducking pieces of debris and falling Poseidon busts, as Jason kept calling, "This way! Come on!"

Then, suddenly, in the middle of the hallway, he halted before one of the doors. "Come on," he whispered urgently, "he's in here!"

Charlotte halted, utterly bewildered. "Who? Jason, we have to go!"

Jason flung open the door to reveal the old man in the aqua suit. Charlotte gasped. She'd completely forgotten about him. And now he was on Poseidon's yacht.

She stared at Jason, dumbfounded. Meanwhile, the man in the aqua suit was staring at Charlotte.

"What's she doing here?" he said, his voice like crackling leaves. He turned to Jason, eyes flashing. "Jason? What did you do?" Another bang hit the ship, and everyone flinched. "What's going on? Did you do this?" He held up his hands to indicate the chaos.

"That's right, Dad!" Jason snarled. "I did!"

"*You* did?" Charlotte exclaimed. Then, "That's your dad?" There were so many things to be confused by, she didn't know where to begin.

"Go ahead," Jason said, voice full of excitement, turning to Charlotte. "Do it."

Charlotte blinked, mouth hanging open. "Do what?"

Jason motioned to the trident. "Blast him!"

"*What?*" cried Charlotte.

"*What?*" cried the old man.

"Blast him! Come on, you can turn him into whatever you want! How about a frog?"

"No!" Charlotte shouted, unable to believe her ears. "Come on, we have to go!"

"Aw, it'll be fine," Jason said dismissively. "Come on, do it!"

"Jason!" said the old man.

"I'm not going to blast your dad!" said Charlotte.

"Thanks, Charlotte!" whispered the old man chummily. Charlotte stared at him. Why was he talking like he knew her?

"Why not?" Jason said. "He's *evil*!"

Charlotte whipped her head back to him. This was getting really tiring. "Because!" she exclaimed, stumbling to the right as another crash shook the yacht.

"Well, then, give it to me and I'll do it!" Jason reached for the trident.

"But," Charlotte protested, gripping her prize close to her body, "you said . . . you can't handle the trident. You have Immortal blood. You said there was a spell on it and it would fry you. . . ."

"Oh," he said with a shrug, "I made that up."

"*What?*"

"Well, I wanted to get back at my dad, and the trident's the only thing that has power over him, and—"

"Jason," interrupted his father, folding his arms, "you're grounded."

Jason ignored him. "I couldn't get Poseidon's trident myself! I'm not *crazy*. He'd kill me! But then I thought you might do it! I mean, you took on Philonecron and Hades. . . ."

"What?" But Charlotte didn't need any further explanation. Jason Hart didn't care at all about her or her parents or all the people on the cruise ship. He hadn't gone to the *Isis Queen* to save her or to save the ship. He'd gone just to trick her into getting Poseidon's trident so he could get revenge on his dad.

"And you did! You're so brave and strong! I wish I could be like you. So now you can blast my dad—"

"Jason!" exclaimed his father again.

"—and then everything's cool. I mean," he said, his voice softening, "I like you, I really do. I really thought we had something. You're the only one who understands me. And just as soon as you turn my dad into a frog or a snail or whatever you want—really, you choose!—we can go, you know, make out!"

"Son!" his father repeated firmly.

"See, Dad!" Jason snapped. "I've finally taken responsibility. You wanted me to do something with myself. Aren't you proud of me?"

His father ignored him. "Now, young lady, give that to me. . . . Poseidon's going to be very angry." He glanced around, as if worried that Poseidon might, in fact, be angry at him. "Really," he said to Charlotte conspiratorially, "I told you to just get over it. It was for your own good."

"What?" Charlotte asked, bewildered.

"See!" Jason said. "He's evil! You don't know what he did!"

Charlotte glared at Jason. "You really are one of them," she spat. A light fixture fell down right next to her and she jumped.

"Don't say that!" he breathed. "Aw, Lottie, come on,

we can save the ship after." He checked his watch. "Probably."

"Don't call me Lottie! My dad calls me that!" And, temper flaring, Charlotte lifted up the trident and pointed it at Jason.

"Charlotte!" exclaimed Jason, eyes widening in fear. He took a few steps backward into the room with his father.

"How do you like it, boy," snarled the old man. "See what you've done? I tried to give you a chance to make something of yourself, impress Poseidon."

"See what *I've* done?" Jason said, rounding on his father. "What about what you've done, huh? You ruined my life, Dad!"

"Now, now," said his father. "I'm just trying to help you understand yourself better. See your true potential! Embrace your heritage! It's a gift, son, a gift!"

"You're nothing. Just because you're a shape-shifter doesn't mean you're great. You're evil, Dad. You're evil, and I hate you. And I'm finally going to do something about it!" He turned to look at Charlotte, who was standing in the hallway, looking back and forth from one to the other in disbelief. "Come on, Charlotte, do it!"

Charlotte screamed in frustration and aimed the trident more pointedly at Jason, then another attack from Sir Laurence sent a tremendous rumble through the wall. From off in the distance, Charlotte heard water rushing.

She lowered the trident. What was she doing? Was she going to turn into Poseidon and start destroying everyone who ticked her off? Just because you can turn someone into a piece of sea scum—just because you might want to very, very much, and just because they absolutely, positively, one-hundred-percent deserve it—does not mean you should. Plus, there was no time; she'd dallied here long enough. So with another scream of frustration, she kicked the door closed and sealed it shut with the trident, leaving Jason and his father to sort out their evil differences for their evil selves in their evil room until some other evil person could find an evil way to get them out again. Then she took off down the hallway again toward the staircase.

Later she would think about Jason Hart and his foul betrayal; now getting to the ship was what mattered. Jason had lied, but there might have been some truth to his lie. The trident should work on the Siren; Poseidon clearly used it to control the sea creatures. Maybe it wasn't really the only way to get the Siren to stop, like Jason had said; maybe Charlotte could have, you know, *asked nicely*, but it didn't matter now. She had it and she was going to use it.

Charlotte ran into the stairwell and headed down

the stairs, avoiding the broken glass and rubble in her path—*just one hallway left*, she thought to herself, *then the deck, then the lifeboat, then back to the ship, you can do this, Charlotte, you can do this*—then ducked out into the main hallway—

—where she found herself face to face with Philonecron.

Charlotte gasped and stopped short. Philonecron's eyes narrowed and he began to clap his hands together slowly in sarcastic applause. "*Bravo*, my dear girl," he sneered. "Bravo. You arranged for all this, I assume?" He held his hands out as the walls shook again. "Well," he sighed heavily, "I see I am going to have to kill you myself. Ah, well, as they say, if you want something done right—"

As he came toward her, Charlotte crouched down and aimed the trident at him. "Just try it," she hissed. At the sight of the trident, something passed over Philonecron's face.

"And where," he asked slowly, "pray tell, did you get that?"

Charlotte just stood there, arms trembling slightly, keeping the trident fixed on Philonecron, struggling to keep her balance while the ship rocked around her.

"Well," he exhaled, "I see I underestimated you, my little nemesis." As he spoke his eyes lingered on the trident. "You are quite something, indeed. Really, quite impressive! Indeed, you are a worthy adversary. But"— he smiled sweetly—"what you have in your brave little hands is not for little girls. Why don't you hand that over to me?"

Charlotte gulped. "Why don't I just blast you, instead," she said through gritted teeth. Yes, why didn't she? Every muscle was poised to do it, but she was rooted to the spot like one of Poseidon's ridiculous statues.

"Ah," said Philonecron with a grin. "Yes, why don't you? Hmmm." He put his hand on his chin in mock thoughtfulness. "Oh, I know! Because I have something you want."

Charlotte blinked. He did?

"Well, perhaps we can work something out." He turned and called over to the wall. "Zero! Come here!"

Charlotte didn't even have time to react to the unexpected words that came out of Philonecron's mouth before a door opened in the wall and a boy walked out, a boy who did not seem at all concerned by the ship's impending destruction, a boy who did not seem concerned by anything, really, because he did not seem quite conscious, except for the whole walking thing. But what he did seem was familiar, very familiar, in fact—

Zee?

Charlotte stumbled backward and nearly dropped

the trident on the ground. Philonecron was too busy presenting his prize to notice. "Come here, Zero," he said silkily. "Look who's come to see you! Your nasty, ill-bred vermin of a cousin! Isn't that precious?"

Charlotte stared at the sight before her, tears stinging her eyes. "Zee?" she said, in almost a whisper. Was it a trick? It had to be a trick. Zee was at home, dating Ashleys and "getting over it" and being a complete and total goon. It was a trick designed to stop her from leaving the yacht. Next Zee would ask for the trident, and she would give it to him because he was Zee and she would do anything for him and then he would turn into Poseidon. Gods did that. Some of the Olympians could take other forms. And then there was Proteus, the old man of the sea, he was a shape-shifter—and Jason's dad was a shape-shifter, and he had been hanging around Charlotte and Zee. . . .

A very, very cold feeling passed through Charlotte and she nearly dropped the trident. Suddenly everything was clear to her. Jason, the old man in the aqua suit, Lulu Zee, everything. "Pr—Proteus?" she squeaked.

"Ah, yes," said Philonecron. "I couldn't have you notice your cousin's absence, could I? So, how did he do? Proteus, I mean. I worried he might be a little too . . . enthusiastic. Our Zero is quite temperate. Did you notice anything? Well, obviously you did. You're here, aren't you. Aren't you clever?"

Charlotte was shaking so badly she could barely keep hold of the trident. Vomit rose up from her stomach and black swam before her eyes. No. She hadn't noticed anything. She was not clever at all. They'd replaced Zee with Proteus, and she'd thought it was still her cousin.

"Now," said Philonecron, "you came all this way—"

Just then a big plaster starfish fell from the ceiling, scattering Philonecron with dust. "ARGH!" he gargled, brushing off his shoulders dramatically. He turned on Charlotte, snarling. "You little—" But then he stopped himself and took a deep and dramatic breath. "Excuse me," he said, smiling sweetly. "As I was saying, you came all this way to get your cousin back, and perhaps we can work out a deal."

"I came to save the cruise ship," Charlotte said dully, staring at Zee. Was he all right? Zee?

"Really?" Philonecron stared at her in disbelief. "You did?" He clapped his hands together as a smile crept across his face. "You mean you risked certain death coming aboard Poseidon's yacht to save a ship full of *mortals*?" He shook his head in wonderment. "That is *adorable*. Really. Moronic, but adorable. I take it that means you didn't know about Zero being here? Goodness me. Well, now that you do . . . Here's what I suggest." He leaned in and looked at her intensely, eyes like flames. "You give me that little prize of yours, and I'll give you your cousin."

*"Right,"* Charlotte muttered.

Philonecron looked wounded. "Upon my honor!" he said, putting his palm to his chest. "Don't misunderstand me! I certainly would like to keep him. We've become so close, and he's such a wonderful protégé! I was even going to get him a cape of his own. But . . . sometimes we must make sacrifices for"—his eyes flickered—"things we want."

Uh-huh.

"Zee!" she yelled. "Wake up! Zee!" Quickly, she jerked the trident over so it pointed at him. A stream of light shot out of it. "Wake up!"

Had it worked? Charlotte stared at Zee, watching for some sign of change. Had his shoulders straightened? Had something passed through his eyes?

"Oh, my dear girl," Philonecron said, rolling slowly toward her, eyes sparkling. "You'll have to do better than that. He's under my control, you see. Just a little spell I worked out, very clever, if I do say so myself. Of course"—he shrugged modestly—"what do you expect?"

Charlotte wrenched the trident back toward Philonecron. "Let him go—"

Just then one of the Poseidon-head lamps came

crashing down from the ceiling right behind Philonecron and Zee. It hit the floor with a tremendous crash, sending glass shooting everywhere. Philonecron ducked, and Charlotte flung one hand over her face protectively, while some shards of glass hit Zee in the back and he flinched.

And then, as Charlotte straightened, she saw Zee do something he hadn't done since he emerged—he blinked.

Zee?

A jolt of electricity shot through Charlotte, and the fog of inaction lifted. She aimed the trident squarely at Philonecron and thought something vague, something very like Jason's words—blast him!—and blue light shot out of the trident and hit Philonecron. Propelled by the stream of light, he went shooting back, wheelchair and all, all the way down the long hallway, blasting right through the glass doors at the end of the hall, over the deck, through the air, and far into the night. Then, with a splash too far away for Charlotte to hear, he dropped into the dark waters of the sea.

Charlotte sucked in a gasp of breath and waited one second, two, five, ten, unable to move for fear she'd be letting down her guard, unable to do anything but look from her zombie cousin to the gaping hole at the end of the hall.

But all was quiet. A great shudder went through Charlotte, and she was conscious again of how much everything hurt, from her scalp all the way to her toenails, but there was no time for that, there was no time for anything.

"Zee," she exclaimed, running over to her cousin, dodging shards of glass. "Are you all right? Zee? Are you in there?" She put her hands on his arms and gazed up into his dark eyes. Was there anything there? A lump rose in Charlotte's throat; she had not realized how much she missed him, how much she needed him by her side. They were supposed to fight together, that's how it worked. Charlotte and Zee, taking on the gods. She'd put all her faith in Jason Hart, the liar, the sneak, when all along what she really needed was her cousin.

"Zee?" she whispered pleadingly.

Then, Zee blinked again, and she saw something pass through his eyes. Was it recognition? She didn't know, but it was life, she could tell that much. There was life in his eyes.

Rage filled her, and she thought again of Jason Hart and Proteus trapped in the room on the yacht. All she wanted to do was run back and show them what happened when they messed with her cousin. But she was not Poseidon, who could have killed her a thousand times already if he hadn't tried to make a show of it. She could not let her anger get in the way of what she had to do. There was no time.

"Zee, we have to go," she said. "I'm so sorry. But we have to go. It's important. Can you come with me?"

He blinked again, and again some light seemed to pass through his eyes. But he did not move.

With a groan, Charlotte took a great step back. "I'm sorry, Zee," she whispered. "I'm so sorry, I don't have a choice." And, tears running down her cheeks, she leveled the trident at him and ordered, "Come with me."

CHAPTER 26

# Ketos vs. Squid

Charlotte took Zee's hand and led him through the long hallway. He ran behind her with plodding steps, ran like someone with no intelligence, no will. If she pulled too hard, he'd topple over. Charlotte's heart was breaking as she pulled him along, but pull him along she did.

They emerged through the doors and, trident poised, Charlotte stopped to scan the deck for some sign of Philonecron. The deck was a disaster. The large aquarium was completely shattered, with only the bottom remaining, as if something very large had swept the fish—and most of the aquarium with them—back into the sea where they belonged. Most of the lounge chairs were gone, though some smashed remnants littered the deck, and one undamaged chair had lodged in the Jacuzzi as if it wanted one last hot tub before the sea monster brought it to its maker.

Charlotte ran across the deck, trident held high, leading her zombie cousin. She climbed over the deck wall, and Zee followed her like the automaton he was. As they climbed down the ladder, a tremendous tentacle swung over their heads with a low *whoosh*. Sir Laurence was still going strong. Gratitude surged through Charlotte. She would repay her debt to him later, once the *Isis Queen* was freed. They had a deal.

But that gratitude lessened slightly when she reached the bottom of the ladder and found her lifeboat had been smashed. A chunk of yacht had most inconsiderately fallen right on top of her getaway vehicle. She grunted. Really, there were four boats lashed to the ship—it couldn't have fallen on an evil one?

Well, no matter. What good is a trident of extraordinary power if you can't use it to hot wire a minor sea god's speedboat? Jaw clenched with determination, Charlotte climbed down into a shiny, sleek boat and unlashed it. Then, after waiting for Zee to mindlessly follow, she tapped the trident on the ignition and felt the engine roar to life. She pulled the throttle into reverse, and as the boat shot backward away from the *Poseidon*, she slammed the throttle forward and they were off.

As the night air whipped against her face, Charlotte cast a glance over to her cousin. He was sitting dutifully in the passenger seat of the small boat. "Zee?" she yelled over the roar of the engine. "Zee, can you hear me? Zee, are you okay?"

He did not answer, and Charlotte couldn't get a good look at his face to see if there was anything there at all. Working valiantly to keep down the lump in her throat, she turned her attention back to the sea in front of her. When she was safely away, she looked over her shoulder at the *Poseidon*, lit by the great full moon. The yacht was covered in squid arms—Sir Laurence, it appeared, had wrapped himself around the boat. A tentacle hung off to the side limply, and Charlotte gulped. But he still had many arms left, and he was using them. Off to one side, she saw two huge yellow eyes floating just above the surface of the water, focused intently on the yacht.

"Thank you, Sir Laurence," Charlotte whispered. "I'll see you soon."

Then she turned back around and went off into the night.

Charlotte used the trident and the boat's compass to go back exactly the way they'd came. She went right through the Strait of Messina without any sign of Scylla or Charybdis, as she knew there wouldn't be; for it had been they Jason had been talking to in the library before the party. Charlotte hadn't been able to place them at first, but when Jason betrayed her, she knew. It hadn't been a mistake that they'd ended up in that strait when they were going to the yacht; Jason had arranged the whole thing in order to make it look like he'd saved her. Not that he'd needed to, for Charlotte was a sucker for boys with nice eyes and rumpled hair and sympathy toward her adventures with the Greek gods. It was her fatal flaw.

What had he been doing, anyway? Proteus must have sent him to follow Zee, not her, to learn more about his life. Because he wanted his son to prove himself to Poseidon. But Jason had had his own agenda: Befriend Charlotte, wait till she got on the cruise, wait until the ship was lost, then show her how to save it. Meanwhile, Zee had been in Philonecron's hands this whole time.

The boat sped through the night-black water, bouncing hard along the waves as it went, wind pounding against Charlotte's face. She had the throttle as far forward as it would go—and it turned out that, on an Immortal's speedboat, that meant you could go pretty fast.

Charlotte couldn't even hear herself think over the roar of the engines and the rushing of the wind, but still, every once in a while she shouted something at Zee, pretending his mind hadn't gone AWOL from his body, pretending he was with her, pretending they were together just as they had been going down to the Underworld. The boat was going so fast that she didn't want to take her eyes off the sea in front of her for even a second, so she couldn't get a good look at him, and in a way that helped. Because the sight of him under Philonecron's spell made her lose all her strength—and if that happened, then all would be lost. If it wasn't already.

And then, a dim light glowed on the dark horizon. The boat sped closer and Charlotte beheld the *Isis Queen*, aglow with lights still on from the previous night, back when everyone was awake and aware and heading happily toward Virginia. At the sight of the distant ship a wave of relief hit Charlotte; her body broke out in shivers and tears sprang to her eyes. The ship was still there. It wasn't too late.

Still, as she got closer to the cruise ship, she saw the sea begin to stir, as if the water itself were uneasy. She peered down at the waves, but saw only blackness. Was the Ketos coming? Was that water churning off into the distance because of the movement of a great monster, or was it just a trick of Charlotte's eye? How much time did she have?

As the waves grew more unsettled and Charlotte sped on, the bouncing of the boat became furious and arrhythmic, so she had to clutch the steering wheel to avoid being thrown from the boat and into the dark sea, but not before pointing the trident at her cousin and yelling at him to hang on. Charlotte's body kept slamming into the driver's seat, and with every hit, her back throbbed and her bones screamed. But she was getting close now—the *Isis Queen* loomed ahead of her, rocking in the restless sea. She slowed down her speedboat and, flicking on the spotlight, started to scan the ship's hull for a place to lash on the boat. When she found it, she eased up to it and tied on the speedboat. Then she turned her attention to her cousin.

"Zee!" she yelled. "You have to come with me!" What was she doing? He had to come with her so he could be eaten by the Ketos? But what was she supposed to do?

Zee was still hanging onto his seat, so hard his knuckles had turned white, but his face was no longer empty. He was looking around vaguely, blinking rapidly, his eyes full of fog—but at least they weren't empty anymore.

She scampered back to him and put her hands on his arms. "Zee . . . Zee, are you awake?"

One blink. Two. Three. Then his eyes met hers. "Char—Charlotte?"

"Oh, Zee . . ." Charlotte exhaled, her eyes flooding with tears. No, no, there wasn't time. "Zee, listen to me, can you walk?"

"I—I—" He pushed himself up, and then promptly fell down again.

"Zee, listen. . . . There's no time. . . . You need to do something for me, okay? You need to stay here. Do you think you can drive the boat?"

Zee looked up at her, eyes wide with confusion. "Y-yes."

"If something happens, something—unusual, I need you to drive away as fast as you can, okay?"

Something passed through his eyes. "Phil—Philonecron?"

Charlotte shook her head. "He's not here. But if you see anything coming toward the ship, I want you to drive away, okay? As quickly as possible. Just pick a direction and go."

"Wh—what about you?"

Charlotte squared her jaw. "I'll be okay," she muttered. (Maybe.)

"Charlotte!" Zee protested. He tried to push himself up and immediately fell again, then let out a gargled scream.

"Zee, I have to go. I'll be okay. I'll come back for you, and if not, go. Promise me."

And with one last glance at her cousin, Charlotte crawled onto the bow and unlashed the boat. Heart pounding, she scampered up the ladder and pulled at the door in the hull. It was, of course, locked—but locks mean nothing when you have a magic trident. But when Charlotte placed it against the door, she realized that the trident was much cooler than it had been, and the gentle humming of the handle was barely perceptible. Too long away from Poseidon, it was losing its power.

Her heart sank, and some other sensation passed over her too, some icy feeling just like the one you get when your doom is approaching. Without quite knowing why, Charlotte turned her head around.

Someone was coming. Someone, or something—a light heading toward her, an oddly shaped glowing dot on the horizon, moving with great speed—were those horses next to it? Was that a tentacle behind it?

No, no, not someone or something, but someone *and* something. Under the bright moon Charlotte saw Sir Laurence, waving two arms in the air menacingly as he moved toward the cruise ship, and in front of him was a towering man in a massive, glowing chariot pulled by four white horses.

Poseidon.

Charlotte yelped. She had had no intention of seeing him again. Sir Laurence was supposed to come—that had been the plan all along. Once she had the trident and had signaled him, he would attack the yacht and create her distraction, and then he would come to the *Isis Queen* and, after she had stopped the Siren, she would change him back to Sir Laurence Gaumm, English gentleman.

Sir Laurence was supposed to be there—yes, but Poseidon was not. But he'd managed to slip away during the fight, and now Sir Laurence was chasing him—to protect Charlotte, and to protect his own chance at salvation.

Hanging off the ladder, Charlotte yelled down at her cousin. "Zee!" she shouted. "Go!"

From his position on the small boat, Zee couldn't see the approach of Poseidon, and he looked up at her, bewildered and still foggy. "Charlotte, what's—"

"Go!" But Zee yelled something else up at her and started feeling his way toward the front of the boat, toward the ladder, toward Charlotte. She narrowed her eyes, pointed the trident at the boat, and whispered, "*Take him out of danger.*" Then, as the boat roared off, she cast one last look at the horizon.

She couldn't tell how long it would take Poseidon to reach the boat—before Charlotte got to the Siren, or after? Before the Ketos attacked the ship, or after? And what was she supposed to do then? How was she supposed to fight off the Ketos *and* the Lord of the Seas? Having the captain hit the gas pedal just wasn't going to do it.

Well, she would deal with that later. Charlotte had gotten the trident to stop the Siren, and that's what she was going to do—for once she confronted the battle brewing outside the boat, there might not be any Charlotte left to save the ship.

Charlotte went through the hull door, then ran through a short entryway and burst through another door to find herself near the doctor's office. Deck Three. Charlotte wanted to collapse on the familiar carpeting and hug the ship, but there was no time to rejoice. She sprinted up two flights of stairs and through the hallway until she came upon the locked doors of the Mariner Lounge.

Nothing had changed. The wooden chair she had used to try to smash the doors lay broken against the ground, and through the porthole window Charlotte could see the heads of the passengers and crew, still mesmerized by the singer. She tried the door once more for good measure.

*"Open,"* she whispered, feeling the trident's hum diminish a little more. And just like that, the doors flew to the sides and Charlotte stalked into the lounge.

Her eyes went quickly over the crowd—her parents had been in the back of the room, off to the side of the doorway, but Charlotte couldn't see them from her vantage point. She wanted to run to them, to fall into their laps—she'd been so scared that she would never see them again, and now that they were so close, her heart tried to pull her body to them. Later, she told herself, later.

Onstage Thalia was singing into the microphone with her eyes closed, as her dark hair hung like curtains over her face and she swayed back and forth in her slinky green dress. She was crooning some horrible ballad, the sort of thing they play in your dentist's office when they really want to punish you for not flossing, and as her stomach turned Charlotte reflected that she could not, for the life of her, understand grown-ups. Drawing air through her nose, she lifted up the trident, which felt nearly lifeless at this point, and aimed it at the singer.

Thalia's eyes popped open. Surprise stopped her cold, and she paused her song mid-note and blinked. Then, regaining her composure, she began to sing again, cat-like eyes fixed intently on Charlotte. As she sang, she articulated her words very carefully.

> *Go away, little girl*
> *Put your toy down*
> *You might get hurt, little girl*
> *Someone's angry with you. . . .*

That was enough of that. "I'll turn you into a toad," Charlotte snapped, aiming the trident again.

The singer's eyes widened, though she still sang on. Charlotte didn't hear the words this time, though, as something outside of the lounge had caught her eye.

The Mariner Lounge lay in the stern of the ship, and its walls featured tremendous windows so its guests could look out upon the sea. Or, at this moment, so they could look on the very large creature that seemed to be rising out of it about a hundred yards from the ship, a creature with a worm-like face, angry-looking pig-like eyes, a massive mouth, and tremendous, sharp teeth.

Thalia followed Charlotte's horrified gaze out the window, then pointed and screamed. *"Ketos!"* she shrieked, and in the blink of an eye she dropped her microphone and sprinted out of the lounge.

Charlotte stared at the Ketos, which was opening its mouth as it approached the ship, and then followed Thalia. She had no idea how long it would take the adults to wake up now that Thalia had stopped singing, and she didn't exactly have time to wait and see. She had a Ketos to kill.

Just outside the lounge was a door leading outside to the small strip of deck that encircled every level of the ship, and Charlotte burst through. And what she saw made her freeze.

The Ketos was moving fast. Its head was bigger than the *Isis Queen* itself, and its worm body stretched on for what seemed like forever. On the horizon, a tail that might be as thick as the ship flickered over the surface of the water, creating great waves in its wake. That was scary enough, but a few hundred yards to the left was Poseidon, who was bearing down fast on the ship in his chariot. When he saw Charlotte, he let out a roar that the waves themselves seemed to cower from. And close behind him was Sir Laurence, one arm reaching for the Ketos, another swinging for Poseidon.

*"Give me my trident!"* Poseidon screamed. He stopped and, raising his arms above his head, summoned a spinning column of water from the choppy sea. The column moved rapidly toward Charlotte, who took a single step back, clutching the trident to her chest. Then a tremendous force slammed her into the wall of the ship. Her head hit the wall hard, and that was when everything went black.

Charlotte awoke to find the trident lying next to her, and a cackling Poseidon galloping toward her. She dove toward her prize, and Poseidon began to shout menacing commands at the sea.

Then a tentacle swooped down and crashed into Poseidon's chariot. The chariot wavered, the horses screamed, and Charlotte pounced on the trident.

Roaring as he righted himself, Poseidon turned and directed a jet of water right at Sir Laurence. It broke harmlessly against the giant squid. While Poseidon's attention was diverted, Charlotte got up groggily and ran around to the stern to make her stand against the Ketos, clutching the trident. Meanwhile, Poseidon had raised his hands to the heavens, and a dense, rolling cloud came in and began to dump thick, sharp pieces of hail on the squid's head. Sir Laurence dove under the sea.

*"Now I've got you!"* Poseidon shouted, propelling his chariot back toward Charlotte.

She took a few steps back, clutching the trident to her. Poseidon reached up toward the hail cloud and directed a stream of icy chunks right at Charlotte. They hit her like knives, cutting and bruising her skin, and she scrambled under a nearby table as the chunks of hail pounded on the tabletop above her. Then Sir Laurence burst back through the water, swung for the chariot, and knocked two of Poseidon's horses down. The horses screamed, the chariot tipped to one side and, stumbling, Poseidon shot his hands out to right them. Free from the hail, Charlotte looked up—and suddenly her head whipped to her right. The Ketos was almost upon the ship now.

With a scream, Charlotte burst out from under the table, lifted the trident in the air, pointed it at the Ketos—and gasped in horror. The trident was ice-cold, and it lay perfectly still in her hands, feeling desolate and void, like a dead animal. Charlotte stared up at it in a panic. Did it have anything left at all? It had to have something left; she needed to stop the Ketos, propel the ship away from Poseidon, and keep her promise to Sir Laurence. She needed it, or all would be lost.

Meanwhile, Sir Laurence had moved toward the Ketos and was beating on him with two arms. As Charlotte watched, the Ketos thrashed him with his tremendous tail. Sir Laurence was repelled backward and fell into the sea with a monumental splash.

"Ha!" boomed Poseidon, now thirty yards away. "Not so strong against my Ketos, is he?" Tears stinging her eyes, Charlotte stared desperately at the sea as it churned over the place where Sir Laurence had gone down. "Now, as for you . . ." Charlotte lunged against the deck rail, throwing her arms and legs around it, and hung on with all her might. Poseidon growled and uttered a command, and moments later a wave pounded against Charlotte. But she held her breath, closed her eyes, and held on.

Surely, when the wave passed, Sir Laurence would emerge again, surely he would have recovered from the impact, surely he was all right, surely he was coming back.

But when Charlotte opened her eyes again there was no sign of her friend.

Choking back a sob, she freed her trident arm from the rail and swung the trident over her shoulder. Pointing her prize at the quiet patch of sea, she shouted, "Fix him!" A long puff of blue steam came out of the trident, and that was it. Tears pouring down her cheeks,

Charlotte looked wildly into the water. But a tremendous roaring noise interrupted her, and she whirled around to find herself staring directly into the gaping maw of the Ketos.

"Stop!" Charlotte yelled, pointing the trident at him. Nothing happened. The Ketos's jaws began to rise over the ship. Slime dripped off its story-high fangs, and a horrible, rotting smell washed over Charlotte.

Another wave came at her with tremendous force, too much for her one-handed grip, and she was sent banging against the wall again. Nearby a window shattered. She felt the world slow down, as if it took seconds to move an inch, and when she hit the wall she felt her grip on the trident slowly release and heard it clatter to the floor.

She bounced off the wall and hit the deck and scrambled frantically amidst the water and broken glass for the trident. But it wasn't anywhere. And Charlotte looked toward Poseidon with dread, expecting to see his prize in his hand, wondering what he'd do to her now— but he didn't have it either.

No, the person next to her did.

Zee?

Propping herself up on her hands, Charlotte whipped her head toward her cousin, who was standing, holding the trident.

Poseidon was yelling at Zee now, insensate with anger. *"Give me that, mortal!"* He began to mutter something to the waters below.

Zee yelled back at the top of his lungs, "You want it? Go get it!"

And with that Zee, looking nothing like someone who had just been under a spell, ran three steps forward, trident poised, and with a loud grunt hurled it like a javelin directly into the Ketos's mouth.

One moment of awful silence, and then a horrible screech filled the air, and the Ketos began to writhe violently. Poseidon roared. The Ketos's enormous tail whipped spasmodically to the right and caused a tremendous wave to crash against the starboard side of the ship. The ship lurched, and Zee lost his balance for a moment. Poseidon turned on Charlotte and Zee and yelled, "I'll tear you limb from limb!" Then with a tremendous crack of the whip, his horses began pulling the chariot toward her. Meanwhile, the still-writhing Ketos's tail had thrashed all the way over to the other side of its mammoth body and came flying toward the side of the ship where Charlotte and Zee crouched. But the tail never quite got to the ship. Poseidon's chariot lay directly in its path, and the tail slammed into it. In blind panic, the Ketos wrapped its tail around the chariot, desperate to hold on to something. Before Poseidon could react, the Ketos's tail coiled around and around until neither god nor chariot could be seen.

Then, thrashing and writhing, with the chariot in its death grip, the Ketos sank quickly into the sea, whipping the chariot this way and that until it, too, disappeared in the watery depths.

The sea roiled for a few moments and then slowly became calm, until all in the world was quiet, the only sound the lapping of the waves against the boat.

Panting, Charlotte collapsed on the ground. The next thing she knew, Zee was crouching next to her, whispering to her. "Char, are you all right? Char?"

"Zee?" Charlotte said, rolling over to look at her cousin, who had the best sense of timing of anyone she'd ever met.

"Are you all right?" he repeated.

She wasn't. Everything hurt. The welts from the hail were bleeding. Her wrist screamed and her head throbbed and her back felt like a bus had run over it. And Sir Laurence—Sir Laurence was not coming back. Grief rose up into her stomach and threatened to choke her.

But the ship was safe. Poseidon was gone—at least for the time being. The Ketos was gone. Her parents were safe. Zee was here.

"Yes," she said quietly. "Yes."

CHAPTER 27

# Home

Officially, the word was that the storm had caused damage to the *Isis Queen*, releasing a gas around the ship that caused unconsciousness and sleepwalking, though preliminary environmental tests revealed nothing out of the ordinary. Something had also gone awry with the ship's navigational controls, sending it dramatically off course. Everyone seemed satisfied with this explanation, despite the fact that it was entirely impossible for the ship to travel four thousand nautical miles in one night. Because if it wasn't something to do with the controls, what could it possibly have been?

No one onboard had any idea what had passed—at least no one who was saying. After the Siren had fled the Mariner Lounge that night, the people in the lounge regained consciousness slowly, as if they'd all awakened from a sleep of a hundred years. The first to really comprehend the situation was the captain, who stumbled toward the bridge to sound the distress call. Other officers and crew followed. It took them some time to realize that they were, in fact, where their navigational system said they were, and even more time to convince the coast guard. Eventually, after long negotiations among the ship, the coast guard, and the Italian government, it was determined that the *Queen* would set sail immediately for the nearest port— Catania, in Italy—accompanied by a cavalcade of smaller boats and helicopters from the Italian coast guard. Coast guard officials came in to pilot the ship as well, while the *Queen*'s officers went through an extremely thorough debriefing.

Everyone else on board was kept inside the Mariner Lounge all night, with the cruise director giving them periodic updates. Most people were too dazed to put up a fight, and the few unruly souls were promptly removed by the ship's security.

The ship's doctor began examining people immediately and discovered that everyone seemed to have survived the experience unscathed—everyone except one thirteen-year-old girl. She had suffered a concussion and a lumbar sprain in her back. She also had big black and green bruises all over her body, tiny lacerations on her face, a sprained wrist, small cuts in her hands and knees, blisters on her hands, and bruised ribs. When questioned, she said she had no memory of what had happened to her—and no one could press her, because they didn't remember what had happened to them, either.

Charlotte spent the night lying on one of the couches, while her parents stayed as close to her as they possibly could. She did not mind at all. This way, she could keep her eye on them.

As for Zee, the cousins determined he would hide in Charlotte's room, as of course he did not belong on the ship at all. He had no trouble getting in, even without a key, because the door had been left propped open.

When Zee first got to Charlotte's room, he went right into the bathroom where he vomited three times. Then he sat down against the wall, buried his head in his arms, and began to shake, steadily but violently, like a man freezing to death. He stayed that way for an hour, maybe two, while the ship started up again and began making its way through the night sea, while helicopters buzzed in the sky and small ships hummed along just outside his window.

And then, finally, he stopped shaking. He pushed himself up off the ground, and took a thirty-minute shower, then he sat down on the bed and thought about all that had happened and about what must be done now.

The next morning the entire *Isis Queen* unloaded at Catania, where they were kept inside the large port facility while a doctor examined them all for contagions and the cruise line worked with immigration officials to get them home. Zee disembarked with them, keeping to the back, well out of sight range of the Mielswetzskis — who did not seem very inquisitive, anyway. They were too busy taking care of their daughter.

Charlotte had to spend the day on a gurney — doctor's orders — though making various excuses, she slipped off from time to time to check on Zee, who was spending the day hiding in a bathroom in an out-of-the-way part of the terminal — not the most pleasant smelling of sanctuaries, but he had little choice. He had been through worse. He spent much of the time thinking about how he was going to get home, because it was easier than thinking about what had happened. And anyway, Zee wanted so desperately to go home.

And then, about mid-afternoon, while Zee was sitting on the floor drinking some water Charlotte had brought him, the door opened. Zee's heart leaped in fear—he had spent the morning hiding in a stall, but after no one came in for hours he had allowed himself to come out.

But fortunately, the man who walked in was not a Mielswetzski, by any means. He was quite striking looking—very pale, with light blue eyes and hair so blond it was almost white, and he wore an old-fashioned white dinner jacket and black tie. His right arm was in a sling, there was a bandage wrapped around his head and another around two of his left fingers, and he looked as if he had been submerged in water and then dried out.

"Pardon me," he said to Zee, then stopped and looked him up and down. "Goodness, it's nice to see someone who knows how to dress these days!"

Zee blushed. He was still wearing a tuxedo shirt and pants, for he had no other clothes and he hadn't exactly been able to borrow any of Charlotte's. "Oh, yeah," he muttered.

The man's face lit up. "You're *English*!" he exclaimed. "How delightful! Where do you hail from?"

"Uh . . . London, originally," Zee said. "But now I live in America."

The man's eyes brightened. "America? . . . Say, do you know a Miss Charlotte Mielswetzski?"

Zee gaped at him.

"Oh! You know her! Capital! Is she all right? Do you know where I might find her?"

"Um," Zee said, blinking rapidly. "She's—" Just then, there was a knock on the door—three short taps. Their signal. "—right here." And he got up and opened the door for his cousin.

Charlotte stood in the doorway, holding herself like a two-hundred-year-old who had just been squashed by a falling piano. "I told them I had to go to the bathroom," she said conspiratorially, her voice tight but brave. "I brought you some food—" And then her eyes fell on the man in the tuxedo, and she shot Zee a confused look.

But the man's face turned as bright as the sun, and he smiled and said softly, "Miss Charlotte?"

Charlotte stared at him for a full second before recognition dawned on her. "Sir Laurence?" she whispered, voice trembling.

"At your service!" he proclaimed brightly.

And then the man opened his arms and Charlotte tumbled into them—and then let out a small yelp of pain as he squeezed her battered body. She backed away slightly and looked at him, tears streaming down her face, and asked, "How—how?"

"Well, funny thing, that," Sir Laurence said. "I'm plummeting through the water, thanks to that nasty blow from that blasted Ketos fellow, and then something hits me and I feel myself begin to . . . change. Then, well, I don't remember what happened then. Everything went quite black, and I thought that was it for Sir Laurence Gaumm! But next thing I know I'm inside a"—he scrunched up his face and articulated slowly—"hel-ee-cop-tor, and some man I've never met before is pounding on my chest and doing something quite shocking with his mouth, and so on and so forth. They thought I was on your ship and brought me here.

"I had a deuce of a time explaining who I really was, of course, then they made me get quite the working over from that doctor fellow, who seemed to think I'd sustained some kind of head injury."

"I can't imagine why," said Charlotte, grinning through her tears.

"Well, the old cove prescribed bed rest for me, but Sir Laurence Gaumm was not going to go anywhere until he found his girl!"

Charlotte turned toward Zee, face bright and wet, and proclaimed, "Sir Laurence, this is my cousin Zee. Zee, this is Sir Laurence. He helped save us."

Zee nodded. Charlotte would explain more later. "Thank you, Sir Laurence."

"I am honored," Sir Laurence said, bowing deeply. "So"—he turned to Charlotte, eyes lit—"tell me! How did you do it, old girl? How did you beat Poseidon?"

So Charlotte told Sir Laurence about the trident and its waning power, about her fight with Poseidon, about the Ketos's approach, and about how Zee's desperate launch of the trident saved the day.

Sir Laurence let out something that could only be described as a guffaw. "Brilliant!" he told Zee.

Charlotte shook her head. "I thought Poseidon would come back to get the ship! You know, once he'd . . . extracted himself."

"Ha!" said Sir Laurence. "No! I think he'll be busy for quite some time!"

Charlotte and Zee looked at him blankly.

"My dear girl," Sir Laurence said with a grin, "he wants his trident back, yes? He might as well not be an Olympian anymore without it! But do you know how long it will take that trident to—oh, how do I say this properly—*pass through* the Ketos?"

"Oh," said Charlotte.

"Oh!" said Zee.

There was really nothing to say to that, and the two cousins and the former giant squid all looked at one another. Then Charlotte asked suddenly, "Sir Laurence, I need to ask you one more favor."

"Anything!"

"Well . . . do you have any money?"

"Gosh!" he exclaimed. "Well, I have a bit of dosh in

the bank. Well"—he considered a moment—"quite a lot now, I suppose."

Charlotte glanced from Sir Laurence to Zee. "Can you help get my cousin home?"

And that was that. Later in the day Charlotte smuggled in one of the travel passes the cruise line was issuing. Zee was quite impressed, but Charlotte said it was hard to deny anything to a girl who looked like she did. And when the passengers were finally let out of the facility, Charlotte hobbled her way back to give Sir Laurence a (gentle) hug.

"I shall see you again, old girl," said Sir Laurence. "You may count on it."

Zee got home twenty hours later, just a little bit after the Mielswetzskis. He had spent the entire day trying to think of an explanation for where he'd been—judging by when Charlotte said Proteus had arrived on the yacht, he'd been missing for at least forty-eight hours—but couldn't come up with anything better than amnesia. But when he arrived home, instead of finding frantic parents and many, many police officers, he found that his parents were still in England and the Fornaras had never missed him. After some investigation, Zee learned that his mother—or someone who could sound just like her—had called Mrs. Fornara to say that Zee wouldn't be coming after all. Apparently, Proteus had wanted to stay by himself as much as Zee did.

Zee called his parents and explained that the Mielswetzskis were back early and he'd be staying with them. He had an urge to ask them to come home, because after you have been turned into an automaton and made into a living doll by your mortal enemy, you really need some parental support. But they were going to be home soon, and Zee knew if he asked, they would be alarmed. They might think that something had happened to him.

So Zee went over to the Mielswetzskis. He did not particularly want to be alone, and he wanted time with Charlotte, who had been confined to her bed for a few days so her back could heal.

When he saw her, his chest tightened. His cousin looked wracked with exhaustion and pain. He knew she had gotten through the whole experience through adrenaline and sheer will (a powerful force in Charlotte indeed). He also knew that if she had not been leaping out of her gurney in the port terminal to check on him, bring him food, and help him get home, she might not be in as much pain today. But that was Charlotte for you.

When Zee sat down, Mew burst out from under the bed with a loud squawk and jumped immediately onto his lap. Zee felt a lump rise in his throat and whispered, "I missed you, cat."

As for Charlotte, she eyed her cousin carefully. There was something she needed to say to him, something there had been no time to say, something important. And even lying there, watching him out of the corner of her eye, she could barely find the words.

"Zee," she said finally. "Um . . . I'm sorry."

Zee blinked at her. "What?"

"About . . . um . . . controlling you with the trident. I'm so sorry. I couldn't think of what else to do, and—"

Zee closed his eyes and then opened them again. "It's all right. You didn't have a choice."

"No, but . . ."

"It's okay, Charlotte," Zee said softly. "It's okay. Just"—he grinned slightly—"never do it again."

Charlotte let out a gasp of laughter, which caused pain to sear through her ribs. She could not even move without pain searing through some part of her or another. That, she thought, is what you get when you go up against the second most powerful god in the whole universe.

The cousins sat in silence for a while. They had not had any chance to talk about what had happened, and now that the chance had come, neither knew where to begin. Finally Charlotte said, "You know, I had a bad feeling. The day you disappeared. I was just standing outside school and I had this horrible feeling. And then I saw

Proteus, but I didn't know. Zee, I should have known."

"I had a dream!" Zee said. "Of you in danger. And I didn't figure it out until it was too late."

And then Zee told Charlotte everything—from his prophetic dream of her on the small boat in the middle of the sea to his abduction and the old man's transformation. And he told her about waking up on a speedboat with his cousin by his side, about how the speedboat took him out of danger but couldn't keep him out, about how he climbed onto the ship and found his way to Charlotte as if by instinct, because it was his turn to save her.

Silence for a few moments, while Charlotte pondered his story. "The dream," she said finally. "That's so strange. Do you think someone sent it to you from the Underworld?"

"I don't know," Zee said. "There was a little girl in it. She was . . . showing me everything. I don't know what to make of her. But if somebody sent it—I mean, it was a warning, not a trap. But who would have done that?"

Charlotte shook her head, and then winced. "I don't know." She thought for a moment. "But it wasn't quite true, you know. I was never on a boat alone. On the way back there was you. And on the way over, there was Jason."

Zee frowned. "Jason who?"

Charlotte sighed. "Jason Hart. He's Proteus's son. He was spying on you to collect information for his dad."

A moment of silence. "Wow," Zee said flatly. "And here I thought he just liked me."

"Yeah," Charlotte said. "Me too."

Then she told him everything, from Jason Hart to the storm and the Siren, to her encounter with Sir Laurence Gaumm, to Poseidon and the trident, to running through the halls and finding herself face to face with her cousin, whom she had missed so desperately, who needed saving.

And the cousins sat in silence some more, each thinking of the other's stories and getting angrier and angrier. After some time, Charlotte asked, "Zee? When you were with Philonecron . . . do you remember?"

Zee glanced over at her and nodded slowly. "Yes . . . vaguely. It was sort of like a dream you can't wake up from."

"Did he hurt you?"

"No. Mostly he played the violin, dressed me in weird outfits, and talked about taking over the universe."

Charlotte's eyes blazed. "We have to do something," she said darkly. "Philonecron. We have to get him."

Zee paused. "No," he said. "No. Not Philonecron."

"But Zee! After what he did to you? He can't do that to you!"

"No," Zee said firmly. "That's just me. Look what Poseidon did to you and all those people. And all those gods on the yacht, who were going to watch the ship get eaten for *entertainment*. They were going to kill all those people, for fun."

Charlotte nodded. "Poseidon . . . you should have heard the things he said about mortals. It's awful. You know, we were so worried about the Dead we didn't really understand that that was just part of it. It wasn't that Hades doesn't care about the Dead, it's that the gods don't care about people at all."

"And I was worried about Philonecron," Zee said in a low voice. "I wanted to get him before I helped the Dead. Even my grandmum . . ."

"I don't blame you," Charlotte muttered. "But—it's like Mr. Metos said, before all this happened. They don't deserve to be gods."

"No," Zee said, "no, they don't."

"The question is," Charlotte said, "what can we do about it?"

The answer arrived several minutes later, after Zee and Charlotte sat in silence for some time thinking of their new ambition, their new burden. Mrs. Mielswetzski came into the room, her face tired and pale, and smiled down at her daughter.

"How are you doing, sweetie?" she asked.

"I'm okay, Mom," Charlotte said. "Are you okay?"

Mrs. Mielswetzski nodded. "Don't worry about us.

We're going to bring you up some pizza later, okay? Would you like that?"

"Yes," Charlotte said softly.

"Okay. You don't tire her out, Zee."

"I won't," said Zee firmly.

"I love you, Charlotte," Mrs. Mielswetzski said.

"I love you too, Mom," Charlotte said.

Mrs. Mielswetzski leaned down to kiss Charlotte on the cheek, then squeezed Zee's shoulder and started to head out of the room. Then she stopped suddenly. "Oh!" she exclaimed. "I completely forgot." Reaching into her pocket, she produced an envelope. "I found a letter for you in the mail. It's addressed to you both."

Charlotte and Zee exchanged a quick glance. Mrs. Mielswetzski handed the letter to Zee, then turned and left the room, shutting the door behind her.

Zee looked at the handwriting on the envelope and nodded slowly at Charlotte.

"You read it," Charlotte said, her throat dry.

And he did:

Charlotte and Zachary,

I have made a grave error. I believe that you are in danger. I thought I could best protect you by keeping away

from you, but I was wrong. The gods
have no interest in me. It is you who
concerns them. I have much to discuss
with you. But first, you must know that
Philonecron is the grandson of Poseidon.
Poseidon does not like it when people
harm his descendants, and I fear that he
will try to exact revenge. Whatever you
do, you must stay away from the sea.

"Oh, great," Charlotte muttered. "I'll do that."
Zee snorted.

More importantly, there is something
afoot, something that may affect the fate
of us all, and I'm afraid you two are
involved. My first priority is to keep you
safe. I will come for you soon.

Sincerely,
Mr. Metos

Zee put the letter down and gazed warily at
Charlotte, who was gazing warily back at him. A moment
passed, then two.

"Huh," said Charlotte.

"Huh," said Zee.

Another pause.

"Doesn't explain a lot, does he?" asked Charlotte.

"Nope," said Zee.

And another.

"Do you think he has a first name?" asked Charlotte.

"It doesn't seem like it," said Zee.

And one more.

"What do you think he means?" asked Charlotte.

"I don't know," said Zee. "But . . . maybe we get to do something."

"Yeah," Charlotte said. "Maybe."

They sat in silence a while longer. Mew got up and spun around three times, then settled herself back on Zee's lap with a satisfied grunt. Zee read the letter twice more, and then gave it to Charlotte to read again. While she was looking at it, Zee sat with his head against the wall.

"Hey, Char?" he asked suddenly.

"Yeah?"

"When Proteus was me? That whole week?"

Charlotte squirmed internally. "Yeah?"

"Did he do anything that I should know about?"

Charlotte blinked a few times, then put on her most reassuring smile. "Um . . . no," she said. "Nothing at all."

# Epilogue

## Under the Sea

Philonecron did not like being wet. At all. Nor did he like it when his clothes were wet, especially one of his nice new tuxedos, which was dry clean only and not meant to be submerged in seawater. Nor did he like it when he had been plunged into the ice-cold waters of the Mediterranean by his mortal enemy, who had, once again, defeated and humiliated him.

As Philonecron sank slowly to the bottom of the sea, he thought about where things had gone wrong and how much he did not like being wet. He did not quite know how he was to get above water again, for he had never been dumped in the sea before and was unfamiliar with the proper procedure. He supposed he could simply swim his way up, but it seemed so undignified. And he wasn't entirely sure he knew how.

It is a very difficult thing to dream of sitting on top of the Universe and then find yourself sitting at the bottom of the sea. Philonecron imagined himself dog-paddling his way back to the yacht—assuming the dread beast that the girl had commanded had not destroyed it completely—but what was the point? Once again his plans had failed, once again he was foiled. He could not go back there; he'd been humiliated, it was the site of his great failure, and anyway all the relentless tackiness gave him a rash.

And do you know what really bothered him? Really and truly? He had been sincere with the girl. Really. He would have traded Zero—ah, his precious Zero! It was never to be, was it? It was a foolish dream, but a beautiful one, nonetheless!—for the trident. It wounded him that she did not believe him. He would have let them go, too, perhaps wiping away a tear as the cousins nobly made their way to safety together, before he zapped her into a pile of ash and wheeled himself back and forth over her remains.

At least the girl would die horribly. Poseidon would come for his trident, and he would make her pay for her transgressions in his own vulgar way. Philonecron would have liked to do it himself, of course, to kill her with his own bare hands in as slow and painful manner as possible. But he was willing to sacrifice for the greater good.

The fact was, there was no place for an evil genius in this world. All he wanted was a little corner of the Universe that he could call his own while he plotted to overthrow Zeus and unleash chaos on Earth. Was it so much to ask? It was cruel that someone with his gifts should be made to suffer so. Really, it was just another sign of the Olympians' ineptitude.

Yes, Philonecron was despairing. If he did not immediately say "Well, this is just another setback, but I am going to get back on the old horse," if he did not say "Buck up, little camper," or "If at first you don't succeed, try, try again," if he merely sat in his wheelchair in the muck at the bottom of the sea watching the bottom-feeders go by, you would have to forgive him. Philonecron was a man of big dreams, and when those dreams came crashing down on his head—well, it hurt. It did. He felt things quite deeply.

So focused was Philonecron on his own bad fortune that he did not notice that the sea had turned very cold and very dark all of a sudden, nor did he notice the way all the life around him seemed to flee, nor did he notice the slow approach of a creature so large it seemed to be bigger than the sea itself. He noticed nothing until a horrible smell overtook him, and then he turned quickly around and found himself staring into the giant, gaping mouth of a Ketos.

"Oh, for the love of—"

But it was too late. The creature swallowed him up, along with everything else in a two-hundred-yard radius. Philonecron found himself tumbling through darkness, accompanied by a great rush of water and slime. Then, after what seemed an eternity, he slammed against some kind of very sticky wall and fell to the floor, where he decided that there were fates much worse than being wet.

Another time in his life, Philonecron might have screamed, have fought, have tried to climb his way out toward the light, but at this moment he simply did not have the will. And truthfully, there was no escape for him—if he started to go through the creature's esophagus, a rush of water would have sent him tumbling back down again. Philonecron would just have to wait. He would be free eventually—though the process of emerging would be very unpleasant indeed.

So Philonecron sat and thought about the great cruelty of fate while the Ketos swam steadily on. Every once in a while, a great rush of water would come in, swirl him around a bit, and throw him against the wall again, but he hardly cared, because when you've been tumbled around by digestive fluid once, you might as well do it a hundred times more.

Then, suddenly, a great roar vibrated the walls around Philonecron and he sighed heavily. Whatever was going to happen now, it was probably not going to be good.

And something did happen. But it was not something bad. The whole inside of the Ketos lit up as if electrified, a piercing shriek filled the air as if the very heavens had been ripped apart, and everything around him began to convulse. Philonecron was thrown this way and that, bouncing from one wall to another, as slime and acid washed over him. Then there was a tremendous sinking sensation—the Ketos was going down, down, down—and then suddenly . . . strangely . . . everything was quiet.

And very still.

Philonecron looked around carefully. There was no movement, no sound, nothing. He had gone from being inside a living creature to being inside a dead one. Which changed everything.

And as Philonecron considered the situation, something came tumbling into Ketos's stomach with him, something long and thin, something shiny and smooth, something familiar and fateful. And Philonecron suddenly realized that his fortune was very good, indeed.

"Well, hello there!"

Quickly he rolled himself over and picked up the trident. It was completely cold and still, like an ordinary object. But of course there was nothing ordinary at all about it. And fortunately, there was nothing ordinary about Philonecron, either.

He reached his arm out and sliced it open with a fingernail. Blood dripped slowly out onto the wheelchair's arm. As it did so, he muttered a few well-chosen words, and the blood began to form four separate pools. One for each grandparent. Carefully he dipped his finger in the first pool and touched it to the trident. Nothing happened. He did the same with the next one, with the same result. Then he placed the blood from the third pool on the trident and, slowly, it began to warm in his hands. A smile crept across Philonecron's face. Using his finger, he sketched a symbol on the trident with his grandfather's blood, and as soon as he was done the trident began to hum.

A few moments and a carefully aimed trident later and Philonecron was standing on brand-new legs. He stretched up and ran a finger lovingly down the handle of the humming trident.

"Well," he said. "I think you and I will be very happy together."

# BESTIARY

## Chimera

A beast with the head of a lion, body of a goat, and tail of a dragon. Has an extra goat head sticking out of its torso, which seems a little unnecessary.

## Delphin

A dolphin who serves Poseidon. When Poseidon sought Amphitrite's hand in marriage, the nymph fled. It was Delphin who found her and persuaded her to marry Poseidon. He proved his loyalty when he planned their wedding—with, we presume, lots of dolphin ice sculptures.

## Echidna

A half-nymph, half-serpent creature covered in mud and leeches. Goddess of sea slime, rot, and plague. Known as the "Mother of all Monsters," she gave birth to the Hydra, Cerberus, the Gorgons, the Chimera, and a whole host of others. Lives in a secluded cave at the bottom of the sea, which is probably best for everyone.

## Empusa

A shape-shifting female demon with hair of flames, legs of bronze, and hooved feet. Not a very nice thing to call someone.

## The Graiai

Also known as the "Gray Sisters," they are three impossibly old she-demons who share one tooth and one eye among them. Cranky, as you might imagine.

## Ichthyocentaur

A fish-tailed centaur. Not as weird-looking as it sounds.

## Indos Worm

A giant worm that inhabits the Indus River in India. By day it rests in the mud at the bottom of the river; by night it prowls the land, hunting for large animals to drag back down to its slimy lair to eat. Gross.

## Karkinos

A giant crab. Looks excellent in formal wear.

## Ketos

A massive sea monster. Interests include destroying sea towns, swallowing ships, and belching.

## Polyphemos

The son of Poseidon. He is the Cyclops who was blinded by Odysseus. Dines on the flesh of people trapped in his cave. Not very nice.

## Scylla and Charybdis

Sailors who pass on one side of the Strait of Messina will be devoured by Scylla, a giant female beast with a pack of dogs below her waist. Those who pass on the other side will be sucked into the horrible mouth of Charybdis. Best to find another route.

## Siren

A female nymph whose irresistible song enchants passing sailors who then dive off their ships and drown. Takes requests.